# THE
# TIGER
# IN THE
# HOUSE

Also by Jacqueline Sheehan

*The Center of the World\**

*Picture This*

*Now & Then*

*Lost & Found*

*The Comet's Tale*

\*available from Kensington Publishing Corp.

"Juxtaposing the past and the present—the gruesome horrors of war with the emotional turmoil of lies and self–discovery—this novel takes readers on an unforgettable adventure. The characters are rich and layered, and the story is brimming with deep, familiar love, the ache of lost love, and the inspiring courage it takes to fight for what's right, even if that road is a rocky one. . . . A story of love, family and discovery."
—*RT Book Reviews*, **4.5 Stars, Top Pick**

"The day I discovered novelist Jacqueline Sheehan marked a great moment in my reading life. In *The Center of the World*, her best book yet, Kate Malloy truly has a heart that is a compass, holding fast to true north as she searches for her daughter. Again and again, Sheehan finds new ways to prove to the world that mothers are the strongest people on earth, and will literally go to the ends of the earth to keep a daughter safe."
—**Jo–Ann Mapson,** *Los Angeles Times* bestselling author of *Solomon's Oak, Finding Casey,* and *Owen's Daughter*

"Jacqueline Sheehan's striking new novel, *The Center of the World,* is a sure-handed exploration of grief and transcendence. I found these characters memorable, the story compelling, the author's ability to make a place come alive on the page a rare gift. Sheehan is a writer with a large heart, and her book is destined to win countless readers."
—**Steve Yarbrough,** author of *The Realm of Last Chances,* a *Washington Post* Notable Book

# THE
# TIGER
# IN THE
# HOUSE

## JACQUELINE SHEEHAN

KENSINGTON BOOKS
www.kensingtonbooks.com

KENSINGTON BOOKS are published by

Kensington Publishing Corp.
119 West 40th Street
New York, NY 10018

All Kensington titles, imprints, and distributed lines are available at special quantity discounts for bulk purchases for sales promotion, premiums, fund-raising, and educational or institutional use.

Special book excerpts or customized printings can also be created to fit specific needs. For details, write or phone the office of the Kensington Sales Manager: Kensington Publishing Corp., 119 West 40th Street, New York, NY 10018. Attn. Sales Department. Phone: 1-800-221-2647.

Kensington and the K logo Reg. U.S. Pat. & TM Off.

eISBN-13: 978-1-61773-899-9
eISBN-10: 1-61773-899-9
First Kensington Electronic Edition: March 2017

ISBN-13: 978-1-61773-898-2
ISBN-10: 1-61773-898-0
First Kensington Trade Paperback Printing: March 2017

10 9 8 7 6 5 4 3

Printed in the United States of America

*To Ruth Lundin. You would have loved the food in J Bird Café.*

# CHAPTER 1

Jen and Richard ate dinner at the seafood place over in South Portland that their daughter raved about all the time. And it was as good as expected. She had the lobster roll and Rich had a mountain of fish and chips. It was the sort of place where you go in and order, pay, and then they give you a number, like Hannaford's grocery store where the deli crew takes your order.

The best part was the picnic table behind the seafood shack overlooking the ocean. Jen imagined how the meal would have gone if they were twenty-five years younger and still had the relentless yearning for each other, or if Rich could think of anything to say at all, even that. They ate mostly in silence. Jen liked it better when they were in the active years of parenting, working as a team, laughing so much.

When they were done eating, they each slid into the Chevy Silverado pickup and buckled up. Rich turned to her and said, "Let's take the long way home, over where they're selling off the big Johnson farm." Okay, that felt good. She slipped in a CD of early Bruce Springsteen and grew a little younger, rolled her window down, and tapped her fingers along the side view mirror. They sailed past sea grass and red-winged blackbirds perched on top of cattails. The houses grew smaller, more like the old days, less monstrously rich. Jen nudged her sandals off and wiggled her toes.

It was the end of August and the hint of lengthening nights announced itself already at eight o'clock.

"Look up there," said Rich, taking his foot off the gas and reaching over to turn down Bruce Springsteen.

A cloud slid over the low-hanging sun. Up ahead, there was a small child in the road, thumb in mouth. The road had turned to gravel a few miles back and they crept along. The gravel sounded like Styrofoam balls crunching beneath the large truck wheels.

The child wore white shorts. There wasn't another car parked along the road, no houses, just a bulldozer that had torn into the earth, making way for a new foundation.

Jen pulled her hand into the truck, getting ready for something. She slipped her sandals back on. The truck would be terrifyingly large to a child.

They pulled up close to the child, who was sucking her thumb. Jen was a small woman and she knew how to talk to kids, and she wouldn't be as frightening as a man or a truck.

The child was a girl with soft brown hair. The white shorts were actually underwear; she wore white underpants and a T-shirt with a faded Disney princess. Jen wasn't sure which princess it was.

She tried to think of something nonthreatening to say that wouldn't alarm the child. The girl looked to be about five.

"Hey there," said Jen, six feet away. The child was barefoot. "My name is Jen. Can you show me where your mommy and daddy are?"

Jen took two more steps to the child and pointed back at the truck. "That's my husband, Rich." She stopped in front of the child and squatted down to be eye level with her.

The girl had been crying; her face was covered with dust, and the tears left two stripes along her cheeks.

"I'd like to help you find your family," said Jen. What was

that along the kid's arm and neck? Jen stopped breathing. It was blood.

"Sweetie, are you hurt?"

The thumb stayed firmly in the girl's mouth. Jen forced a smile.

"Everything is going to be okay. You wait right here."

She turned at the sound of the truck door closing. "I've already made the call," Rich said, sliding a cell phone into the front pocket of his jeans.

He had a Windbreaker in his hands. "Here, put this on her."

# CHAPTER 2

"It's not that they live forever, but they should," said Delia. "Instead, dogs live in an accelerated universe, parallel to ours."

She was helping Ben, the local vet, at his annual Spay & Neuter Clinic. He had called her when one of his volunteers quit. They started at six in the morning and wouldn't end until seven or eight that night. Ben made tiny stitches along the nether parts of a female terrier mix.

"You don't usually talk about parallel universes. I suspect it's the atmosphere of anesthesia talking. But in general, I know what you mean." Ben wore his special glasses for surgeries, the same as reading glasses, but larger, the kind that old people wore in the eighties, large and round, circling their eyebrows and the tops of their cheeks. Thick black frames.

Delia wasn't a vet tech, but she had known Ben since junior high. He was a good friend of her father's. His last remaining friend. The best thing about Ben was that he knew the worst parts of her family and she didn't have to explain anything.

Ben straightened up, rolling his shoulders back with a groan. "This girl is ready to go back to the recovery room."

This was the part that Delia liked above anything else at the S&N clinic. It was her job to carry the still-anesthetized animals in her arms. She didn't have kids of her own, never had the feel of a babe pressed against her chest, and she wouldn't claim that hoisting freshly neutered dogs and cats was the same as a carrying a baby, but there was something about it that stirred her. She protected the animals when they were vulnerable and unable to care for themselves in the postsurgical moments. Not unlike her job as a caseworker with foster kids.

She slid her arms under the small dog, careful to hold up the wobbly head, and walked to the back room, where other dogs in various stages of consciousness were placed in wire crates. The techs put old towels on the bottoms of the crates. Delia knelt down and edged the terrier onto the towel. She placed her hand on the warm belly and felt the thumping of the heartbeat.

She retraced her steps and returned to the surgery room. Ben stretched his arms overhead, then placed both palms on his lower back and pushed his hips forward.

"My wife tells me that my posture is terrible. She says my profile looks like a question mark. She wants me to go to yoga or tai chi. I don't think that I'm old enough for tai chi. I saw old people on a TV show moving in slow motion doing something called qigong. Please tell me that I'm not there yet."

Ben was in his early fifties, and Delia knew age had nothing to do with his reluctance to exercise. He'd been an athlete as a young man but never made the transition to sports that an older man could enjoy, not tennis or biking, never mind the more esoteric areas of tai chi. His old days as a high school football player resulted in a recent knee surgery. He was six months post knee surgery and still limping.

The next dog, a female mixed breed somewhere between beagle and boxer, was brought in and quickly anesthetized. Ben picked up the scalpel, leaned over the spread-eagle patient. The scalpel clattered to the floor. He picked up another scalpel from a stainless steel tray. "Clumsy today," he said.

Delia reeled between two things that pulled at her attention. What was different about Ben? He was a stellar vet. Animals loved him. His staff, almost all young women who were vet techs, liked working with him. The staff at the animal shelters said he was their best vet, always willing to work on injured animals even when no owner could be found to pay for the expenses.

She didn't hesitate when he called her for help. How could she? He had been there for her and her sister Juniper when their parents died. She would do anything for Ben, including assisting him so that fewer animals might end up abandoned at the shelters, terrified and bewildered at the turn in their lives.

But something was different, so slight that if she hadn't known him well, it might not have registered at all. Delia, cursed with a powerful sense of smell, had sniffed an acrid overlay from his usual older-man scent, as if a new chemical had been added to his molecular mix. And the way he reached for his scalpel, a premature surge of his wrist, faster than his slow, deliberate pace. Then dropping the surgical instrument. The movement lost something in the jerkiness, a bit of connection with the dog that lay anesthetized, her lower belly ready for the slice that would take away all future puppies. No, it must have been Delia's lack of sleep, her newfound restlessness since she had actually handed her resignation to Ira, with three months' notice, which was too long for Delia but not nearly long enough for Ira. She now had four weeks left.

Jill, the receptionist, opened the door. "There's a phone call for you, Delia, from the foster care place over in Portland."

How could Ira possibly know that she was working at the S&N clinic? She had turned off her phone when surgery started. He must have called her sister. This was going to be bad.

Delia followed Jill back to the reception desk and picked up the phone.

"Hi, Ira," she said.

"Sorry to pull you out of the clinic," he said, "but we've just had a request for an emergency placement. We're going to need you."

# CHAPTER 3

Delia sat in the parking lot of Foster Services. She was keenly aware that she hadn't filed her latest case notes, becoming less organized, for the first time ever, as her job drew to an end. She pulled out her laptop and typed furiously before meeting with Ira.

She hadn't typed her notes from yesterday yet. She imagined titles for her case notes, which would be frowned on by Ira, potentially viewed as minimizing a child's tragedy or mocking the disaster of parenting gone haywire by alcohol, drugs, mental illness, or general meanness.

She never kept the titles, at least not yet, although they remained in her head. Sometimes titles captured an entire life or just a single interview. "Transformer Joe" for a boy who changed from sweet to tyrannical in an instant. "Don't Take My Blankie Away" for a child who had traveled through the worst of times with a shredded blue blanket, now the size of a paperback. "We're Just Atoms Combining and Recombining," a title for a family of four kids who had been dispersed among three foster families until Delia had campaigned hard for one family to take all four kids.

Imagining the titles was part of what helped Delia remember the most important details of a person's life, like labeling a photo in an album. But so few people still had photo albums. They had photos on their phones, or in the cloud. Although she was embarrassed to ask, she didn't clearly understand what the cloud was. And specifically, if you put something in the cloud like a photo or a kid's placement file, could you ever take it away from the cloud? She'd ask one of the interns. One of the great things about graduate interns was that you could peel the latest technology right off them.

Her last intern said, "How old are you? You seem a lot older than you look." Her comment could have been in reference to Delia's lack of cloud technology. She hoped it wasn't the way she looked, at thirty-two. But she felt older, sometimes decades older.

When Delia told her boss, Ira, that she was leaving, Ira had not accepted her resignation easily. "This is about Juniper, isn't it? You can't keep taking care of her forever."

The truth was, resigning was about Delia and starting a new life that was bright and beautiful, without social services.

Ira, director of Southern Maine Foster Services, had worked his way up through the ranks. He had been a kid in the foster care system by the time he was eight years old, fresh out of the burn unit at Shriners Hospital in Boston. Delia never asked him for details about the abuse; the burn scars visible along his arms were all she needed to know about a little boy who had been through unspeakable trauma. He was one of the survivors. He had only been in two foster homes before he landed with a family who wanted to adopt him. His biological mother died from a drug overdose and his remaining biological parent, who was in prison, did the best thing he'd ever done for Ira by relinquishing all parental rights. But someone like Ira saw everything, every twitch, because he had learned to be vigilant when he was a kid, on the lookout for any sign that his parents had gone from benign to dangerous. Now he was like one of the dogs that were trained to sniff out seizures moments before they felled their owner.

"It's the accumulation," she had told him, avoiding the comment about Juniper.

Delia finished her notes and filed them, snapping her laptop shut, and headed for whatever awaited her with Ira. Even now, walking along the hallway, she could smell it, the fear and anger of children who had come through the foster care system. A steel-wool-meets-linseed-oil smell that children gave off when they'd been hurt by the ones they loved.

Delia did all the right things that she'd learned over the years at the professional development workshops. Most recently she had attended yet another workshop about establishing clear boundaries. Buzzwords for not getting traumatized by the pain of your young clients. Bystander trauma.

She exercised, had friends, took every bit of her vacation time, and listened to music on her drive to and from work rather than the news. Even so, with each child, a droplet of something had found its way into Delia, like acid rain eating up the paint on her car. The accumulation finally hit her personal high water mark.

Delia saw other people in her profession who had missed the signs. She did not want to become the bitter, fatalistic curmudgeon that others had morphed into.

As of today, she had thirty days left. Time to sensibly close out her cases, transfer them to others, and withdraw from the world of uphill battles. But Ira had called her, and she did not, absolutely did not, want to know what waited for her. The underside of her chin itched, as it always did with the worst cases. She had stopped trying to explain the telltale itch to others. It just was, and she had learned to listen to it. *Scritch, scratch*, like little creatures rambling about along her jawbone. This meant the case was searing hot with abandoned kids and parents in a tailspin. Or worse.

She rubbed her chin, trying to rub out the familiar twitch. She paused at her desk long enough to read the new file. A gift from Ira. He had already penciled her name on the front of the file: Delia Lamont.

She closed the file after reading it. The child was five years old and had been released from the hospital. Blood was found on the child, but it was not her own. The pediatrician noted symptoms of malnutrition, a good deal of dirt under her fingernails, and mosquito bites that had become infected. She came in at the seventieth percentile for weight.

They had reason to believe that she lived in a house on Bakersfield Road. Because the house was a crime scene, the on-call caseworker had not been able to get into the house to check for something that might be special to the girl: a blanket or a stuffed animal.

There had been three adults at the house, all shot at close range. One woman, two men. The woman had been identified by her driver's license as Emma Gilbert, twenty-six, from Florida. The two men had no ID's on them, as if they had been stripped of ID's or maybe they never had them. The house was a rental. A local management company received cash, one month in advance, deposit, and rent for part of August and September, for a total of $4,600. The name on the rental agreement was Russ Tiggs. The police said that upon checking, his ID was false. No one named Russ Tiggs existed. There was no information about the child.

This wasn't the first time a child had arrived in emergency foster care without any records at all. Children could fly under the radar for years, never see a doctor or a dentist, and never go to daycare or preschool.

She had been found by a local middle-aged couple who stayed with the child until the police arrived. They requested to be notified about the well-being of the child. When the first cop on the scene had asked the girl what her name was, she answered without hesitation. "Hayley." When asked for her last name, she had shrugged.

Delia was glad that the job of locating relatives of the girl was up to Ira and not up to her. She looked at her job as surveyor of disaster, sort of a one-woman hazmat crew. Despite the media portrayal of foster care as the devil, foster care couldn't even enter the equation unless a true shit storm happened in a family where kids were in situations that looked like war zones. Or sometimes kids were just left with nobody, dangling, free-floating on their own.

No one wanted to be the kid who had to go to foster care, because that meant something cataclysmic happened, and one of those things might be that your parents didn't care enough about you, or weren't able to care about anyone, not even them-selves. If kids at school knew you were in foster care, it was a neon sign on your forehead that said you weren't worth loving.

She paused in front of Ira's door, calming herself with several breaths. It wasn't working. Delia slid the file across Ira's desk and said, "Were there really no family members for this child to stay with?" She looked down at the file again. The child's name was written on the file tab, not a nameless girl, but Hayley.

"What's going on here and why have you called me in? This child may need someone who can stick with her long term. Why not someone else?"

"Because you're the best. Don't you think we should give this child the best that we have?"

She could never say no to Ira.

There were parts of her job that Delia never got used to and she prayed that she never would. The first was the smell of fear when a child was left alone. Not just alone for an hour, but un-speakably alone, and Delia's job was to bring them (after clear-ance by the police and the hospital) to an emergency foster placement. If anyone had asked her to describe what this kind of fear smelled like (unlikely since she had never mentioned it to anyone, not even Juniper), she would have said that she had forgotten. And it would have been true, or mostly true, because she tried so hard to banish that scent.

The second was the lack of oxygen when a kid's parents had died. She had seen photos of the forest around Mount St. Hel-ens after it erupted and how all life was snuffed out, choked in ash, and the trees all fell like toothpicks in a strange art instal-lation. That's how the kids looked. If she ever grew accustomed to this part of the job, she'd quit. Well, she had quit.

What humbled her was the way that memory softened the blow for children, the surprising kindness, perhaps an evolutionary safeguard for humanity, that the brain protected itself from shattering by simply forgetting. The way Delia had forgotten.

This was precisely what Delia wanted to avoid with the girl found on the back roads of South Portland. The child had to remember. She was approximately five years old, and she had been with the three adults who were killed in a home invasion/robbery. The girl had been found walking along a gravel road almost a mile from the house where the murders took place.

With file folder in hand, Delia had headed straight to SPPD after calling Detective Lt. Michael Moretti. He was one of the newer additions to the South Portland Police Department. He was younger than the other cops and somehow, Delia hadn't yet crossed paths with him officially. He walked around his desk and sat in a chair near her. She wasn't expecting the way his hands looked, fingers braided together, resting on his thighs, or the way his eyes softened when he looked at her. A photo of a young girl on his desk announced that he was a dad. It seemed like all the men she ever met were married.

"Murders like this either have to do with passion or drugs, and my money is on drugs. I wouldn't have said this fifteen years ago, maybe even ten years ago. The drug trade, mostly heroin, is like an airborne fungus, and it has spread into every crevice of the country. There were traces of heroin found on one of the bodies."

Delia liked his voice, even when he delivered harrowing information. Some men had the right warm tone, a wavelength that was easy to hear.

"Was there any evidence of identification with the child? Were the victims related to her?"

"We're checking DNA right now," he said. The detective tilted his head slightly, not the coquettish way that a young girl might, but as a sign that he might be ready to choose his words carefully. "I want to be clear with you about what we are up against. This case gives me every indication that larger crime syndicates have moved into the area to manage the heroin pipeline and its related little brothers: street prescription drugs. These victims might have stepped into someone else's business. At any rate, they made someone very angry."

He smelled like the outdoors, like a breeze.

"We've always had some heroin in the city, this is nothing new. And crack," said Delia. She liked looking at him, his neck and his Adam's apple. She crossed her right leg over the left.

"I was hired because of my experience with the drug trade in Rhode Island, precisely because something *is* different now. Heroin has followed a phenomenon that started back fifteen years ago, when doctors wrote prescriptions for OxyContin and the rest of the pain meds. Big Pharma neglected to spread the word that Oxy is chemically one hair's breadth away from heroin. So let's say you've had a hip replacement or a car accident and your knee is shattered. You get pain meds, and for lots of people, they became addicted. Solidly addicted. Like brain glue addicted."

He stopped, exhaled, and rubbed the back of his neck. He slid one foot in closer to his chair, the rubber of his running shoe leaving a black streak on the old linoleum. Something was driving him other than the demands of his job.

"Is heroin personal for you?" she asked.

His brown eyes flashed. "My niece. Senior year, basketball player, scholarship to North Carolina. In the spring before graduation, she had a car accident and broke her ankle. We all thought she was getting better, and she was, well enough to work on a house painting crew that summer. What none of us knew was that she was addicted to Oxy and bought it off the street." He stopped. "I haven't told this to anyone outside the department."

Delia uncrossed her legs. "Your niece sounds like she was close to you."

He closed his eyes for a moment. "I was close to her. She

was an awesome, smart, beautiful kid with a free throw record that still stands at her high school. That summer she started on heroin. A bad batch came into Providence and she overdosed."

Delia's throat tightened. "I am really sorry."

He looked down as muscles twitched along his jaw.

"What I didn't know back then was that this was happening all over, times fifty states, times one hundred towns per state. There is now huge, and I mean enormous, money to be made in this drug industry, because heroin moved to the suburbs and rural areas of states like Maine, Vermont, and Massachusetts. Everywhere. It has exploded. Until you're like my niece, sitting in your two-story house in white America shooting up in the basement. And our three dead victims are linked into it."

His phone buzzed. "I'm sorry. But I have to take this call. I'll let you know anything about the girl's identity as soon as I find something."

Delia wanted to stay longer in his office. She knew from experience that all of the police went into hyperspace when a child was involved. When a child was a victim of a crime, the police took it personally. This detective had a daughter of his own. But he also mourned the senseless death of his niece.

She gathered her purse and the file and gave a small wave to him as he settled back behind his desk. He looked up and nodded.

The bad guys were Moretti's job. Delia was accustomed to working with the police in Portland who handled domestic problems, not homicide. But she had never worked with the South Portland Police and never with Moretti. Her job was to provide an assessment that would safeguard the child and ensure the best emergency placement for her. Ira said only his best-trained foster families could offer this type of placement.

# CHAPTER 4

Delia and her sister walked the Eastern Promenade along the waterfront of Portland several times a week. They had just passed the place where people left sculptures made from the rocks well-rounded by the ocean.

"That child looked terrified in the photo," said Delia.

"What do you mean terrified?" said Juniper.

Delia tossed her paper coffee cup into a trash bin. "What I mean is a five-year-old kid in a police photo, dressed in white cotton underpants and lavender T-shirt with a princess on the front. I mean her eyes, I mean the way a mouse doesn't move when a cat has it in his jaws, doesn't move its eyes left or right. The way the muscles have frozen up."

Delia imagined the child's intestines either frozen up or, more likely, voiding everything out of her system, the way soldiers do under fire.

"I read the report. The child was not physically hurt. She wasn't assaulted physically or sexually, but she had been found walking along a back road in South Portland. The child hasn't spoken other than to give her first name and could not say where anyone else was. Like Mommy or Daddy or brothers or sisters."

Delia could talk about a case as long as she didn't exceed the details that were public knowledge. The newspapers reported about Hayley, excluding her name. The sisters ended their excursion at Juniper's car, parked near the Italian Market.

When Delia was still in college, she had volunteered with the Red Cross right after Hurricane Katrina hit. She had been sent to Meridian, Mississippi, where thousands of evacuees from New Orleans had landed. People who had evacuated New Orleans were scared in a way that turned them inside out, whacked them senseless. Delia met with hundreds of people at the makeshift shelters in churches and schools. But it was a cat that unraveled her. A young man and woman had rescued their cat from the storm surge in New Orleans, put it in a cat carrier, and carried it on top of their heads for miles in chest-deep water to get out of the city. When they arrived at the Red Cross center, dazed and looking for a place to sleep, the cat sat in the vinyl carrier and looked straight ahead. You could snap your fingers right in front of its whiskers and it wouldn't blink, wouldn't follow your hand from left to right.

That's what this child looked like.

After the walk along the Promenade, Delia and Juniper drove into the parking lot at the Whole Foods Market.

"We can get the last of the local peaches," said Juniper. "I'll make a peach pie. Or I'll roast peaches on the grill."

Delia heard the hopefulness in her sister's voice, the desire to offer something soothing. She envied her sister's absolute certainty that food was the ultimate salve. Delia was soothed by her soon-to-be career in baking also, but not with the conviction of her little sister. On her good days, it was only envy. On her worst days, she saw the monsters skulking the shadows for Juniper, and Delia was forever on the alert for the tweak in their DNA that might steal Juniper away. The way her father had been stolen from them.

# CHAPTER 5

Delia's father, Theo, smoked furiously. Camel cigarettes, a retro choice even then. The smoke had drifted into most of his jackets and sweaters, the things that were hard to wash or have dry-cleaned. He didn't smoke in the house during his good times, needing only occasional nudges from her mother, Susan. "Sweetheart, would you mind taking the cigarettes outside?" But during the bad times, he lit one cigarette directly from the other and they would have had to blast him with dynamite to get him outside. Delia was eleven, in the autumn of fifth grade.

When his clothes were stale or he was adrift in his paranoid thinking, the smell hit her like a chemical bomb. She learned to calculate how the day would go by the scent of cigarette smoke. Too much smoky resin spelled disaster.

One day when the autumn sun was warm, it must have been a Saturday, and he wasn't head down in his office writing his food reviews, Delia and her father were under their largest maple tree, the bell ringer that announced autumn for the neighborhood. He had softened around his jaw, and the scent of cigarette smoke was nothing but a teaspoon of seasoning. Most of his syndications had canceled him, but a few newspapers in Maine still carried his reviews.

"Delia, let's rake these leaves into a dragon, like a dragon sand castle. We'll surprise your little sister and Mommy when they come home from the grocery store."

She startled at the word *dragon,* fearing that making a dragon would bring out the real monster from its lair. She looked at his eyes; his pupils weren't dilated and dark with failed medication. He was here, fully here with Delia. This was what it felt like to rake leaves in the backyard with your father.

"Oh, come on, kiddo. I'm okay. It's only a dragon made of leaves. What do you think I am, crazy or something?" He winked at her and tossed a rake toward her end of the leaf pile.

They raked and sculpted the leaves, making a dragon that looked more reptile and snake than regal dragon. Her father worked up a sweat. He dropped his jacket on a plastic lawn chair.

"We need spikes for his back, something to make him look fierce," Delia said, standing back to admire the creature.

"I believe you're right," he said, and set off for the refuse pile in the farthest corner of the yard, by the fire bushes that had overnight turned magenta. "Would you get us some lemonade?" he asked, looking over his shoulder at Delia.

Did she take too long? Should she have searched the cabinets for the Ritz Crackers that he loved? Had she taken ten minutes to get two glasses of lemonade from the plastic pitcher? She balanced the two glasses along with a cereal bowl filled with the crackers and walked toward the dragon. Where was he?

Delia found him shuddering behind the fire bush. He pointed to a trash heap of sticks, a broken ladder, and an abandoned tire swing. "Who put those there?" he said, looking past Delia, forever past her. "Who did you let into the yard? Were they men? Did they ask for me? What did they say about me?"

Delia's heart thumped, and she counted the minutes until her mother would be home.

"No, Daddy. There was no one here. I would have seen them.

Let's go back to our dragon, please," keeping her voice as steady as she could. She handed him a glass of lemonade. He took it and stared at it as if it might hold poison. His eyes flicked to hers and he poured out the liquid.

"Did they tell you to give this drink to me? They'll try anything. They slipped something in this to track my movements."

He walked across the yard, past their dragon, and into the house, where he filled an ashtray with his Camel cigarettes.

One week later, after a new round of medication deflated his delusions, Delia walked into the kitchen after school, opened the fridge, and heard the muffled voices of her parents on the back porch. She tiptoed to the window. "I can't stand to hurt you all," her father said in between sobs. Delia edged closer like a spy and looked out the side of the window. Her mother squatted next to her father. She surrounded him with her arms.

"She's afraid of me, my daughter is afraid of me. I can see it in her eyes," he said, his face pressed into his wife's shoulder.

Delia prayed for her father's schizophrenia to go away, for a cure that would excise his demonic hallucinations. More than anything, she wanted her father back, the good dad, all the time. She would have done anything for her dad.

# CHAPTER 6

It had been a bad summer for their father, for all of them. Delia was ready to start her second year of college in one week, and Juniper was in eighth grade. Public school had already started for Juniper. Delia had a summer job working at the front desk of the YMCA, checking in members and handing out towels. She wanted more than anything to live on campus in the fall, but the thought of leaving J Bird as the sole recipient of her father's bad days was unbearable.

Juniper's nickname, J Bird, was new that summer. At first it had been a taunt from an older boy who called her *Bird Legs*. Delia's little sister didn't carry the family legacy of being deeply hurt by ridicule. Juniper instead tossed the insult back at the boy, flapping her arms and saying, "I'm bird, a bird, a J Bird!" The nickname stuck, and once people grew to know her, they graduated to her nickname. When Delia thought of her, she was still Juniper, but she gave in to the new moniker. Even her father, even during this horrible summer, had taken joy in her feisty name-taking.

Her mother left her job writing the political coverage at the newspaper and now worked in distribution. The editor suggested the change when Delia's father missed too many deadlines and the syndications fell away. "This way I'll be home evenings for J Bird," she told Delia with a forced enthusiasm that tore at Delia's heart. Her mother loved the heat and drama of state politics.

For the hundredth time, her father had decided to go off the medication that muffled the voices in his head but dulled his senses. His paranoid thinking opened a cascade of terrors for all of them. The wires were yanked out of the TV again, the batteries removed from her boom box. He insisted on a PO Box instead of a mailbox on the house. He was on a path of shutting down all of the invasive dangers from the outer world, from the government, from the UN, and from beyond.

Their mother interceded, acted like a social lubricant, soothing him, stepping between the man who sometimes resembled her handsome husband and her often terrified daughters.

"Delia, take J Bird out tonight, to a movie or to the mall," she said when Delia came home from the Y. Her mother met her in the driveway. Something crashed on the second floor of the house. Her little sister sat on the black asphalt, her back pressed against the garage door, with a new school backpack at her feet. Head down, picking at a crack in the drive.

"It's a school night. Doesn't J Bird have homework?" They both knew this wasn't the question that hung over them. It was the galloping paranoia exploding in her father that was the only question.

"I have a call in to his psychiatrist," her mother said, tucking her shoulder-length hair behind one ear. She had talked to the psychiatrist and the ER doctors a dozen times over the summer. Her father's stubborn schizophrenia challenged even the seasoned psychiatrist. Her mother battled the conundrum of convincing someone in the grip of paranoid delusions that it was safe to take medication. Delia thought her mother might just collapse from exhaustion. They all might.

What was worse, the tyranny of his delusions holding them all hostage by the outside invaders that only her father could detect, or witnessing the bottomless remorse of her father? The medication brought with it the horror of realizing his illness. The delusions and the medication worked as collaborators to keep her father from writing. If he wrote while in the grips of hallucinations, the result was a jumble of false starts, panicked half sentences. If he tried to write while taking Thorazine (an old drug that the desperate psychiatrist was trying after all else failed), it dulled his senses and he spent all day writing one paragraph that hit the page with a joyless thud.

The heat of the day, absorbed into the black asphalt of their driveway, radiated up through Delia's shoes to the soles of her feet and traveled up the bones of her legs. She was exhausted from standing all day behind the counter; she only wanted to go inside her own house and sit down on the couch, or stretch out on her bed. But no, not in this family, because her father had gone insane again. Why couldn't her family be like others, even like the families where parents argued or someone drank too much? At least they didn't have bare wires sticking out of the walls, they could at least use the bathroom, call a friend, watch television. Why couldn't she invite her boyfriend in? The last time she tried to have Tyler in after a date, her father had mortified her by shouting at Tyler, "They told me about you! Stay away from my daughter!"

Delia didn't want to have to say it, but she longed for more time with her mother. She wanted to go to an ice cream stand, go shopping, or take a walk along the beach without her mother constantly ready to sprint back home to reel in her father. He was convinced that he heard the neighbors across the street plotting to dig a tunnel under the street and invade their house.

"I know he's sick, but when do we get to have a normal life? Do we all have to pay for his sickness? I know you want to leave him," said Delia. "For God's sake, just do it."

Delia had never said this out loud before, only to Tyler in a tearful state of exhaustion.

Her mother squinted against the setting sun, putting one hand over her eyebrows. "When we first met, I knew that I had found the most brilliant, handsome, funny man. I knew there would never be anyone else like him." She looked away and squeezed her eyes shut. A breath shuddered through her. "I have to hang on to the brilliant parts of him, to the part of him that loves us. If I let go, he'll be lost. Take your sister out for a few hours. Please."

She handed the car keys to Delia. "Go do something fun, just the two of you."

"I have a date with Tyler! I already broke a date with him last week when Dad refused to let me leave the house," she said.

"You'll have lots of dates with Tyler. Please, Delia. I wouldn't ask you unless it was important."

In a silent acquiescence, Delia slid the keys into her pocket.

"I love you girls. I know this has been hard for you," said her mother, tilting her head, imploring something like forgiveness.

Delia, honeycombed with anger, didn't respond to her mother's unspoken request for a hug, for an emotional understanding. She glanced up and saw her father at an upstairs window, his once angular face bloated by medication that, while absent in his system for weeks, still left its puffy mark.

She turned and said, "Come on, J Bird. Let's go to a movie."

She called Tyler's house and left the message that she had to cancel.

# CHAPTER 7

Delia had always taken care of Juniper and patrolled for any hint of her father's illness. Delia watched Juniper for signs all through high school and her early twenties. If they had the bad gene for breast cancer, they could have their breasts removed in a preemptive strike. But what can you remove to stave off madness of the worst sort? Not the brain, where all the trouble is.

What if Juniper took drugs and it jump-started a cascade effect, rumpling her brain? What if a car accident flipped the switch? Or worst of all, what if the thief came for Delia, voices warning her of conspiracies, screeching in her head? What if it happened and she didn't realize it, and then who would Juniper have?

Her little sister was now twenty-six, nearly in the safe zone, and aside from picking ghastly boyfriends for a solid seven years, she seemed no worse for wear. And what of Delia? Aside from her heightened sense of smell and a chin that itched a warning with difficult cases, she was past the age, at thirty-two, when schizophrenia was likely to raise its skeletal hand from her father's grave and grab her.

What was your risk of being doused with the schizophrenic gene if you had one parent who had schizophrenia? Delia knew the numbers by heart; she'd known since she was a twenty-year-old student in a psychopathology class. Thirteen percent. She and Juniper had a thirteen percent chance that they would start wearing aluminum hats to keep out invasive radio waves. In the general population, less than one half of one percent of people were cursed with psychosis. And it was a curse, a thief, leaving Delia with a father who was so afflicted that he believed radioactive air was being pumped through the water pipes. When Delia was a senior in high school, weary from trying to outwit his delusion, she tried to reason with him by saying, "But, Daddy, these are water pipes. . . ." He shoved his contorted face into hers and said, "I'm not stupid. There's air in water, it's $H2O$, O, get it?"

What else did Delia glean from her early psych classes? That the life expectancy of someone like her father was ten to twenty-five years less than average. Her father hit the average like a bull's-eye, dead at forty-four.

Today, everyone loved Juniper. She made people laugh. Customers at the Bayside Bakery, where she worked, swooned over her muffins and her baked concoctions of raspberries and cream cheese. Delia would have given anything to shed the layer of seriousness, of too-early adulthood, that came with the death of their parents. She wanted what Juniper had, the way her perfect lips didn't crack in the winter, the easy way she talked to men, the way she danced if she felt like it, even at the bakery, even with her huge white apron on.

When disaster struck their family, Delia had been nineteen, almost a sophomore in college, and Juniper was only thirteen, an eighth-grade girl with small nubs of breasts. Delia had to take over. But now, she wanted someone to notice her in the way they noticed J Bird, she wanted someone to say, "Hey, you've got the moves, Delia!" She was ready for the unbearable weight of being the stand-in parent to be lifted.

It wasn't that she wanted Juniper to be someone else. She adored her little sister and was proud of her. What Delia didn't want were the feelings of resentment, those unspeakable feelings that no one was supposed to have. There were days when her lungs couldn't expand and she couldn't shake the oil and water mixture of loving and resentment. The unholy combination made her heart squeeze up like beef jerky. There were days when she was jealous of her little sister, and it was wrong in every way possible. She would do anything to excise the pettiness that swamped her at times.

Change the thought and she could change the emotion. Wasn't that the mantra of Oprah, Deepak Chopra, and Wayne Dyer? Hadn't she watched an entire PBS fundraising special on the power of changing thought and vibration while she ate a bag of corn chips, dipping into the salsa jar with regularity? She tried a visualization of an angry wart on her big toe (as far away from her heart as possible) and pictured a drop of liquid falling on the wart, melting it away. Everyone on the fundraising special agreed that the unconscious mind understood metaphor, and what better metaphor than a wart for the ancient, crusted-over feeling that crept over her? Wasn't it time to be done with a coping mechanism that had overstayed its welcome? Juniper was a fully functioning adult. Delia didn't have to keep taking care of her. Her little sister had escaped the family disease.

When Delia pictured Juniper, it was her thirteen-year-old version of her sister that rose up. When Juniper thought of Delia, was it the nineteen-year-old model? Maybe not. And as if the universe was conspiring to keep Delia in a perpetual do-over, she had chosen a profession where she was responsible for children who were in need of safekeeping.

But Juniper was safe now, wasn't she? Weren't they both safe at last? Weren't they in the blessed doldrums of adulthood?

The sisters had no physical artifacts from their family home. No favorite chairs, no dishes from Great Aunt Heddy, no photos of the four of them, no clothing except what they had worn that night, no trinkets, no sports awards, school records, hairbrushes, toothbrushes, shoes, or hair clips. No copies of *Goodnight Moon*. No food from the fridge. No fridge.

Pick off the thinnest scab when the sisters were together and their little girl selves burst out, sticky with sweat and braces.

The phone chirped in Delia's pocket. It was Ira. Thanks to caller ID, she had a few seconds to prepare. Nobody could pull her back to the present like Ira, offering her disasters other than her own to focus on.

"The blood tests are back," he said. "None of the three people in the house were related to Hayley. None of them were her parents."

# CHAPTER 8

*J Bird*

Juniper's soulful golden retriever, Baxter, was due for his rabies shot. They had been together for three years after Ben called her from his vet clinic, saying that someone had just brought in a stray dog and would she be interested. Ben was the family hero, helping Delia through college and telling Juniper that she deserved the best boyfriends, not the worst.

Ben was as close to a parent as Juniper would have for the rest of her life. He'd been there for her when she couldn't even call Delia for help. He'd picked her up at a high school party when she was so stoned that she could barely stand and some guy she didn't know pushed her onto a bed. Ben came to get her, taking the last ferry over from Peaks Island. As soon as she saw his car pull up, she rushed to the door, collapsing inside, sobbing.

"It's okay, J Bird," he had said. "We all screw up sometimes. I'll always be here for you."

Now, there was a question about Baxter. While she had avoided the question since the day Baxter came into her life, others at Bayside Bakery dropped subtle and not so subtle suggestions about the dog's fertility status. Technically, Baxter belonged to both of the sisters, since Delia never balked at walking Baxter in even the worst possible weather, but like a biological parent versus stepparent, Juniper was the ultimate decision maker about his welfare. At least with Baxter, she was the grown-up.

Baxter was an intact male. He was the proud owner of a mighty set of testicles that he tended to with such frequency and care that Juniper couldn't help but think that the dog was showing off. They were the first bit of business for the golden retriever in the morning, just a sniff to see how the mighty sacs fared overnight. He nudged them with his black nose, as if to say, *Good morning, boys.*

Wasn't the very cornerstone of all responsible pet owners to spay and neuter? And Juniper had been, until Baxter's arrival, the most strident advocate of neutering. Wasn't she an unbearable hypocrite, advocating one thing for the masses but offering a privileged existence for her dog?

Baxter had not, to her knowledge, ever procreated. Nor was he aggressive with other dogs. He walked through life with the easy confidence of a large, barrel-chested dog, sure in his ability to safeguard his pack if he had to. He didn't need to bark in a histrionic fit like a small dog, or put up his hackles when another equal-sized dog approached. In fact, Juniper wished she were more like the consistently happy dog, sure of her place. Maybe if she were more like Baxter, Delia would stop hovering.

Baxter was a dog unlike all others in her life, and even considering the end of his life was excruciating. Big dogs squeezed a lot of living into a relatively short life. Would it be so terrible, Juniper asked, just this once, if she had a dog who could pass on his DNA, if a lovely sweetie was found to Baxter's liking and, if the moment was right for both the four-leggeds, there could be a happy moment of dog humping with a litter of puppies as a result?

It was time to talk this over with Ben. Since Baxter needed his rabies vaccine, Juniper would broach the subject.

She was twenty minutes late; an accident on the bridge had delayed her. And she had purposely scheduled at the end of Ben's office hours. She was relieved to see his truck was still in the parking lot, so it was worth a try. She pulled in next to his ten-year-old Toyota and turned off the engine. Baxter, riding shotgun, raised his eyebrows up in a peak when he saw where they were.

"I'm only researching the subject, that's all," said Juniper, opening her door.

She came to the passenger door, and the dog disembarked with deliberate slowness. At the clinic door, she tried to pull up the handle, but it was locked. She knocked loudly and peered in to see if Ben was still rattling about. The light from the exam room offered a vertical slice. Ben stuck his head out, saw Juniper, and gave a half wave. He walked around the reception desk and opened the door.

Sweat beaded around his hairline, and he had an unfocused look.

"Hard day?" she asked, stepping inside.

"What? Oh, yeah, it was." He ran his fingers through his hair and looked away.

She knew how hard a bad day could be.

"Sorry to be late. There was big accident on the bridge," she said. "And I'm sorry you've had a bad day."

Ben looked at his watch. No one her age had ever worn a watch, a device that only did one thing. Delia was more like Ben's generation than Juniper's. Six years made a big difference, not a generation gap by any means, but still, Delia always was the parent and she gravitated toward more parental responses. Ben was solidly in their parents' age demographic.

When Juniper graduated from high school, it was Ben and his wife, sitting next to Delia, who whooped and hollered as she crossed the stage. But still, he was more like their unofficial big brother. After the graduation ceremony, he found her, and said, "Don't worry, pip-squeak, if you ever need me, just call."

Juniper had only seen a few men like Ben. She called them the big easies. Men who loved animals, spent all day with some sort of mammal tucked under one arm, always knowing where to put their hands to calm a dog or a cat, and married, the big easies were always married. Just like Ben, married and living on Peaks Island.

So why did Ben have this extra sizzle of something today, a low hum of static electricity with his facial muscles pulled a little tighter?

The clatter of Baxter's claws came to an abrupt halt in the reception area, midway to Ben's examining room. The dog tilted his head, blinked hard, and flared his nostrils, somehow filtering out hundreds of scents from terrified cats and dogs that had passed through. Some other scent stopped him. Baxter regularly forgave Ben for all his sharp needles and pokes and prods and had always approached Ben like an old comrade, as if they came from the same neighborhood. Now, he hesitated.

"This isn't a good time," said Ben. "I've got to pick up the kids."

Wait, his kids were in high school now. One had just graduated. They needed picking up? Hadn't she just told him about the snarl up on the bridge?

"Then you'd better call your wife because you won't make the next ferry," she said. Juniper might not have the nose that Baxter did, but she could smell a brush-off a mile away, and coming from Ben, the sting went deep into her flesh.

Then she softened as she walked back to her car with Baxter. Even the big easies have bad days.

# CHAPTER 9

*J Bird*

Juniper had worked in cafés and restaurants since she was sixteen years old. When she was a freshman at Fairfield University, she woke up five days a week at four a.m. to bake muffins at Sticky Fingers Café. By the time spring break rolled around, she developed a muffin recipe with grated ginger and peach puree that eventually caused her to be fired. "I own that recipe," her boss declared. This was his first restaurant, and he was convinced that he owned his workers and the air that they breathed.

Juniper had just enough nineteen-year-old strength in her spine to smile and say, "No, you don't. And you don't own me either." When she was fired on the spot, she took the secret ingredient of the famous muffin with her, which her boss could never figure out. The secret essential ingredient was Juniper, with her full frontal love of food alchemy and how it restored the soul, how it had saved her time and again since the death of her parents.

She had developed a loyal following of older motorcycle riders who spread the word of her ginger/peach muffins through their Google riders' group, and when they showed up as usual one Saturday morning, their leather chaps squeaking against each other, their helmets humbly in hand, a static silence filled the bakery when they were told that Juniper had been fired.

Her coworker Angelo told her later that there was an alarming sit-in on the following Sunday of twenty-five motorcycle guys, who filled the café with their broad backsides and black leather. They occupied every available seat and sat in silence, not ordering anything, as if they were at a funeral mass. They stayed for thirty minutes, and after thoroughly unhinging the owner, they stood up and tossed some twenties into the tip jar.

Juniper tailored college to her cooking. History classes were doorways into Renaissance pastries and slow-cooked meats. She studied enough French and Italian to spend her junior year abroad studying literature, which somehow always came back to food, the chilled butter of perfect croissants, the almost indiscernible tang of a few drops of buttermilk in pastry shells, custards, and the hearty crepes with ham and cheese sold by street vendors.

In Italy, she learned to make fresh ricotta and mozzarella, topping them with basil, tomatoes, roasted garlic, and fresh olive oil.

Delia was already a caseworker when she visited her little sister in Italy, scrupulously saving her vacation time to be with Juniper at Christmas. Delia grudgingly followed Juniper to a corner pasta factory no bigger than a frozen yogurt shop at home. The woman who owned the shop showed them how to make pasta, passing it through the roller again and again until it was thin enough to go through the slicer, spilling out strings of pasta to the waiting arms of her assistant. The pasta hung on dowels around the shop, looking like miniature laundry.

Delia always credited all the sensuous talents of cooking to Juniper. "J Bird, you're the cook in the family, everyone knows that." The family meant the two of them.

But their father, who wrote food reviews when he was free

from delusions, taught both of his daughters to savor food, to discern food that was prepared without finesse and love. He once took them to a local restaurant in Portland on two consecutive nights and ordered the same dish, shrimp scampi. He said nothing to the girls, gave them no hint of his preference until they had consumed their second meal of glistening shrimp.

"Tell me which one makes you happy," he said.

Juniper, who was only nine at the time, didn't wait for her big sister to answer. "The one yesterday was more delicious. It made me hum a song the whole time I was eating," she said.

He smiled. "Each dinner had exactly the same ingredients. The difference was the chef. Sheila cooked yesterday, and she loves food, she respects the crustaceans, and she is an artist. The chef this evening was Philip, a man who wouldn't know love if it conked him on the head. It's about skill and proficiency, but the main ingredient is the transference of energy."

But during his bad times, and increasingly so until the end, food spoke to him with threats that her father endured until he could no longer taste the pleasure.

Until the day in the pasta factory, when the small Italian woman held the wet strands of pasta over her arm, Juniper might have continued to believe that she was the only sister who understood food, who tasted the layers of flavors, the comingling of savory spices. Delia had all but convinced her that her big sister was good for one thing in this life: taking care of J Bird and then taking care of the kids traveling through foster care.

But there had been a sea breeze off the Mediterranean in the small town of Minori, the zest of lemon was everywhere in the shop, the sweet notes of the semolina flour wrapped around Juniper. Delia looked transported, stunned, as if a long-dormant part of her brain had creaked open, lubricated by the molecules of fresh pasta bouncing unrestrained along the corridors of her olfactory center.

"Ask her if she'll teach me how to make this pasta," Delia said. She spent the remainder of the day with the woman, rolling, cutting, and hanging more pasta. Juniper left the two of them in the small kitchen. They spoke a language of food, unable to communicate otherwise.

Delia returned to their hotel and stretched out on the single bed next to Juniper.

"I didn't know, I didn't understand before. This is the good part of Dad. He left it for us, this way of seeing food."

If ever there was a time to be smug, to say *I told you so,* it was right then with Delia softened up like a slice of baguette with warm brie. But it was so comforting to Juniper that Delia could finally see her world that she smiled and handed her sister a bowl of olives, purchased that morning at a small storefront grocery.

The pasta maker later told Juniper, "Your sister has the nose. She can smell anything, that one. The semolina opened up its secrets for her."

It had taken Juniper five long years to convince Delia that they could open a bakery, and now they were only two months from opening.

She had found the location on her daily outings with Baxter. On Willard Beach in South Portland, prior to nine a.m., dogs were permitted off leash. In fact, she had walked Baxter on this beach four days a week since he was a puppy, which meant that for a total of three years, she had passed by the one-story building, which had, until one particular day, cloaked itself.

Back in March, five months ago, Juniper stopped to shake sand out of her blue Nikes, balancing on one foot as she shook one shoe, then the other. Maybe it was the shaking or the balancing on one foot, a change in perspective. She looked across the street at the building for sale, an old storefront that still had the faded letters DRY GOODS over the covered entryway, but which had last been a real estate office.

The morning light, not far from the spring equinox, caused the window to glitter, a word she would confidently repeat to Delia. The window vibrated, the light bouncing and jumping. The old storefront was at a crossroads to the beach, the place where everyone who knew about this beach (dog beach in the early a.m., runners next, track teams later afternoon, strollers throughout the day) passed by. She had never truly noticed the building before.

Juniper snapped the leash onto Baxter's collar and crossed the street. She pressed her hands against the glass and peered in. Everything that could have been ripped out had been. A few wires dangled from the ceiling where lights had been. Two large ceiling tiles sagged from their aluminum frames. What was beyond the tiles?

Baxter bumped her leg with a stick that he carried from the beach. She looked down to nudge it away, and when she looked up again, a ruffle of soft wind, sweet with the promise of summer, blew her hair, and in one devastating instant she saw people at café tables with croissants and sandwiches, steam coming from mugs of tea and coffee, clean, gleaming windows, an open kitchen, bread boards, two industrial ovens, large tubs of Canadian flour, and Delia. She saw Delia as clearly as she had ever seen her, elbow deep in dough with a kind of happiness on her face that she had never seen before.

Juniper blinked, looked down at Baxter, the stick, up again at the former dry goods/real estate office. Had thirty seconds passed? Five minutes? No matter. Juniper found something that had been there all along, waiting to be seen. A café/bakery. And she needed Delia to make it happen.

Two days later, on a Saturday afternoon when Juniper was done with her early shift at Bayside Bakery and Delia was not on call, they stood in front of the storefront.

"Even if I thought this was a good idea, it would have to be gutted, plumbing installed for a restaurant," said Delia. "ADA requirements, ramps, grab bars in the bathrooms. Permits, building inspections," she said, already rubbing her hand along the storefront glass.

Delia, so conditioned to be the parent, the serious one, seemed compelled to point out every single drawback. "I have a job with benefits, insurance, stability," she said.

"That's right," said Juniper, "soul-sucking stability." Baxter sat on her feet, trying to emphasize her point. "We have a choice.

Dad didn't have a choice and we do. Mom made a choice to give up what she loved doing to take care of Dad. You can stay in the world of social service and meetings and tragedy forever. Or we can take a chance."

Baxter stood up and pressed his head into Delia's hand, wagging his tail.

"Okay, Baxter, I can see you're in on this campaign," she said, kneeling down to nuzzle the dog. "We can try it for two years. If we're dead broke by then I can always get a job again."

# CHAPTER 10

After the epiphany in the pasta shop in Italy five years before when she visited J Bird, Delia began to bake bread on the weekends. Once a month she made pasta. She was not the tart, muffin, or chocolate éclair maker that J Bird was. That was a different language. Delia found her culinary home with breads and pasta and used her researcher's brain to understand yeast, the texture of crust and rye flour versus wheat. She read everything she could find about yeast, fascinated by the entire life form that had previously been unknown to her. Pasta was uncomplicated compared to the variability of bread.

Her first loaves had been unbalanced, lacking a critical amount of salt, or having too much salt. Bread was something she wanted to get right. There was so much about foster care that was never going to be right, a patched-up lifeboat for some kids. Within her own family, there was no going back, no extraction process of the gene that had caused her father's schizophrenia. But with the bread, she felt a kind of absolution. Perhaps it was because she baked only on Sundays. The bread became her holy day.

The living, breathing yeast drew her in. Delia relied on packaged yeast for the first year until she learned how to make her own starter. She caught on quickly to the life cycle of yeast, how the organisms could drink food straight from the atmosphere, catching molecules of salt air as it streamed by, the iron-rich moisture of rain, and even her own cast-off breath, all forming a natural yeast. She let the organisms evolve from the flour itself, along with the moist air off the Atlantic, the occasional loud dog burps whenever Baxter supervised, and every bit of her life that swirled around their kitchen. If she was absolutely quiet, closed all the windows, and turned off the music, she could hear the yeast mixture bubbling and exhaling. Once, she pulled her hair back with a scarf, put her ear close to the mixture, and closed her eyes. She was startled by a series of sighs, *ahs,* and *ohs* from the bowl, an orgasmic chorus as the yeast expanded into its own delicious passion.

*Careful, be careful,* she thought, pulling back suddenly. Her father heard voices coming from places far less strange than frothing yeast. This was the legacy of schizophrenia; were it not for her fear of inheriting the raging delusions of her father, she could give in fully to the beauty of the live yeast and its passionate, symphonic universe. She should stick to her highly developed reliance on smell, which was bounty enough with the aromatic bread.

She would have to be content with working the dough, mixing the flour, delighting when the perfect skin formed on the dough that contained the methane bubbles coming from the life cycle of the yeast community. The outside world fell away, the tedium of documentation in protective services, the memories of her childhood that held her hostage. They were no match for the visceral experience of kneading, nudging, baking, sniffing, and tasting bread made by her own hands.

J Bird noticed Delia's bread with her keen sense of foodie appreciation. "Good texture. Crust noticeable, but it doesn't need a jackhammer. Let me take a sample to Bayside Bakery and get their opinion."

That had been a year ago. Juniper grabbed onto an idea like

a hound dog, and the taste of Delia's bread launched her into the idea of the café.

"You and me, why not you and me? Why should I keep baking for other bakeries and why should you keep working in foster care when you bake the best bread I've ever tasted? I know the business part of a bakery, how to order, where to get the best supplies, and I know how to make the fancy stuff. But your job would be the bread and pasta."

The idea had seemed frivolous, irresponsible. Other people might be free to take a chance, to respond to artistic whimsy, but not Delia. She spent her childhood ever vigilant for the spikes in mood that would turn her father into the terrified and terrifying man who was so unlike her real father. Shielding her little sister from the worst of his paranoid delusions had been natural to her. After the fire, it was her job to take care of J Bird. But now, was it possible that she could shed the constraints of caretaker? The café loomed in the future, a dim star that grew brighter every day.

# CHAPTER 11

Delia packed her briefcase, cleared her breakfast dishes, and freshened Baxter's water before she left for the day. By the time she arrived at work, she smelled the remains of Ira's breakfast, something with eggs, onions, and beans; likely a burrito stashed into a desk drawer before she arrived.

"Have you found any relatives who can be guardians for her?" asked Delia.

If extended family could be found, Ira could do it. He could reach into the tangled ether of Social Security numbers, previously known addresses, or scraps of paper found at the crime scene. She had no doubt that Ira, the master of foster care in Southern Maine, kahuna of lost, neglected, and abandoned children, would find an aunt, uncle, or grandmother to care for Hayley.

He kept one eye on his aging desktop computer, his desk awash in papers. He spread his hands directly in front of him, rearranged his spine, possibly stretching for the first time since he'd been at this desk since eight a.m., and said, "No. Nothing yet."

The child had been in the emergency placement for three days when Ira delivered the news about her parentage, or more precisely, her lack of discernible parentage. A shadow of dread crept up Delia's neck. Ira always had a lead by now. Alienated grandparents emerged, stepdads with vital information, a critical morsel from a social service agency in another state, a women's shelter. But now, nothing.

She wondered about her own parentage. What if she and J Bird weren't related by blood to her father? But they were.

Delia had twenty-seven more days. She balanced on her tiptoes at the edge of her new life, ready to dive into the world of serving deliciousness: croissants, oatmeal bread, and homemade pasta with fresh lemon. The dream of the café with Juniper was within reach.

But there was no one for Hayley, and if there were, Ira would have found them by now. She sank back on her heels.

"I only have this, found in the pocket of one of the male victims. It's a receipt, cash, unfortunately, for a store in West Hartford."

"What kind of store does it come from?" Relief entered the picture again.

Ira picked up a copy of the receipt, a photocopy of the crumpled rectangle forming an island on the paper.

Ira held the paper in front of him, stretching his arms out to accommodate his aging eyes. "Artemis Hardware Store. West Hartford, Connecticut."

"There's really a hardware store named Artemis?"

"I wouldn't make that up. Probably a family name."

Ira handed the paper across the desk. In the upper right-hand corner was stamp that said, *South Portland Police Department.* The receipt recorded three items: four boxes of Ziploc bags, a flashlight, and eight D batteries. Were they planning on making a lot of sandwiches? Unlikely.

As if he heard her thoughts, he said, "Remember, the police are already suspecting heroin traffic. The location fits the drug pipeline. Heroin dealers are great supporters of plastic baggies."

Hayley's photo, taken at the hospital where she stayed the first night, sat on top of the thin file folder. Her brown doe eyes caught a glint of light in the room from an overhead fluorescent light in the hospital. Her hair, still embroiled with a piece of bubble gum on the left side, near the crown, was soft brown.

"They were unable to get a last name from her. When they said, 'Hayley what? What's the rest of your name?' she shrugged and honestly didn't seem to know. It makes me wonder if her parents had been too busy doing something else, like running heroin, to teach the child her full name. At least there was no answer. She also had no response to the deaths."

Delia had been at this long enough to resist the urge to make assumptions, to set them aside until the facts rolled in. Ira was normally ready to wait for all the facts too, but something about Hayley brought out a simmering anger that Delia rarely saw in him. The full blast of over identifying with a particular child could hit any of them, at any time.

"Have the police faxed the photo to authorities in West Hartford? Did they take the photo to the hardware store?"

"Yesterday. Nobody remembers the girl. The woman who generally works the cash register at the hardware store thinks she remembers a man buying the Ziploc bags. But he wasn't someone she knew."

"What happens next if we can't find relatives?" asked Delia.

She wasn't new at this; in fact, she'd been at her job too long. Her personal expiration date had come and gone.

Ira pushed up from his chair, his fifty-something belly, not huge but the size of a soccer ball split in half, had grown since she started her job ten years ago. Juniper reminded her often that ten years was enough.

"You know what happens next. We take her out of the emergency placement and find an extended placement for her." He grabbed his car keys from the top right drawer. "Come on. We're going to see if there is something that Hayley can tell us."

Delia rarely saw Ira interacting with kids anymore. His reward for being a competent, sensitive, exacting caseworker meant that he rose through administration like a hot air balloon. His job was filled with the big picture of fund-raising and dancing around regulations.

Delia caught up with him in the hallway after gathering her dark brown L.L. Bean briefcase.

"Is she in Portland?"

"No, South Portland."

The parking garage was in the same block as their office. The brief respite of fresh ocean air filled her nose with light salt and fish that had been fried in olive oil along Commercial Street.

They took Ira's RAV4 Toyota that he and his wife had used to haul their kids to soccer games, music lessons, and camping trips. The last daughter was in college but they held onto the car, the two of them rattling around in the all-wheel drive vehicle. Ira paid for a monthly rate at the parking garage rather than hunting for parking spaces on the street as Delia often did.

They hadn't teamed up on a case in several years, not since Ira was promoted to director, right about the time that Delia refused a promotion into administration. But here they were, like an old couple reuniting after an amicable divorce, seated next to each other amid the intimacy of the SUV. They left the parking garage, skirted the daydreaming pedestrians along Commercial Street, and crossed the Casco Bay Bridge into South Portland.

They pulled up in front of a ranch house that had been renovated with an added second story. The first level was covered in vinyl siding, the second was covered in shingles stained with a gray/white oil that the entire neighborhood seemed to be fond of.

Delia had long since noticed that people in the gated communities, or who lived in the five thousand-square-foot houses, rarely signed on to become foster parents. The houses where foster parents lived were modest: three bedrooms, two baths, small rooms, white Corelle plates, thin towels, and big hearts. At least all the families that Ira trained.

Ira was meticulous about training and accepting foster parents. Having gone through the system as a child, he knew that even one foster parent who turned their home into a child version of a dog kennel would doom the whole system. He was wary of foster parents who treated their kids with anything less than bountiful, loving care. On a good day, the system teetered on the edge. Newspapers only covered the worst disasters in foster care, not the hundreds who found a safe harbor.

"Which family did you put her with?" she asked. Normally she would have asked this first thing. With her resignation, she was slipping, not as careful. She had to pull herself together; she was still working for the kids. She wasn't done yet.

"Erica and Tom. They're relatively new, but I trust them. They understand that she might well regress, wet the bed, act out, have nightmares, stop talking. They have one child of their own who is in high school, a girl, and a very friendly Maine Coon cat. I didn't start doing this yesterday." Ira tilted his head and did something with his lips that made one side of his well-trimmed mustache jump.

"I'm still afraid of making a mistake, of making this situation worse," he said, doing a slow nod. "I remember when I first started and it hit me like a truck. What if I make this horrible situation worse? What if I make a mistake and trust a foster parent who flips out and can't handle a kid who starts raging and tossing their toaster around their kitchen? What if I put a kid with a foster parent who was really a sexual predator, the kind who's been waiting all of his adult life to have little kids put into his care? Terrifying, isn't it?"

This was exactly what made Ira the best. He knew how wrong everything could go with one weak link among the foster parents. He never forgot, never got complacent.

Two tricycles marked the edge of the driveway.

"Has the art therapist been here yet?" asked Delia, opening the passenger door.

They passed the trikes and the last of a row of petunias, already going leggy before the cold nights of fall.

"Not yet. She's on vacation," he said, pressing his fingers on the beige doorbell. The door opened and a wave of cooking smells tumbled out.

"Hi, Erica. I smell dinner cooking. You never disappoint."

# CHAPTER 12

Erica ran her hand through her dark blond hair. "What you smell is dinner, but so far, Hayley's favorite thing to eat is a hotdog, plain, no mustard and no ketchup."

Delia followed Ira into the house. "This is Delia, the caseworker I told you about. We thought we'd visit with you and Hayley for a short time."

Delia shook hands with Erica. Her touch was warm and soft. Strong. Erica's dark blue pants, made of the indestructible fabric that hikers wear, stopped right below her knees. She was barefoot, but a tan line along the tops of her feet came from the pair of Tevas in the corner.

"Are you a hiker?" asked Delia.

Erica laughed easily. "My husband says I look like a model for the Appalachian Mountain Club. We get out whenever we can. My daughter doesn't love it as much as we do, but we're good at bribing her. I was just telling Hayley about a little walk we could take and have a picnic."

Erica looked back into a room beyond. "She's in the kitchen now, helping me with some mixing." She wiped her hands along her pants. "Hayley has never gone on a picnic and tells me that Emma is waiting for her."

Emma Gilbert? The female victim? Not Mommy, but Emma. *Is there a Mommy,* Delia wondered.

Erica stepped back and pointed toward the kitchen. "Come in and join us. I'll make some fresh coffee."

Erica already understood Ira's insatiable coffee habit.

The kitchen was hot. Erica took a peek into the oven and said, "Sorry about the heat. I cook several meals ahead on days when I can." The sliding glass door was open. Erica's head spun around. "Hayley? She was just here."

Any comfort that Delia felt when meeting Erica evaporated, and in its place, her solar plexus braced for an assault. A missing child was one thousand times worse than a child of unknown parentage.

Erica ran to the door and stepped onto the deck. "Hayley?"

Delia and Ira were one step behind her. There in the backyard was a girl, standing in the middle of a raised garden bed, holding a cucumber. A Maine Coon cat, as large as a beagle, pressed its head against the girl's leg, looking every bit like a guard dog. When the girl looked up, she put the cucumber behind her back.

Delia sighed. Thank God for children who were inquisitive and went no farther than garden beds. She looked out at the yard. And thank God for fenced back yards, which Delia normally didn't like, but at this moment, she appreciated the benefits.

Erica hopped off the Trex-floored deck and walked calmly to Hayley. "Do you like cucumbers? I do too." She sat down on the wood rim of the raised bed. "Can you show your cucumber to my friends Ira and Delia?"

This was their cue. Delia walked over to the garden bed and sat down on the grass. "Hi, Hayley. I like to pick cucumbers too. Can I help?"

Hayley's light brown hair, freshly shampooed with something floral, hung to the top of her shoulders. Everything that she wore was new. The few clothes she was wearing when she was found were part of the crime scene and were taken from her at the hospital. To her huge credit, Erica found clothing that looked similar to help Hayley feel comfortable. Her yellow T-shirt didn't have a princess on the front but it did have a friendly looking dragon with wings. Her blue shorts were too big, ballooning around her skinny thighs. Her legs, dappled with scabbed insect bites, were strangely flaccid for a child. Wouldn't she have been running, jumping, and skipping wherever she had been?

"Emma likes cucumbers," said Hayley.

No one had made the leap to tell the child that Emma was dead. While it was likely that Hayley had either seen the murders or the aftermath, making the final conclusion was not straightforward for young children. She had blood on her body when they found her; she made contact with the victims. This was far too complicated for a first visit. A therapist and Erica would be the best people to present the ultimate truth about the dead woman.

Hayley brought the cucumber in front of her. "Emma is dead." She nodded solemnly and reached down to touch the cat's head. "I told Louie and he is sad."

Delia never knew how young children would respond to death. For some, the death of a parent or caretaker was beyond comprehension and the child blocked it from their reality. For others, they struggled to understand the forever absence that death caused and talked about it with a frankness that caused adults to crumble. Hayley was in the latter camp.

Erica reached over and stroked the large cat. "Our cat's name is Louie," she said in a tender voice.

"What helps Louie when he is sad?" asked Delia, not wanting to lose the thread, yet venturing as lightly as she could.

The cat, a hefty twenty pounds at least, chose the moment to swat a bumblebee from midair with his large paws and eat it. "He likes cat food. It comes in a can," said Hayley. She looked at Erica. "Will the bee sting him in the mouth?"

Erica smiled. "He likes bumblebees and I don't think they've ever stung him. I'll go get a can of food and we can feed him together so he won't be so sad about Emma."

Ira knew what he was doing when he picked Erica. The woman had dialed into this child.

Erica rattled around in the kitchen and returned with a can of Friskies and a small red bowl. She pulled the tab on the can and the sound ignited Louie, ears up, eyes alert. "Hayley, take this spoon and please give Louie two big scoops."

Had she fed a cat before? Or was this the first time? Delia watched for everything that might help.

"Do you have a kitty?" she asked.

Hayley shook her head. "Emma says we can't have a cat in our car."

Did they live in a car? There was no car at the crime scene.

"Do you sleep in your car or do you sleep in a house? I sleep in a house," said Ira. Delia was so focused on the moment that she almost forgot Ira was there.

Hayley squatted near the bowl and carefully scooped out two spoons of cat food. "Louie sleeps with me. I have a bed now," she said, pointing to the house.

Erica tilted her head toward Ira. "He doesn't have fleas and he's sort of a love chunky. All the kids love him. I hope that's okay."

Delia could think of no one who would begrudge this child the simple comforts of the furry creature.

"Did you and Emma sleep in a bed?" asked Delia.

Hayley peered at Louie's fine dining with fascination. "He likes his food." She ran her hand along his spine. Louie, without a one-second delay in eating, raised his back in a curve to meet Hayley's palm.

The maze of talking with young children was fraught with dead ends. When the path was open with kids, Delia could sense a difference in the light. The path wasn't blocked yet.

"Is Emma your mommy?" Delia said, while reaching to pet Louie. If the cat would stay put, Hayley might keep talking. According to the emergency workers who were at the hospital, the only thing Hayley said was her name. They were in the midst of a conversation cloudburst now.

"Emma reads books to me. We sleep in the car when the tigers come."

Delia slowed her breathing. She felt the end of the path closing in, the light changing.

"Did the tigers hurt Emma?" She rubbed the back of Louie's head while he cleaned his face with one paw.

Hayley pulled her hands into claws, opened her mouth wide and roared. "Like this," and she roared again. "Tigers are bad. Louie said he will fight the tigers if they come."

The door of words slammed shut. Hayley put her thumb into her mouth and turned away, rocking side to side.

Ira and Delia stood up, both knowing how long a child could endure what must feel like an onslaught of hard questions, dragging Hayley into dark days with dangerous tigers.

"It's time for us to leave. Good-bye, Hayley. Thank you for showing us the beautiful cucumber. Good-bye, Louie," said Delia.

Erica walked them back as far as the kitchen, looking over her shoulder at the child, who hummed and rocked while sucking her thumb. "I'm going to stay outside with her and read a story. I understand now why she feels more comfortable outside."

"We can see ourselves out," said Ira. "I'll call you later."

Back in the car, Ira backed out of the driveway. "What was Emma Gilbert doing, dragging that child around? And who were the tigers?"

Delia pushed a button to roll down her window. "We know they weren't the good guys. Thank God for Louie. Maine Coon cats are more dog than cat. I'm surprised Louie doesn't bark." Delia kept seeing the small girl comforting Louie, offering the cat what she so desperately needed after the carnage.

Ira turned right and eased out of the neighborhood, past the buzz of a lawnmower, the flashing light of a mail truck.

"That's what makes tigers so dangerous. You don't hear them coming."

# CHAPTER 13

*Hayley*

**"A** re there tigers in kindergarten?" asked Hayley. She had a bowl of Cheerios in front of her on the dark blue kitchen island. If Hayley were able to fly above the kitchen, the kitchen island would look like a pond. Emma told her a pond was smaller than a lake.

This was not the kind of cereal that Emma gave her, not the chocolate kind with little chips of dried marshmallows.

Erica was the lady who took care of her now. Emma was gone. Hayley told Erica that she understood dead. She was not a baby. Emma was dead, although Hayley still wondered at times if Emma would surprise her by coming back, drive up in the car with her *Star Wars* sleeping bag in the back seat and say, "Time to go, Miss Sweetie Pie. Hop in."

Now she was stuck in this tall chair with a bowl of small, donut-shaped cereal and there was nothing special about it. The cereal was small, hard, dry, and dull. Erica thought she should eat the whole bowl. Hayley couldn't. She'd rather do anything than eat this cereal.

Erica loaded up a blender with yogurt and green stuff and bananas and dry powdered stuff. She pushed a button that made a noise as loud as ten pots and pans all clanging together. Then it was quiet again.

Erica poured the gooey stuff into a glass and drank it with tiny sips. She probably didn't like it either. How could she? "Why do you think tigers might be at school?"

Hayley's stomach tightened. What if Erica tried to make her drink the green goo?

Erica put her glass on the counter. "Don't worry; nobody except for me likes to drink this for breakfast. Tom and Sarah call it pond scum."

Sarah was Erica's daughter. She was a big girl and went to high school. She braided Hayley's hair yesterday.

"Oh," said Hayley, unclenching her hands and her belly. "Emma told me never to go into the house with tigers."

Erica put the empty glass in the sink. "I think Emma took good care of you. Did you ever see the tigers?"

Hayley saw pictures of tigers in books. "Yes. They live in the jungle and they can eat you. They have sharp teeth and big claws."

Erica rummaged in her red purse and pulled out a phone, looked at it, and put it on the counter.

"The kindergarten class doesn't have tigers, only children like you and two teachers. Today, you and I can look at the kindergarten. I'll show you where your backpack goes and where you'll sit. Then we'll come back here and you can play with Louie while I work. Where is Louie? Here, kitty, kitty."

Erica made her voice go funny when she called Louie, higher, almost like singing. Hayley heard Louie meowing as he ran into the kitchen, talking and talking as if he were saying, "Coming, I'm coming, right here, coming, coming."

Erica crouched down and stroked Louie, starting at his head and finishing at the end of his tail. This was the first time ever that Hayley had a friend who was a cat. Erica had showed her how to pet Louie.

Erica looked up at Hayley. It wasn't often that she was higher than grown-ups, where you could see the tops of their heads. Erica's hair smelled just like the shampoo Erica used last night on Hayley's hair.

Louie made everyone happy. She was sure that he was the best cat in the world. He was big. Erica told her that Maine Coon cats were big, with extra-big feet that looked like furry slippers. When Hayley first came to this house, she was afraid of Louie. Now she wanted to be with Louie all the time.

"Climb on down. You can let your breakfast be. Louie wants to tell us his cat story before we go to kindergarten."

Hayley slid off the stool, hanging on the edge of the island until her feet touched the floor. She sat next to Erica and the cat. He rubbed his head into her chest and toppled her into the woman. He pawed her arm but kept his claws tucked inside.

"He's trying to tell you that he wants you to pet him. Here, sit in my lap and then Louie can get on your lap. Louie and I will make a Hayley sandwich." Erica took a pretend bite from the top of Hayley's head. "Yum! You taste like peaches!"

Louie was heavy, so heavy that Hayley was sure she couldn't lift him. But his body was warm and his purring motor vibrated right through the bones in her back.

"Can Louie come with us to kindergarten?"

She rubbed Louie's face along his jawline like Erica showed her. Louie pushed into her hand, wanting more.

"Cats can't go to school," she said. "But he'll wait for you and be right here when we come home from school."

If the tigers came to Erica's house, Louie would help her. They would run, run as fast as they could.

# CHAPTER 14

How could Delia possibly think of online dating when her mind was filled with Hayley, when the most important thing was finding guardians for the child before Delia came to the end of her job in twenty-six days? She made this date a week ago, before Ira hooked her back into the new case. But Juniper had said, quite clearly, "Go! In the name of all that is holy and delicious, go!"

This was Delia's third coffee date in six months via Match.com. Despite everything, the tragedies at work and starting the J Bird Café, she had to make time for romance. Her sister was right. Even Ira had lectured her, along with Ben. She was thirty-two and beginning to feel a grim reaper of romance clipping along her heels with the sudden realization that she might be single all her days.

She was certain that J Bird would never remain untethered to a man, since they swarmed around her like bees. When she walked into a room, even men who had their backs to the door swiveled around as if they were on a lazy Susan serving plate, pulled by the fragility of her face, the open, guileless way she stood, moving, doing something delicate with her hands.

Men thought they knew J Bird, even before they spoke to her. Did her vulnerability translate as sexuality? Delia was sure that it did, and her sister often verified this in their late-night sister talks with more detail than Delia wanted. Given that J Bird could have pulled in any man, she had selected tragically until now. If there was a cinematic type for Bad Boy, she found all of them, complete with sulky, brooding stares, hard-driving sex, and demanding monogamy while they slept with as many women as possible. Collier, her most current ex-boyfriend, had offered a reprieve from high drama. He was in law school part time, taking classes at night while he worked at Whole Foods to pay the bills. To J Bird's utter astonishment, he had broken up with her over the summer, pleading emotional exhaustion. J Bird could have that effect on people.

Delia shook her head. Here she was waiting for the coffee date to arrive and all she could think of was her sister. Her plunge into the dating site was a step toward pulling her head out of her little sister's love life, accepting Juniper as an adult. She did not want to become a character in a nineteenth century British novel who grew old tending to her beautiful sister.

The Daily Grind was a café on the top of the hill in Portland, out of the trendiest parts of the city that edged along the port on Commercial Street. The coffee was rich and dark, the buzz of noise rose to a pleasant hum, an espresso machine hissed like a steam engine, spoons tinkled against the mugs of foamed milk, plates with scones slid across the copper-edged stone counter. The perfect place for a meet and greet date.

Or not. Who came up with this idea that you could get to know another person within an hour while hunched nervously across a small, round café table? Rather than a coffee date, perhaps a type of competition would be better, a version of Hunger Games for the dating crowd. Fight against a common enemy. Jousting? A pool tournament, even a card game, something other than what almost everyone dreaded, the interview date.

But these were the rules when meeting someone for the first

time, offered by all the online sites, not only Match.com. You meet in a public place, as if either one of you might be danger-ous and the café would offer protection.

He was five minutes late. If he was ten minutes late, she was going to get up and leave casually, as if she had come here with no other purpose than coffee. Already the feeling of re-jection lit up in her belly. And if he was fifteen minutes late, what would that predict for the future? Delia was terrified and fought against her preemptive reaction that she didn't want to have a second date anyhow.

"Delia? Are you Delia? I've been sitting in the other room, out by the patio, and it occurred to me that I should come in here and check."

There was a patio in the back? Why would someone on a first date hide out in the back?

"Jeremy? Nice to meet you." Delia held out her hand. She knew they would size each other up in the first ninety seconds, maybe less. He was pale. He hadn't seen the sun all summer, not even walking to his car. But his hand was moist, and this evoked a human connection for Delia. He was afraid too. Ei-ther one of them could reject the other on the spot. Online dating was the new emotional blood sport.

"Um, should I come to your table?" he said, doing something with his upper body, a loose, almost comic swivel between the back room and the front. "I already ordered a coffee, I can bring it up here."

"Sure," she said. He was going to come to her, and in the minutiae of the first date interview, this was a plus. She tried to slow her breathing.

Jeremy turned and went back to the rear of the café, where he might have been sitting for who knows how long, to retrieve his drink. This truly was a jousting competition, in a slow, in-terpersonal give and take. She sat back in her chair, recoiling when her spine hit the metal of the chair. Did the chairs have to be so unforgiving? She turned to look out the large window near the entrance and froze.

Tyler. Was she hallucinating? Was dating so stressful for her that her father's illness had found a portal of entry? No, it really was Tyler. Not so different after thirteen years. He was broader in the chest, taller, if that was possible. Did boys keep growing after they were nineteen, when she had seen him last? Maybe he would keep walking by and she could pretend that she didn't see him. Surely the light was so brilliant outside that he couldn't see in. And her date would be back any minute.

Tyler pushed open the glass and metal door. As if there were no one else in the place, he looked directly at her. The sound of the coffee machines faded away. He tilted his head to one side in surprise. Or like he was seeing a ghost.

"It's been a long time, Delia."

What could she reply, frozen in place? Could she say something about the muscles along the sides of his eyes, the tiny muscles around his nose, how he looked down for only a second, composing himself, as ripped into the past as she was? It had been a long time, yes, several lifetimes, two dead parents, two daughters surviving the disaster. She was too stunned to speak.

Three memories of him popped up, a triptych of images. The first was at the foot of her hospital bed after the fire, when Delia was treated for smoke inhalation. He said, "I'm sorry, I'm so sorry," his eyes red and puffy. He had pulled Delia out of the house, so they told her later, after she forced her way in, using her key to unlock the door of the house, convinced she could save her mother and father, who for years gave every evidence of not being able to save themselves.

Tyler came from her other life, back when she had to be pulled out of infernos and dragged to the safety of moist green grass, the air filled with smoke, heat, and fire sirens.

The second image was the funerals. Plural. Two funerals. But all of Portland was there, funneling through the Belmont Funeral Home, squeezing through the point that focused on Delia and J Bird.

And the third image—

Jeremy banged into the table, spilling his coffee.

Tyler looked at Jeremy and made a quick assessment of the

situation. He pulled a card out of his wallet, scribbled something, and said, "Please call me. I'm back in town. This is my cell." He put the card facedown on the table and walked out.

Jeremy mopped up the spill with a wad of napkins and piled them near the edge of the table. "Who was that? You look sort of stunned." He sat down.

Tyler was here. They were going to see each other. There wasn't anything else she could think about as she sat facing Jeremy across the small table. "I knew him a long time ago. He was my boyfriend."

Jeremy, looking even paler in a moment of crystal clarity, said, "We're not going out with each other, are we?"

It was such a relief to talk with someone who spoke the truth, who didn't try to soften, pretend, or modify, that Delia hesitated for a moment before she said, "You're right. Thank you. I mean, I wasn't expecting him to ever show up again. I never thought I'd see him again." She was going to be Jeremy's bad Match.com date story, the one who changed her mind before she even sat down after seeing an old beau. If she said she was sorry, it could make it worse, make him feel pathetic.

Her bag hung on the back of the chair, and she reached around to pull it in and stood up. "Jeremy, you just dodged a bullet." Oh, my God, that was even worse. Now he could add that stupid line to his story and his friends would shake their heads.

She fluttered a good-bye wave and made for the door, heading in the opposite direction of Tyler.

The third image of Tyler flooded every part of her. Tyler leaving her when she had needed him so much.

# CHAPTER 15

Delia left Jeremy to formulate his online dating story. She felt wretched and almost wished she had been the one abandoned on the uncomfortable metal chair. The midafternoon temperatures were warmer than usual, as if autumn had been waylaid. She opened her car door and heat billowed out. She slid in, opened all the windows, and leaned her forehead on the steering wheel.

Tyler's business card slid around in her pocket, darting like a fish in the shallows of a river, alive, vibrant, hiding from the sun and predators. Tyler was now thirteen years older, eyes more shadowed by a furrowed brow, hands oddly soft. It was shocking to see his earnest, younger self peeking out. Was she still who she had been when she was nineteen? No, absolutely not. But still, a warm circle pulsed around her belly button, spreading out from an ember core. He had been the exciting new kid in high school, arriving in their senior year.

Tyler Greene, M.D. He was a physician? He had scratched out a number from a clinic in San Jose, California, and scribbled a new phone number. Why had he returned? The third image of

Tyler that popped up was somehow the worst, when she thought she had one thing to hold on to, one person she could count on.

Hadn't he and his family moved three thousand miles to the opposite side of the continent that horrible summer, a return to their extended families on the West Coast? The fire that had killed her parents incinerated most of her memories from those months. When she came up for air, after the funerals and the fire investigators who said their conclusion was that the fire was intentionally set, she realized that Tyler and his family were loading up a moving van.

She had driven back to the charred ruin of their house to collect anything, a melted mercury dime from her mother's coin jar, a plate, a piece of wood from their staircase. The moving van in front of Tyler's house sagged under the weight of the Greenes' household possessions. Tyler, his hands still pink from his burn injuries, a hank of his blond hair charred by the fire, carried his six-year-old sister on his back.

Delia got out of her car and walked in a daze toward the moving van.

"What happened? Why are you moving? Why didn't you tell me?"

Before the fire, they had been new, a year of dating once the scrutiny of high school was behind them. And then there was the world-shattering asteroid of the fire. Delia had not come out of the disaster zone mode of living for two months. The vortex of taking care of Juniper, deciding how to live as orphans, where and how. Basic survival took over. Ben had rushed in, taking care of the horrible details of death, the funerals, standing by their sides ever since.

Tyler swung his sister to the ground. "Go inside, Becky," he said. He wiped his hands on his jeans. "I was going to call you. Or write. My father got a job at Boeing. He's on their cockpit designing team."

The filaments holding Delia together disintegrated from exhaustion. She felt foolish. Surely if he had cared about her, even in their fledgling relationship, he would have stayed. He was in college; he didn't have to follow his family. But who wouldn't if they had a choice? If she had a family like Tyler's, parents who made pizza from scratch on Friday nights and held hands when they walked through the neighborhood, she would follow them like a bloodhound.

Although Ben and his wife wanted them to move to Peaks Island with them, Delia insisted that they stay in Portland. Ben's mother was ready to sell her house on Montreal Street and move to North Carolina. With Ben's signature on the mortgage, Delia and Juniper moved in.

Still, Tyler's nineteen-year-old self had resurfaced in the coffee shop, and she could think of nothing else. Everything that she had to deal with was so much more important, like a small child without parents, and terrifying, like starting a café business with Juniper. She didn't want to go home yet. Given her options, the café was the most manageable. She pointed her car toward South Portland.

Delia stopped at their café to see how the remodel was going. She wanted to meet Greg, the new carpenter that Juniper hired. This was the future, the one void of childhood traumas.

She walked around the café storefront to the back of the lot and saw a man on the peak of the shed roof. He looked familiar, but a lot of people looked vaguely familiar to Delia, and sometimes it was only the daily repetition of passing the same people on the sidewalks. He was older, several decades older than she was able to imagine being, the sun striking through his thin hair. He looked up and waved.

"I'm Greg," he said. "J Bird said you were stopping by." He superglued a porcelain elephant to the cupola of the shed roof in back of their new café. Juniper said it was good luck to have an elephant with a raised trunk.

Delia waved back, looking up at him.

"I'm retired, but you wouldn't know it," he said, while he straddled the peak of the outbuilding. He pointed to the elephant. "Your sister said this was good luck." He swung one leg over, as if he were dismounting a horse, and slid his legs to the edge.

"Hold the ladder steady, would ya?"

Delia braced one foot against the bottom of the extension ladder and leaned into it with her arms.

"What are you retired from?" she asked, when he was back on the ground. One of the bakers Juniper worked with had recommended Greg.

At first, they needed an extra handyman to help with renovations, not a full-out licensed contractor, but someone who would know how to frame out a door on a shed, or how to attach something porcelain to wood that might survive the winter elements in Maine. But somehow, Greg had advanced from handyman to general contractor after J Bird had a meltdown when the plumbers wouldn't return her calls. Now Greg was the intermediary, sort of the vice president of operations right under the sisters.

"I did some stuff with IBM," he said, carefully placing each foot on a ladder rung.

"What kind of stuff? And you can't be retired because we've hired you."

Greg reached firm ground. "I opened up the Asian office back in the day."

She should have known. People came to Maine through portals that Delia had given up hoping to understand. A woman from Boston with her PhD in anthropology worked at the homeless shelter. The best plumber around lived with his longtime partner, who was an editor for an online fantasy journal. The white-haired guy with a hunched-over back had been a physicist at Brown. There was no way to predict. Now she learned that Greg, the handyman turned general contractor, had delivered IBM to China.

"Where's that boyfriend of yours?" he asked. He tucked the plastic bottle of superglue into his jacket pocket.

What boyfriend? Greg must have seen her with the guy from the online dating parade. Well not a parade. She had dated three men in the last year, each one remarkably unsuited to her. Or maybe it was Delia. She was unsuitable.

"Where could you have possibly seen me with a date?"

"I frequent The Daily Grind. I can't give up my daily espresso."

That's why he looked familiar. He was one of the regulars, likely head down into the *Wall Street Journal,* or faced into his smartphone.

"I'm sort of taking a break from dating," she said, completely aware how overused this sounded.

Greg's hair, a mix of white and brown, was thin enough that his pink scalp was visible.

"That's what I told IBM when I was about fifty-five. *I need a break,* I said to them. Except I never went back. That was ten years ago. We all knew they were going under." He pulled a tape measure from his toolbox. "Don't take a break for too long or you'll end up supergluing elephants to shed roofs."

A gold wedding band on his left hand announced his marital status. "How did you meet your wife?" she asked. "You didn't have Match.com back then."

"The old-fashioned way, at college in Chicago. Our first date was at a Pink Floyd concert, and neither of us could hear one word the other said. She told me she was more of a Marvin Gaye, Carly Simon kind of gal. I had never listened to any music where the bass didn't pulverize my skull, but I sort of liked her music. Weird, isn't it, how people find each other?"

Weird? Was there something beyond weird, something that drew people together beyond what we could see or touch, a kind of vibrational wave designed for only two people? Radio wave matchmaking? Her parents had found each other at their college newspaper. Ira and his wife met through friends and knew the second they were in the same room for ten minutes. Ben and Michelle were married for twenty-five years, all without the aid of Match.com. Well, Ben did say they met at a bar, but Ben had been bartending his way through vet school.

Delia slid one finger into her pocket and touched Tyler's card.

"Nice to meet you, Greg. I have to get back to work. Juniper said she gave you a list. She knows more about the requirements for the café than I do."

"Juniper? You mean J Bird. She told me to call her that."

Her sister had already pulled Greg into the fold of her life.
He gave a wave, not quite military, but still, his fingers started
at the side of his head and then pointed toward her. "Any time
you need a tester for baked goods, I'm your man," he said.

Delia walked back to the storefront and felt a soft ocean
breeze filter in between the houses and caress her face. How
did the breeze find her, whistling in like it knew she was standing right there? How had Tyler found her?

# CHAPTER 16

If Delia was going to see Tyler again, she wanted a buffer. Perhaps several. She had been rejected by Tyler once, and did not want a tête-à-tête, meaningful looks, a possible too-long hug, fingertips grazing over a menu. His business card felt magnetized, drawing the iron from her blood. Did she know anyone else circling their thirties who handed out business cards? Maybe he was professional all the time now. Mr. Medical Doctor. Maybe he wasn't Tyler anymore.

It was like seeing a ghost, and Delia had plenty of those to go around. She hadn't given Tyler a number to call, certainly not an address. Yet when she came home from putting a coat of paint on the bathroom of the café, he had already called.

"Delia, you'll never guess who called and left a message. Tyler. Didn't you guys go out? Wasn't he the guy who moved to Portland in his senior year, all cool and West Coasty?"

Her number was listed, making it easy enough for Tyler to find it. But still, the feel of him reaching out permeated her marrow.

Baxter trotted to the front door and greeted Delia with his

full-body gyration, head pressed into her thigh, a purring whine that melted her every time. How could a dog with such a dignified profile make such a silly sound?

There were times when Delia and J Bird devolved from *we are both adults* together now. J Bird became thirteen and Delia became nineteen again. Or worse yet, Delia was thirteen and J Bird was seven, brand new to second grade, and Delia knew how to keep her occupied while her parents were off to the psychiatrist again for another round of promising medications.

"Did you hear me?" said Juniper from the kitchen.

Pans clattered, and the whoosh of water running down the sink meant she was cleaning up after a baking episode. Delia smelled sage; these must be the new scones. Freshly ground pepper, sage, and a hint of finely ground caraway. The latest experiment.

Delia dropped her ever-present shoulder briefcase, big enough to hold her laptop for work. When she finally left Foster Services, she would never carry a briefcase again. She longed for the feeling of bread dough, full of promise and life.

Fragrant scones cooled on a metal rack. J Bird was never happier than when she had successfully concocted a slight variation in a recipe. She held out her arms, palms up, and took a bow. Baxter took his favored position under the kitchen table, his head resting on his paws, brown eyes darting from sister to sister.

"These are definitely going on our menu," she said. Her auburn hair was held out of the food zone by a purple scarf rolled into a headband. Even sweating, with tendrils of her hair tumbling past the scarf and wearing a white baker's apron, J Bird was beautiful.

Delia pinched off the nose of a scone and popped it into her mouth. "Nice. The ground caraway is a third-level taste, not as prominent as in rye bread. I've never understood why they put caraway seeds in rye bread. Biting into them is like a caraway grenade."

Juniper put her hands on her hips. "The Tyler guy?"

"Okay," said Delia, "I saw him today. He's moved back."

"He would like you to call him." J Bird vacillated between being an annoying thirteen-year-old and the blistering hotshot baker she had become.

"How can I? I don't have time. I need to work on this last case. And the café needs so much work before we can open; I'm afraid we won't make our deadline for an opening."

Juniper untied the apron and threw it on the counter. "Let me ask you this. How did your Match.com date go? Another *improbable pairing,* to use your words?"

Baxter saw the apron toss as a sign for a potential walk. He stood up and went to the door that led to the backyard, looking back at them for confirmation.

Delia conceded the point; she would call him back. And she already knew where they'd meet. Tomorrow morning at seven a.m. when Willard Beach at South Portland allowed dogs off leash, she'd bring all eighty pounds of golden retriever with her and J Bird. Two layers of buffer between her and Tyler should do it.

Delia, J Bird, and Baxter arrived at the parking lot in front of Willard Beach at six forty-five a.m. Great Danes squeezed their way out of two-door Corollas and teacup poodles emerged from V-8 Land Cruisers. Every car that pulled in held a dog, or two, or three. Since the moment he saw the sisters put on running shoes, Baxter's level of anticipation remained sky high. His muscles flickered with each bump of the journey that meant beach, water, sticks, gulls, and the occasional decaying fish. He pressed his black nose against the window and whined a slow, high-pitched sound that was unique to beach arrivals.

Delia opened the back door for Baxter, and he leapt out in a detonation of joy. Delia wished that she could be as happy as this dog, forgetting all wrongs from the past and planning no more than five minutes into the future. Was Baxter's present moment larger than both her past and future? She had asked Ben this question several months ago while Baxter gracefully submitted to his vaccinations. "That's it exactly," he said, "sort of like a perpetual high."

"Tyler isn't here. He's probably not coming," said Delia, trying to keep a lightness to her voice, keeping a lid on her deep disappointment. She'd been awake since five and had changed her clothes three times, settling on jeans that looked the best in her gray-dawn mirror. Her stomach churned on too much coffee and nerves.

J Bird was accustomed to being up this early. Baker's hours started at four thirty. She managed a shift change with another woman at Bayside Bakery in order to be with Delia this morning. She wore a skirt from the Dusty Rose Gently Worn clothing store. The black skirt hugged her butt and ended midthigh. Even with running shoes, the outfit was pure J Bird.

A car door closed, and both sisters turned to the sound across the parking lot. "Oh, my God, is that Tyler?" asked Juniper. She jumped up and waved as large as one woman could. "Tyler!"

Even from a distance, Delia could see that his legs were still tanned from years in the California sun, not white like most of Maine's inhabitants. J Bird did a fancy birdlike dance, arms overhead, high-stepping all the way across the parking lot while Tyler opened the back door of his car and released a dog, a Chesapeake Bay Retriever. Baxter, who trotted beside J Bird, immediately raised his tail and puffed out his chest. Tyler's dog must have been a female.

Delia tucked the car keys on top of the passenger side rear wheel and followed her sister, feeling ordinary, a black-and-white image compared to J Bird's full-color print. Would Tyler remember the times that were anything but ordinary?

Without hesitation, J Bird opened her arms and hugged Tyler, squealing as if she had won the lottery. As Delia approached, Tyler looked at her over J Bird. He mouthed, "Hi."

He grabbed J Bird's shoulders and said, "You are still as bouncy as when you were a kid, but honestly, it's going to take me a minute to accept the fact that you're all grown up."

J Bird launched in for a second hug, laughing. J Bird and Tyler were midhug while Baxter and the other dog investigated each other head to butt. Delia was alone, not knowing where to put her hands, where to look.

"I think the dogs like each other," said J Bird, releasing him. Tyler's chestnut-colored dog lowered her chest to the ground, butt up, in a clear invitation to play. "Let's get them out of the parking lot. I mean, I'll take them out of the parking lot. Come on, pups." She ran with the two dogs toward the beach.

"Delia," he said. "It's so good to see you." He took two steps to her frozen island and wrapped his arms around her. The scent of him sent Delia reeling, eight layers deep, the soft claret of his sweatshirt, worn at least four times, his hair, shampooed this morning, soap, something that had to be from years of California air, and beneath it all, his skin, embedded like hers with the lingering hint of smoke, trapped beneath the epidermal cells, emerging in fearful sweat.

She had to remember this wasn't a class reunion, this was a reunion of catastrophe. Tyler was a marker in time of fire/hospital/funerals and the sight of his family's moving van pulling out.

"I was shocked to see you yesterday," she said, pulling away. Did her voice tremble?

"I knew that I'd run into you. Actually, I only arrived here last week. Mercy Hospital offered me a position that I couldn't refuse."

Isn't that what his father said about the job in Seattle that yanked their family three thousand miles away? Of course you could refuse a job. Delia was three weeks from refusing hers.

"Come on, let's catch up with J Bird and the dogs," she said.

Fog rolled in from the ocean and covered them with a fine mist. Tyler hadn't shaved his head like nearly every other man their age when they looked in the mirror and saw the first hint of receding hairline. Tyler's hair, the color of golden sand, was a relaxed thicket, short enough to show a tight, defined line along his neck, long enough that the mist curled a top lock across his forehead.

They crossed the parking lot and took a paved path to the beach. J Bird was near the water in the vortex of two whirling dogs.

"What's your dog's name?" asked Delia. She took off her shoes, wanting to feel the abrasiveness of the sand.

"She's not my dog. She belongs to my landlord. When they heard that I was going to Willard Beach, they begged me to bring her. Her name is Lucy. They said this beach is known as the Canine Riviera."

The sand was cold, infused with salt.

"You always loved to go barefoot," he said, smiling.

They had spent hours on the beaches along the coast when they were dating. Was he as pulled back into the past as she was? She was slipping out of her skin, rushing headlong into the other life before the fire, swimming like a fish in the shallows with Tyler, wrapping her legs around his waist, immune to gravity.

Delia dragged her weightless body back into the present. "Look at them," she said, pointing at the dogs.

The dogs played a game that looked very much like tag. First Baxter ran up to Lucy and slammed his front paws on the ground, butt up, then ran away. Lucy chased him at top speed, her jaws open, eyes wide. They ran side by side for an undetermined amount of time until they stopped and Lucy pounced on her front paws, butt up, and she ran off with Baxter in pursuit. J Bird tried to keep up with them, zigzagging around, head back, laughing.

"So you went to med school. I didn't see that coming at all. What made you decide that?" said Delia. A Frisbee flew low over their heads. It was caught in midair by a standard poodle, ears flying, front paws tucked in, looking more like Pegasus than a dog.

Tyler walked on the ocean side, wearing a kind of heavy duty flip-flop. So West Coast.

"It's a long story. And a little sappy. Please don't laugh if I say it was because I wanted to help people, because it's true. I went to Stanford." He kicked a long strip of seaweed out of the way. "But I wanted to come back here to Maine. I must have been implanted with a homing device that went off about a year ago, pulling me back here. California was too unrelentingly sunny and happy for me."

Should Delia stop pretending, chatting on the surface while her emotions rolled like earth tremors? Could you ever pick up where you left off, especially if where you left off was orphaned, smoke-charred, watching the back of a moving van bump along the street?

He bent over to pick up a piece of driftwood. He rubbed it with one palm. "How about you, Delia? What are you doing?"

What was she doing? "I work with kids who need foster care. I've done it for ten years, but I'm leaving soon to start a bakery with J Bird."

Tyler stopped rubbing the bleached piece of wood. "Don't tell me you're involved with the little girl who was found at the murder scene? That was the first thing that I read when I moved back."

"If a child needs an emergency placement, that's exactly what I do. But I can't talk about my cases. You should know that." Delia stopped walking and put her hand on his arm. "This feels awkward. I'm not good at dodging the issue. It's hard because the last time I saw you was all mixed up with the fire and my parents' deaths and you breaking up with me. Why do you want to see me now?"

Her voice didn't sound like her own; it was mixed with the collision of love and death. Tyler's deep brown eyes did not waver or seek shelter on the horizon or the dogs galloping around them.

"One of the things that I've learned about being a doctor is not to show when I'm petrified of doing the wrong thing. Like right now. Like when I walked into the coffee shop and saw you. Part of me wanted to run away and the other part of me was so glad to see you. . . ."

Delia's cell phone went off with the now-ominous cricket sound of Ira. She dug the phone out of her jacket pocket.

"I have to take this," she said. "Work." She took a few steps from Tyler and turned away.

"Sorry to bother you," said Ira, "but I just got a call from Erica. Hayley told her that she talks with her mommy on Skype.

She actually said, 'The Skype.' Where are you right now? I know it's early but can you get over to Erica's house and find out more about her mother? I don't want to lose the thread of this."

"I'm in South Portland at Willard Beach, not far from their neighborhood. I knew it! This kid has family out there. She has a mother. Okay, I'm leaving right now," she said.

One child, untethered and dangling in the stratosphere, could be reunited with her mother. Or at least the possibility was within sight. Each time this happened, each time a child was reunited with a parent and the outcome was at least adequate, Delia felt like she was rewriting history. Parents did come back. They did look for their lost children.

"I have to go. Can you give J Bird a ride home? Oh, God, I don't even know where you live? Do you live in Portland?"

Tyler held up both hands, palms facing Delia. "No worries. Do what you need to do. Please call me."

She hadn't meant for him to hear her end of the phone conversation. The location of foster kids was never revealed to the public. But Tyler wasn't the public, and she hadn't said exactly where Hayley lived.

Was Tyler relieved that she was leaving? Had it all been a mistake to get together? Her bones shifted deep beneath her skin; she was the one relieved. She knew how to do her job; she didn't know the terrain of Tyler.

Delia waved her arms at Juniper and shouted, "I have to leave for work. It's important. Tyler can drive you and Baxter home. Okay?"

Her sister trotted over, and the dogs followed her. She smiled a huge smile at Tyler. "Okay with me, except I'm not ready to go yet. Are you? These dogs are insane about each other. Can we stay until nine, when the beach switches over to anti-dog time? And then I can show Tyler where J Bird Café is."

Tyler looked at Delia and shrugged. "Sure. Lucy probably hasn't had this much fun in a long time. Her people said they never give her as much exercise as she needs."

Delia walked back to the parking lot, her shoes tucked under one arm and her heels sinking with each step into the sand. She turned and looked back. Tyler and J Bird were already walking side by side along the water's edge.

An old twinge rose up her throat. Could old lovers return in anything but storybook romances? They weren't kids anymore.

Her chin itched as if an ant were crawling along her jawbone. Just one more indication that this case would be harder than she imagined.

# CHAPTER 17

*Hayley*

After seven days living in the blue room at Tom and Erica's house, something tingled beneath her ribs, and it was dank and gray and wanted to devour her. What would become of her if the thing erupted from her belly, blasting its way out? Hayley saw what happened to a squirrel that Uncle Ray shot. The center of the squirrel exploded. Is this what would happen to her? Had the squirrel lost her family too, like she had back at the house?

Erica said they were going to sign her up for kindergarten, and they visited the classroom. What exactly did that mean? Were kids in kindergarten like her, with no family? Would she have to live at kindergarten?

"Delia is here already," said Erica, when the doorbell rang. How could Erica know so quickly? Hayley was sure that Erica was extra smart, like Emma was. "Remember I said your caseworker is going to come for a visit this morning?"

No, she didn't remember. Sometimes Hayley slipped away by

thinking of other things, like Louie. The huge cat helped her to slip away. Sometimes she liked to think of nothing, just colors, or better yet, songs. She liked to hum songs in her head.

Was this the same lady who drove Hayley to this house from the hospital? Or was it the lady who liked cucumbers? It was hard to remember all their names. The lady who drove her from the hospital told Hayley that she must sit in a booster seat. Uncle Ray said booster seats were for babies and seat belts were stupid. When Uncle Ray wasn't looking, Emma would quietly slip the seatbelt over Hayley. She was glad that Uncle Ray wasn't there to see her in a booster seat and strapped in with a seat belt.

She had told the lady, "I'm not a baby."

Maybe she didn't know as much as Uncle Ray or she didn't have kids. Hayley was a big girl.

The lady said, "This is how big girls ride in my car. This is the big kid booster seat. Try it and let me know how you like it."

That was how she came to stay with Tom and Erica, riding in her big kid booster seat. Erica taught her how to buckle herself in, which felt better because she didn't like Erica hanging over her to buckle in the seat belt.

Erica opened the door and one lady came in. This lady was different. She was the one from the garden who liked Louie and the cucumbers. She was going to tell this lady to take her home.

"Hi, Hayley. Where's our friend Louie?" The lady put down her bag and squatted in front of Hayley.

Where was Louie? He knew when she was afraid.

"Hold on, everyone. I'll go get the Lord of the Manor. He's outside stalking bumblebees," said Erica. She had so many names for Louie. Lord of the Manor. The President. The Big Kahuna. The Boss.

"You and Louie have names that sound the same at the end, Hayley and Louie," said the lady.

Grown-ups looked different close up. Mostly she saw grown-ups from below, looking up at them as their voices sailed over her. The Delia lady came down to Hayley and she looked into her face.

"I brought you some books and a lonely bear who needs a home. I'd love to read these books with you. My favorite is *How Do Dinosaurs Say Good Night?*"

"I'm ready to go home now," she said.

The Delia lady's face changed from good and happy to worried or mad.

"I know you are," she said. Delia glanced up at Erica, who followed Louie from the kitchen. They both looked sad. Or mad, as if Hayley said the wrong thing. This place was not for Hayley.

Louie wedged his body between Hayley and the lady. There, that was a little better.

# CHAPTER 18

Delia was on the way to Erica's house in response to Ira's urgent call. As she pulled out of the parking lot, she turned down Plymouth Street past the J Bird Café, which was on the way to Erica's house. She slowed to ten miles per hour and put the wipers on slow mode to wipe off the mist. Brown paper covered the large windows in front, but the front door was open, giving her a view of a circular saw set up on a metal table. The carpenters had arrived early. She saw Greg's truck parked along the street. Good, if he was on the job, they didn't have to worry. She didn't stop; talking to Hayley was more important.

Would there ever be a time when she wasn't juggling so many things? Had there ever been? Now it included Hayley, leaving her job, opening the café, and suddenly, Tyler, who was presently back on the beach with J Bird. Multitasking was the curse of the human race in the twenty-first century. Her head felt like it was going to erupt.

Fifteen minutes later she pulled into Erica's driveway. Ira said he would call ahead to let her know that Delia was on her way. She slowed her breathing; longer exhales than inhales.

Kids didn't respond well to anxiety in grown-ups. They recoiled from it the way horses and dogs did. Could young children smell the mixed chemicals of fear? Maybe they couldn't smell it, but it registered in their survival instincts, and they retreated to the backs of their caves. Long exhale. Again.

Delia kept a plastic box in her car with kid supplies: stuffed animals, books, and fish crackers. She pulled out a book about a dinosaur, which was really a book about kids learning self-soothing techniques so they weren't afraid to go to bed, nicely camouflaged as a dinosaur book.

Erica opened the door, and Hayley stood beside her, one hand lightly placed on Erica's leg. Before Delia left the foster care system, she was going to give this woman an award for being the best emergency placement site in history. Erica was a safe port in Hayley's long storm.

Once they were settled on the couch with Louie draped over both of them, Delia read the dinosaur book, and then two more at Hayley's request. Louie kept his hindquarters pointed in Delia's direction and his head pressed tenderly into Hayley's ribs. Delia understood the message from the cat; she was not the important one in the equation. If Louie helped this child feel safe, then Delia was his biggest fan.

She closed the cover on the third book, one of the many Berenstain Bears books that focused on family. On mothers and fathers.

"I'm trying to find your mommy. Can you tell me where she is?" asked Delia.

Hayley stroked Louie. "He likes to be petted from head to toe, not the other way, toe to head," said the girl. "Do you want to pet him?"

"Oh, yes. There's plenty of him to go around. I think Louie is big enough that four people could pet him at once."

Hayley smiled. Not so much a smile, but a softening of her face.

"Emma said my mommy is waiting for me to come home, but it is very far away. And I will have to be a good girl."

Delia inhaled and exhaled slowly. She stroked Louie from head to toe.

"What is mommy's other name?"

"Just Mommy. But Daddy calls her Sweetie. Her other name is Sweetie."

*Oh dear God, there is a daddy.* Why did Delia assume there was no father? Somewhere there was a father and a mother for Hayley. This was where Delia must be careful; the focus must stay on the child and not her old fantasy that slithered out when she least expected it. There would never be a magic moment for Delia when suddenly her parents appeared. And yet she could smell her mother's body lotion, something with lavender, and she could smell her father's medication pulsing hot from his skin.

"Let's play magic. Pretend there is a magic wand and it has a star on the end, and if I point it at something, I can make it be whatever I want," said Delia. She pointed the imaginary wand at a wingback with cat-scratched sides. "Razzmatazz, that chair is now a throne for a princess. And razzmatazz, your shoes are silver slippers. Do you want a turn?"

Hayley accepted the imaginary wand and sat up tall. "I turn the house into pink candy. We can eat the whole house. I turn Louie into a dragon who breathes fire." The girl shrank back into her seat and handed the wand back to Delia. "I have to be good. Emma said if I am a good girl, my mommy will come and get me."

"Did Emma talk to mommy on Skype? Did you talk to Mommy on Skype?"

Louie was getting restless. He stood up and stretched. Delia reached over and rubbed him behind his ears, hoping to lure him back down again.

"I heard that you talked to Mommy on Skype? Did she say where she was?"

This was too much; she shouldn't have asked so many questions.

The cat leapt off the couch, using Delia's legs as springboards, allowing the claws of his hind paws to pierce her pants.

Hayley shrugged her bony shoulders. "I don't know."

As clearly as a vault door closing with a thick thud, the child was done, and Delia knew it.

This child had a mother and a father. Why wasn't she reported missing?

# CHAPTER 19

Delia waited until she was back in her car before she phoned Ira. It didn't feel right calling from Erica's driveway. Here was the balance between confidentiality with a child and protection for them. So many children had been instructed to keep secrets, and part of Delia's job was to make kids feel safe enough that they would break the well-kept promises. She pulled into a grocery store near the bridge.

"Ira. She wants to go home. That much is clear. I only wish we knew where home is. She confirmed that she speaks to her mother on Skype. And there's a father. She said her mommy's other name is Sweetie because that's what her Daddy calls her. This kid has two parents." Delia paused, considering the worst image. "Or she did have parents."

Delia turned off the engine. No use creating a cloud of carbon monoxide around the patrons as they pushed their carts from the store.

"Nothing else?" he asked.

"No. And we're not likely to get a sense of time from her. She's too young. She could have been with Emma Gilbert for two years or two weeks and it would all feel like an eternity to Hayley."

Ira knew all about the developmental stages of kids. Delia was thinking out loud.

It was only nine thirty in the morning. Two men came out of the store wearing shorts and sandals. Tourists. As they passed by her, one of them beeped the car open. A silver Mercedes two-door sedan. A hint of cologne made its way into her car, something robust and dark, the way she imagined whiskey and spice smelled, followed by a hint of a tropical flower.

"We have additional information. I called Detective Moretti at the PD this morning, just to see if anything new was forthcoming about the murders, something that we could use to help us find her parents."

Delia knew he was in his office with the door closed. He would already have put his brown bag lunch in the staff refrigerator.

"They ran fingerprints on the two male victims. The police only just shared this with us. They must have assumed they're the only ones looking for her family. They were able to identify one man. The other one didn't have fingerprints in the system. The one with prints is from Tennessee. He had a brief criminal record: possession of a controlled substance with intent to sell. But he had a very good lawyer. He was on probation. Raymond Blanchard."

The two men in the Mercedes pulled out of the parking lot.

"Won't the police contact the victim's family in Tennessee and then find out who the other guy is? This puts us one step closer to figuring out why Hayley was with them. Right?" she asked.

"They're contacting next of kin today."

Delia felt a stream of relief run through her. She hadn't realized that she was so worried about Hayley's placement. "That's enough information to keep Hayley in the emergency placement with Erica. We're not putting her into another foster home, are we?"

"Technically we should find a longer placement for her. Erica is well trained as our emergency placement specialist. But I can make an exception. If we can locate the parents or other family members within the next two weeks, then there's no need to move her."

Delia pictured Hayley back at the house, her small hands resting on Louie's back. She would not be able to bear the sight of Hayley chipped away by multiple placements until she disappeared down a narrow tunnel. She had seen too many kids lost in the shuffle of placements.

"Has anyone told you that you're good at what you do?" said Delia, breathing a sigh.

She pictured him smiling. "I'm trying hard not to say this every day, but I wish you weren't leaving us," he said. He wasn't smiling after all.

"The detective said one more thing. He said it is critical that we do not release Hayley's location. To anyone."

"Why was he so adamant about it? He knows that we keep all the information about families confidential," she said.

"They're taking extra precautions because of the scope of the heroin business. I liked Maine better when the worst thing that happened was the fishermen got mad at each other."

# CHAPTER 20

Delia brought Ira a latte from The Daily Grind. She knew it was his guilty pleasure. Ira and Delia spread a map on the conference table.

"Maps help me think better," said Ira. "I'm still stuck on the receipt to the hardware store. Remember? One of the few bits of evidence found on the victims?"

"Isn't West Hartford all chic and filled with outdoor cafés, bookstores, and baristas with black aprons?" asked Delia.

She went to West Hartford with her father when she was in high school, accompanying him on a job during a good stretch of nondelusion. Between bites of pasta covered in a lemon and cream sauce and light-as-air fresh ricotta, her father said, "This kind of food will change the city." He closed his eyes as the food spoke to him, igniting his palate with colors and music. "Sky blue and a Chopin tune." He opened his eyes, satiated with pleasure.

Back then, West Hartford wasn't a hip city, but she had learned to accept her father's ability to see the world through food, and even see the future of a city when it was still scarred with gang-related graffiti.

The receipt from the hardware store came from West Hartford. The crumbled-up receipt was found in the pocket of one of the men found dead at the homicide scene.

Ira squinted his eyes at the map and then took out his reading glasses. "The last time I was there, I realized that a level of hipness was happening that was beyond my comprehension. Why are all the women wearing black-framed glasses? And are skinny jeans in or are they out?"

"Don't try and keep up with glasses and jeans," she said. What would life be like without Ira? The generational difference between them was reassuring to her, and the first pangs of missing him seized in her chest. She only had a few more weeks with him.

"We could look at this on Google Earth," she said. "I know you prefer maps, but let's try the computer. I want to zoom in on the neighborhood."

Ira spread his hands along the paper map with a degree of reverence. Delia's parents had been the same way. Their car was stuffed with maps, old AAA Trip Tik maps, dried, shredding maps of Boston, Montreal, Nova Scotia.

"Look, we'll use your map and I'll open up Google Earth," said Delia.

Ira folded the map into a smaller section. "Was that your best effort at not sounding condescending? You wait, you're going to need this map. For example, how far is the store from a major roadway like 84 or 91? Did they just hop off the highway, stop at the first hardware store they saw, buy their stuff, and back on their way? Or is this a neighborhood store, tucked into a residential area?"

Delia didn't have the heart to tell him that all of those questions could be answered on Google Earth. She opened her laptop. She was sure her resources could be more helpful.

"Look. I'm going to zoom in on this address and we'll check out the whole neighborhood."

The scene was far from what Delia expected around a hardware store. No chain-link fences, no abandoned lots. Diagonally across the street were a library and a park.

Ira squeezed in next to her. "Wait a minute, go back to the library. Stop. What does the name over the library say?"

Delia zoomed in and angled over. "Lillian Tiger Library."

"What did Hayley say? Something about a tiger in the house? Emma Gilbert told her they had to stay away from the tiger in the house?"

Delia's chin began to itch the way it did when a case with a kid was hard, something that she had never shared with Ira. How could she, a child of a schizophrenic? She couldn't say, "I get strange bodily sensations, specifically facial itches on the left jawline, when a case is going to be heartbreaking."

But it did itch and not like an insect bite or a rash, or dry skin. This was her body saying be careful here. Her itch sensor was close to her father's musical interludes with Chopin when the pasta sauce was superior.

"Is this where we call the police and put the two things together for them? Little Hayley's admonition about tigers in the house and the name of the library across the street from the hardware store?" Delia asked.

Ira was the director, no matter how sucked into the case he was, how much he identified with a child. He knew when to call in the police. Delia's adrenaline trickled through her torso at first, like melting snow running down the street on the first warm day of spring.

"If it's about the heroin, then yes. If it's about tracking down her family, then yes," he said. He stood up straight, no longer leaning over Delia's shoulder, staring at the Lillian Tiger Library. He rubbed the back of his neck.

"It's late, and it's Friday afternoon. I don't know if this is about heroin. But I'll call and leave a message for Mike. He said to be sure to let him know if Hayley gave any additional information."

"You mean Moretti? How can we call him anything but Moretti? With a name like that he should be a chef, or an actor, or the mayor of Boston."

"You call him Moretti. He gave me instructions to call him Mike. What do you have going on this weekend?" he asked.

"My sister has a new catering job. She wants me to help her later in the day," she said. "How about you?"

"Oh, Marie probably has something cooked up for us to do."

At least one of them was lying. Ira folded up his map and waved a good-bye to Delia.

# CHAPTER 21

Delia was not on call with Foster Services, and she knew exactly where she was going the moment she woke on Saturday. She was up before the sunrise, checking the Web page of the library in West Hartford to see what time they opened on Saturday. Nine a.m. MapQuest said the drive would take four hours.

If she left at six, she'd arrive at the library while the staff was still fresh and sparkly. She and Ira left a message with Moretti with their most recent speculations regarding Hayley's fear of tigers. Could the Lillian Tiger Library be too thin of a thread? Coincidental and unrelated?

Moisture from the ocean rode in on the warm air of the last summer days. Soon enough, the windows would be closed, but now, the windows hadn't been pulled shut for months, and Delia took a moment to breathe it all in; the last cup of coffee, a few bread crumbs on her plate from the toast, the heel of a loaf she'd baked two days ago in a fit of self-soothing. Her cell phone rang and Ira's special tone, a chirping cricket, jarred her. Why was he calling so early? Why was he calling at all?

"Delia, you're going to West Hartford, aren't you? My Delia Lamont radar was ticking all last night. Stop and pick me up. I'm coming with you," he said.

The man could see inside her brain, and she didn't like it. She picked up her car keys.

"Okay, maybe I was thinking about it," she said.

"You're on your way out the door, I can hear the car keys jangling. I'm coming with you." Click.

Could she say no to him? He was still her boss and he was as tuned in to Hayley as she was. She rearranged her spine, letting go of the solo adventure, switching over to Ira sitting next to her for the four-hour drive. She filled another water bottle. That man was not going to dehydrate in her car.

They were on the road south by six thirty. She had showered. Ira had not, and he smelled like a more condensed version of himself than his work week self. It was always better if she kept her heightened sense of smell to herself.

For the first hour and a half, they flowed through the light traffic. The sun was muted by a thin layer of clouds. By ten thirty they were on the outskirts of Hartford.

"Who would want to be known as the insurance capital?" said Delia, adjusting the air in the car, turning the air conditioner up one notch. The city skyline loomed in front of them with the Connecticut River on their left.

"They could have been the Colt Single Action Gun capital," said Ira. "They had that going for them too." He tapped his fingers along the window. "By the way, I installed an app on my phone last night, Google Maps or some such thing. But I have the real map with me just in case."

Ira's phone app guided them to West Hartford and finally to Cleveland Avenue where the solid nineteenth-century library sat.

"Stop for a minute before you pull in; I want to find the hardware store. Just pull over," he said.

"You bet I'm pulling over. I had to pee about an hour ago. I'm parking in the back," said Delia as she swung the car into the driveway that promised free parking for library patrons.

Ira craned his head around. "Okay. Oh, there it is."

Delia didn't want to spare any extraneous movement that was not related to peeing. She parked the car and made a rapid march to the front door of the library.

"I'll catch up," he shouted to her.

Delia loved libraries that didn't hide their bathrooms. She saw the sign immediately after she pulled on the brass handles to the front doors.

Ira caught up with Delia in the nonfiction section. Biographies: political, corporate, religious, literary. Delia had blasted her way through college, ripping through the courses that led directly to graduate school and to a job. By the time she was twenty-four, she was employed full time. Prior to that, she'd worked part time with Foster Services while she hammered out her graduate degree. She had Juniper to consider in all of her career choices. She didn't pause to read fiction, not often, anyway. All of that could change. Now she wanted to sink into a bathtub and read a story. She rubbed her pointer finger along the spine of a book. She pictured a time in her future when she could meander through the stacks in Longfellow Books in Portland.

"What did you find out at the hardware store?" asked Delia, opening a copy of Obama's prepresidential story of growing up with his grandparents and single mother.

"I showed Hayley's photo to two clerks, and no one remembered her. Maybe she was never in the store."

"What was it that the police said? Were there security cameras in the hardware store? Aren't there cameras everywhere?" she asked.

"I don't know, but let's check with Mike when we return."

Delia and Ira had never been together in a library before. Why would they? They worked together for years, but there was no reason for them to cruise a library together. She felt misaligned, uneasy.

"When we get back home, our first stop needs to be the police station. If heroin was coming through Hartford and if these two buildings were a regular part of the route, we are now officially out of our area of expertise. Let them look at security footage," he said.

*Only operate within your area of experience and expertise.* This was drilled into the trainees during graduate school, and now Delia felt far from her area of knowing anything.

But they didn't leave the Lillian Tiger Library. They sat in the periodicals section on the beige couch. They walked up a broad staircase to the second floor trying to see why a small child might have been warned off this library by Emma Gilbert. Why Emma told her never to go inside.

They came to the corner of the library designated for audio books and DVDs. She tugged on Ira's shirtsleeve and whispered, "If you were transporting, let's say, ten thousand dollars worth of heroin and needed a drop-off place that would look totally innocent, invisible, wouldn't a library be a perfect location?"

Ira's eyes darted around the room, refocusing. "City libraries are a respite place for homeless people. They come in during the day when they are booted out of the shelters. People need to use computers to find work. They use the bathrooms to clean up. They could provide a screen for people dropping off and picking up drugs. What I mean is, a lot of transient people now use libraries as a home base, making it perfect. Who would suspect one more unknown person coming through to use a clean bathroom?"

Delia walked to the checkout counter for the DVDs. "Do you have a children's section?" she asked. The young man behind the desk was thin with black-rimmed glasses, skinny jeans.

"Garden level," he said. "You can take the elevator."

Delia and Ira walked down the two flights of stairs and emerged into the children's level. The area smelled slightly of mold and cleanser. Small chairs, miniature couches, a riot of colors and banners. On the checkout desk was a colorful stuffed tiger, abundantly large, bespectacled with tortoiseshell rims. Around its neck hung a sign that said, LILLY THE TIGER LIKES TO READ. HOW ABOUT YOU?

She grabbed Ira's arm, then quickly let go, remembering the

scars along his forearm. "She was here, I know it. Or Emma Gilbert was here."

Ira tapped a little bell on the counter. A woman stood up who must have been deep into the lower shelves behind the counter. She was young, with hair shaved on both sides, counterpointed by a clump of bleached blond hair that draped over one eye.

"Can I help you?"

Ira slid open the envelope with Hayley's photo.

"I was wondering if you recall seeing this child. We're with foster care in Maine, and we're trying to locate any family members."

She looked at the photo and shook her head. "I only started working here a few days ago. There was a volunteer librarian before me, but she left. And she wasn't the world's best librarian either. The place is a disaster."

Ira put the tips of his fingers on Delia's arm, like hitting the pause button on the universal remote.

"Thanks for your help," he said to the young woman.

They headed for the stairs. "This just went beyond our know-how," he said. "I'm calling Mike. He needs to know about the library."

# CHAPTER 22

Delia drove northeast on 84 until they hit the Mass Pike, then north toward Maine. The sun sliced along Delia's left shoulder, making her sweat by the time they crossed over into New Hampshire. She'd had a one-hour reprieve driving east on the Mass Pike, but now she was in for a long, slow bake until they hit Portland.

She turned up the air conditioning one notch.

"I'm freezing over here," said Ira. "Can we settle on cool and not cold?"

"Close the air vents on your side. Or put your jacket on."

"My nose is cold. I can't put a jacket on my nose. Maybe I should drive the rest of the way so I can warm up," he said, and cupped one hand around his nose for emphasis.

They had called Mike Moretti and left a message for him at the station. After speculating about people using the children's section of the library as a drop-off for drug trafficking, they still had no idea how Hayley figured into the picture. Delia was talked out, left with buzzing images that made no sense about a trio of adults running drugs with a totally unrelated child with them.

Delia pulled into the first stop in New Hampshire, the state liquor store that sold tax-free liquor. The parking lot hummed with a steady flow of cars, people pulling in with expectations of saving lots of money and leaving with shopping carts full of beer, wine, and hard liquor, and monster bills on their credit cards.

"Do you want to go in?" asked Delia. She stepped out of her car, feeling blood start to move through her legs again. She flopped over in a forward bend, letting her head dangle.

"No, thanks. I'll wait for my favorite cabernet to go on sale in Portland. Maine can have my tax dollars." He slipped into the driver's seat.

They had decided that they would land on Mike's doorstep on Monday morning and hammer away at the link that Emma Gilbert and possibly Hayley had been in the Lillian Tiger Library in West Hartford. Delia's first priority was the child, and she was pretty sure that the first priority of the police was the murderer, followed by Hayley.

"How is your dating experiment going? That is what you called it, isn't it?" asked Ira, easing the car out of the liquor mega market.

For once Delia welcomed Ira's peek into her love life. Any topic would be a relief after the immersion into Hayley's baffling origins. She opened the plastic air vents on her side of the car so that the cool air pointed directly at her.

"I wish I lived during a time period when people still met each other in vivo and not through the wisdom of computer algorithms." She slid off her shoes and pulled one knee up, wrapping her arms around her shin and resting the side of her face on her knee as she looked at Ira. She figured he had about thirty minutes of warming up and then he'd be as roasted as she was.

"So the Match.com dates didn't go so well?" he said. He adjusted the rearview mirror.

"No. I mean they're perfectly fine guys for somebody, just not me. They probably thought the same thing about me."

"But you didn't give them the chance. You were the one to say no. Am I right?"

"Yes, but why did you assume that?"

"Come on, Delia, you know this from psych. Kids who lose their parents tend to seek out parental replacement figures for partners or they reject anyone who shows interest for fear of losing them. I didn't make this up," he said. Ira did a little grimace that made his mustache bounce. She had never seen his upper lip and now she didn't want to. It would be like seeing Ira in his underwear, which she didn't want to see either.

"We get longing confused with desire," he said. "Notice that I'm including myself."

"You're going to keep going on about this, aren't you? You have me captive in my own car and now you're going to try to improve my poor romantic life." She released the hold on her knee, straightened out her leg, and tilted the seat back one setting. She hadn't told Ira about Tyler.

"The path to a real relationship is hard enough, but for those of us who lost parents, we are focused on what we don't have, rather than what we want. We think we're looking for love and we are, but it's the lost love," he said.

Ira had a heavy foot; he clicked the left blinker and passed the few cars that were actually going the speed limit.

"Wait a minute," she said. "Your parents abused you and abandoned you. How did you end up with a marriage that, from all appearances, looks pretty damn good," she asked. She opened the glove box and found an unopened plastic bag of Twizzlers. She ripped open the bag with her teeth and pulled out a red rope of artificially colored and flavored food. Some days she needed a counterpoint to all of J Bird's superior food.

She offered the bag to Ira, and he pulled one out. "Two things. But I was lucky in both. I was adopted by the best parents one could ever hope for. That made up for a lot. I was able to see grown-ups in love, working together, being kind to each other. And they let me know that they loved me. Even so, I still looked for the missing mommy. So the second thing was, Marie let me know rather firmly in our second year of marriage that she wasn't my mommy. I had to dig deep to understand that. I had to give up longing for something that was gone, so that I could desire something fresh. It was like emerging from a dark cave. Our sex life got a lot better after that too."

"We have two more hours until we're home. We are not talking about your sex life for the remainder of the trip," said Delia. Both Ira and Ben were a little younger than her father would be right now, but they did fit the need in her for a dad, sort of. Maybe she wouldn't ever have to marry a stand-in if Ira was right.

"I don't want to talk about my sex life, which is just fine, thank you. I'm just offering you a small nugget of unsolicited advice. In a few weeks, you won't be able to get this free advice from me on a daily basis."

She pulled out another strip of red Twizzler. "Which is what, exactly? Please limit yourself to one sentence." She bit off a hunk.

"Don't look for what you've lost. Look for what you truly want," he said. Now they were passing the cars that were also speeding.

"Is this a Jewish thing?" Ira wasn't a practicing Jew, but she had a feeling he was practicing something. "And that was two sentences."

"It's my version of Jewish Buddhism. We are a small slice of the spiritual pie," said Ira, passing a logging truck. "I don't like following those trucks; I'm sure that one of the logs is going to pop off and come through our windshield."

"Could you keep it in a range that won't ignite the State Troopers?"

"I shall say no more." He turned up the air conditioner and pulled back into the right lane. "It really is hot over here."

Where did Tyler fit in? Was he a lost love that she had been longing for? He wasn't a stand-in for a father. He was in a different category.

# CHAPTER 23

It was almost four in the afternoon by the time Delia arrived home. She stepped into the house and crinkled her nose and said, "Lilies. Stargazers."

She was exhausted from the trip to West Hartford, but she had promised her sister that she'd help with this catering job. They weren't delivering until tomorrow.

Juniper was in the kitchen, grating ginger with her latest gadget. "You haven't even seen them. What if I told you they weren't Stargazers? What if I just happened to have a few gay guy friends in the living room?"

Baxter greeted her from the living room, where he was banished while baking projects were in the works. Delia let her black bag slide to a kitchen stool. "But you don't have gay men in our living room, and those are Stargazer lilies. You can't bear it when I'm right. Are you prepping for scones? Please tell me yes. And where did the flowers come from?"

For one ridiculous moment, she wished that Tyler had sent them to her.

Juniper did not have the super sniffing ability of Delia. Juniper's nose was well above average, honed from years of baking. She smelled a banana when it was past ripe, detected grease molecules in the air at the local diner and could suggest when they should change the oil, but she mercifully could not smell the cornucopia of odors that Delia confronted.

Delia knew she was in the same category as a bird expert, with binoculars dangling around her neck, wearing a tan baseball cap and sturdy hiking shoes, able to identify a scarlet tanager by the first note of its song. Except with Delia, the world's song was purely olfactory.

"One of my customers bought them for me. Is it too much for you? They're powerful," said Juniper. "Just say so and I'll put the vase outside. I know how sensitive your nose is." Juniper slid the grated ginger into a Pyrex cup of buttermilk.

"That would be a relief," said Delia. "I won't be able to concentrate otherwise." She was so glad that she hadn't verbalized her desire about Tyler, that she kept one mortifying fear to herself.

Delia had to concentrate on bread, not Lilly the Tiger in West Hartford, or Stargazer lilies pumping out waves of perfume from a vase.

Delia constantly navigated the world on a tsunami of scents thundering toward her, layers and layers of complex high notes and low notes, some competing with each other for prominence, like onions and sauerkraut, or garlic and thyme. Some things should not be in the same one-mile radius of each other. On the other hand, she admired the complexity, the synchronicity of other combinations, say turmeric and cumin, or the natural marriage of cinnamon and a fresh rub of nutmeg.

Delia could see that even though Juniper was baking, she was preparing to go out. Or rather, she could smell it. Once her scones and cupcakes were on the cooling rack, she could leave, unlike Delia, who had to babysit the bread dough.

Her sister had showered, shampooed, and used her new, expensive conditioner with its faux mint scent, and had anointed her body with Burt's Bees honey and vanilla because Juniper now believed smelling slightly like a cookie or a crème brûlée would have an intoxicating effect on men. In this one way, she had followed Delia's advice. "Men generally have an inferior sense of smell, but they do respond unconsciously to something more foodlike. I mean, you don't want to smell like a rare New York strip or garlic-embedded shrimp scampi. Go for sweet or chocolate."

Her sister had taken her advice.

"Where are you going? And with who?" Whoever it was, he was going to be swept away by the honey and vanilla scent of J Bird.

"Just some people from work. One of the new guys has a boat. It's just a skiff, or bigger than a skiff, I haven't seen it yet. But the plan is to take it out, bring a bottle of wine, and watch the moon come up over Casco Bay," said Juniper.

Collier had been the best guy her sister had ever dated, and Delia had struggled with feeling left out. How mortifying to be the big sister and feel left out. Now that J Bird was single again, she vibrated to an urgent search mode. Or at least that was what had always happened before. This time, Juniper swore she was too busy for the shenanigans of a relationship. "After we open the café," she had said. But the void in Delia's love life was Grand Canyon wide, just as deep and long-lasting. J Bird was her dating coach, and so far all of her expertise with men felt wasted.

If Delia was lucky, they'd talk about the upcoming boating excursion, the now and future; she didn't want to get sucked into the past. But a sister was a magnet for the past. Sisters knew you when you blew fart bubbles in the bathtub or threw up on the kitchen floor. All of Delia's past lived in J Bird, or at least the part of her past since the arrival of her little sister.

"Was I just imagining things or was your old boyfriend trying to reconnect with you? I saw him looking at you with *The Look*," said Juniper.

Delia opened up a new sack of King Arthur bread flour. "What look? I didn't see a special look," said Delia.

"That's because you don't know the look. You can smell a gumdrop a mile away like a freaking bloodhound, but you're blind to the way men look at you."

Maybe her sister was right. Maybe she had been so busy taking care of J Bird and working that she had ignored the very basic cues of romance. Juniper understood the solace of romance, every nuance of flirtation, lust. It was how she sustained herself after their parents died.

"How was the trip to West Hartford?" Juniper asked, expertly avoiding comparisons of social lives. Delia was both appreciative and resentful that Juniper had dodged an obvious topic.

"It's the new truly awful case. It's not the kid who's awful; it's the whole gut-wrenching, I-can-never-fix-it scenario. We can't find any family to claim this girl. But Ira and I found some threads that might lead us to her family. And that's all I can say about it."

Delia balanced client confidentiality constantly, hoping that the kids in foster care could keep a few shreds of privacy once their families were blown apart. She sat down and put her head into her hands, elbows on knees, pressing her fingertips into her forehead.

Juniper pulled a large green bowl out of the dish cabinet. "Here. I started some bread dough for you. I was worried that you'd get back too late and not have time to get it started. I figured you might need it after working on this case. I don't have the finesse that you do with bread, but once the café is open, we need to be the backup for each other. Suppose you're sick one day and I have to make the bread?"

Delia wanted a backup. She was exhausted by feeling out in front. The last time the sisters went cross-country skiing after a heavy snowfall, Delia had immediately taken the trailbreaking job, slogging through the snow so that J Bird would have an easier time. After a water break, J Bird launched off first, not hesitating. The reversal felt uncomfortable, wrong in every fiber, until J Bird collapsed into a snow bank, laughing. "So this is what life is like in your world. We'll have to do this more often."

That's what the J Bird Café was all about: working together, letting J Bird take the lead.

Delia dusted the countertop with flour. She formed a fist and punched down the sourdough that had expanded like a hot air balloon. Deflated, the dough sagged in the middle, falling in on itself.

"I had a wild dream last night," said Juniper. "Daddy explained the family secret to me."

Delia stopped; a deathly hand clutched her heart.

What secret could the dead tell her sister? The age-old protectiveness rose up in Delia as it had when they were kids, when she needed to push the dresser against their bedroom door when their father wanted to rip the wiring out of their room, when Juniper had huddled in the corner farthest from the door while he pounded and shouted.

Juniper pulled a tray out of the oven, the miniature cupcakes that people devoured sans guilt.

"What was the secret?" asked Delia, pressing the heel of her hand into the smooth, elastic dough. The day had turned into that rare thing, a perfect ratio of warmth and humidity vs. crisp air and whatever else it was that made yeast flourish. An ocean breeze blew the heat and humidity inland. What would happen to the dough now that the darkness of their father had entered the kitchen?

Juniper set the tray of mini cupcakes on a wire rack. "He looked like he did when he was good. Even better than good, like pure Dad essence. He held up two vials of liquid, the kind from a chemistry lab. He set them in little hangers. They were both the same except one of them had a little black dot bobbing around in it."

"That's it?" said Delia. Her hands hovered over the dough. She wanted more than a black dot.

"That's it. That was the big explanation, the black dot. But I wish you could have seen the kindness on his face. . . ." Juniper stopped, her voice catching on a ledge of longing.

They only had each other, there was no one else who understood what they had been through. Ben was as close as they could hope, and they both knew he would do anything for them. But there were times when just the two of them talked about their parents, and it lanced the infected wound. Not something you ever looked forward to, but the effect was cleansing.

It was a dream, a projection of Juniper's desires, her struggle to understand their father, not a visitation; she couldn't accept a visitation. Delia pounded the dough again with power from her arms, her shoulder blades, and the spot between her shoulder blades that held grief.

Juniper fed eggs, flour, sugar, milk, grated lemon peel, salt, and baking powder into the large stainless steel bowl for the next round of cupcakes. "I think the secret was that there was this one dot in him that was wrong, his chemistry, his chromosomes or something, and that it caused him to be schizo." She switched on the fat blades that whirled around the bowl in a robotic dance.

Delia bristled at the label. Their father wasn't schizophrenic, he was their father, who had schizophrenia in the same way people had diabetes or cerebral palsy. Except those diseases didn't cross-shred a family into bits, or make a mother choose a father over the kids.

Juniper switched off the mixer. "I used to pray that Mom would leave him." Her voice was rough, dragged through the rugged terrain of the past. "I used to pray that we could leave, just the three of us, and I wouldn't be afraid all the time. And it hurt so much because I loved Dad, but he scared me witless."

Delia kept one hand on the dough. "I know." She gulped hard. "Right before the fire, I begged her to leave him."

This was new territory, unexplored by the sisters, honeycombed with shame for wanting to leave their father. The words expanded the walls, bulging out.

"She should have protected us too, not just Daddy. Didn't she love us?" Juniper slumped against the counter, her chest sinking.

"She did love us, but she loved him too. She knew him when

he was brilliant, kind, and handsome, not all beat up by a major thought disorder. She was never going to leave him. We were all held hostage by his illness, not just Dad," said Delia. Her last image of her father, bloated by medication and defeat, rose up and gripped her heart.

"Surviving the mental illness hostage takeover doesn't feel so good. Like in some weird way, I wished for it, I wanted him gone. And now he is, they both are, we lost them both," said Juniper.

Delia dipped her fingers into the bag of flour, forcing them to move. "Do you think he knew that we wanted Mom to leave him?" Delia whispered.

Juniper looked startled by the shift in her big sister, their usual roles reversed.

"Hey, you know what? If they could see you making this freaking awesome bread, they would be cheering for you. They'd be shocked, but happy," said Juniper. Her voice sounded tender.

Delia was grateful to her for the attempt at comfort. "It would be a surprise for them. And the café would just make them faint," she said, forcing a brightness in her voice.

Delia glanced at the clock; it was five. J Bird had to deliver the breads, scones, and cupcakes by seven the next morning. The art department at the university was hosting a regional conference off campus and they had agreed to try J Bird's new catering service. The sisters had plenty of time. Besides, this was where her little sister excelled, the timing of baking and the choreography that brought all the baking to a sumptuous conclusion at just the right time. Delia could relax and let Juniper hold the reins.

Juniper finished frosting the cupcakes, slid them into the fridge to safeguard them from Baxter, and ran out the door with a bottle of wine. Delia was left with four loaves of bread for their final rise.

But had a black dot of their father been deposited in either of them? Were they truly in the safe zone yet, barricaded by age? She wanted to believe so. And she wanted to believe that her mother truly had loved them.

# CHAPTER 24

The next afternoon, they collected the serving trays from the grateful academics. The rave reviews from the organizer stayed with them as they drove to the café. A few hours of painting awaited them.

Juniper screwed a paint roller to the end of a broom-length pole and dipped it into a tray of fuchsia paint. Everything was going to take two coats.

"Delia, where was I when you ran into the house? It feels so weird and disconnected not being able to remember. I mean, I was almost fourteen."

Delia never told her sister about what she heard, so long ago, when she ran into their house before the fire engines came screaming down the street, before Tyler dragged her from the building. Why did Juniper want to know now, thirteen years later? Couldn't they keep that one bit sealed over?

The demon of the fire haunted Delia, but it had been her fire, never fully explained to Juniper. She owned it, chained it securely in a dank cave and visited it from time to time to be sure that its incarceration held firm.

It had been wise to keep details of the fire from Juniper when she was thirteen. The important details were clear enough. Their parents were dead, as inconceivable as it was to the sisters; their parents were gone. Now J Bird was twenty-six. She had survived a string of boyfriends unfit even for themselves. She had survived drinking too much in college and too much Ecstasy. But for the last few years, J Bird had left behind the remnants of her wild girl identity, the one who would do anything, and exchanged it for this new, more exciting version, the one who could run a bakery. Her future was bright and boundless.

J Bird's true north was baking, and she drove the effort to open the café in seven weeks. Seeing her sister's expertise, the way she knew just where to buy a good used baker's oven, where to attach the cooling racks, how to order supplies, had lowered Delia's vigilance monitor by a few degrees.

So why now? Why did her sister want to know the details now? Delia had held the demon chained up in the cave for so long. She wasn't sure if she could talk about that night again. Except for the fact that Juniper had been pecking at her for hours.

"Can't this wait? I have the worst case of my entire career weighing on me, Tyler has come back into town, and my online dating project was awful. Do we have to scratch off this scab now?"

The clatter of Baxter's claws on the hardwood floors caused them both to turn their heads. He had a dayglow green tennis ball in his mouth. He looked at both of them, raised his eyebrows, and walked to the door. Tail up, three wags. He had to go out. Delia was suspicious. She was sure that Baxter was intervening in a discussion that probably sounded like arguing to him. Were they arguing? She suspected that hearing his two main people argue was the most complicated situation for him, far worse than keeping them safe from outside forces. How could he protect the sisters, whom he loved, from each other?

"Okay Mr. Peacekeeper, I'll take you out. I've got to change out of these painting clothes before I do," said Delia. She had on ancient yoga pants that were blotched with paint and had a hole in the crotch. She slipped off the pants and pulled on a stretchy skirt free of paint.

"Come on, we could both use a break. Let's walk out to the marsh," she said to Juniper. Baxter wiggled his entire body, offering them his trademark retriever smile, even with the ball in his mouth.

They wrapped their brushes and rollers in plastic bags and headed out. It was easier for Delia to talk if she was moving.

"There was a fire, our parents were killed. It was arson, and most likely our father set the fire in the midst of his last raging psychotic episode," said Delia. "You know all this. What else is there to know? Dead is dead." Even as she said this, she knew it was too harsh, not what J Bird deserved.

The serenade of katydids looking for love filled the air along the quiet street that bordered a marsh. Juniper still wore her flip-flops, unwilling to give in to the approaching fall.

"After we talked yesterday, I remembered something. You made me go to the Clarks' house. Then you ran into our house. I saw you from their living room window. So did Mrs. Clark. She screamed and held on to me; she wouldn't let me follow you. I heard the sirens, but you ran in before the fire truck arrived. What did you see?"

Had they come to a time when the past could be untangled? Would talking about it help?

Muscles along Delia's rib cage woke up and tightened. They relayed an alarm that marched outward, toward her arms and legs. "The smoke was already so thick, I couldn't see much. I dropped to my hands and knees where the smoke wasn't as thick."

"Did you call to them? Could you hear them?"

Delia heard the demon in the cave jangling its chain, whipping it from side to side.

The gravel crunched under their feet. Baxter jumped into the first water access he could find in the freshwater marsh.

Delia's voice constricted, the sides of her throat conspiring to silence her. "Yes, it was the first thing I did. I thought I heard them, I thought I heard Dad. But then my lungs filled with smoke, or at least that's what it felt like. I couldn't see and I couldn't breathe." She remembered the sound, the roar inside their house, the blast of hot air that hit her like a wall.

Baxter ran back to them and shook off, spraying his people with marsh water. J Bird picked up his tennis ball and hurled it into the water. Baxter dashed off, the tips of his ears bobbing, his powerful body stretched low and long, in full retrieving mode. There was nothing he wouldn't do in his quest.

Delia scuffed her paint-splattered running shoes in the dirt. "Let's go back, okay? Talking about this feels like I'm being dragged in the dirt behind a pickup truck. I forgot how it felt to picture that day. It doesn't get easier. Please. But I did call to them. And I'm not sure that I heard Dad."

Juniper jammed her hands into the pockets of her painting pants, jeans with shredded knees. "I know you don't like to talk about it, but I missed something that you were able to have. You got a little bit more of them that last time, in the fire. I want to see it all," she said.

Baxter returned, dropped the ball at their feet, and shook off, fully prepared to do it all over again.

"Sorry, big guy, we've got work to do. No more," said J Bird. The center of Baxter's eyebrows rose, as though he were crushed by the terrible news.

They walked a two-mile loop in silence, punctuated with ball tosses, and returned to the café. Baxter claimed the spot by the front door, where his stainless steel water bowl awaited him.

Delia lined up planks of baseboard trim between two sawhorses and dipped her brush into high gloss white paint. She looked down at the boards, giving a sideways glance to her little sister. "What made you think of the fire today?" Delia said. She only wanted to know why now, but the question was sure to open the door to more questions.

Juniper rolled a twelve-inch-wide swath of fuchsia up the wall. "It's just that you and I are starting this business together, and Dad would be so happy about all this great food and Mom would be proud of us. If ever I wanted them to be back, you know, alive again, it's now. I feel like they're here, watching us sometimes."

Delia gripped the paintbrush. She didn't want her dead parents in the new business. She wanted a clean break from the sadness that defined their lives. But if J Bird wanted to feel closer to their parents, if that was the reason tied up with starting the new bakery café, maybe she should share more. J Bird was all grown up.

Delia took a breath. "I was glad that our neighbors, the Clarks, kept you across the street while they called 911. Remember, we had just come home from the mall and saw the smoke coming from the upstairs bedrooms. It was getting dark." A furnace of heat started deep in her stomach and rose unabated to the top of her skull.

"I sort of remember. I liked Mrs. Clark even though their house always smelled like hamburgers. I remember she had on a sweater, something itchy. Wow, I'd never remembered that before, even when you made me go to the therapist after Mom and Dad died."

Delia's vision blurred along the periphery, and she swallowed hard. Maybe this would be enough for Juniper, maybe the stupid scratchy sweater would be enough and they could go back to painting and nothing more.

Juniper ran two more rows of paint up the wall, coming dangerously close to the ceiling.

"I remember now; you had on flip-flops and tan shorts." Juniper eased the roller back into the tray and set it down. She licked her lips and pressed her bottom teeth along her top lip the way she used to do when she was a kid.

Delia's paintbrush clattered to the tarp covering the floor. She picked up a rag and mopped up the puddle of white paint. She couldn't look at her sister.

"There was too much smoke. The smoke was so thick, I couldn't see anything," said Delia.

"But you said you could hear Dad. What about Mom? Could you hear Mom? Do you mean they were both still alive then?"

"I don't know! For God's sake, J Bird, please stop. I don't remember."

Baxter was suddenly at Delia's side, pushing his head into her hand. His fur, still damp, took on all the odors of the marsh, rich with plant life, amphibians, and muck.

The torrent of emotion caught her off guard, the heat of her tears unstoppable. Delia turned her head away, embarrassed, and covered her face. Baxter planted his butt on her feet and pressed his entire body against her legs.

J Bird put down her paint roller. "Jeez, I'm sorry. I forget that it was different for you. I forget that maybe it's harder to have memories that you want to forget than to not have enough memories. Let's go home. I can come back tomorrow after my shift and finish the painting."

# CHAPTER 25

*Juniper*

Juniper finished her shift at the bakery by ten on Monday morning, went home, walked Baxter, and headed straight for the J Bird Café. The opening date galloped toward them, and she would have to spend every spare moment getting the building ready. Greg and his minions weren't there today.

"If you want to hire a painting crew, just let me know," Greg had said. "Otherwise, call me when you're finished. We can't do anything else inside until you finish painting."

Painting soothed her almost as much as baking did. She liked the rhythmic movement of rolling paint on a wall, watching the fuchsia and melon walls emerge after decades of beige. They chose high gloss white for the trim. Greg had uncovered an old tin ceiling, and once it was cleaned and painted silver, Juniper thought it looked like the night sky when the moon was full, the kind of soft silver light that reflected off the ocean.

She couldn't remember seeing Delia as undone as yesterday when Juniper had pressed her for details about the fire. She could at least make it up to her by getting the café ready for the oven delivery.

She'd been painting for hours. Everything seemed to take longer than she imagined. Juniper knew the restaurant renovation meant the bathroom had to be up to code. The doorway had to be wide enough to accommodate a wheelchair, there had to be ventilation, and besides, who didn't want ventilation in a bathroom? In a bakery, the aromas rolling through should come from breads and soups, coffee and tea, if tea had a smell, and Juniper wasn't sure that it did. But she wanted the bathroom to be rather odorless.

She didn't want to put up the compulsory sign that said, EMPLOYEES MUST WASH THEIR HANDS, as if there were a question of whether she or Delia would wash their hands after using the toilet. Or that they were raised in a home without running water. How could anyone look at them, with their firmly tied aprons, their hair pulled back, carrying a tray of croissants from the oven to the display case, and imagine that they wouldn't wash their hands?

The sign was part of the state health code, but it seemed to be more of a reassurance to customers. Juniper was determined to come up with a better, friendlier sign for the handicapped accessible men/women's bathroom. Maybe, LET'S ALL WASH OUR HANDS.

The window above the toilet was the kind that slides to one side. Juniper put her left hand on the sink and stood up carefully on the closed toilet seat. The seat and lid were old, but thick and sturdy, made from either a massive hunk of plastic or possibly wood with glistening white laminate paint.

She picked up a wet cloth from the sink, intending to wipe the window, but a branch from a tall bush caught her eye. A lilac bush brushed against the building, and two leggy branches caressed the window. This was the south side of the building, and the lilacs would bloom early. There would come a time in the spring when the bathroom would smell like lilacs, just the way her bedroom had when she was growing up, when the lilacs had pressed against her upstairs window. One day her mother had opened her bedroom window and reached out with a pair of clippers and grabbed a handful of the fragrant blooms. "These are for you, J Bird." They filled a canning jar with water and placed the dark purple lilacs in a jar. It seemed like they lasted forever.

The back door creaked open and she jumped, dragged out of her childhood reverie. "Anybody home? I need a chocolate éclair."

It was Ben. His big brother voice hit a familiar place with her. Where would they be if not for Ben, finding housing for them after her parents died, helping Delia fill out student loan forms? Baxter was back home or he would have greeted Ben with his ticker-tape-parade wiggling and dog serenade.

"Hey! I'm back here in the bathroom. Look out; there's wet paint everywhere."

Ben stretched his head and neck around the corner. "So that's why my buddy Baxter isn't greeting me. Goldens don't make good painting companions, unless you like doggie tails dipped in paint."

Juniper hopped off the toilet seat and held the paintbrush high while she hugged Ben.

"What do you think of our place so far?" She felt like a teenager angling for a compliment.

Ben turned around slowly, taking in everything with exaggerated concentration. "What you've done with the sawhorses and brown paper over the windows is, well, stunning. And the drop cloths on the floors. Just beautiful," he said, stroking his chin.

"Oh, come on, really, what do you think?"

She wanted him to see that their business venture was in the final stretch. Correction: She needed some of Ben's magic praise, the kind that had sustained her as a kid.

"I'm so proud of you. Once people taste anything that comes out of this kitchen, they will be helplessly addicted to the J Bird Café. You'll own them. By the way, exactly where is the kitchen?"

"Right in back of you. See, the ovens go against that wall,

cooling racks over here, and a partial wall goes here so that people can see the bread coming out of the ovens. The ovens are coming tomorrow, so that's why we've been pushing to finish the painting."

Ben took a few steps toward the back of the building. The limp was still there, slight but noticeable.

"I think you should get your money back from the knee surgeon. Aren't those surgeries supposed to be foolproof?" she asked.

Ben leaned over and rubbed his knee, frowning. "Nothing is foolproof with surgery. You'd be surprised by what can go wrong. I'm taking care of it."

She'd be glad when Ben was back to normal again, without protecting his knee all the time. It made him look older than he was, a bit drawn around the mouth.

"And by the way, what the heck was wrong with you the other day when I stopped in at the clinic with Baxter? You've never given me such a brush-off before," she said, hands on her hips.

Ben looked out the side window. "Don't take it personally. Please. I haven't been feeling all that great after the surgery and a couple of bouts with the flu. Don't get old like me, sweetie."

"Old? Don't say that!" She reached up and wrapped her arms around his neck. "You are not permitted to get old. Or sick. And stop limping right now."

Ben laughed and gave her a big squeeze. "Okay, I promise. Your job is to keep me stocked up on chocolate éclairs."

"Our grand opening is the first weekend in October. I want you to put it on your calendar and put a big sign up at your office. Tell all your patients that it's mandatory for them to come to our café. But mostly I want you to be here, with Michelle and the kids."

Ben had kicked in money to cover some of the startup costs of the renovation. Seven thousand dollars, which the sisters insisted was a loan. They'd even written a contract that all three of them signed to say that payments would begin within two years, or sooner if they turned a profit. He had been there for them every step of the way since the fire. When Ben's mother moved to Florida, he cosigned the loan so they could buy her house.

"I wouldn't miss it. I just wanted to stop by for a quick check on how you were doing. It looks great, kiddo. I've got to run; I'm meeting a friend for a dog consultation. I told him to cruise by here and I'd help him out." Ben looked upward to the right corner of the ceiling. "Cool tin ceiling," he said, patting the doorframe. "You can always call on me if you need grunt labor. I can haul trash or plant flowers in the window boxes. Just don't ask me to do anything that requires actual carpentry skills." He winked at her and left.

Juniper rinsed out the paintbrush and roller. She opened the side door to put the brushes outside to dry when she heard Ben and another man talking. She took a few steps into the side yard and saw the back end of a sage green Camry. Ben leaned into the passenger window, looked left and right, and then slid an envelope into his pants pocket. He took several long steps to his pickup truck and drove off.

Juniper sat on the step and picked paint from her fingernails. Ben had done house calls in the past, usually when an old dog needed to be euthanized and the owners wanted the dog to die at home. But was he taking payments outside the office, a little tweaking of the books by not recording cash?

Ben was her model for how to be an adult, how to be responsible and still have a good time, how to find a good partner and stay married, how to love what you do, how to be kind and generous. He was out of sorts lately; that was clear when she stopped by his clinic with Baxter. But today he was the old Ben, the last friend that her father had, the one who didn't abandon him when he was at his worst, bloated up like a whale on medications. Sometimes you just had to let people be who they were, let them have their highs and lows. If Ben wanted to pull in a little cash without running it through the clinic, then Juniper wasn't going to say anything about it, especially not to Delia. She had Ben's back. It was the least she could do for him.

# CHAPTER 26

Two years ago, Ira changed the old Mr. Coffee machine in the staff room for a single cup brewing system. It was true that the staff meetings were no longer a battle zone for who would clean the glass coffee pot, empty the grounds, buy the coffee, or remember to turn it off at the end of the day. There were no longer signs in the break room, posted with anonymous anger, YOUR MOTHER DOESN'T LIVE HERE. . . . CLEAN UP AFTER YOURSELF!!!!! But Delia still cringed at the environmental carnage of Keurig K-Cups in their individual plastic firmness, destined to fill landfills right next to mountains of disposable diapers. It was eight forty-five a.m., and she popped a French roast K-Cup into the holder, closed it, and waited for her cup to fill.

She and Ira had arranged for a morning meeting with Detective Moretti in Ira's office. Foster Services had a close relationship with the police. In the case of abused or abandoned kids, the two agencies needed each other. Delia didn't want to overstep her role by telling the police that they needed to dig deeper to help them find Hayley's family, and yet that was exactly what threatened to burst out of her mouth as she sat down next to the detective in front of Ira's desk.

Moretti was a big man, a couple of inches over six feet. Delia sometimes saw him at night at the Y, headphones on, jogging on the treadmill with a white towel draped around his neck. It was hard not to notice him, but she assumed that he didn't want to engage in small talk any more than she did while she was sweating away on the elliptical machine. They would nod an acknowledgment at each other.

Today, he looked like he'd already been at work for hours.

"We immediately followed up on your lead about the library in West Hartford. The Hartford PD told us there are no security cameras in the library, so we were unable to use that technology. We were already checking into the security cameras at the stoplight closest to the hardware store based on the date of the receipt, but it's unlikely we'll be able to narrow down a vehicle, since there was no vehicle at the murder scene," he said.

He spoke like he'd been trained to exclude all extraneous information. Delia grew up with a father who was bombarded by extraneous information: the messages delivered by katydids in late summer, the patterns of the bar codes in the grocery store, the secret directives sent through television commercials.

Delia sipped her coffee. She was sure that a residue of plastic made it into her cup. "What about the woman in the library, the one who worked at the children's desk? The one who disappeared around the time of the murders," she said.

This time he turned his head to look at her. "She didn't check out. She'd been a volunteer for about six months, and the library sometimes uses a shortcut for verification in order to save money. The only official identification that the library required of her was a driver's license, and that was bogus. Every CORI check costs the library fifty dollars, so if nothing pops up with the license when they send it to the local PD, they take a chance and skip the CORI. It turns out that she had stolen the identity of a teacher in the area who never knew her ID was stolen. She was smart; no claims were made on the stolen credit cards, so there were no red flags."

Ira tapped the fingers of his right hand along the edge of his desk. "But you must have a description of her from the people at the library."

"Hartford police sent us a compilation of her description."

Was this guy only going to answer direct questions? Delia wished he would bend a little in their direction.

"The longer that Hayley spends away from her family, the more traumatized she is. Our entire goal is to find her family as quickly as possible," said Ira. "We're not intruding on your territory, Mike, it's just that we feel strongly that she has parents out there. We told you about the Skype calls that were made between Hayley and her mother."

Moretti leaned forward slightly. "I know. You guys do good work. But I am more and more certain that these crimes are part of a large heroin network, larger than we've ever seen in Maine. Technically speaking, we have a lot of unconnected dots. We have heroin residue at the scene of the murders, three people killed execution style, we have a receipt for a hardware store in West Hartford, we have one vic from Tennessee, another male unidentified, and Emma Gilbert, who lived in Florida. Emma had no priors, and she had been reported missing by her boss at a radio station a few months back. And now we have a library volunteer with a falsified identity who left the library around the time of the murders. My guess is that the crime organization moved the library girl out and we won't see her again," he said.

Ira stopped tapping his fingers. "And we have Hayley. She's a five-year-old girl who wants to go home," he said.

The detective's stick deodorant pulsed a wave of scent to Delia, carried on increased body heat. He had saved something for last, something that he didn't want to say.

"We've seen an exponential increase in heroin in the last two years. The state is struggling to stay in front of this, and we're not winning. We've already had sixty-one deaths by heroin overdose this year in Maine. This case may be our entryway into a major supply line of heroin coming up from Mexico through Nashville, Tennessee." He paused and shifted his feet. "I need to interview Hayley. I need to ask her about the killings."

Delia swallowed hard. She knew this was coming now that Hayley was more settled at Erica's, enrolled in kindergarten, talking freely. She and Ira had been expecting it.

"I want to do the interview," said Delia. "What if you come along, but I ask the questions? I know how to talk with Hayley, and I know when she's not going to stop talking."

He tightened his lips. "I have a daughter who's ten. I understand what you mean. But you don't know what information I might need, or how to follow a thread."

Ira's wall clock was a cheap, battery-powered replica of the kind that was in every classroom in schools. The ticking filled the silence between the three of them.

"Then tell me exactly what you need to know, what you think this child might be able to tell you. I'll call Erica and set up a time, and I'll make sure Louie is with us," she said.

"Louie? Is that one of the foster mom's kids?"

"Um, no. He's a Maine Coon cat. Are we good? I'll do the interview?" asked Delia.

Moretti put his hand on a cell phone that vibrated in his pants pocket. "Do you have some time now? We can go over what I would normally ask. I will need to be there. But if you skip something or lose a thread, I'm going to ask her a question. This isn't my first rodeo, and I've worked with kids before. Excuse me while I check this call."

Leaning to one side, he extracted the cell phone from his pocket, looked at the screen, tapped it, and returned it to the pocket. "I need to be back in the department in an hour. Can we go over the details now?"

Ira stood up. "You two can work out the details without me. I need to look at applications for a caseworker."

Delia felt a twinge of guilt. Hiring a replacement was time-consuming, fraught with phone calls to references and also with scheduling interviews. It was hard to balance her excitement about J Bird Café with the burdens she was going to leave behind with Ira. And right now, it felt like she was never leaving, at least not until Hayley found her family. Ira didn't look up as Delia and Moretti left his office. He was already deep into a pile of applications, most of them from people brand-new to the profession.

The detective and Delia squeezed into her small office. The man took up a lot of space. Delia grabbed a pad of paper and rolled her chair several inches away from him when he sat in a manspread posture. "We have to remember two things when we interview Hayley," she said. "First, her memory is probably impaired by trauma, and if we force her to remember things that are too traumatic for her to tolerate, she is going to reexperience the trauma and retreat even more. Second, she is only five years old, and her understanding of the world is part magical and part real. If we force her to be concrete, you aren't going to get what you want."

He tipped his head once. "Understood. And you understand that three people are dead and my job is to find the bad guys?"

She pulled a pencil off her desk. "Understood. Tell me what would be most helpful to find out from Hayley."

He held up one fist and extended his pointer finger up. "One. Did she see the shooter? Can she tell us anything about what they looked like? And I mean anything. Male. Female. How many? Did she hear anything?"

Delia wrote furiously. "What else?" she said.

He held up his middle finger. "The car. They traveled to South Portland in a car. I know she won't be able to tell us the kind of car, but anything that she can tell us about the car would help. Did it have a sunroof? What color was it? Was it a van?"

These were all questions that she expected. He held up the next finger.

"What was the other guy's name? And then these are long shots, but did she know where they were going, or why she was with them?" He opened his hands, palms up. "If we can get answers to any of those questions, it would help us. And hopefully help Hayley."

She'd worked with him before, but only for short periods, like in a hospital emergency room when a child was brought in with suspected abuse and once when she had to consult with him about the Somali community leaders when a ten-year-old

Somali boy was kicked out of his house. But never tucked away in her office, nearly knee to knee.

"Okay," she said. "I'll call the foster mom, Erica, this morning and see what we can set up. I'll call you."

He didn't move. "How about if you call her right now. The longer we wait, the harder all of this gets for everybody."

Delia stuffed down a sense of irritation. This was her domain, and she knew what she was doing. In the end, she called Erica and set up a time for later that afternoon, after Hayley had a rest from kindergarten.

# CHAPTER 27

Delia worked her way through files in her office. She and Moretti were scheduled to meet at Erica's house at three. She pulled the office shredder next to her desk, and she slid in any scraps of paper that were no longer relevant to a child's file or only meaningful to Delia, scribbles that the next caseworker wouldn't be able to decipher. But she was distracted by the shocking return of Tyler. And on the back burner of her attention, the detective simmered.

She didn't want to pretend not to notice that Tyler was back in Portland. Something about being thirty-two had sheared off the varnish of her skin, revealing what wanted to push through. She called Tyler's cell, hoping he wasn't in the midst of a medical intervention.

"Hey," he said. She heard the welcome in his voice. "I'm here with a Realtor right now. Can I call you back in half an hour?"

"Sure. Are you free for lunch?"

"I think so. I'll call you back."

Was he buying a house? Was he settling in Portland permanently? When she first saw him, she assumed Portland was a stopover, a place to work until he moved on.

She was going to help train a new caseworker during her last week of work. But you couldn't just drop seventy cases on the new person. That would be like teaching someone to swim and forcing them to drag a barge behind them. Delia would have to assign two thirds of her cases to the other four caseworkers in her office, at least temporarily. Right now, she had to figure out which child would go with which worker. And she couldn't let any of the kids fall through the cracks.

For ten years, she'd lived with the tickling fear that she might just do that, forget a child, that multitasking might start to shrink up the part of her brain that needed to remember every child on her caseload, every parent, every foster parent. Were they working on reunification or adoption? Did the foster parents need more training, more resources, was she on a weekly visiting schedule with the child or twice a month? Her brain felt like an Excel sheet.

But now, she had transferred nearly twenty of her cases, much to the groaning exasperation of her already overburdened coworkers.

She was leaving Foster Services mostly intact. There had been no horrible disasters like the two cases in Massachusetts: a young boy, forgotten by his caseworker, who was killed by a flagrantly abusive stepfather, and another boy who had been starved into a coma. She had escaped the vilification that came with one mistake in this high-stakes world of understaffed workers and overloaded caseloads.

As the eleventh hour of her career chimed, Hayley appeared, the five-year-old without a family whom no one had reported missing. Hayley, who wanted to go home. She'd been working on Hayley's case for ten days and so far, nothing had budged other than the possible link with Lillian Tiger Library in West Hartford. Every avenue was blocked, every tried and true technique, every inquiry to other agencies all resulted in the same response. No one had reported this child missing.

Delia continued to update and transfer files until her phone rang. Her heart jumped when she saw Tyler's name on caller ID. "Can you stop by and meet me for lunch at a house that I'm looking at? I need a second opinion. I've never bought a house before," he said.

She had felt the heat of him since the day he walked into The Daily Grind. His return was like the great seventeen-year cicada cycle, except in this case, it was the thirteen-year cycle. He returned to Portland and *whoosh*, the old raw burn in her was ignited.

Hearing him was still disconcerting to her, blending his adult voice with the voice of a teenaged boy. Was there a way to extract her memories of him from before? The first sex, the flood of desire, the open reservoir of trust in him, crying in his arms when she confided all the family's tightly held secrets about her father, how she and J Bird were so afraid of him at times, embarrassed to invite their friends over, and how much she loved her father when his true self peeked through the mental illness.

Delia locked her office and drove to the address that Tyler gave her, 29 Woodlawn Avenue. The address was in an old residential neighborhood filled with houses built in two waves. The first wave of building had been in the flush of wealth in the 1920s, and the second surge came right after World War II. All the houses were squat and solid Craftsman-style homes, some reputed to have been ordered directly from the Sears catalog. Not unlike the neighborhood where she and Tyler grew up.

She pulled her car to the side of the wide street. Two girls pedaled along the sidewalk, each one helmeted in matching purple headgear, both of them riding on the sidewalk instead of the street because they were eight years old. Ten years in the business of foster care made Delia an expert in assessing the ages of kids. And she knew these two girls weren't in foster care. They had a home, and the filaments of their home trailed them with their bodily ease and matching helmets.

The front door was wide and welcoming with thick, angled

pillars on either side of the steps leading up to the open porch. She liked porches. Her father loved to sit on the porch, writing the first drafts of his food column on a yellow legal pad. He would greet the young Delia as the yellow school bus dropped her off from school. "I've spent the day writing about artichokes," he said. "Please tell me your day was more exciting." But when he was overcome by the onslaught of delusions, the front porch terrified him. "Get in the house, Delia! We're being watched."

The front door to 29 Woodlawn was open. "Anybody home?" she said.

"In here." Tyler's voice echoed through the empty house.

Delia felt the weight of the house and Tyler's ownership as soon as he walked out of the kitchen, the way he touched the thick molding around the door, giving it a rub with his thumb.

His heat was already in the house, the way men can spread their aura around like dark honey. A woman's voice reverberated from an empty room upstairs.

"The Realtor is making calls while I show you around. Tell me what you think so far," he said. "No, wait. Let me show you around before the pizza gets here." He reached for her hand so easily, as if no time had passed.

"Come on, you've got to see this sunroom. That's what sold the house."

"You already made an offer? Have you been looking at other houses or is this the first one?"

He squeezed her hand and released it.

"I told the Realtor what I wanted and this was the first house she showed me. That's why I called you back. Well, aside from wanting to see you. I need a reality check. I haven't signed anything yet. I'm calling her back in an hour."

A flutter ran through her, a culmination of being with Tyler in this house, his enthusiasm about buying it, his desire for her opinion, and the hand squeeze. Was she so deprived of romance that even a hand squeeze felt dramatic? The erogenous zone of their palms, pressing against each other?

Tyler led the way through the living room, through the

French doors, to the sunroom. "The sunroom was an addition back in the nineties. The owners were young, and they decided to add the sunroom instead of flying away to an island every February."

The floor was lined with terra cotta tile, oversized squares of it, ready to absorb the heat of the sun through the glass walls and roof. Delia pictured the tiles exhaling puffs of heat in the cold afternoons of January and February.

"Look up," he said. "There's an awning that covers the ceiling during the hottest days of the summer." Tyler reached for a remote control device, sitting on the one piece of furniture in the sunroom, a wicker couch with bright blue pillows. He clicked the remote and an interior awning slid across the ceiling. "Shade cloth," he said, sitting down on the two-person couch. He patted the space next to him.

"What do you think? You've hardly said anything," said Tyler.

Delia hesitated before sitting close to this man who was her first young lover, who had slid his hands along her breasts, fresh from midnight skinny dipping in Sebago Lake. She could still hear the thumping of his heart when she had lain across him, her ear pressed to his chest. Everything about Tyler had been an antidote to the daily tragedy at home as her father's illness accelerated. He had been everything fresh and healthy when her home was encased with sadness.

She turned in the small space, angling her body so that she could look directly at him. "I haven't said anything because we are skipping a huge block of our history. I'm not good at pretending. If I ever had that social skill, it incinerated thirteen years ago along with my mother and father."

Tyler winced, his entire torso trembled as though unprepared to step back in time.

Did she have to be so abrasive? Had she gone too far in the direction of speaking the truth?

She cleared her suddenly dry throat. "I'm glad you're here. It's amazing to see you, but I can't fake it; seeing you brings back a lot of emotional turmoil. Okay, tons of turmoil. I'm completely undone, sort of time-traveling to age nineteen and back to right now in my overwhelming, oh-so-adult life, and it's giving me whiplash." She didn't mean to say so much about being undone.

"Whiplash?" Tyler laughed, the skin around his eyes crinkling. "Finally we're talking about something that I actually know about." He paused, took a huge breath, and slowly exhaled.

"Did they teach relaxation breathing techniques in med school?" she asked.

"Delia, it was California. Of course they did. Reiki and acupressure were also offered, although they were optional and I couldn't fit them into my schedule." He put his hand on her thigh for an instant. "In some strange way, I don't feel like any time has passed at all. I didn't plan this, although I seriously hoped that I would run into you in Portland. I wasn't even sure you were still here."

Delia took the remote out of his hand to have something to do. A tremor ran through her. She pushed the button to retract the shade cloth. A small motor whirred. "You didn't plan what, specifically?"

He took the remote from her and set it between them. "That it would matter to me if you liked the house that I bought, that you would look more beautiful, that your eyes would still make me go all goofy, and that I would still sound like I was nineteen. I swear to you that I am a fully functioning adult and I don't sound like this when I'm fixing broken bodies when they come through the emergency doors."

Delia stood up. "You're an emergency doctor? It is almost impossible for me to wrap my head around this. I'm sorry, but you aren't old enough to drink. You are nineteen. Me too." She could only address one part of his comment. Not the part about her eyes or any of the rest.

"I've embarrassed you. And me. I didn't mean to say that. It's the combination of seeing you and having my younger, more impulsive self leap to the foreground. I promise you that I can take care of car accident victims at three a.m., and kids with croup who have freaked out their parents when they started barking like a seal, and everything else without blathering like this."

The doorbell rang and echoed throughout the house, unmitigated by furniture, drapes, or rugs. Both of them jumped a bit.

"Let me get that. The Realtor said we can't bring food into the house, but there's a neighborhood park at the end of the block. We can eat there," he said. He rushed out of the room to the front door.

When she had been nineteen, after the fire, after he and his family drove away, she longed for Tyler to suddenly appear, to drive back from the West Coast, to answer her e-mails, to offer her salvation from the collapse of her family. After Tyler didn't respond, after months of hoping, she closed the door on him. She rarely spoke of him, excised him from her life. When she had needed him the most, he left her. The current version of Tyler sliced open the old wound with a scalpel.

The front door closed and Tyler returned, holding a flat cardboard box of pizza.

"Let's eat," he said. "I promise not to let the nineteen-year-old out again. I just sent him to his room without supper." He paused and then went to the bottom of the stairs. "Jessica, we're going to the park to eat. You can lock it up. I'll call you later this afternoon."

A woman trotted down the stairs, cell phone in one hand, large black handbag in the other, blond hair pulled back with clip. "Great. I'm sorry you can't eat here, but we can't allow prospective buyers to bring food in the house. Are you sure you've seen everything that you need?"

"Don't worry about us. It will be nice to eat outside."

Delia followed him through the kitchen and out the sliding glass doors to the patio, and Jessica locked the door behind them. They walked along the side yard to the street and the half block to a small park with one set of swings and a picnic table. They sat across from each other.

"Did you take away the nineteen-year-old's ability to call or e-mail also? Because that's what happened once before." She didn't want to spare him anything, or pretend, or eat pizza. She was glad that the thick planks of wood separated them.

Tyler's hand hesitated over the cardboard box. "Time has made you even more direct." He sat back, hands beside him along the bench. "My family needed me. No sooner had we moved than my father became ill. Lung cancer. He told me not to transfer to the West Coast, told me to live my life, but I couldn't do it. I wanted all the time I had with him. I didn't have anything left to give to anyone else."

Tyler closed his eyes and bent his head down for a moment. "My dad lived for about eighteen months, a good long time for his kind of cancer. When the dust settled, I was too ashamed to contact you. I mean, you had to take care of everything, I know. You had to take care of your sister."

When he looked up, his eyes were red, blood vessels bursting.

"We could have helped each other. That's what people do," she said.

"How? We were suddenly three thousand miles away. But you're right; I've never regretted anything as much as what I did," he said. "I should have called you. I should have done a lot of things."

A sudden breeze rustled the treetops, a harbinger of autumn. They were in the shade of a large sugar maple that was sure to turn orange or red as the days grew shorter. Gooseflesh rose up on Delia's arms.

"I have to meet a colleague in South Portland," she said, getting up. "If you like the house, you should buy it. This is a good, solid house." She swung one leg over the picnic table bench and then the other. "I'm sorry about your father." She knew she had to say more, but what was enough in the face of so much death? "You don't ever have to apologize again. We can't go back to being kids again. Both of us made it through awful times, and I think we're okay now."

"Delia, wait. I want to see you again. We can stay right in the present and do something ordinary, like dinner. Could we be ordinary people at dinner? I'm on twelve-hour shifts for the next few days, but after that?"

She did want to see him again. She wanted to see what he had grown into.

"Okay, I'd like that," she said.

Tyler walked with her back to her car, the pizza box filled with cooling pizza. When she slid into her car, her chin began to itch. Chin and left jawline. Of course, it was the case again. It had to be Hayley.

# CHAPTER 28

"Hi again, Hayley," said Delia. "Where's my favorite cat, Mr. Louie?" It was midafternoon and Erica had directed them to the back deck of her house.

Hayley looked up from a child-sized plastic Adirondack chair on the deck. Erica picked squash and cucumbers from the raised garden bed. Delia knew she had one ear cocked toward Hayley, ready to intervene if the child became distressed.

Delia and the detective sat near Hayley on the edge of the deck with their feet nestled along the stone walk. Delia had warned Moretti that he needed to shrink considerably. Now they were close to eye level with Hayley.

"His name is Louie, not Mr. Louie," she said.

At the mention of his name, the bobcat-sized Maine Coon cat emerged from beneath the large leaves of a dark green hosta. Louie settled in front of Hayley, easily coming to the height of her knees.

"Michael, this is Hayley, and she's in kindergarten."

"Hi, Hayley. My daughter is in fourth grade," he said.

So far, so good with the detective. He kept his voice soft, kept his arms and elbows tucked in and didn't do the manspread with his knees. Delia hadn't done an assessment of a young child with him before. Often, there wasn't a need for the police to be present during the ongoing assessment. And Delia had never worked a case where there were no family members at all.

"We know that you want to go home, so we are trying to find your mommy and your daddy," said Delia. She reached into her pack and pulled out a floppy stuffed rabbit about the size of Moretti's large hands. "So I brought my friend, Igor the Rabbit, and he will whisper questions to me that he wants to ask you. Is that okay with you if we play this game? And please ask Louie if it's okay with him."

Hayley looked at Delia with eyes fresh and unstained by time. "Okay. And Louie can't talk," she said.

Delia set the toy rabbit on her lap. "If you say so, but Louie can let me know when he likes something and when he doesn't. I know he likes you."

Hayley leaned forward and slid her small hand along the cat's spine.

"Oh, wait, Igor has a question." Delia put the rabbit up to her ear. "Got it. I'll ask her."

She put Igor back on her lap. "Igor wants to know if Mommy lives in a house with a driveway and a place to park a bike in case Igor wants to visit."

The detective stroked his chin. "Good question, Igor. Sure, I've got a driveway. Oh, you're asking Hayley! You mean Hayley's mommy."

Hayley approached a smile.

"My mommy has a blue car. Blue is my favorite color."

Delia shook the rabbit around her ear again. "Oh, sorry, yes, I'll ask her." Louie flicked his tail. They wouldn't have long with this game. She figured ten minutes, maybe fifteen.

"Igor wants to know the color of the car that you and Emma traveled in." She turned to Moretti and said, "Igor is so nosy today."

Hayley frowned. "Not blue like Mommy's car." She looked around as if searching for a reference color.

Moretti leaned to one side and pulled a laminated card, no bigger than a deck of cards, from his pocket. It was covered with cartoon-looking cars of different colors. With one finger, he covered the blue car. Why wasn't this man wearing a wedding ring? Maybe they didn't when they were on duty. "So, not this blue car. But which color was the car with Emma?"

He was right; this wasn't his first rodeo. Hayley pointed to a silver car. "Like this car," she said.

"Thank you, Hayley. Hey, Igor, she says it was a gray car," he said. He winked at Hayley and smiled at her.

Delia wiggled the stuffed toy, bobbing it around her ear again. "Okay, I'll ask her."

"Igor wants to know who was with you and Emma Gilbert. The two men."

"Only Uncle Ray," said Hayley. She frowned.

Delia made the rabbit jump up and down. "Igor says you have answered three questions! He is so excited. Please calm down, you wild rabbit."

Louie stood up and stretched. If he walked off, Hayley was likely to close down again. Delia was ready for him this time. She reached into her pocket and pulled out a plastic bag of something called Kitty Kibble Treats. She tore open one corner and gave one to Louie. For the first time since she had been coming to Erica's house, Louie looked directly at Delia.

Igor whispered in Delia's ear again.

Moretti pulled a pad of paper out of his pants pocket and wrote something in large print and passed it to Delia.

*Who hurt Emma and Uncle Ray?*

Delia dreaded the part where Hayley must be escorted back into the memory of bloodshed and trauma. She had to keep her eye on the goal: find out why Hayley was with Emma Gilbert and Ray so that hopefully, they could backtrack to Hayley's mother.

"Igor wants to know who hurt Emma and Uncle Ray. Tell Igor what they looked like," said Delia.

Hayley shrugged. "I don't know," she said. Her voice lost air, like a deflated balloon. She rocked forward and back in her chair.

The detective held out his hand to Delia and Igor. "May I?" he said.

Did she trust him enough to channel questions through a stuffed rabbit? She hadn't noticed how blue his eyes were before now.

"Yes," she said, "but Igor will need to go home soon. He gets very tired when he's out and he still has to dig up lots of carrots to eat." She handed over the rabbit, giving him a look that she hoped communicated a dire threat if he took Hayley too far.

As soon as Igor reached Moretti's hands, the detective fell back on the deck. "Ow, ow! Igor, don't bite my ear! I promise to stop at the store and buy you an entire bag of carrots. What? You want chocolate ice cream too? Okay, I promise, but no more ear biting."

Hayley squealed with a surprised laugh, forgetting everything else for a moment. Delia put a check mark in the category of *This Guy Knows Kids*. He just gave the power to Igor and minimized his own presence.

He sat up and rubbed his ear. He addressed Louie the cat. "Be careful of this rabbit. I hope he doesn't like to bite kitty ears." Louie's ears rotated minutely forward. The cat seemed as intrigued by the performance as everyone else. The detective placed the stuffed toy on his shoulder and bobbed it around.

"Where were you when the people came and hurt Emma and Ray?"

The silly act softened Hayley. She answered without hesitation. "Emma told me to hide behind the dresser. I hide flat as a pancake. Emma said not to come out until she said it was okay."

Delia didn't know one thing about Emma Gilbert except that she had saved this child from murder, and for that she was grateful. Emma cared about Hayley. What the hell was she doing with killers and the heroin trade?

"What did you hear when you were hiding?" said Moretti. He didn't go through the rabbit.

"Big bad voices and then *pop, pop, pop.* I waited a long time but Emma didn't come for me." Louie pushed his head into Hayley's hand. "A tiger came in the house and hurt everyone with his big teeth and made them bleed. I found Emma. The tiger killed her."

Delia was continually stunned by the deep subterranean life of children, where they held unimaginable demons and hopes, a place too terrifying for most adults. She hoped that speaking the words out loud, with Delia, the detective, Louie, and Igor as witnesses to the carnage, would take some of the toxin out of the scene. But how could it?

Erica stood up from the raised garden bed with an armload of squash and cucumbers. She stepped up on the deck and headed for the kitchen door.

Moretti remembered Igor again. He bounced him around his ear. "Igor says you are a brave girl to stay hidden behind the dresser. Can Igor give you a hug? He says you are a good girl."

Hayley nodded yes, and he handed the stuffed animal toward her with his hand cupping the backside. She wrapped her arms around the toy and then held him out at arm's length. She pointed one finger at the rabbit.

"Naughty bunny. No biting ears! If the tiger comes, hide." She patted the rabbit on his head.

An icy fear descended through Delia's body. Could the tiger come here? Would there be any reason for the drug traffickers to locate Hayley? There had been enough reason to kidnap her. Hayley looked so small and vulnerable, with only a large cat, a terrific foster family, and a wooden fence between her and people who were willing to kill for the heroin business.

Moretti smiled an enormous smile at Hayley that could have melted the Arctic ice cap. "I am an official tiger fighter. Bad tigers run away when they see me and they squeal like little babies. What we have here at Erica's house is a tiger-free zone."

As if on cue, Louie stood up, stretched, and yawned, showing his formidable teeth. The interview was over.

Erica, who had been standing in the doorway to the kitchen,

said, "Time to wash your hands for dinner. I need help stirring when I make brownies and I know just the girl to help me."

Hayley stood up. "I washed my hands before snack."

Erica said, "I know, but if you want to help me cook, we all have to wash our hands."

Hayley and Louie walked into the house, headed for the bathroom. Delia knew Erica wanted the child out of earshot.

Erica looked at the detective. "Should I have my daughter stay at my sister's house while Hayley is here? Is it possible that the people involved will come looking for her?" She was scared, but not once did she hint that she didn't want Hayley at her house. Delia loved this woman and wanted to clone her.

"There's no way to trace the location of a foster child," said Delia. "We have firewalls on top of firewalls on our computer systems. This is the safest place that Hayley has been in for a long time."

"We're going to increase the patrol around your house. And here is my cell if you notice anyone unfamiliar in your neighborhood. Don't feel weird about calling," said Moretti.

They waited until Hayley was back from the bathroom and stationed at the kitchen island with a wooden spoon at the ready.

"You could stay for dinner," said Erica. "Tom is picking our daughter up at soccer practice. They'll be here in a few minutes."

Moretti hesitated and looked longingly at the brownie batter. Didn't this man have a home to get back to?

Delia said, "I'll have to take a rain check." She looked at Hayley. "That means I have a special ticket for the next time that you make brownies. Yum, these already smell delicious! Let's go, Mr. Tiger Fighter, I have to get back to my office."

In the driveway, they stood between their cars. "I'm not sure how much help that was for you. A silver car is what you have from the interview," she said. Her hand was on the edge of her open door. He had one foot in the door of his car. Across the street, a trio of crows made a sound like laughing. Or barking.

"I have a lot more than that. I know that Emma Gilbert was taking care of Hayley and that she saved her life. And Hayley's mother drives a blue car. We need to look at the possibility that Emma may have been kidnapped too," he said. His jaw muscles twitched. "Seeing kids in danger never gets any easier for me. It pretty much makes all of us on the force go nuts."

Who wouldn't go ballistic in the face of a child being hurt? But Delia had stopped trying to answer that question or the other questions that went along with it. Adults hurt children, and sometimes they didn't mean to but other times they did, whether in a fugue of rage, reenactment of their own childhood abuse, mental illness, or everything that came along with drug abuse. But she was glad that Moretti was on this case, that Hayley had ignited something in him.

"Go home, Moretti, and give your daughter a big hug. I have a feeling you're a great dad," she said.

He swung into the driver's seat. "I would do that, except she's at her mother's house until the weekend. I'll save my hugs until then. I have a gigantic supply. And would you please do me a huge favor?"

"What?" said Delia.

"My name is Mike. Michael if you're up for two syllables. But you sound like a street thug when you use my last name. Would you mind?" He looked up at her from the driver's seat, head tilted, just enough of a smile.

Delia reached into her pack, retrieved Igor the Rabbit, and made the stuffed toy dance on the edge of his door. "Okay, Mike, or Michael. I'll give up my street thug talk."

Mike reached over and patted Igor on the head, brushing Delia's fingers.

"Much appreciated, Igor. And Delia."

She had to ask. If J Bird were here, she would have put all the signs together and figured this out much sooner, or she would have asked long before this. "Are you divorced?" said Delia.

Mike started his car. "Yup. Too young, too much police work

at crazy hours and all the rest fits into the vast cauldron of irreconcilable differences. Stay in touch. Let me know anything that you find out," he said as he tapped the computer screen on his dash.

A tributary that had been dammed up with the debris of charred rafters broke open and a ripple ran through her. She shook her head, not unlike the way Baxter shook himself after a dip in the ocean. All this because the man could make a child laugh, talk with a stuffed rabbit, and make a traumatized child feel safe? Or was it because Tyler was back and she could feel the pull of him?

# CHAPTER 29

Delia's job was to continue with the assessment for Hayley, which could take up to a month for any child who was removed from a dangerous or neglectful home. Delia had to be fully informed about a child's physical needs and schooling so she could locate the best fit for a foster home and, with most kids, arrange visits with the immediate or extended family. No family visits for Hayley; that was the big puzzle. No family.

Regina, the art therapist, was back from vacation and had already paid one visit to Hayley. Regina was a consultant, hired occasionally by the state for special cases. Delia could imagine the political uproar in the newspapers if Foster Services had a full-time art therapist on salary. Any libertarian worth their salt would run wild with a news item like "Taxpayer dollars go to art therapist."

"The good news," said Regina, one day at Delia's office, "is that I feel like an artist, coming and going all over the Portland area, sitting with children, drawing and painting with them. I get to see their world without a filter, and it's quite beautiful."

The downside was that Regina had no health benefits, no

anything. She wasn't even paid mileage. Amazingly, the woman seemed happy, without the bitterness or rancor that Delia was sure she'd have if she were in Regina's shoes.

Today she was meeting Regina at Erica's house for Hayley's second session. She wished she could put in a special request, like where is the mother, or what town, what state did Hayley come from? But this was when Delia had to take deep breaths, slow down, and listen.

Regina's car, a twelve-year-old Honda stacked with art supplies in the back seat, was in the driveway when Delia pulled in. Erica answered the door, and Delia heard voices from the living room. Hayley and Regina were already engrossed in a project. Each of them was seated on the floor, side by side, next to an oval coffee table, paper spread out in front of them, crayons and colored markers scattered.

"Can I color too?" asked Delia, sliding down to the carpet.

Regina and the child looked up, too deep into their world of coloring to fully notice Delia. Regina was thin, her skin pulled tight along her arms, her legs crossed under a short, flowered skirt. Her small size made her less intimidating to children.

"You can have the red ones," said Hayley. "And the brown."

Clearly these were the cast-off colors.

Regina slid a sheet of paper to Delia, who tried to take the smallest space on the table. Listen, her job was to listen.

"We're drawing favorite animals," said Regina.

Good. Delia would draw Baxter with the red marker and the brown. Baxter was actually a gorgeous burnt orange, but no one called a golden retriever orange. Invariably he was called a red dog. She drew a seated version of Baxter, with one paw up in an offered handshake. Paw shake. The whole drawing was one step up from a stick figure, but she soon felt the spread of childhood comfort, sitting around a table and drawing. No wonder Regina liked her job so much.

"Your dog is good," said Hayley. This was the first thing Hayley had said to her that wasn't in response to a question.

"Thanks," said Delia. "His name is Baxter. He likes to chase sticks and balls. And he likes to swim and shake water all over me." And this was the first uncalculated thing Delia had ever said to Hayley. She didn't want to leave this island of safety. The smell of crayons, paper, and markers, all rolled up in Hayley's almost indiscernible little girl aroma of soap and maple syrup, was a balm to Delia's adult world. She slid down the portal to grade school, where her old teacher, Mrs. Conz, handed out drawing assignments, and the change in the seasons from summer to fall knocking at the windows felt like a soft blanket.

"Can Baxter fight tigers?" said Hayley.

Delia crashed back into her adult body. Why hadn't she thought of this before?

"Would you like to meet Baxter? Tigers are so afraid of Baxter that we've never seen a tiger at our house. Not once. Or in all of Portland. But what about Louie? I'll ask Erica if Louie is okay with dogs. Some cats are afraid of dogs."

"Who lives at your house with Baxter?" said Hayley.

Sometimes, but not often, children wanted to know about Delia's family. Mostly when they were looking for a safe harbor to land in, and sometimes she answered the questions directly and other times she sidestepped, directing the kids to the best way to adapt to their new surroundings. But she saw that Hayley was drawing a family, not a favorite animal, and Delia didn't want to do anything to break the spell.

"I live with my sister. She is almost as good of a cook as Erica, but nobody can make brownies the way Erica can." She was supposed to be listening, not talking. Delia looked over at Regina, who pushed a blue marker around the top corner of her paper.

"I see three people on your paper," said Regina as she drew a gray mouse with huge whiskers. "I wonder if my mouse has a family. Who is that?" she asked, pointing to one of the figures on Hayley's drawing.

"That's the daddy," said Hayley. He was the least detailed figure, no arms, all legs and torso, and no mouth. He was also far away from the other two figures.

Delia kept drawing, adding in a ball for Baxter and stylized ocean waves for him to dive into. She needed something to do to quell her rising anxiety as Hayley formed what looked like a family. Where the hell where they? The murky land of art therapy demanded a different language that was more like poetry, all symbols and metaphors.

"He's so far away. Can those two see him or hear him?" said Regina. She started in on another mouse, following Hayley's lead.

"He can't talk. See, he doesn't have a mouth," said Hayley, with a tinge of exasperation at Regina's inability to see the obvious.

"And who is this?" Regina said, pointing her marker at the larger of the two remaining figures. Hayley drew two tear lines cascading from of the eyes of the figure that had hair, eyes, a mouth, arms, and a triangular skirt.

"This is Mommy. She says, *be a good girl.*" Then Hayley took a black crayon and drew a line under the mommy, then a dark line over the top of her head, and finally two wobbly lines that connected the two, forming a sort of box. "Uncle Ray said, Mommy was naughty and tried to run away with me. Now she has to stay in the naughty place."

Delia dropped her crayon. Her heart knocked against her ribs. Regina, undaunted, forged ahead, keeping her voice even, soft, and interested, and sticking with the drawing. Delia was familiar with Regina's approach. "If you talk about their drawing, not their life, suddenly they have the safety and freedom to talk," Regina told her when they first started working together several years ago. Delia trusted her, even though now she had to squeeze her lips together to keep from asking this little girl for precise details.

"Can the little girl see inside the naughty place? What color goes in the naughty place?" Regina asked. She started to draw an enclosure around one plump mouse. "I'm going to give my mouse a door that she can open."

Hayley looked at Regina's drawing. She reached across the coffee table and stroked the mouse. "Come out, Mama Mouse. Baby mouse is waiting for you. She is sad," said Hayley. She turned back to her drawing and picked up a green marker. She colored a rough green blob in the corner of the naughty room. "Mama likes plants. This plant is for her."

Regina took a green crayon and drew a single green stalk of a plant, reached over and took Delia's red marker, and made fat red circles. "Mama Mouse likes flowers too, big red ones, like roses. Oh, they make Mama Mouse wish they could all be together again."

Delia felt like she was watching a split screen TV. On one screen, a diminutive woman and little girl drew on their papers with crayons and markers, talking about mice and mommies and flowers and naughty rooms. On the other screen, Delia saw a father, distanced from his young family, and a mother who was sad, punished for running away with her child. Both screens were veiled in fog, the dialogue in a foreign language without subtitles.

Tingles of pain brought Delia back to the present. One foot squawked from lack of circulation. She shifted her weight and massaged the abused foot and ankle. Regina wouldn't go on much longer. She kept her sessions with young children short, twenty minutes, maybe thirty.

"Mama Mouse has a door on her house." With her fingers, Regina walked an imaginary mouse out of the enclosure. "Come with me, baby mouse! Let's go," said Regina.

Louie the cat, absent for the art session, chose this moment to make his entrance, tail held high, stalking in with his mukluk-sized paws. Or maybe he was just announcing the end of the session. He pushed his way between Hayley and the table. Delia wondered if this cat wasn't more of a butler or personal assistant to Hayley. Or a self-ordained familiar, a spiritual protector.

Regina, forewarned about the cat, reached in her pocket and took out a kitty kibble. Louie leapt over the table and followed Regina's hand to a spot behind her.

"Where does the mommy run with the baby girl?" said Regina, absently coloring the sky again. This was a quantum leap for the art therapist, and Delia was grateful.

Hayley's eyebrows rose up in the middle, her lower lip pulled up over her top lip. "Not the bacca barn or Uncle Ray will find you." She stood up. "I need to pee," she said.

"Okay, Hayley. I really liked drawing with you today," said Regina as the child ran out of the room.

Delia stood up. "You are amazing. Can you send me your report later today? I'm going to make some notes as soon as I leave here, but your reports are so much better than my notes."

Regina picked up each crayon and marker, putting them into zippered pouches. "There is so much sadness pumping off this child," she said in a low voice. "I'd like to keep working with her if only to give her an outlet. I know you want information, but that can only be a side effect of these sessions."

Regina's professional voice always startled Delia, the sharp departure from little mice and crayons to the woman who had logged every emotion that poured out of Hayley onto the drawing. What did it look like inside Regina's brain?

"I agree. You can work it out with Erica, and I'll let Ira know that you're going to keep working with her," said Delia.

From the other side of the house, a toilet flushed.

"I need to wrap things up with Hayley," said Regina, grabbing both drawings and shouldering her bag of supplies.

Hayley and Louie cuddled on the love seat that faced the kitchen island. This was a house centered on the kitchen.

"Can we trade drawings? You can have my little mice and I'll take your drawing. What do you think?" said Regina.

All twenty pounds of Louie pressed against Hayley's legs. Hayley shrugged in response to Regina.

Erica took the mouse drawing from Regina. "This looks like it needs a place of honor on the fridge." She found one vacant spot on the fridge door and slapped on a few magnets. "Perfect."

"I have to run, but I wanted to ask if I could bring my dog, Baxter, to visit the next time. How does Louie like dogs? I won't bring Baxter if there's any push-back from Louie," said Delia.

Erica smiled. "Louie has frightened more than a few dogs, but we can try it. Just don't expect him to back down. Let's give it a trial run."

That wasn't the answer Delia was expecting. She had second thoughts about Baxter's safety, the possibility of his tender nose shredded by the long claws of Louie the palace guard.

"I'll warn him not to underestimate Louie. But I think you would like Baxter. I'll see you all next time," said Delia, heading for the door.

"Delia?" said Hayley. This was the first time she had addressed Delia by her name.

Delia turned back.

"Show your drawing to Baxter," she said, petting the cat along his chin.

"Oh, my drawing. I almost forgot it. . . ."

Regina handed her the canine portrait. "We didn't forget it."

# CHAPTER 30

Delia wasn't surprised that the instant she stepped out of Erica's house, Mike drove by at a ridiculously slow crawl down the street. And it wasn't his police car. It was a black Maxima, sleek and fast, like a panther. Funny, that wasn't what she expected him to drive. She took him for a pickup truck kind of guy.

He stopped at the end of the driveway, one elbow resting along the edge of the open window. Delia walked to his car, rolling her drawing into a tight cylinder.

"You're off duty, aren't you," she said.

He smiled up at her. "The Dalai Lama once said that we should all be good to our mothers. That directive stopped me in my tracks. I was in college at UMass and I managed to get a ticket to see him from my favorite criminal justice professor. I thought he would say something more profound," he said. "And then I realized just how profound it was."

He looked smaller when he wasn't in his high-tech cop car.

"You're patrolling the street because of Hayley, aren't you?"

He glanced in his rearview mirror as a car approached.

"I must have missed the topic sentence about the Dalai Lama," she said.

"I know what you mean," he said. "It's like a Möbius strip. What if the mother is terrible, does drugs, and can't or won't take care of her kids? What was the Dalai Lama talking about when he said be good to your mother? It's a chicken and egg kind of thing. If everywhere, all at once, we were all good to mothers, would it make us all kinder people who didn't cause mayhem?"

"Have you been driving up and down Erica's street thinking about this?" she asked.

A blue jay started scolding someone with a sharp squawk, and Delia suspected it was aimed at Louie the cat behind Delia's house.

"I think about this all the time but in a background kind of way," he said. "What if Hayley really knows where her mother is, but Raymond threatened Hayley that he'd harm her mother if she said anything?"

It was like Mike was walking arm in arm with Delia and Hayley, as if he'd been in the room when the child drew black lines around the mommy on the page. Or was he just that good?

"The Dalai Lama also said we're screwed unless we keep the global population below six billion. I try not to think of that one."

Delia wanted to keep talking about the conundrum of mothers, slide into Mike's car, tilt her seat back, and watch the clouds through the moon roof while he drove. She longed for a moment like that.

"Change of topic," she said. "I was just sitting in on a session with the art therapist and Hayley. There's something you need to know. But we should get out of their driveway. Erica tries to live a normal life here. She has neighbors that are probably wondering right now who we are."

Mike contracted, his muscles firmed along his face. Detective Moretti was back. "Can we go someplace nearby?" he said.

J Bird Café was already a place, not quite finished, but it held who Delia would soon become. "Follow me. There's a place near Willard Beach."

Delia led the way in her car. Her eyes flicked to the rearview mirror, watching the outline of Mike, sometimes catching the whites of his eyes latched onto her. The four-mile drive took forever.

She pulled in front of J Bird Café, and Mike pulled around in front of her. Must be a cop thing, she thought. They both stepped out of their cars.

"What do I need to know?" he said.

The squeal of a Skilsaw came from behind the café. J Bird said they'd be working on the back deck for the next few days, a last minute addition.

"Hayley said that her mother is in the naughty place, that she tried to run away with Hayley, and they hid in the 'back barn' or in back of a barn, and Raymond found them and put Mommy in the naughty place," said Delia.

All ruminations about the Dalai Lama were gone. Mike pulled out a small pad of paper. "I'm going to have to talk with her again," he said. He had a way of looking through Delia, measuring, anticipating, remembering. A leaf might fall from a tree, land on his car, and he wouldn't forget it.

"Please wait. This all just came out in the art therapy session. Regina hasn't even had time to write a report. She promised it to me by the end of the day. But those were close to Hayley's exact words."

"Anything else?"

Delia had almost forgotten the first part of the drawing. She was glad that Regina was going to send her a detailed report. "Yes. It was a classic family drawing. She drew a father but he was farthest away. And he had no mouth and no arms." It was low tide, and even from several blocks away, Delia smelled the large, flat ribbons of seaweed glistening in the sun.

"I need to talk with her tomorrow. We don't know if this is fantasy or wishful thinking, but if I can get any shred of information from Hayley that helps us find the mother and find the link to this heroin, I've got to do it," he said. He wasn't asking, but he gave Delia the sense that he respected her and wanted to work with her.

Every part of him straightened and tensed.

"I need to be there when you talk to her. I'll call Erica after I read Regina's report," she said.

"Is Igor coming with us again? The puppet was helpful, but I need to ask her very direct questions," he said. There it was, the smile, his smooth lips, a tiny spot near the cleft in his chin where his razor had missed the black hairs.

The Skilsaw stopped and something hard, hopefully wood, hit the newly built deck.

"No. This time I'm bringing my dog, Baxter. Well, he's my sister's dog, really. Kids love him. There's a chance that he could be a distraction to questioning, but I have a feeling that he'll increase Hayley's sense of safety. Plus, he's a giant hunk of burning love, and she could use every bit of his special brand of affection."

"Okay. Let's hope he works as well as Igor," he said.

Mike looked like an engine idling, getting ready to charge up. Was he was ready to leave, call headquarters, plug in more information, look again at reports of missing kids nationwide, searching for Hayley's face? And yet she wanted a few more minutes of him. She wanted to pull him into this next world of hers, currently covered with brown paper over the front windows. How would he fit into her next world of baking bread, white aprons, wiping crumbs off their new counter? Could she keep him here a little longer?

"Is it easier when you work with adults, when you can ask someone directly who did what and when and how? I wish Hayley's superpower were that she had a secret part of her brain that spoke adult, and she could tell us where her mother was. Or that we could take a picture of her brain and print out a memory card with everything on it like license plates and addresses. I feel more like an archaeologist deciphering hieroglyphics than a caseworker," she said.

Mike slid the notepad into the back pocket of his jeans. "You'd be surprised how similar art therapy reports are to interviews with adult witnesses. I've learned a lot from my daughter, the way kids don't have a filter installed when they speak the way adults do. The trouble is, their world is one big magical kingdom, and pulling concrete information out is the challenge," he said. Mike leaned against Delia's car, letting his legs angle out in front of him.

Where had this man come from?

"But how is that similar to adult witnesses?"

He tilted one shoulder toward her. "We each have a filter of perception that is unique to us. When you see a car accident, what you see will be different from what I see, or anyone else. Two eyewitnesses might not even agree on the color of a car, or the color of someone's skin. If your art therapist asked each adult witness to draw a picture of the same car accident, she would have decidedly different images," he said. "But investigators would go on the core similarities, the things that can't be denied, and it might be something important that the witnesses didn't know was important, like they might all have a hazy image of a pedestrian stepping off the sidewalk."

While he spoke, a part of him looked farther away, distracted by the drawing of a child like Hayley.

"You sound like a therapist. Or a profiler. Or a weird shaman dressed up like a detective," said Delia.

"I get the 'weird' part all the time from the other cops," he said. "Don't you dare tell them that I was spouting about the Dalai Lama. Now would you tell me why you chose this particular place to stop?" Mike said. "Are you involved in this place?" He turned toward the J Bird Café.

So the detective didn't know everything. "This is the bakery-slash-café that my sister and I are opening next month. I'm leaving Foster Services in a few weeks. She is a master baker, and I'm a baker in training. Hayley is my last case. Come on in; I want to show you my new venture."

"You're leaving your job with Foster Services?" He sounded incredulous, his voice deepening, hovering above them.

"Don't tell me that I've surprised the detective. I thought you knew everything about South Portland." Surprising this man gave her a surge of pleasure. She reached into her purse and found the keys to the café. "Come on."

She doubted very much that he didn't know about J Bird Café. An image of him came to mind; a dragonfly whose head was primarily taken up by multiple eyes, able to see everything at once except for that which trailed behind him. What trailed behind the good detective?

He checked his watch and hesitated.

"You can't do anything about the report until Regina turns it in. We've got to give her until the end of the day," said Delia.

The cry of gulls was carried to them on the breeze.

"It's not that. Well, it is that, but I'm also due to go to my daughter's soccer practice. It's my day to bring cool and original snacks. That was the exact assignment from my daughter," he said, "even though I don't know what could be cool or not cool about snacks."

There was nothing like a daughter to flummox a dad. When J Bird was six, she threw a crying fit because their dad put the wrong barrette in her hair. The barrette was blue and she would only wear the purple one. Their father searched every drawer in the bathroom vanity until he found the perfect barrette. Even later, when medication and delusions exhausted him, Delia never would have drawn a family picture with him far off on the edge of the page, a man with no mouth. She would have drawn him holding her hand, his arm around their mother, and little J Bird in front of them, pressing her head against their father, the purple barrette firmly in place.

"Bring anything, orange slices or fruit Popsicles. Believe me, they will just love that you're there," she said, looking down to kick a small stone off the sidewalk. She swallowed the memory of her father and her mother.

When she looked up, he was watching her, full bore, all of his dragonfly eyes fragmenting her. Had he seen her shift into memory?

He lifted his chin toward the café. "Let's take a look at your new career venture." He pointed to the front door. "After you, Madam Barista."

The front door was already open. A pile of round tables crowded the right corner, surrounded by stacked chairs. Two of the walls were painted coral and fuchsia, two more were primed, looking fresh and clean. Greg must have just finished installing the wood trim yesterday. But there was still no counter or display case, and much to Delia's disappointment, only one of two ovens had arrived.

"When did you say you were opening up?" asked Mike. He walked into what would be the kitchen. "Nice oven."

"Yes, but there were supposed to be two ovens delivered. See, this is my new life, worrying about ovens."

The door to the deck was open. Delia announced their arrival. "Hey, Greg, is that you back there?"

The new deck was gray, but unlike so much of the weathered wood along the coast, this wood was recycled plastic, possibly from mountains of single-serving coffee pods. "You'll never have to do anything to it," Greg had advised them when Delia and Juniper asked him to build a deck. "This stuff will last longer than I will."

Greg leaned over a sawhorse, his right leg bent, the other leg stretched behind him, the saw pressed down on a length of eternal plastic wood. He wore ear protectors and safety glasses. Delia waved her arms to get his attention. He looked up and moved the safety glasses to his forehead. He took off the ear protectors, set the Skilsaw down and unplugged it. J Bird often accused Delia of being too methodical and not spontaneous enough, but Greg outclassed her by a mile. IBM would still be top dog if Greg had been the CEO.

"Greg, this is Mike Moretti. He's a detective and we were just consulting about a case with one of my kids," she said.

Both men took a long step forward and extended right arms as far as possible for a handshake while keeping an amazing amount of space between them. The male greeting system.

"Greg is the head honcho on the remodeling project to get the café ready for opening. He has already saved us from inspection disasters a dozen times," said Delia.

"We could always use another place for cops to get coffee and pastries. And just in case you think that's a stereotype, it's not," said Mike. His smile was on half wattage, but still enough to crinkle the skin around his eyes. "Nice work on this deck," he said, with an appreciative nod to Greg.

"These two sisters are keeping me out of trouble. I plan to be a permanent customer when they open. Right now, I'm also their official taster," said Greg.

Delia knew that Mike was itching to go, called by both his daughter's soccer team and the desire to check back with his headquarters. She imagined his social exchanges had been stretched as far as they could go.

"Thanks for coming in, Mike. I promise to call you as soon as the report comes in," she said. "I know you have to run. Remember, all those little girl soccer players will think you are the coolest dad."

Mike nodded to Greg and Delia. Rather than going back inside again, he stepped off the deck, as agile as a deer with his long legs, and jogged along the side of the building to the street.

Greg crossed his arms over his chest and smiled. "Interesting," he said, "very interesting."

"What?" said Delia, suddenly self-conscious under Greg's appraising eye.

"I believe the good detective has his eye on you. And you'll have to trust me on this one. You might be the expert with bread and Juniper knows cakes. I know when a man has his eye on a woman." He reached down to plug in the saw again.

"We're working on the same case. He's a super observant guy; that's what you're picking up. I mean, he has to notice everything, that's his training," she said.

"I'm too old to pretend that I don't see what I see," he said. He slipped the protective eye gear back on. "That's only for young people. Although, from my vantage point, it seems like a terrible waste of time."

Greg put the ear protectors on and switched on the saw.

Should she believe Greg? If J Bird were here, she'd be able to tell in a nanosecond if a guy was interested or not. Was there anything else she couldn't see?

# CHAPTER 31

The next morning at work, her phone rang before she had truly dug into the day. "I did it," Tyler said, "I signed the papers for the house. The inspection was a piece of cake."

The pile of files that she needed to transfer to other caseworkers was now down to five. Even Ira had been forced to take some of her cases.

"Congratulations," she said, talking on the speakerphone. "No dickering back and forth? No horrible disclosures from the inspection like radon gas or cracks in the foundation?"

She pictured Tyler rattling around in the house. Did he say it had three bedrooms? It seemed a strange purchase for a young, single doctor. She imagined him living there, eating breakfast alone, sleeping, and putting on his blue scrubs to mend broken bones. He picked a family home, the kind she left behind after the fire. The clean lines of the house that she lived in with J Bird held no hints of ancestry.

"I have a moving van arriving in two days. Well, not a moving van exactly, more like the two pods that I packed up in California that have been in storage. But I have to buy a dining room table and chairs. I was wondering if you could help me pick out something that was, I don't know, comfortable," he said.

She remembered moving vans. She remembered Tyler and his family pulling out of town with their moving van when she could still taste the fire in her throat. Since he couldn't see her on the other end of the phone, she shook herself. She had to let go of that. It was old news.

Delia pictured a drive to Boston, a tedious selection process in furniture stores while her clock ticked away at her job, while Hayley came closer to being assigned into permanent foster care if her parents couldn't be found. Tyler would have to wait because Hayley could not.

"I can't help you, Tyler. I have double the work these last two weeks."

"Oh, I didn't mean a shopping expedition. I meant online. It's not like I need to try on a table," he said.

Of course, J Bird was right. Delia was oddly out of step. Naturally Tyler would shop online for everything.

Dark clouds galloped in from the northwest, framed in Delia's window. The season was changing and soon the leaf peepers would be in town from points south and from Europe and Asia. It was time to button up for the coming winter, time to find Hayley a safe port. In case her parents weren't found, she had to find the best possible foster home for her.

"I can meet you after work, around six," she said. "But not The Daily Grind." Delia now associated The Daily Grind with Match.com coffee dates.

"How about the Portland Hotel? They have a quiet bar," he said.

By the time Delia arrived, Tyler was already set up, his laptop in play at a corner table. It was a low decibel bar with thick carpets, no TV, dark wood. For a moment Delia wanted to live there, her meals prepared and served to her by the young waiter in black pants and white shirt, the massive vase of flowers wafting its scent to her from the fireplace hearth. No children needing homes, no upcoming sad good-byes when she left her

job, no jumping off the career cliff hand in hand with J Bird by
starting a café.

Tyler hailed her with one arm. The soft, glowing light of a
wall sconce caught the sun-lightened glow of his hair. She could
live here in pretend land for an hour or two. Was Tyler part of
pretend land, or was he real?

"I'm on call," he said, "so let's visualize no rush on the ER
tonight."

Delia ordered a glass of white burgundy, drinking too quickly,
then self-consciously putting the half-empty glass on the table.
Tyler stuck to iced tea in deference to his on-call duties. He
turned the screen to face Delia. Four pages were marked, all on
the screen at once.

"Which one do you like?" he asked.

This felt like a question a guy would ask his girlfriend. Delia
wasn't his girlfriend.

One table was oval, oak, and uninspired. Another was light
wood, Scandinavian and sleek, not one unnecessary curlicue
to be found. The third was oddly familiar. She swallowed more
wine, but this time a drop of it slipped into her windpipe and
she choked as if she were drowning. The table was round, central pedestal. Sloping claw feet gripped the floor, all shrouded
in a warm brown finish. So much like the table she had grown
up with. She pictured her father, mother, little J Bird, and herself all hunched in forward toward each other at dinnertime.

Tyler's eyes widened in alarm. "Are you okay?" Then his physician's training kicked in, and he settled down. "Just cough it
out. It's only a few drops of wine that took a wrong turn."

Her throat pulsated with spasms, sending her body into full
alarm. A surge of extra blood would turn her face red, something she knew from experience, and tears already breached
the rims of her eyes. "I'll be right back," she choked out as
she headed for the ladies' room. She could at least convulse
in private. As soon as she pushed open the two doors of the
bathroom, one for the outer sanctum and one for the inner
sanctum, her throat relaxed. She leaned against the dark pan-
eling in the bathroom.

The kindness of soft lighting couldn't hide the fact that she looked a mess. What remained of the mascara that she'd put on this morning was now smudged along her cheekbones. Her eyes were bloodshot, and, to complete the picture, she'd spilled wine on her shirt, her one expensive splurge at a store in Boston. She ran her hands through her shoulder-length hair, a brown that eerily matched the dark wood of the hotel.

Did Tyler know what he was doing? Was he recreating her past? Or his past? She splashed water on her face, used some of it to run through her hair, and sighed. People recreated their pasts all the time. It was called nostalgia, and except in Delia's case, it seemed to be a perfectly delightful thing to do. Magazines were devoted to it. Nineteen fifties furniture was all the craze. Nineteen seventies ranch houses were turned into something modern with austere retro lines. But not for Delia. Their present house was without a past, furniture designed entirely by IKEA.

Delia took one last look in the mirror; her red eyes were returning to normal, and while the mascara was gone, her face was clean and no longer splotched with red. She pulled open the door to the outer sanctum and pulled open the door to the restaurant.

Tyler had put away his laptop. A fresh glass of wine waited for Delia. For a second, Tyler looked so young and expectant, the way she remembered him when they'd been together, when he'd been her one confidant about her father's deteriorating condition. He was once again the boyfriend who would do anything for her. That's what he had whispered to her when they had curled entwined in her dorm room. But what he did was leave.

She slid into her seat. "That table that you showed me is a replica of the table I grew up with. My parents bought it when they were first married. It was one of the things that my father didn't deconstruct in his paranoid delusions. I was caught off guard when you showed me the photo." She carefully sipped her wine and swallowed deliberately. "Why is it one of your choices?"

Delia wasn't sure she wanted to know the answer.

Tyler sat back and closed his eyes. His Adam's apple rode up and down. "I thought you would like it. I wasn't in your house very often; you wouldn't let me come in except for a few times. But I remember how much you loved that table. Do you remember the day that you let me come in when your parents were out and you were looking after Juniper? You two told me how you used to play beneath the table, making a tent with a huge blanket, and you called it your tiger house because of the clawed feet."

*Tiger house?* When Hayley spoke about a tiger in the house, it was a dire warning from Emma Gilbert. What had the tiger house been for J Bird and her when they were growing up? Was it really the childhood playhouse that Tyler described or had it been a place for little girls to hide when a rampaging father, who was nothing like their good father, threw all the pots and pans from the cabinets looking for listening devices? Or were all tigers inherently dangerous?

Part of her had wanted Tyler back since the day he left Maine. Not a loud or public part of her, but in a tight and twitchy sealed-off room. She tried never to speak of him, and even when Ben had asked about Tyler after the girls went to live in the house his mother sold to them, she responded lightly. "Oh, that ended. We talked about it and decided not to try a long-distance relationship." They had never talked about it because Delia didn't know he was leaving until she was hit in the face with fumes from the moving van.

And now, here he was, with a deed to a house in his pocket, enticing her with beloved furniture from her childhood home. Something was wrong.

"You're going to buy furniture because you want me to like it? I'm not nineteen anymore. We can't just leap ahead like this. We've skipped too many steps," she said. Every word scraped out of her with jagged pain, picking away at the very thing she had secretly wanted for so long. Tyler. She started to get up.

"Wait, Delia. I can see this wasn't the right thing to do. I'm not trying to entice you into my new house with haunts from the past. I swear." His eyes were moist. She settled back into her seat, yet tigers growled in the background, the dangerous ones who attack and the ones who protect little girls.

"You're exactly right; I wanted to skip all the hard steps and magically have you back again. When I first went to medical school, an older doctor told me that I'd learn everything about the human body and nothing about meaningful social interactions. His wife said he was socially and emotionally delayed when they met and that it took him years to catch up. That might make me emotionally equivalent to a teenager. And you know, guys are delayed anyhow."

A little self-effacement went a long way with her. It was always the characteristic that made Delia stop and listen.

"Then let's slow way down and get to know the new and improved, grown-up version of each other. And I want to know why you broke up with me when you did. You didn't just move away, you broke up with me," she said.

Tyler reached across the table with both hands and grabbed hers, rubbing his thumb along the top of one hand. Delia felt the zing of the connection run up her arm.

"No more furniture selection, I get that," he said.

This was the old Tyler, or the essence of Tyler tucked inside the grown-up doctor, the one who understood her right away, who wasn't blown over by her directness. Could she have it back again, that feeling of being understood, of loving someone full out, feeling loved?

In a quiet bar, you could hear everything, even a phone set on vibrate.

The center of his eyebrows rose up. "Oh, no. I've only given this out to a few people including work. I have to look," he said, withdrawing his hands.

He pulled the phone out and frowned when he saw the number. "Work." He took the call, and Delia knew instantly that he would soon be running out the door, that medical emergencies awaited him. "Fifteen minutes," he said into the phone.

"You didn't pay someone to call you at this exact time, did you?" she said. Teasing him felt natural.

"Yes, I have a special device that signals for help when you have me by the short hairs," he said, smiling. "I will call you."

Tyler left first, and Delia finished her wine alone.

# CHAPTER 32

*Juniper*

Juniper's phone gonged with the Tibetan bell sound that she'd assigned to Delia's text messages. If her sister knew that she'd been characterized in this solemn, echoing way, she'd pitch a fit. It delighted Juniper each time that Delia sent a text, which wasn't often. It had been hard to entice Delia into the world of texting instead of phoning. What other thirty-two-year-old in America was this averse to texting?

She was still at the Bayside Bakery, finishing up with prep for the next day. She was nearly finished with rolling out pie dough for sixteen pies, fitting the circular dough into pans, and sliding them into the supersized freezer. This made her morning shifts so much easier. Cold pie filling scooped into frozen pie shells, slid into an oven made the rhythm of the morning start like a NASCAR race, but in a good way. Pies never crashed into each other.

There were still a few clean places on her white apron, even after seven hours of baking, and she wiped her hands before reaching for her phone. She looked at the message.

"Can Baxter come to work with me tomorrow? He needs to snuggle with a little girl."

Was Delia serious? Baxter was made for kid snuggling, or any kind of continuous body contact. She texted back: "Sure."

Response: "Thank you."

The other thing about Delia was that she refused to abbreviate. J Bird wondered if her sister's precision with all forms of communication had to do with her career with children and never wanting to make a mistake with the kids, or if it had as much to do with their father. Because his form of communication became so muddled during his delusional state, Delia swung as far as possible in the other direction. Exactness at all costs.

But what was it that their father had told her in the last year of his life, during the briefer periods of lucidity? "J Bird, you're okay. It's your big sister who worries me. She can connect the dots when she shouldn't, like me. She might have only a drop of my messed-up thought disorder, but I see it in her. You take care of her," he said, one night when Delia was out with Tyler.

At the time, she rolled her eyes and said, "Oh, Dad, are you kidding me? Delia?" But it was the kind of thing that stayed with a kid, tucked away, especially when all she had was Delia. And it was something that she never shared with her worrywart big sister.

The life of a baker was not in sync with the rest of the world, and maybe their father should have been worried about her and not Delia. She started at four a.m. and was done by one p.m., four days a week. On work days, she had to go to sleep by nine p.m., aided by a gummy bear–style melatonin and an eye mask. Her schedule didn't exactly match that of her peers. But it worked well for Baxter. He was not alone for such a huge stretch of time. He had a quick pee break in the backyard when she woke up and then again when Delia woke, hours later. If Delia had time, she and Baxter went to Willard Beach. If not, J Bird took him on a long walk when she got home. It was a good tag team approach to dog care.

If Delia took Baxter to work, he would be in a place beyond happy. He would ratchet right up to euphoria.

Delia didn't get home until after six. By then, J Bird was dressed in cutoff sweatpants and a tank top, binge-watching the first season of *Once Upon a Time* with a bag of Doritos stationed between her knees. Her sister looked more frayed than usual. Baxter greeted her with his usual adoration-style welcome, wrapping around Delia's legs. Who wouldn't want to be greeted every day like that? The dog should teach couples' counseling. Step one: Rush to the door when your beloved comes home. Step two: Tell them you love them and that you missed them. Step three: Make body contact.

"Doritos?" said Delia. "We're getting ready to open a high-end bakery and your food of choice is Doritos?"

Juniper felt no guilt or shame over the Doritos. "Sometimes junk food does exactly what it's meant to do. It's culinary recreation, an adjunct to binge-watching Netflix," she said. "You look terrible, by the way. Are they working you extra hard for your last few weeks? Tell Ira to quit it."

She held out the bag of fried, Day-Glo orange chips to Delia, who sank into the couch next to her. Delia dipped her hand into the bag. Juniper hit the mute button just as the bad witch revealed her true nature to the heroine, the beautiful blond sheriff.

"It's my last case, the little girl in emergency foster placement. If we can't find her family, any family members, soon, then we have to move her into the system. Into a regular long-term foster placement."

Baxter stretched out between the sisters on the floor.

"And on top of it, I met Tyler at the Portland Hotel for drinks. He wanted me to help him pick out a dining room set," she said.

Juniper skidded to a stop, a Dorito chip between her thumb and finger, paused in mid-ascent to her lips.

"That's a girlfriend job assignment. That's like saying, what's our color scheme for the kitchen? Do we want granite, soapstone or butcher block?" said Juniper.

"I know. That's what I told him," said Delia. Her sister passed the bag of chips, but Delia shook her head. "This is very close to breaking confidentiality, which I have never done, but I want to tell you something strange that just happened. Promise me that you won't repeat it?"

Juniper was used to the lead wall that Delia erected around any information pertaining to the kids who went through Foster Services. There had never been a crack in the wall before. Why was she changing course now? Juniper held up her right hand and said, "I promise."

Delia inched back on the couch and crossed her legs. "Do you remember the dining room table at our house, the one with the clawed feet? When we played under it we called it the tiger house."

Baxter lifted his head and looked from one sister to the other.

"I remember playing under the table and hiding under it," said Juniper. No breach of confidentiality here, just good memories along with the bad.

"Tyler showed me four choices for his dining room, and one was a close replica of our table growing up," said Delia.

"What? Now I am officially freaked out. I mean, he's gorgeous and he's obviously into you, but that is creepy. Why would he think that would be a good thing? Please don't tell me he's creating a replica of our old house or I'm calling the police right now." She was only half kidding about the police. The skin along her neck quivered.

Delia ran her hands through her hair. "Stay with me and put aside the Tyler part of it for now. The important thing was that I'd forgotten all about the claw-foot table and how we called it the tiger house until he showed me the image. The little girl that I'm working with, my last case, said a similar thing. She said that the woman who was her caretaker, or kidnapper, told her to avoid a certain place because it was a tiger house. How strange is it that both places were related to danger, like when Dad was delusional, and they were both called tiger houses?"

Had Delia been working too hard? Was she under too much pressure with starting the new business? She was connecting dots that were only distantly related, if at all, and missing the big warning sign about Tyler. She sounded like their father, and few things could be more terrifying. Baxter stood up and licked her hand.

"Don't. Don't connect points on a map that are unrelated. Lots of people have dining room tables with clawed feet and they probably played under the table as kids. That doesn't mean that your little kid is connected to them. And frankly, you sound like Dad when he was going off, and you can never, never do that. Do you understand me? If you do, I'll have nobody," she said. The last words caught in her throat and came out in a sob. She put her hands over her face.

Baxter whined and pushed his head into Juniper's lap. The dog was an emotional Geiger counter; when one of the sisters was upset, he went on red alert, chest up, nose flickering. At that moment, nothing else seemed to matter for Baxter. He was like an astronaut, highly trained for one specific duty, to save the mother ship by keeping his pack harmonious and safe. If Juniper or Delia were in pain, Baxter went to work offering the kind of solace that was unrelenting and irresistible.

Delia put her hand on Juniper's knee. "So does this mean you think I've gone too far?"

She smacked Delia with the bag of chips. "Yes, you big geek, you just went too far! You just hit the Dad parameter, the electric fence of screwed-up connections."

Elbows up in mock self-defense, Delia said, "Okay, okay. I will use you as the reality check. The two tiger houses are officially unrelated. Coincidental."

As Juniper looked up at the silent screen, the dark queen on the television gazed into a glass ball and viewed the hapless heroine, who was totally alone in her knowledge of the queen's identity. She clicked off the power.

"I think we're both working too hard, getting the café ready to open and finishing up our other jobs. Maybe we're both frayed around the edges," said Juniper. Which she mostly believed. But she wanted to talk to the person who knew Delia almost as well as she did. Ben.

# CHAPTER 33

The next morning, Delia concentrated on the details of clearing out of her office. She would pick up Baxter in the early afternoon, give him an enormous walk, and then head over to Erica's.

Most of the furniture in Delia's small office was either cast-offs from Ira or pieces that she had picked up at the used furniture stores around the Portland area. She appraised the three chairs with padded seats, an oval coffee table, and a three-foot-tall bookcase placed strategically to give the illusion of a room divider. The only thing that she really wanted to take with her was the round blue and beige area rug from IKEA. She would have it cleaned from all the wintery mud that had dropped off shoes and put it in their spare bedroom on the main floor. She dropped down to her hands and knees to take a closer look at the rug to check on a stain that looked like mashed crayons and scratched at it with her fingernail.

"I was in the area and thought I'd stop by to find out when you were going back to Erica's, but I see you're involved."

Delia looked up. Mike stood in her doorway, white paper bag

in hand. She popped up as gracefully as she could, brushing off the knees of her black pants. "Melted crayons," she said. "I keep crayons in here for kids but I can't even explain how they ended up melted."

He walked in and set the paper bag on her desk and extracted one cup of coffee. "Once, just on a hunch, I looked under my daughter's bed and there were a dozen cheese sandwiches stuck in little hidie places beneath the box springs. It turned out they were offerings to the monsters that used to live under her bed. You never know with kids." He pulled out the other coffee. "I took a wild guess and thought you might like coffee. Cream and sugar is in the bag."

He had come bearing gifts of coffee. This was a welcome break, a respite from closing out files. "I do like coffee. Black." She pulled off the plastic top. "Please tell me that you're here with good news about Hayley's family."

The detective sat down close to the coffee table. "Not exactly. But from what we've all noticed on the street, the heroin market took a big hit with the deaths of Emma Gilbert, Raymond, and the third guy. We can't conclude causality, but their deaths coincided with drugs drying up on the streets." He took a sip of his coffee. "Until now. Something has changed, and whoever took over the business is dumping heroin again."

Ira's road atlas was on the coffee table. Delia had brought it in from her car and intended to return it to Ira. Mike picked it up.

"Can I show you something on the map?" he asked. He opened it to the map of the entire USA. "Here's Nashville, the destination point of the new heroin link from Mexico. What's happening is that heroin comes into Nashville and is then dispersed in all directions, but mainly east." He flipped to the map of Tennessee. Highways struck outward from Nashville in a starburst pattern. All roads led to, or out of, Nashville. Mike ran his pointer finger along one major highway that went from Nashville due east.

"This is Dalton, where Raymond was from, about forty miles from Nashville. If you're a smart business guy in the heroin trade, you take it directly to New York City, where you will turn an incredible profit, especially if you cut it down. But if you want to charge even higher prices, you bring it to places like Vermont, New Hampshire, and Maine." Mike traced a line on the map of the USA along route 81, through a spiderweb of roads to New York, then angling up to Hartford, to Portland.

"Heroin costs more here than in New York City?" she asked. Delia wasn't new to the topic of heroin, but her reference point was always the kids and parental fitness. Alcohol remained the top wrecking ball for most families.

"That's right," he said.

She took a sip of the hot coffee. Mike was a Dunkin' Donuts man. "Let's pretend there is a new kingpin in the local heroin trade. What does that mean for Hayley, and what does it mean for her mother?" she asked.

Mike crushed his empty cup and tossed it into the metal trash can by Delia's desk. Overhand. "I wish I knew. This whole case feels like it's shrouded with a veil, just dark enough that I can't see clearly. I woke up at four a.m. with something scratching at my brain about Hayley. Does she seem like a kid who was abused to you?"

Both she and Ira had speculated on the same thing. "No. She's a kid who is traumatized because of separation from her parents. I'm even going to guess that to the best of her ability, Emma Gilbert took good care of Hayley," she said.

He closed the road atlas. Whatever scratched at his brain was still at work. Mike frowned and ran one hand along the side of his face. Most cops looked like they all went to the same barber and gave the same instructions. Shave it. But Mike had real hair, deep brown, neatly trimmed along the back of his neck but threatening to break into a wave.

She would need to tell Ira that his road atlas was more helpful, this one time, than all of Google Maps. Delia moved it across her desk. She needed to look at it again after Mike left. Something about Dalton, the way it hugged the highway coming out of Nashville, Emma Gilbert, Raymond, and the mystery man all began to dance around. It was like whatever Mike had was contagious, and the inscrutability of Hayley's origins grew.

"The third guy at the scene? We're beginning to think that he was collateral damage. It's likely that a bigger heroin trader came after Raymond and wanted to put him out of the business. And given that big drug dealers aren't known for their good behavior, the third guy was killed to get rid of him for any number of reasons, with the prime reason being that the others could get a larger piece of the pie," he said.

Why did Mike always start a sentence that answered a question in Delia's head? How did he do that?

He raised one dark eyebrow and winked. "We've been thinking a lot about the third victim." He glanced out her window. "So, Delia, is there a boyfriend in the picture?" asked Mike.

The man could change topics with heart-stopping speed. "No. But I need to qualify that no to a suddenly-I'm-not-sure. An old boyfriend has reappeared." She was glad for the change in topic, but unprepared for the direction.

Mike typed a few notes into his phone. He looked up. "I've never had an old girlfriend show up. I married so young that there won't ever be an old girlfriend from long ago. How long ago are we talking about in your case?" he said.

Did she really sense a bit of nervousness with the detective, a change in voice, a junior high blush?

Delia stuffed a few files into her bag. These weren't case files about kids, these were personal files, notes from workshops and conferences. She was gradually emptying her office, closing this part of her life.

"Thirteen years ago. We were just out of high school. We had one year of college under our belts and had seen each other nearly every weekend, and we were sure we were in love. Then he left Portland abruptly, his family moved to California not long after . . ." Delia pressed her lips together. She hadn't told this to someone new in a long time. "After the fire. My parents were killed in a house fire."

Mike slid his phone into his front pocket. "I'm sorry. That's terrible. I'm sorry," he said. He sat down, hands resting on his thighs, giving her full attention. Either he was an incredible actor, or he really didn't know about the famous house fire that claimed the lives of her parents.

For the first few years after the fire, people would say to Delia or J Bird, "Oh, you're the two Lamont girls whose parents were killed in the house fire. I'm so sorry." It was their identity. But Mike didn't grow up in Portland, which she knew because she had Googled him. He had grown up in Rhode Island. Apparently he hadn't Googled Delia, otherwise he would have known about the fire. She was disappointed in a surprising way.

"We've always assumed it was arson, likely set by my father, who had schizophrenia. The fire chief told me that arson is one of the hardest things to prove conclusively. But the old boyfriend, Tyler, is the one who saved my life. He pulled me from the house when I ran in to find my parents," she said.

Sometimes when you retell a story, a true story, after not telling it out loud for a long time to an outsider with fresh ears, the story sounds different. New bits show up.

"He saved you how exactly?"

Or sometimes a new person asks just the right questions to adjust the lens.

"I was overcome by smoke and Tyler pulled me out. He suffered burns on his hands when he saved me," she said. Delia pulled a few therapy books from her bookcase that she planned to take with her. She touched each one and then replaced them. Let the next person have them.

Mike tilted his head the way dogs did trying to decipher a strange noise. "He pulled you out. He was on the scene of the fire and he burned his hands. Were you burned too, or was it primarily smoke inhalation?"

No one had asked questions like this since the initial investigation after the fire. She rubbed the center divot in her collarbone with her thumb. "I didn't have any burns but my lungs took a big hit, and I was hospitalized for a few days. I don't know why his hands were burned. I never really had a chance to ask him. My world was upended. I was only nineteen and hollowed out by grief. I missed my parents so much, I still do. But I couldn't stop to be reflective; my sister was six years younger and I had to take care of her."

There was a knock on her door, and both of them were startled. Ira opened the door and said, "I saw the summary from our art therapist. I need to talk with you, Delia."

As if a magician had snapped his fingers, the smoke and calamity cleared from the room and Delia was back in her office and not in the nightmare of the burning house.

"Sure. Five minutes, in your office," she said.

Mike stood up, nodded to Ira. Ira glanced from Mike to Delia, noted something that Delia was positive he would mention later, and pulled the door closed as he left.

"So now Tyler is back and you are in a maybe-yes and maybe-no place with him. After thirteen years." He managed to ask questions between statements. Why was Tyler back? Did she still have feelings for him or was it an old fantasy?

"That is what I'm trying to figure out," she said. "But everything has to take a backseat to Hayley. Old boyfriends resurfacing will have to wait." She picked up a file. "I've got to go. My boss beckons. And I almost forgot to tell you; I'm going out on a visit to Erica's this afternoon with my dog, Baxter. You said you wanted to be there. I need to go over the art therapist's report, which just came in this morning, but I'll be there at three today."

He frowned. "I wish you had called me before the chief assigned me to a review panel. If I can get out of it, I'll be there. If not, please tell that dog of yours to bring back some concrete memories from Hayley."

Mike opened the door for her, which felt odd since this was her office. Wasn't she the one to welcome people into her den and to wave bye-bye when they left? Men; they claimed territory wherever they went.

"You had your hands full," he said, answering her unspoken question. How could he tell what she was thinking? Would he notice the extra hum of vibration in her solar plexus?

"Thanks, Mr. Detective," she said, opting for playful, light.

She stopped in the doorway, and the pull of Hayley found her again, stripping away anything light. "Do you think we'll find Hayley's parents? All we have is a vast amount of geography between here and Tennessee and the mom might even be somewhere else entirely." A conspiratorial space grew between them, forming a capsule tinged with desperation for a child who wanted only to go home. He relaxed his shoulders and leaned closer to her.

"Someone knows where the mother is being held. And we need to get to her before this whole thing implodes on us. It's possible that the husband is being manipulated in some way and that his wife and Hayley were the negotiating point. Your work with Hayley has been important," he said. He didn't lie to her, he didn't say, *Don't worry, we'll find her.* And for that, Delia was grateful.

He touched her elbow with one finger, so lightly, but his finger must have landed directly on a meridian to her chest, along the ribs that protected her heart. "I'll let you know if we find anything concrete," he said.

"Me too," she said. Although her information was woven into puppets, art therapy, and soon, dog therapy. Not concrete at all.

# CHAPTER 34

With the file tucked under one arm, Delia knocked on Ira's door. He called her in.

It was still early in the morning, so she wasn't surprised by the heavy aroma of coffee and peanut butter. No one drank coffee darker than Ira. But peanut butter?

"You either had a peanut butter breakfast or you just dipped into an early lunch of your favorite PBJ," she said, sitting down in front of his desk.

He looked puzzled. "How could you possibly know that? And it was the latter."

Delia tapped the side of her nose with one finger. "You know I have a delicate nose. Don't tell me that you're already forgetting everything about me," she said. "I'm not gone yet."

"No, you're not. And I plan on using every bit of your time left with us. No early dismissal for good behavior." The printer behind his desk shot out two pieces of paper. "Regina's report just came through. I wondered if you'd seen it, but then I saw you were occupied with Mike."

She ignored the emphasis on *occupied,* as well as the slight jump in his mustache that begged for further commentary.

"I'm impressed with how good he is with kids. If he weren't a detective, you could offer him a job with Foster Services," she said.

She settled into the chair by the side of his desk. Ira passed the one-page report to her while he looked at his own copy. "I've read it once online but I prefer a hard copy," he said.

Delia scanned the report, appreciative of Regina's descriptive approach to Hayley's demeanor, her replies to Regina, and the drawing. The printer clattered again, producing the drawing. It was the summary at the bottom that Delia wanted.

> Hayley's ability to amplify her emotions on paper, to explain her circumstances as she understands them, and her willingness to engage with adults continues to improve even from the first art therapy session to the second. She appears increasingly comfortable with her caseworker, Delia, and her foster mother, Erica. She does not draw the images associated with long-term abuse or neglect. She does, however, use classic images of sadness and related depression. In the family drawing, the father is distant and uncommunicative, and the mother is depicted as imprisoned and sad. Recommendation: further sessions to allow Hayley to express the distress that she is experiencing.

Ira pulled the drawing off his copier tray and looked at it. "I know we can't use a drawing as fact, and she may just be drawing out a story that is representative of loss. But I am hopeful for her. She doesn't show either parent as angry. The father is ineffective for some reason, which could be the result of simply not seeing him much, but it's her commentary along with the drawing that sent shivers down my spine. She has parents and she feels wanted," said Ira.

"But most kids, no matter how horrific the abuse, long to be home," she said. Someone in the room had to play devil's advocate, and today it was her turn.

He put down the copy of the drawing. "I didn't," he said.

In years of working with Ira, he rarely mentioned details of his childhood, the burn scars on his arms, his slow recovery in the burn unit, and his gratitude at finding loving parents through adoption. "We've all worked with the parents who were a danger to their kids, who should never be parents. I'm not Regina, but every bit of my experience tells me that her parents are not the problem. Let's share this with the detective."

Delia cleared her throat. "He's already heard the highlights." She told Ira about finding Mike driving by Erica's house, going to J Bird Café, and giving him the pertinent parts of the art session.

He pulled his head back in mock alarm. "The detective has been to J Bird Café and I haven't? What does it take to get an invitation?"

For a man who gave limited details about his past, Ira was relentlessly interested in romantic opportunities for Delia.

"You have an open invitation. Come to the grand opening and I'll give you a free ginger scone," she said.

They were making nice about her leaving. Ira was saying all the friendly, teasing things he should say when a colleague was ready to launch a new career. But still, it felt like an old grass-covered landfill of resentment with occasional wisps of waste matter seeping out. Resentment and encouragement. Sadness and pride. She felt it from everyone still working at Foster Services, and if she were in their places, she would struggle with the same conflicting emotions.

And why had fire been the topic of conversation with Mike and then Ira in such a short span of time? How often did that happen? With Mike, the fire had burst out fully engulfed, flames and black smoke from the genie bottle of her memories. Moments later with Ira, his touch had been subtle, a simple reminder that some things that adults do to kids are beyond redemption. His history of fire rarely emerged, yet it drove his career and his empathy with kids.

Delia would miss this man, her fire cousin, both of them born again from the disaster of flames. "If you wake up a little earlier in the morning, you can come to J Bird Café every day. We'll make you something fancier than peanut butter sandwiches."

It was better not to talk about fire, about how much they'd miss each other.

"Just keep me in the loop with your assessment visits with Hayley," he said. He pushed away with his rolling chair. Delia stood up to leave and stuffed Regina's report into the file.

"Hey, do you know what I miss?" he asked.

Dang it. She thought they were going to skip this part.

"What?" She braced herself.

"I miss the days before heroin moved into town like a steamroller. I miss our crackhead mothers who finally got clean, our alcoholic parents who latched onto AA. They might not be stellar parents, but they were good enough. Heroin brought the bad guys to town," said Ira.

"I know," she said, reaching for the door handle.

"By the way, try to remember to bring my road atlas back. When you're done making fun of it, I'd like you to return it, please."

"Sure. I must have left it at home. I'll make a note of it."

She'd bring it back after she finished scratching the itch when she looked at Tennessee.

# CHAPTER 35

There were few creatures happier than a golden retriever in a car. They were the premier road trip partners, enjoying the journey and the destination, one feeding the other in a constant loop of anticipation. Delia left the office just in time to pick up Baxter and head for South Portland before the traffic on the Casco Bay Bridge turned thick and cumbersome. They pulled into Erica's driveway, and Delia turned off the car. The passenger window was partway down; Baxter's black, moist nose already sniffed the air for information. He'd never been here before, and a new environment offered him unlimited olfactory stimulation.

"Okay, here's the situation," said Delia. Baxter pulled his attention from the partially opened window and looked at her. "This little girl wants to go home to her family, and you and I have to help her find them. Your mission is to turn on your full throttle dog love, and my job is to ask just the right question at the perfect moment."

Baxter stood up, which took up the entire passenger seat

area. Whatever Delia had said, he was ready to proceed. His answer to almost everything was, *Yes.*

"One more thing. There is a large cat inside. This is his house, and you have to mind your manners. He is not a seagull; you cannot chase him. Besides, if you did, he would probably hurt you."

She snapped the leash on his collar.

This was where the word *manipulative* could not be denied. She promised Hayley that she would bring Baxter to Erica's house, which was true. But if she were strapped to a lie detector, she would be found lying if she said the trip was just recreational. She understood the overwhelming power of a dog, especially a dog like Baxter, the koala bear of the canine world, with his affable smile, brown eyes, and pink tongue at the ready for kisses. If Hayley felt safe enough, distracted enough, some bit of memory might just fall out, a link, an address, without Hayley being drilled into a state of withdrawal.

"Heel," said Delia. Once outside, he stepped brightly to her left side, and she looped the leash over her wrist. The big unknown was Louie the Maine Coon cat, Hayley's bodyguard and familiar.

They walked to the front door, but before she could knock, the door to the ranch house swung open.

"We've been waiting for you," said Erica. "I think every child in Hayley's kindergarten class knows that Baxter, the big red dog, is coming to visit today. News of Baxter was Hayley's share today."

The child peeked from behind Erica. "Hi, Baxter," she said.

If Delia's level of anxiety transmitted through the leash to the dog, this could go badly. She was worried about animal territory, worried that Louie with his razor-sharp claws would lay siege to Baxter. She pictured his black nose in shreds, then Baxter growling and attacking the cat (which he had never once done in his entire life), blood streaming, the child screaming, and perhaps a bit of feline urine sprayed in the house to complete the picture.

"Where's Louie?" she asked. She stepped gingerly into the

house, scanning the entryway for the twenty-pound cat with large paws.

It was hard enough to keep track of human interactions, what with the unconscious lobbing grenades that the conscious mind wouldn't take responsibility for. Animal language posed a greater dilemma because Delia could only react when all the messages had long been delivered and there was little she could do.

"Louie's in the garden. Hayley and I thought it best to all meet outside."

Delia knelt down on one knee next to Baxter and said, "It's okay to pet him. In fact, you could pet him all day and he'd be happy about it."

The dog was excited by the prospect of meeting new people to sniff, to rub against, to please, and yet he remained seated while Hayley stroked his head, then his neck. Delia released the lead. Hayley's small hands soaked in what Baxter offered, the strum of his heartbeat, his energy coiling along the back legs, and his tail swishing along the floor. She leaned into him. Would it be a good thing or a bad thing that Hayley was now covered in dog smell? How would all of this register in the small yet specialized brain of Louie? How was it that two animals that were predators ever agreed to be domesticated by humans? Or were they domesticated?

Erica picked up a few pieces of paper from a basket marked SCHOOL WORK and said, "Let's head outside and I'll bring some of Hayley's school work for you to look at."

When Delia stood up, Baxter followed her example. "Destiny awaits you," she said to the dog.

"His name is Louie. That's who awaits him," said Hayley, leading the way through the kitchen to the sliding glass doors.

Delia was frequently surprised by the vocabulary of young children, how quickly they absorbed new words and understood the meaning from context.

"You are correct. Baxter, Louie awaits you," she said.

Hayley pulled open the sliding glass doors with some difficulty. She was a slight child and however long she'd spent with her abductors had taken a toll on her overall health. But she had now been in foster care for almost three weeks, and despite the trauma of her circumstances, her vitality was improving. Three weeks ago, muscling open the sliding glass door would have been impossible for Hayley. Delia must remember to mention this in the case notes.

Once on the deck, all of them scanned the area for Louie, from the right side of the fenced yard, along which grew borders of hostas backed by sunflowers now bursting with seed, to the back side of the deep yard where the portable soccer goal had tipped over. No cat. On the left side of the yard, a series of raised beds still produced tomatoes, cabbages, dark, curly greens. The garden closest to the deck still produced Hayley's favorite plants, cucumbers. Still no cat.

Sometimes the best course of action was to ignore animals, especially cats. "Hayley, please show Baxter and me your school work," said Delia, sitting down on the steps that led to the garden. She still had the dog on the leash.

The one constant of kindergarten over the ages had to be glue. There were no family drawings, but instead, three pages of bright bits of paper glued to a tree, a farmer's field, and an apple orchard. "Look how Hayley glued all these colors on the apple tree," said Delia, holding the paper in front of Baxter. He sniffed the page, then relaxed his face into a retriever smile.

But his attention was not held for long. Alerted to a noise that none of the humans heard, he swiveled his head to the side yard as Louie emerged from one of the broad-leafed hosta plants. If Louie was alarmed at the sight of a dog in his paradise, he didn't show it. The cat walked easily with his tail held high in a question mark, pausing to bat at a bumblebee that flew too close and scooping it in for a snack. No arched back, no low, stalking body posture. Just a quick display of his prowess.

Delia swallowed and exhaled, ready for whatever might explode. Baxter sniffed the air again, decoded the hundreds of complex scents that swirled around the receptors in his nose, and stood up, ears alert, body idling at about fifty percent power. Louie took one effortless jump and landed on the deck and stood in front of Baxter without hesitation, without a question of who had animal priority. He didn't make eye contact with the dog, instead, he pressed against the dog with a casualness that screamed confidence.

Baxter's eyes grew wide and he froze as the introductory comments passed from cat to dog. As Louie curled his way along the side of Baxter, the dog lowered his head and chanced a butt sniff, which the cat permitted. Delia could only imagine what Baxter, and all other dogs, gleaned from butt sniffing: gender, diet, possible proclivities for aggressiveness or submission, and overall health. Whatever he concluded in summary caused him to sit down. There would be no cat chasing, even Delia could decode that message.

"Louie likes him," said Hayley. "He's lonely for another animal like him. He needs a friend. I'm his friend, but I'm a girl."

This seemed as good a comment on interspecies relationships as any. "Let's take a walk around the yard with Baxter and see what happens. Would you like to hold his leash?" said Delia. She held out the lead to Hayley. If all went well, she'd take off his leash after a stroll around the yard. "He wants to smell everything in the yard."

Without hesitation, Hayley said, "Come on, Baxter."

The dog glanced at Delia. She said, "Good boy." And off he went with the girl, trailed far behind by the cat.

Erica crossed her arms over her chest and leaned against the doorframe. "Baxter is the first dog who hasn't been totally intimidated by Louie. I don't know what they just said to each other. Wouldn't you like to hear what goes on in their brains?" she said.

"More than that, I'd like to photograph everything in Hayley's brain: street address, town, last name. Did your daughter know her street address by the time she was in kindergarten?" said Delia.

"Yes. Address, telephone number, and her grandparents' address. And, of course, her last name. It's really unusual that a child Hayley's age hasn't been taught this kind of critical information." She pensively rubbed one bare foot along the other. Her tan line from sandals formed a large V across the tops of her feet.

From the far end of the fenced yard, Hayley led the furred companions on a tour of garden beds.

"But aren't addresses and numbers just abstract ideas for kids this age? How did you teach her all of that information?" asked Delia. Baxter wagged his tail enthusiastically when he found a small stick to carry.

"We taught her the same way a lot of parents do. We inserted our address into a song that the kids would know. We used *Twinkle, Twinkle Little Star.*" She stopped, mouth open. "Oh, my God, I wonder if Hayley's parents used a song." She pushed off the edge of the doorway.

Could it all be this simple? Was her address embedded in a song? All the agonies of a small child could be healed and parents found. Delia pictured the phone call to Ira and Mike, the euphoria, the relief, this one terrible crime that had blasted a family apart could now be solved. Among foster care caseworkers, this would be like winning the Nobel Prize for family reunification.

Hayley returned to the deck with Baxter. "He wants to give me the stick. He keeps dropping it at my feet," she said, marveling at the event, wanting to share this discovery with Delia and Erica.

"He wants you to throw it," said Delia. "He loves to chase the stick and then return it to you so that you'll throw it again." She could barely contain her anticipation about this new avenue for finding Hayley's family.

Erica was unable to contain her excitement. She nearly levitated. "And after you throw the stick, we need to learn a song about the address of our house. It is a very cool song that my daughter, Sarah, learned when she was in kindergarten. And you can teach us the song about where you live with your mommy."

Would Delia ever meet Erica's daughter? Like most kids that she knew about, she was pretty tightly scheduled.

Hayley dropped the stick. "No. Emma said not to sing a song about my house. And I could never tell anyone where Mommy is. She said no songs or Mommy would be sad. Uncle Ray took away my special blanket when I sang a song. I cried so long." Her lip quivered and her shoulders shook.

Baxter's ears perked up. He stepped over the stick and stood directly in front of Hayley. He nudged his head under her elbow. She leaned forward slightly and wrapped her arms around the dog. She whispered to the dog, "Uncle Ray threw the special blanket out the car window."

The momentary structure of happiness collapsed in Delia, crumbling like faulty concrete. Delia had seen so many children clinging to a relic of safety, a stuffed animal, a soft blanket, an action figure, and she understood the magnitude of such a loss, the final disassembling of children pulled from their family.

She squatted down by Baxter. "Uncle Ray was wrong to take away your special blanket. I think Baxter understands that sad feeling inside you. You didn't do anything wrong, Hayley. You are a good girl, a very good girl."

The cat pushed against Delia in some kind of weird group hug and then weaved in between Baxter's legs. Erica dropped down to a cross-legged pose. "You can sing any song you like here. All of your songs are okay," she said. Her eyes brimmed with tears.

"I don't have any songs," said Hayley. "They are all gone."

They were going to be crushed in sadness, all of them. And then Delia remembered J Bird's parlor trick with Baxter. Would he do it with Delia?

"Hey, wait just a minute. Baxter knows a song." She ruffled the fur along his neck, hoping to dust off the misery that had descended on them. "Come here, boy."

Delia sang, "*Home, home on the range, where the deer and the antelope play . . .*" a song that J Bird and Baxter sang together. It turned out that "Home on the Range" was a very popular song with dogs if one were to consult YouTube.

Baxter flung his head back and howled, yipped, and howled again. With each refrain, he sang with total commitment, his great head back, his throat open to the world, his wolf genes awake and powerful.

He would sing as long as Delia did, and she figured the demonstration was good for a few rounds. But then Hayley dropped to her hands and knees and howled, mimicking Baxter, leaning into him, her eyes closed, letting her small voice travel straight up, not ready to sing words, but now chancing a different kind of song. In the spirit of the moment, Erica began to howl with the duo, leaving only Delia to lead the chorus in words. For Louie, this was too much dog music, and he hopped on the picnic table and showed his lack of interest through personal grooming.

Breathless, they simultaneously came to the end of the song. Something ancient and wordless reverberated through Delia.

Hayley rocked back on her heels. "I sent that song to Mommy. I want her to come and find me. Now she will know where I am," said Hayley, with a kind of assurance that left Delia reeling.

There had to be more that she could do to find Hayley's mother. Delia knew she would do anything.

# CHAPTER 36

*Juniper*

Three text messages and no reply. What was wrong with Ben? He could always be counted on to return her messages. And he was the only person she could talk to about Delia and their father. After their conversation last night about Tyler and the ghosts of their childhood furniture, her mind had twitched and tightened all night. Ben had been her father's best friend, the only one who still treated him like a friend, not just a guy with schizophrenia.

Today was Juniper's day off, and she had to meet Greg at the café. He had just called to say that the second oven was being delivered. She headed out the door with Baxter as she called Ben's vet clinic to see if today was a crazy, busy day filled with emergencies. Maybe she could stop by if she called him on the way.

She was sure the whole thing about Delia was stress; she was freaking out about leaving her job and that little girl. Juniper had never seen her so obsessed with a case. Delia had always been the model of firm boundaries with her clients. Maybe it was nothing to worry about. Then again, when Delia tried to make a connection between the tiger feet on their dining room table of their childhood and the tiger-in-the-house fears of the little girl, Juniper went on red alert. Crazy alert. Ben was the only one she could talk to; he would understand crazy alert. She could always count on him.

"South Portland Animal Clinic," said Jill, the receptionist.

"Hi, it's J Bird. Is Ben able to take a phone call or is he too busy?"

"He's home sick today. Some kind of flu. This is the second time in the last two months that he's come down with it."

In the background, a cat yowled pitifully.

"That's funny, I just saw him a few days ago. I had no idea he was sick. He's been having a tough time, on top of the whole knee surgery, which doesn't look all that great to me. Is he still limping around?" said Juniper.

"Yeah, his knee doesn't seem to get all that much better. I thought knee surgery was a guaranteed improvement. We really need Dr. Ben back, healthy and full time again. It's been hard on all of us."

"I just tried texting him and he won't answer. You don't think he's mad at me for some reason, do you? Mostly people don't get mad at me anymore now that I'm a grown-up and especially since I make such awesome desserts." Juniper made a note to bring the vet staff some cinnamon rolls. The power to soothe people through baked goods never got old for her.

"Maybe he's annoyed because you still haven't had Baxter neutered," said Jill.

She had reminded Juniper of this shortcoming several times. Even though Jill was joking around, Juniper felt pushed, and she didn't like being nagged about something so important.

"Didn't I tell you? Delia and I are thinking of starting an illegal puppy mill. We figure Baxter could spawn hundreds of golden retrievers," she said.

"Okay, I see that you're sensitive on the topic of Baxter's virility. And besides, Dr. Ben would never get mad at you, and you know it. You're family to him."

"Thanks. I'll bring you guys something that will temporarily make up for my deficit in canine family planning," said Juniper.

Ben was part of their family. He had been there for them when they could've kept falling, after their parents died, but he had swooped in like a superhero. He had walked them through the funeral preparations, interfaced with Juniper's school when Delia had her own college classes to attend to, and promised them that he would always be there for them, no matter what.

Did he really have the flu? Was he in trouble financially and he had no one to confide in? He and Michelle had two kids ready to go to college, one this coming year and one the following year. She would do anything to help him.

She texted him. "R U OK? I saw you with the guy outside the café. Call me." She slid the phone into her bag, grabbed Baxter, and headed to her car.

The day was a bell ringer for fall: a brilliant blue sky, with the first maple trees tinged with red, as if their leaves had been professionally and expensively highlighted. Baxter leapt into the backseat. After meeting with Greg and catching up on renovation details in the morning, she'd shop for baking supplies at Whole Foods. As she snapped her seat belt into place, her phone rang. Ben.

"Where are you?" he said. He sounded tired, his voice deeper than usual, as if he had woken up moments ago.

"I'm on my way to the café. Where are *you?* Jill told me you had the flu." She paused, dreading the direction that she had to take. "Are you in trouble? You can talk to me. I'm not a kid anymore."

The staggered breath came through the phone, an exhale that shuddered. "I'm not far from your place. I don't want to meet you in South Portland; I don't want anyone from the office to see me. Can you meet me at the 7-Eleven near you?"

"Jesus, Ben. You sound terrible. Sure, I can meet you there. I'm only a few blocks away."

* * *

Juniper parked on the far side of the convenience store. She kept her eye on the rearview mirror, waiting for Ben. After ten more minutes, he pulled in next to her, driving the old pickup that he drove to work every day. He turned his head her way and cupped his hand in a sign for her to come into his truck. She rolled down all her windows halfway for Baxter.

"Stay. I'll be right back," she said, turning around to face Baxter. But she knew in dog language that translated into, *You are being abandoned.*

She slid into the passenger seat of Ben's truck. He hadn't shaved this morning and possibly not the previous morning.

"What's wrong with you?" she said. Delia always said that losing their parents had burned the chitchat out of them.

"Nice to see you too, J Bird. Can you give me a minute here?" He wrapped his hands around the steering wheel, straightened his arms, and pushed back against the seat. "This isn't easy for me. I haven't told anyone that this is a problem. . . ."

"Look, I saw you with that guy outside the café. Are you in financial trouble, taking cash payments off the books? Everybody does that once in a while. That's what all my bosses have told me. A client pays you in cash and you don't report it. You don't have to go all desperado about it. You're not perfect," she said. For so long, Ben had been her gravitational center, and she wanted him back again.

Ben looked confused. He slid his upper teeth along his lower lip. "Cash payments off the books? If only that were the problem." He rubbed one palm along the side of his face. "I don't want you to worry about me, kiddo. I'm not going renegade with the financial books." He closed his eyes for a moment. "God, sometimes you remind me so much of your mother. You are just as beautiful as Susan," he said.

Ben was the only person other than Delia who ever mentioned her mother or her father. Even hearing her mother's name felt like sunlight. "Then what is it? You can't fool me; I know you too well," she said. She heard the pleading in her voice, sounding more like the teenager she left behind.

He rubbed his hands along his chinos. "I started taking pain meds right after the surgery. Everybody does, right? My knee didn't heal up like they said it would and I had to get back to work, so the doc kept writing the scrip. I tried to stop taking them twice, and I was so sick that I was sure that I was going to die. It's like having the flu times one hundred. J Bird, I'm addicted to pain meds."

Not Ben, not their Ben. For a few breaths, she stared at him, this trembling, unshaven man who had served as her personal landing pad when she had tried all the usual drugs in college, when she didn't even tell Delia, when she thought she was pregnant but wasn't, and when Ben found her the best dog on the planet to be her pal. He had called her three years ago and said, "I want you to come down to my clinic. There's someone here who needs you." No one had truly needed her before Baxter. Ben had known that about her; he knew everything about her and still loved her, just like her mother and her father would have done.

"Are you flipping kidding me? Have you not received the worldwide memo about pain meds? That they're addictive?"

He squeezed his eyes shut. "I know, I know. It wasn't the surgery so much as the physical therapy. I just couldn't stand the ongoing pain. It took up all the space in my mind. The oxy got me through the day so I could go back to work." A bead of sweat rolled down his right temple.

"Could you turn on the ignition so we can roll down the windows?" she asked, suddenly overwhelmed by the rising temperature in the cab of the truck as well as the heat that rolled off Ben.

"I can't. I'm freezing," he said. "It's like there's an intruder in my brain."

He wore a sweatshirt with the University of Southern Maine emblem on the front. If Juniper had on a sweatshirt, she'd pass out from the heat. She reached over and touched his chilled and damp hand. "Have you told Michelle" she asked.

"Not yet. I will. She thinks I have the flu and she's mad at me for not ever getting a flu shot. She's never taken a drug in her life, not when the kids were born, not ever. She doesn't even take aspirin. This would be hard for her to understand."

"Are you working with a doctor to help you cut down?"

Ben glanced up to the left. "I thought I could handle this on my own. But you're right, kiddo, I'll call my PC, and we'll work on a more gradual decrease. I promise." He nodded nervously, signaling that the topic was coming to a close.

"Wait. Who was that guy who drove up to the café? He gave you something. What did he give you?"

He turned his face away, fogging the window as he spoke. "Street oxy. My doctor cut me off and said I shouldn't keep taking it." Ben turned back to her again. "He didn't know that I was addicted. And there's a limit to how much anyone, even doctors, can provide now. But I found this guy and he sold me a bag of oxy. Don't ask me where he gets it because I didn't ask him. I doubt that the answer is through legal means."

Juniper's personal landing pad evaporated. Something had Ben, something owned him.

"You're buying street drugs?" She couldn't keep the incredulity out of her voice. "I want my Ben back again. You've stepped over a line, and you've got to turn back. Make an appointment with your PC and then call me, because I'm coming with you. If you don't, then I'm calling your wife. Do you understand what I'm saying?" she said. She was ready to cry, to hit him, honk the horn, or kick the inside of the cab until all of her toes broke.

Ben looked at her, nodding his head like a bobblehead doll, and squeezed his lips together. "Yeah, okay, okay."

"And keep that trash away from J Bird Café. I can't believe you used the café to meet your dealer. Did you hear what I just said? You have a dealer!" She opened the truck door. "I mean it, Ben. Call me as soon as you make the appointment or I will do exactly what I said." She slammed the truck door as hard as she could, turned around, and mule-kicked it. She didn't look at him as he drove away.

Inside her car, Baxter greeted her as if she had been gone for hours, not minutes. "Our guy's in trouble, Bax. We've got to help him."

# CHAPTER 37

Delia gripped the sheets and pulled herself from the clamoring dreams. She had slept badly after seeing Hayley the day before. Her father's dream voice rang in the gray light of morning. *Tennessee spring lamb.*

How could Delia tell Mike or even J Bird that she heard her dead father's voice as she was finally drifting off to sleep at five a.m.? And it wasn't even an entire sentence that she heard, just a fragment. *Tennessee spring lamb.* How could she explain that only her father would have said that and only Delia would understand it? Worse yet, that now she had to go to Tennessee and sift through information that they had already covered?

Baxter, ever the meter for distress, had nosed her awake. It was nearly six. That meant J Bird already left, otherwise the dog slept as close to J Bird as he could manage.

"Good dog, Baxter. You've saved me from sleeping too late." Delia walked the already exuberant dog to the back door and opened it so that Baxter could relieve himself. The backyard was small and not Baxter's first choice for anything except peeing. She looked at the clock on the microwave. Six thirty. She had plenty of time to take a brain-cleansing walk with Baxter on Willard Beach.

"Let's go to the beach, big guy," she called to the dog. When he heard one of his favorite words, *beach,* he spun circles around her while she pulled on jeans, tank top, and jacket. Was she ever as grateful for anything as Baxter was for a good walk on the beach?

By the time they pulled into the parking lot at the beach, all the regulars were there. Baxter greeted his dog friends, the Great Dane, the standard poodle, and the Australian cattle dog. She followed along behind as the dogs ran together, occasionally stopping to slobber each other with dog kisses.

Delia couldn't shake the dream about her father issuing his spring lamb proclamation. She was already worried about how disembodied voices and amplified scents might merge into a kind of thought disorder that could bump her off the track of normal people. Did she just say normal? Did she just say anything aloud, or was she only thinking?

She'd been at the business of human tragedy long enough to know that in the midst of disasters, anyone could look delusional, that the senses either sharpened like a Japanese Santoku knife, or the person dissolved into a sludge of muddled thinking. For most people, the altered state was temporary, and if the disaster could be modified (abusive husband arrested, housing arranged, teenager goes into drug rehab), they could return to whatever their base rate of coping with life had been before. Not always, but it was what Delia hoped for. But for some people, the new normal crushed them and pulverized the bones of their psyches.

She took off her sandals and let the moist sand rub the rough spots off her feet. Better than any pedicure.

Her dead father hadn't delivered a message to her before, but she firmly believed it was from him. It was just like him to get in a triple-layered message. Just like him on his good days. Smart, complex, funny.

His annual food column about spring lambs had caused him more distress than any of the others. His favorite restaurant in Portsmouth, New Hampshire, specialized in offering spring lamb. The chef prepared it with a reverence that made it possible to eat something as sweet and innocent as lamb. It was one of her father's major food conflicts and even if he hadn't suffered from schizophrenia, the magnitude of the dilemma could have kick-started a breakdown in a sensitive person.

Rare. The best roast lamb was rare, with a side of scorched rosemary and roasted baby red potatoes, drizzled with butter. Did she still have one of his spring lamb columns about the horrible, yet delicious, sacrificial lamb dinners that he ate once a year? His columns were syndicated; she could still find them online if she needed to.

*Slam!* Baxter delivered a piece of driftwood by bumping it into her leg. He dropped it at her feet and then slowly backed up, his eyes flicking back and forth from Delia to the stick. She picked it up and tossed it into the shallow waters of low tide. Baxter took off like a rocket, leaping into the salt water.

Delia was sure that the spring lambs in Portsmouth were local, not from Tennessee, but would she really have known that when she was a teenager? Or did the message mean that Hayley was the spring lamb? She didn't need an ancestral visitation to figure that out. Most kids in foster care were the spring lambs, or they had been at one time. Bleating little kids, searching for the scent of their mamas under every leaf, confident that all would be right with the world if only they could find her.

Delia couldn't shape the rest of it into words without sounding crazy. She was sure that if her father really slipped through the veil to give her a message, he picked his words carefully. If he said lamb, then he understood that this was the hardest thing for Delia, because despite his illness, he understood his daughter and she understood him. Spring lambs were the most painful dilemma. And secondly, a lamb couldn't make it without a mother. Otherwise they turned into sacrifices.

Lastly, there was Tennessee. Two of the victims were from Tennessee. That was where she needed to go. No, she was not going to try to explain this to Mike, Ira, or J Bird. Especially J

Bird. Although J Bird's mental health looked robust enough, the habit of protecting her little sister was well entrenched.

After a dozen more tosses of the stick, Delia turned around to head back to the parking lot. Baxter was shocked by the horrible turn of events. There was rarely a middle ground with him; life was either breathtaking or soul-crushing.

"Come on, Baxter, I have to get to work," she said, as if he understood anything but the tone of voice that signaled an end to the walk.

Did the dead still suffer from schizophrenia? Was it entirely a physical affliction, improper wiring and a bad mix of chemistry? Could she count on her dead father now, when in life she had been so often bludgeoned by his paranoia and delusions? And how long would it take to drive to Tennessee? No, she didn't have time to drive. She had scrupulously saved up miles on her credit card. She would fly.

Mike said that the most recent heroin line ran from Mexico to Nashville. But Raymond Blanchard lived outside Nashville in Dalton. Or he had lived there. Once she was at her office, she'd look up the nearest department of child protective services to Dalton. She might not know the world of heroin traffickers, but she did know the world of protective services better than anyone.

She would tell J Bird that she had to fly to Denver to pick up an unaccompanied minor to return him to Maine. She would tell Ira that she had to take a personal day, despite how close she was to the end of her days at foster care. She would tell Mike nothing at all for fear that he might sniff out a lie. There was no one who would understand why she'd do something so irrational, so unlike her.

She rinsed off Baxter at home; the salt water wasn't good for him or their floors. He adored the rubdown with his special towel, smiling with pleasure as Delia indulged him.

When she arrived at her office, she went straight to her laptop and to the Kayak Web site; flights to Nashville and one night in a motel somewhere between Dalton and Nashville. She'd be in and out of Tennessee before anyone even noticed.

# CHAPTER 38

*Tennessee*

The dark smell of cigarette smoke clung to the entrance of the Dalton Family Services Center and jettisoned Delia into the past again. Cigarettes meant mental illness roaring through the kitchen, spilling off the counters, when her father locked the door against imagined invaders.

There had been a national campaign against smoking for decades. But none of the tobacco companies had capitalized on the connection between smoking and mental illness, at least not in a forthright manner. It would have been too insensitive, creating a campaign that honed in on an already maligned population. Delia could have written the advertising script for them: *Crazy people crave the smoke from cigarettes, huffing away in slow suicide, trying to subdue the monsters of mental illness.* She could hear Ira, shocked at her sudden lack of compassion. And just as quickly, she could feel her mother's devotion to Theo, the love of her life, her patience with anything that soothed him, including cigarettes.

In Portland, smokers were the scorned underworld. Here in Tennessee, where children still picked tobacco on family farms in the summer, smoking was a sign of defiance against all things new. It marked a loyalty to a way of life that had both supported them and annihilated them for generations.

Delia felt the memory melt her flesh as she pulled open the glass doors of the child protection office. She shook off the past, as she did numerous times each day, and attended to her present challenge.

Previous occupants must have been a real estate office, or even a medical facility. Now a worsening economy, lack of jobs (thanks to the growing ranks of nonsmokers), and increased drug use created havoc for children. When Delia called to set up an appointment, she learned that the agency was struggling to address the kids who were the carnage of the surge in drug use, those left parentless.

If Emma Gilbert had not left some mark on social services, Delia's trip would be a bust and little Hayley would be about to enter foster care with a permanent family back in Portland. Hayley might get lucky, but her chances of going through multiple foster homes was high. All of this would be for nothing: the early morning drive to Boston for the quickest flight out of Logan, renting a car in Nashville, and lying to J Bird and Ira. Tyler had called twice, the last time with the message, "I need to talk with you." She had not answered him.

She didn't want her last case to be the worst, the failure she'd never forget, the one that would mark her final days with foster care. Surely in her ten years she had learned enough of the ins and outs to get one kid back with relatives who could take care of her. This was about Hayley. Or was it about Delia saving herself, and not some ego-laden attachment to taking care of kids?

It wasn't like she'd have to hunt through case files; every single person who came through this door would be in the computer system.

In the reception area, a young black woman with exceedingly good posture sat behind a counter with a glass enclosure. The castle guard. Delia said a prayer. *Please let her be interested*

*and willing. Please let her have had her favorite breakfast, eggs just
right, with toast golden brown. Please don't let her think that everyone
from the north is a big know-it-all. Please let her hand over the hall pass
to let me in. Don't let this be the day when she has decided that all of the
services in the world for shattered families are useless.*

The woman slid the glass window open. "Do you have an appointment?" She kept it neutral. Delia knew it was her job to
start assessing people the minute they walked in the door. Un-
officially, of course. She waited to hear Delia's voice. Reception-
ists and administrative assistants ran every organization, in a
stealth, massively underpaid sort of way.

"I don't exactly have an appointment, but I called yesterday
and spoke with Pat Garvey. She said she'd try to fit me in this
morning. I know I might have to wait."

There, she'd heard Delia's voice and was figuring where she
was from.

"I'm from foster care in Portland, Maine," Delia said, offering a token that could move things along.

What had her father said during one of his stays in a hospital,
where they filled him with a cocktail of medications to soothe
him? She and her mother visited him in the family room of the
psych unit.

"When we all have so little, we will fight like starved dogs for
the scraps. Last night there was a fight between two men over
the remote control," he said.

Delia didn't want to arm wrestle this woman for admission
to their office of broken families. She heard an electronic buzz,
and a door to the left released its lock.

"Thanks," said Delia.

"Second door on the right," said the receptionist, with a
slight toss of her head.

Delia pushed open the door and followed the clipped directions to the director's office. She wanted Pat Garvey to be the
Tennessee version of Ira: smart, ethical, friendly enough, but
down to business. More than anything, she wanted this person
to have enough caring left in her for a kid stuck in emergency
foster care in Maine.

The people here had tried hard to make the place softer, if not beautiful. They made an effort to curl the edges of concrete block from right angles to curvilinear with the help of murals depicting the surrounding mountains dotted with friendly animals, Disneyesque versions of cows, horses, owls, and deer with white tails.

Delia tried hard to shut down her overly sensitive olfactory system, but the layers of fear swirled through the hallways and made their way into her throat with their sticky tendrils. Maybe she should try dotting her upper lip with a drop of lavender, a barricade to the assault of a world of scents.

Even for people with average nose ability, memory worked in collaboration with smell, pairing traumatic images with the scent of burning toast, rubber dolls, or Dove soap. Would children coming through this hallway forever link the mural images of animals with abuse, neglect, and abandonment? If Delia had a say, which she clearly didn't since this wasn't her office, she'd say skip the murals, go soft and neutral, include water, maybe a fish tank, plants, and something for people to nosh on. Food, something with carbs that people could hang on to. Big bowls of Goldfish crackers.

She knocked on the door. Surely Pat Garvey had been notified about her arrival.

"Come in." The doors were cheap, hollow core. It must be terrible in this office when families started trumpeting and the sound vibrated the flimsy wood, when rage and fear battled it out and children were at stake.

Delia opened the door and took a quick visual tour, left to right, sweeping the room. It was not what she expected. Pat's desk faced the left wall, but the opposite side of the small room held a semicircle of three comfy chairs. A kid-sized chair, a box of Legos in a blue plastic tub, another box of two-inch-tall superhero action figures, and in the center, an oblong coffee table that had never seen a coaster in its life.

Pat sat in a small version of a wingback chair with roughed-up blue brocade. She was anchored by a laptop. Manila folders were stuffed between her left side and the edge of the chair.

Her feet rested on the coffee table, where another stack of files leaned dangerously to one side. Pat started to get up, and Delia was sure that the entire rig was going to topple over.

"Please don't get up. I'll just sit right over here," said Delia.

Pat looked older than Delia, late forties, solid build, a white blouse over a tank top, sensible beige work pants made of something that didn't have to be ironed.

"You know that the police up your way have already checked with us about Emma Gilbert and the child. Neither of them came through our system," she said.

Good. She was just like Ira. Pat didn't need a prologue.

"I know. You mentioned that on the phone. And I don't doubt the thoroughness of the police, but . . ." Delia's voice caught on something hard, a memory of suddenly being orphaned, being shot out into the universe, untethered.

"I've been in this business for ten years, and this is my last case. I know that what I'm doing is not normal; caseworkers don't chase down hunches in other states about their existing kids in foster care. Hayley is just so . . . I mean, I have a feeling that someone is looking for her. She told us that she talked with her mother on Skype. If I can catch a thread that might lead me to her family, if she has a family, then . . ."

Delia couldn't shake the emotion that rolled through her.

Pat waited patiently, putting down her reading glasses and an open file.

"Then you thought you could end with a success? Saving one kid," asked Pat.

Delia knew what she sounded like, that this was more about Delia than the girl back in South Portland currently being guarded by a Maine Coon cat.

Delia let out a rumpled sigh, gaining traction again. "Yes, I would prefer a happy, fantasy reunion for my final case. But there's more to it. My gut tells me that this child has somebody, that she's telling the truth about the Skype thing even though no one has been able to trace it. My boss, sort of you in my parallel Maine universe, is more invested in this case than I've seen in a long time. There is something ticking in the background that I can't quite wrap my brain around, and I'm willing to dig hard until I find it. She's worth it. They're all worth it."

"Spoken like someone who is either brand new, or leaving the business with your soul intact. Why are you leaving?"

Delia put her feet up on the coffee table. "My sister and I are starting a bakery café together."

Pat laughed with a deep, throaty alto that could have belonged to a nightclub singer. "Oh, please take me with you. I can wash dishes. Did you bring any samples?"

Delia wished that she had scooped up some of J Bird's chocolate éclairs on the way out. "That would have been wise, but I've been awake since three a.m. and all I could think about was coffee and my GPS."

"Oh, well, a girl can dream. Tell me again how you think I can help you," said Pat.

Delia glanced at the wall behind Pat. Master's degree in social work, Penn State.

Delia's glance was not lost on Pat. "That piece of parchment both helps and hinders me. As we say here, it's the bottom fact. With doctors it gives me credibility, with my clients it's a hurdle that impairs their ability to trust me, and that makes my job harder. What about you, does it help or hinder you?"

Oh, she was good.

"You've guessed that I've never been to rural Tennessee before, and you're right. What I'm hoping for is a thread that the police might have missed. I've got a child in Portland, Maine, who was with three adults who were killed. Emma Gilbert was one. She had no police record. And one, Raymond Blanchard, was from Dalton, with a record of possession," said Delia. She saw no harm in repeating what Pat already knew. She often did this with kids and parents in foster care.

Pat leaned back. "And I told the police that Emma Gilbert had never come through our system. And yes, they showed me a photo of her. You know that her family was contacted, all of whom live out of state. Emma attended college in the area, but she graduated more than five years ago. The other man who was identified, Raymond, was never part of our system. Which means both of them had good enough parents or they had good luck. I can tell you that Raymond's lawyer is well known in these parts. If you have money, you hire him, which is what Raymond did. He paid him enough to wake snakes, and the result was probation for a drug charge. He's white, too, which in the legal system was a point in his favor."

Delia relaxed a little, felt her pelvis uncurl from her crouched and ready posture. She trusted Pat. She liked the speed at which this woman's brain traveled.

She slid a photo of Hayley out of a file folder and gave it to Pat. "This is the child. Hayley had never been to school before, but is there a way to get this photo around to local preschools? I know this is a long shot, but she may have gone to day care when she was younger," said Delia.

"The local police already shined all over town with the photo. Pediatrician's offices too. But no one recognized her. Kids are tough, though. Their looks change nearly every day," said Pat.

"What about Raymond? You sound like you knew him. Or knew about him. Why would he be involved with heroin? And why would anyone want to kill him?"

"There are only two answers, and you already know both. He was capitalizing on the unprecedented rise in heroin use and embarking on a career in drug running, or he was a user who didn't pay his bills. There is a third option, which is that he was addicted and running a business, but I hear that heroin preoccupies the brain almost entirely so he wouldn't have made much headway in selling if he was addicted," she said.

Pat had skipped part of the question, and Delia returned to it. "Did you know him?" There, that should be direct enough.

Pat slid the stack of folders out of the nook of the chair and onto the table. "I know we're supposed to have all the files computerized, but it's taking us time to catch up. I've only been the director here for six months, and wheels turn slowly. I knew of Raymond's family. Everyone in town knows them. His father is the mayor."

She was closer now. Even though he was dead, she could come closer to Raymond and make him tell her where Hayley's mother was.

"He wasn't exactly one of the kids in town who still spend August picking bacca," said Pat.

Delia blinked hard several times trying to decipher the unfamiliar term.

"Tobacco picking. The kids call it *picking bacca*. We don't say tobacco here, more like, *tobacca*. I should write a translation app for our part of the country and make a fortune," said Pat.

Delia felt something struggle to rise up out of the sludge of too much information in her brain. Tobacca. Bacca barn. Is that what Hayley had said? Not *in back of the barn,* but *bacca barn.* The kid was precise, and Delia had tried to alter her words without really listening. Had she been repeating what Raymond said? Bacca barns? That's where the naughty place was. That's where her mother was.

On the trip to Hartford, she and Ira had commented on the pastoral beauty of the tobacco barns that dotted the Connecticut Valley, where the specialized tobacco that was grown for cigar wrappers was still dried. The long barns seemed a thing of the past, like playing horseshoes, or women in long aprons.

"Maybe I'm connecting the dots where I shouldn't," said Delia. "It's a family trait. But Hayley said her mother tried to run away, and then that's when they took her away from her mother, and now her mother is in the bacca barn."

Pat lifted the remaining files off her lap and put them on the coffee table. "Well, Jesus Christ. There's only about a hundred tobacco barns in Tennessee, and now we're going for the industrial bunkers that aren't near as pretty. I think this all might be beyond our pay grade. It's a slim lead, but I'm with you connecting those dots. I'm on a first name basis with the police in Dalton. I'll call them when we're through here. Are we through?"

There had to be more. Her father had crossed the veil to tell her about Tennessee, the Tennessee spring lamb. It wasn't just a tobacco barn that she came here to find.

"I'd like to talk with Raymond's family. Can you give me

an introduction to them? I'm only here for one day. My flight leaves tomorrow morning," said Delia.

Pat projected a large presence until she stood up. She was shorter than Delia had imagined, probably not more than a few inches over five feet.

"I can try. They held the funeral a week ago. No matter if Raymond was running drugs or kidnapping small children, he was still their son, and I expect he was once a sweet little boy. That's who they buried, the sweet little boy. I'm going to count on you to remember that. The parents are shattered to the core."

"I understand. I wouldn't ask unless I thought it might save this child," said Delia.

Pat looked at Delia again, as if she was trying to look into her. "I'll walk out with you. Sitting is the curse of the twenty-first century."

On the sidewalk, Pat stretched her arms up. "Why in the world would a car rental company give you a red car? Who does that? Rental cars should blend into a gray or beige background of invisibility."

Delia patted the roof of the Ford Focus. "The Chinese regard red as the color of prosperity and good luck. Hayley and I need every bit of that. Thanks, Pat."

# CHAPTER 39

The Blanchard family lived in a house overlooking the town. Delia's mother would have predicted as much. One day while driving around Portland, her mother had said, "The ship captains, the company CEOs, and whoever is on top of the pecking order will always pick a location that is physically above the rest of us, a strategic holdover from the days when you had to have a clear sight of the enemy before they climbed over your walls." Her perspective was based on history and current political maneuverings.

The housing development looked less than ten years old, with three-car garages and lawns manicured by people who didn't live in the houses. The Blanchards brick and stone house perched on the highest edge of the cul-de-sac. But unlike every other house on the street, theirs was not festooned with pots of early fall chrysanthemums. Even before stepping out of the red Ford Focus rental car, Delia knew there would be a great room and that the view would look over the town, with the rolling hills as a backdrop.

She rang the doorbell, still unsure exactly where to start,

how to ask grieving parents to help her. Could she have helped anyone else after her parents were killed? John Blanchard had agreed to a brief meeting before he left for Nashville to pick up his wife, who had been with her mother since the funeral.

He'd been waiting for her. John opened the door. Delia was expecting someone different, rougher, meaner, someone who would try to shuffle her out the door after a few political non-statements. But as soon as he opened the door, she was struck by how unvarnished he was. Like Ben, or Ira. Just a man with dark circles beneath his eyes, chino pants that had recently become too large, and the unrelenting molecular fumes of grief.

"Delia? I'm John, come on in."

"Thank you for seeing me. I'm very sorry for your loss," she said, wishing she knew what else to say, but knowing that she had to address the power of death.

He led her into their kitchen. "Do you mind if we meet in here? Can I get you something to drink? Iced tea?"

He needed normalcy, and his upbringing cushioned him with its rules of hospitality.

"I'd welcome a glass of water."

After carefully placing a glass of water in front of her, he joined her at the end of the island counter.

"I promise to keep this short. I know the police have spoken to you. . . ."

"Several times," he said.

"I'm not concerned with the crime as such, but with finding the child's mother. The girl's name is Hayley. I've never done anything like this before, and I've worked in protective services for ten years. The girl is just five years old. She maintains that she was permitted to Skype with her mother, so I am convinced that the mother is out there and is being held against her will." Delia took a breath. "I didn't offer much of a lead-in and I apologize, but I know that you will understand a parent's agony in this situation."

Delia wondered if the man had eaten in the last few days. There was no lingering scent of food, no hint of reheated casseroles delivered by anguished friends. His digestive system must be on hiatus, unable to take in nourishment, sanded raw by the death of his son. She understood the terrain that he was thrust into; all the rest of life would seem miniscule, irrelevant.

"I will leave it to you to know how helpful my information will be to your case. I can only tell you about our son. Raymond."

What could she pick out that the police might have missed? She had to start somewhere. To the left of the kitchen island, a small ledge served as the family desk, where people kept track of grocery lists, and the weekly schedule. A framed photo of a young man looked out from a moment of hopefulness, a place that would never be the same again. Golden-haired, a hint of scorn around his mouth, the top edge of one side of his mouth rising up, but handsome, killer handsome. The kind of man that women with a few broken parts would flock to.

"What was one of the best parts of Raymond?" she said.

He squeezed his eyes shut for a moment. "No one has asked us anything about the good parts of him. I appreciate that, I truly do. If you are honestly asking, and not just trying to be polite in the face of my grief, I will tell you. He was a wonderful storyteller, right from the time he started school. He could spin a story that would keep you on the edge of your seat," he said. John cleared his throat. "He could make you believe anything, always the fantastical, over the top." He rubbed his fingers along the edge of the counter.

"The idea of day-to-day work, like most of us do, did not appeal to my son. It was like he wanted to show me that he could outdo me, although I must have told him hundreds of times that I didn't so much care what he did as long as it was good, meaningful work. I told him that he'd find the kind of work that would make him happy. My father never would have given me that kind of advice. He would have said happiness was for other people, not us. My father said we were meant to work hard. I wish I had given Raymond less and asked more of him." He rubbed his thumb into the palm of one hand. "Do you have children?"

Almost all parents asked her this. Did she belong to the parental club? Did she know how it felt to have her heart beat to bits with a cleaver like parents did?

"No, not yet. And I don't know if I ever will," she said.

He went on as if he hadn't heard her. "He worked a few years as a pharmaceutical rep, but he wasn't good at working for other people. Raymond had huge plans, first with the Internet, but if he couldn't be Steve Jobs, it wasn't enough for him. Then for the last two years, he told us he was going into business for himself."

Delia wished for an open window to let in fresh air. She felt the vibration of air conditioning, still necessary in Tennessee during September. The air that circulated throughout the house was heavy with death, filled with murmurings that their son would never come back. The back of her throat grew thick with the stale air of mourning.

Before she could ask anything else, John looked to the right, to the great room, as if he viewed their family diorama. "My wife said Raymond wanted to surpass me. We had bad years of locking horns back when he was a teenager, but what father and son don't? She said that I should have paid attention to what was going on, I should have asked questions about where the money was coming from in the last year. But he could be so defensive. If I questioned anything, he took it as criticism."

This man was on a search of every word, every glance from his dead son. "You may never find an answer that fits the tragedy, but I know you have to look. Do you have other children?" she said.

He looked back at Delia, seemingly surprised that he was speaking to another person, not just to himself. "No. Only Raymond."

"Did you ever meet Emma Gilbert, the woman who was with him when he died?"

"No. I told the police that I'd never heard of her before the . . ." He didn't have a word for the execution-style slaying of his son. And Emma Gilbert and the other man.

Raymond had been young, handsome, possibly manipulative, and driven to show his father that he was more important. There had to be more women. She was counting on the fact that Raymond would have used women. Would he have sacrificed them to his cause of empire-building?

"Did he have girlfriends, women he brought home to meet you?" she asked. The right question eluded her.

John took a breath and exhaled an unpleasant cloud tinged with the scent of someone who was sick. "Not for the last year." He looked down and examined one of his fingers, picking away a few flecks of blood from the closely bitten nails.

There it was, the way he looked down, avoiding her question. Finally something. "If I can't find Hayley's parents, she will be put into the foster care system. No one has reported this little girl missing, and she has given us every indication that her mother is being held against her will. If you know of someone who might have understood what was happening with your son, someone like a girlfriend, please tell me. A slim thread of information might be all I need to find her mother. Hayley wants to go home. Hayley and her parents still have a chance."

She could tell that he knew more. John had found a shred to hang onto, he had salvaged something from the wreckage of his son's death. But why should he tell Delia? He didn't know her. Their conversation would soon be over. She had to offer him a token, a sign that she wasn't only asking him to give her what she needed.

"My parents were killed in a house fire when I was nineteen. It is likely that my father set the fire. My sister was just thirteen at the time, and there is something that I've never told her about the fire, that I've never told anyone," said Delia.

John stopped picking at his fingers. She had pulled him back from the full weight of his son's murder. This man had gone through the agony of flying to the East Coast to identify and ultimately retrieve his son's body. There was nothing more horrible left for him. Delia did not want to believe that the human heart was designed for this much suffering. But what if it was?

"Recently my sister has been demanding details of the fire. I went into the burning house before the fire trucks arrived. I never told her that I heard my mother calling. She must have been trapped upstairs. She was yelling for my father. They were still alive, and . . ." Delia stopped, caught between two worlds: one of fire and the other of Raymond.

John's eyes cleared. He said, "And they died. No matter what you did, they died." He stood up, went to a cabinet, and pulled open the door. He pulled out another glass and filled it at the faucet.

"No matter what I tried to do, I couldn't bring Raymond back from his obsession with the big deal, striking it rich. But I never imagined he would enter the world of marketing heroin. Not in a million years," he said. He looked at the water in the glass as if he were seeing it for the first time. He took a long drink, nearly emptying the glass. Delia wondered if this was the first thing that he had ingested all day.

"Raymond did have a girlfriend, or she thought she was his girlfriend. She showed up here last week. She told me she'd been living on the streets in Nashville and somehow read about Raymond's funeral. I've been trying to help her; my wife doesn't know. No one does," he said.

Delia could almost taste the man's need to stay connected with his son.

"She's in a rehab center on the outskirts of Nashville. I agreed to pay her bill if she'd just stay, if I can visit her and when she's able, she can tell me about who our son had become. You know, did he talk about me? Was he angry with me?"

"Is she addicted to heroin?"

He nodded yes.

Delia couldn't threaten the tenuous lifeline that John gripped. "If I could talk with her, it might help me find the girl's mother. She might not know anything, but John, I don't have anything else to go on. I am lost. Would you help me? Please."

Now he could get back to familiar territory. He was the mayor, public servant. He had the power to say yes or no. Delia waited for him to gain equilibrium and prayed that he would make the decision in her favor.

"I could stop at the rehab center before I pick up my wife at her mother's house. You can follow me. I can't guarantee that Courtney will talk with you."

Delia could breathe again. "Thank you." The young woman had a name: Courtney.

"She doesn't always make sense. They're evaluating her for what they called dual diagnosis."

Addiction and mental disorders. Delia was back on familiar territory.

# CHAPTER 40

Mid-September in Tennessee felt like July in Portland. It was just as humid, except in Maine, the sodium chloride in the air combined with the water in the atmosphere and swirled above the land until a breeze started up farther north in Damariscotta and ran down the coast, pushed by the muscled shoulders of Canadian air, and took the whole murky mess out to sea. Then the ocean opened her throat and swallowed.

Here in Tennessee, the moisture built up and formed a bond with the blossoming cloud of carbon monoxide from Nashville and the highways that spiraled out from the city. The only thing that could carry away this blanket of dank air was a thunderstorm, maybe a tornado. Even so, the moisture would only rise again, pulled up by the heat, and start all over again.

It was four o'clock and Delia's blouse was wet under the arms, damp wherever it touched her skin.

Delia's picture of a drug rehab center was dashed by the upscale setting where John pulled up his black Jeep Wrangler. The façade of the two-story building was painted white brick, and the landscaping rivaled John's neighborhood. If he was paying for Courtney's treatment, his bank account was taking a big hit.

"They'll be eating dinner soon, and their schedule is not flexible. We only have a short time to talk with her. I wasn't expecting the traffic snarl-up."

John led the way into the rehab center, which was camouflaged as just another house on the outskirts of Nashville. The front door was huge. The thick metal door was made to look friendly yet secure, with decorative trim outlining an inner rectangle.

In her peripheral vision, she noticed a workman with a carpenter's belt strapped onto his waist, not worn and softened to his shape as Greg's was, but new and stiff. She turned to glance at him as his hammer swung from a leather loop. His shirt, the blue of shattered bird eggs in the spring, bore no soiled spots, no paint splatters. He didn't wear work boots, but running shoes, New Balance, with a large dark blue *N* covering the sides of his gray shoes. A baseball cap was pulled low over his eyes. Shouldn't he be careful with saws and hammers, the sharp rasp of metal tools on his vulnerable toes?

As John pulled open the front door, the workman turned away, picked up a crowbar, inserted the sloped end to a window frame, and thumped until one piece of wood screeched against old nails. He looked over his shoulder and said, "Rotten wood. It's best to get rid of it." If she had to guess, she'd say the workman was a recent graduate of the program.

Inside, John pressed a button on the wall to alert an attendant. Delia looked up; security cameras covered the front door. Delia picked up a pamphlet on a side table. *The Phoenix House, treatment center for addiction.*

"John, it's always good to see you. We weren't expecting you today. Are you here to see Courtney?" said a woman who appeared from the hallway. Her blond hair was pulled back in a tight ponytail, white blouse, sleeves rolled up to the elbows, wedding ring, black pants, shoes with a heel but the kind that wouldn't rub out a blister after walking three blocks. This woman could easily clean up for a fundraiser, blow-dry her hair, pull on a little black dress, and slip on shoes meant for show.

"Carolyn, this is Delia. She's visiting from out of town," he said.

He didn't say, *South Portland, where my son was murdered.* He didn't say, *We've come to ask Courtney to help us.* He didn't say, *Courtney is all this woman has, she's the last hope.*

Carolyn extended her hand. Delia's hand pulsed with heat. Carolyn's hand was cool and dry after a day in the air-conditioned climate of The Phoenix House.

"I'll let her know that you're here. She's just finishing with a group meeting. Her thinking is still compromised. We're working with her, though. Next week is the full clinical review to determine the least restrictive environment."

Delia understood a therapeutic bailout in progress. The treatment center was having a hard time handling Courtney for whatever reason, and they wanted to move her elsewhere. She wondered if John understood the clinical jargon.

The muscles along his jaw tightened. He understood.

"Please wait for her in the living room," she said, clicking open a door that led to the main portion of the house.

"May I use your bathroom?" asked Delia. She hadn't peed since she'd left Pat's office, hours ago.

Carolyn pointed the way. The bathroom revealed the lineage of the house before The Phoenix House bought it. Black and white tile on the floor, old pedestal sink, and a family bathtub that now held plastic shelving filled with cleaning supplies. She needed a moment alone before meeting her last hope.

By the time Delia returned to the living room, Courtney, all twenty-one years of her, twitched on the edge of one fat-armed chair. The couch and chairs were covered in sturdy tan canvas, the kind you could use to hoist a sail and catch the wind for a ship. They were on casters, mobile, able to be reconfigured at a moment's notice. Courtney's hip bones peered out from the rim of her low-rise jeans, the flesh around her belly button exposed and leading the charge. Brittle-limbed, she pulled one leg under her and flopped onto the seat of the chair.

John, now Courtney's confidant, or wanting to be, hung on to this perilous remnant of his dead son, this girl/woman. Raymond's companion, he had said. He rolled his chair closer to Courtney.

"Who's she?" said Courtney, tilting her head toward Delia.

This should be interesting. How would John introduce her?

"She's from Maine. She's trying to help the child who was found with Raymond."

A speck of light changed direction in Courtney's brown eyes. Withdrawal from heroin was one thing, but Delia sensed the presence of another medication announcing its ownership of Courtney's eyes and her skin. Suboxone? If Delia were to come closer, her overactive nose might detect the alteration in the blood and oxygen pumping erratically through Courtney's young body.

"I have a favor to ask you. Can she ask you a few questions?" he said.

"Did you bring me anything to eat? Did you forget what I need?" she said, turning her entire body to John.

"Oh. I forgot, I mean, I wasn't planning on coming today or I would have stopped to get them."

"I can't talk with her without them."

What could be so important to Courtney? What food would possibly induce her to respond to his request for a favor? But Delia knew that John would do anything to keep his link to Raymond alive.

He forced a smile. "Courtney likes a special kind of donut. . . ."

"Chocolate covered cake donuts," said Courtney, curling back into a corner of the chair, looking satisfied now that she was sure John would comply.

"I can run out and get them now," he said. To Delia, "The donut place isn't far from here, but Courtney is still required to stay within the house for the next two weeks." He jangled the car keys in his pocket and left.

No matter where Delia went, food was the carrier of comfort.

Just how muddled was Courtney's thinking? She was relieved that John was off on a mission; it would be easier without him here, having to buffer his grief.

"I'm looking for someone, and I'm hoping you can help me."

Courtney turned her head at an odd angle, more like a bird than a human. "Everyone is looking for someone."

The door to John's car thudded shut. How long would it take him to fetch donuts for Courtney?

"You knew Raymond, at least that's what John told me. Did you know Emma Gilbert too?" How much should Delia skip? She could ask her so many things, but the only thing she really wanted was the location of Hayley's mother. Or her name.

"Do you think I'm like Emma Gilbert? No, wrong again. Emma wouldn't have even been in this story if she hadn't poked her nose into my affairs with her goodie-goodie questions. 'I'm worried about you. Why are you so sleepy all the time? I care about you. I only have one sister and it's you, Courtney.'"

The police report said nothing about Emma Gilbert having a sister. They had spoken with her family in Florida. "She was your sister?"

"Big Brothers Big Sisters. Big college girl was assigned to me from on high," said Courtney. Her body stayed in a kind of small, erratic motion. Her torso rocked from side to side. She tapped one foot, then the other.

Delia remembered the language of metaphor from her father and no one spoke it more fluently than a person in the midst of delusional thinking. Or was Courtney being obscure on purpose?

"Did Emma know you when you were a kid? Did she visit you as part of the Big Brothers Big Sisters program?" Courtney was still so young; being a kid was not that long ago.

Courtney looked at the door. She nodded yes to Delia. "Emma wasn't like us."

How far away was the donut shop? "Like you and Raymond?"

She whipped her head around toward Delia. "Do you have a phone?"

Even someone as adept as Delia struggled to keep up with Courtney's pathways. Courtney popped out of her chair and sat down cross-legged next to Delia on the couch. "What do you have for music?"

Going on instinct, Delia handed over her phone to Courtney, who tapped her way through it until a torch song by Adele came on. Courtney rolled her eyes in disappointment. She set the phone against a stack of magazines while the song played.

"Listen to me," she hissed, testing the volume of her voice against the music. "I was Hayley's nanny." The music masked their conversation. Courtney didn't want anyone else to hear.

Delia turned to the girl, her heart pumping madly. "Go ahead."

"You understand that Hayley was the leverage, right? So, just think about it; leverage for what? Keep thinking. You know that her mother was being held in the naughty place? Raymond loved that name, The Naughty Place. But what about the father? What could the heroin business squeeze out of the father by holding his wife and daughter? Come on, I won't have time to tell you everything."

Delia took a chance and restated the obvious. "You know that Raymond is dead, that Emma is dead, along with some other guy?"

The twitch in Courtney started with her face, ran down her neck. "I only know about Emma and Raymond. There was no other guy. This is so messed up." She tugged at her hands, pulling from each wrist to the ends of her fingers. "Someone, or a couple of someones, are looking for that little girl. And I'll tell you why, and this might help you a little bit, more than a little bit if you're smart. Are you smart?"

"I'm trying, Courtney. I want to find Hayley's mother. Otherwise we have to put Hayley into the foster care system, and I don't want that to happen. And I'm very worried about Hayley's mother."

The girl's eyes were wide, frantic. "The police are looking for the carriers of the heroin pipeline. They might catch a few, they might slow it down on Tuesday only to have it surge on

Thursday. But really, once heroin slid along the granite covered kitchen islands of white America, the police should have called the game on account of not being able to win."

Courtney was sounding totally lucid. Why had she been acting so confused before?

"Ray, by the way, had everything given to him. But he was after some kind of financial superpower and he saw a road that looked almost too good to be true. And say he sets up someone like me, after he introduces me to his hand-picked oxy, and I advance to heroin in record time, and I'm the nanny to the little girl. I don't want to distract you with how I thought he loved me, because even I don't believe that now."

Courtney pounded her thin thighs with her fists and rocked back and forth. "Good girl, Hayley. Good girl. I'll take good care of you. Don't be afraid."

Courtney wasn't pretending. She dropped in and out of psychic pain like a swimmer, coming up for air only to have a wave crash over her and push her down.

"Aren't you glad that you can put all this into your little caseworker file? You only want to know where Hayley's mother is and you think that will fix everything."

"You're right, that is really what I care about. I'm not the police, I'm not your counselor. Courtney, please. Those two things. Where is her mother? What is her name?"

"Don't we care about the father? Look at Ray's father. He's . . ." Courtney swallowed hard. "He's sad. All the time. Not like Ray."

"Yes, okay, the father, the mother, the name. I know John is sad, but he's trying so hard to help you. Please, Courtney. John will be back soon and I think that you don't want to say any of this in front of him. Those donuts are on the way."

"I was the nanny," said Courtney, looking again at the door. "Let's see, the father could be a pharmacist. Nashville is the drop-off place from the link in Mexico. What could the father do that would need such extreme persuasion, like kidnapping his wife and child? What happens when you dabble a bit in something like opioids, say stretching out an OxyContin scrip for some of your friends who were cut off by their nervous doctors? The friends should know better but they can't imagine getting addicted to something that pours honey directly into their brains. Hang onto that thought. I didn't say this was going to be easy."

"I'm following you," said Delia.

"How is it that Emma had to show up right when we're ready to take Hayley and her mother, right at that exquisite moment? That was pure Emma, ever on guard for something she could fix. Raymond said, 'Who the hell is this?' and I said, 'She was my Big Sister.' And he said, 'We can't let her go; she'll tell someone.' And because, even if I am shooting heroin five times a day by then, I'm worried that Raymond might really hurt her, I say, 'Bring her with us. She can help us.'"

"Raymond used you to kidnap your employer and her daughter? And Emma interrupted the plan by coming to see how you were." One of the first things that Delia learned in graduate school was to restate what clients had said, first to acknowledge that she'd heard them and then to verify if she had understood them correctly.

"Yeah, that is basically what happened. You can't imagine how high I had been the night before, and Ray arranged it so that I wouldn't get another bag of heroin until Claire and Hayley were stashed in the van. And then Emma had to show up, with, her 'Hey, I'm so proud of you, I was just driving through visiting friends from college and thought I'd stop by. . . .' See, I had written to her ever since high school."

Oh, my God, Hayley's mother had a name. Delia kept her voice even. "Her mother's name is Claire."

"Emma whispered to me as we drove away with Hayley and her mother tucked in the third row seats of the van. 'Are you crazy?' She watched me shoot up and I told her about the oxy and the heroin, and she started to cry and I said, 'Why are you crying?' because it didn't seem that bad right then because heroin had become so essential like part of my blood. It still is. We drove all day and Emma was quiet as anything. That night, she said to me, 'You have to get help, right now. You've gone too far and you may not be able to swing back, but here's what you're going to do.'"

Any minute, John was going to pay for a bag of chocolate covered donuts, the kind that J Bird scoffed at. The clerk was going to put on plastic gloves, pick out the donuts, and put them in a white paper bag. He'd pay for them with cash, check his watch, maybe call his wife to say that the traffic was hell, he was going to be late, and then drive back to The Phoenix House.

"What did you do?"

"We were spending a few hours in a hospital parking lot so Ray could sleep. They let you park a van in some hospital parking lots and don't hassle you, that's what Ray said. All the doors were locked and Hayley was asleep. Claire wouldn't look at me and Ray told her not to speak. I did what Emma told me. I found another bag of heroin when Ray was asleep and I took a bigger hit than I've ever taken. Emma told me that the hospital had Narcan, they all do now, and that I wouldn't die because Narcan reverses the effects. She said that after the hospital took care of me, I had to go to the police and tell them about Raymond and Hayley and all of them."

"Emma told you to overdose?" Should Delia believe her? This was incredible. But what would she have done if she were Emma?

"She said Ray would dump me out at the hospital; she'd make him do that. I don't remember what happened, but I woke up in the hospital. After the Narcan, they released me. It was some hospital in Philly. I needed another hit. Someone like you wouldn't know how the brain screams for heroin, it's louder and stronger than any other voice. Five hundred times stronger. I hear it right now." She touched the side of her head with her pointer finger.

"You never called the police?"

Courtney rocked back and forth and hummed a dirge-like tune, repetitive and disturbing.

Delia took this as a no, the police were not called. "You kept doing heroin. How long ago did this happen? When did you and Ray take Claire and Hayley?" Delia pictured Courtney on the streets of Philly, doing whatever she needed to do to score a bag of heroin, making her way back to Nashville.

The sound of their names seemed to violate Courtney and make her cringe.

"It was cold in Philly. The shelters took me in at night, but in the day, I had to find someplace to be. Maybe March. Yeah, I think March."

A car door slammed and both women startled. "Where did he take Claire? And what is her last name? Hurry, Courtney."

"The bacca barn, I told you, the naughty place! That's all I know. He said he bought property and that it was perfect. He never loved me. He dumped me out like garbage, that's what they said in the hospital, not even in front of the ER. He left me in the parking lot under a lamppost." Courtney's eyes filled and her nose instantly began to run.

"Where is the bacca barn? Here in Tennessee?"

The front door opened. Courtney whispered, "Way past New York, that's what he said. It was a perfect place." She curled back into a corner of the couch and whimpered like a pup.

Footsteps. "What's going on in here?" said John. He glared at Delia. "What did you do? She's sick. This is a treatment center, not an interrogation room."

"I'm sorry. I didn't mean to upset her," said Delia. She turned off the torch songs of Adele from her phone and stood up.

"I think you should go," he said. John sat down on the couch next to Courtney. "Come on now. I've brought your favorites." He reached for a box of tissues on the side table and pulled out several, handing them to Courtney.

"Thank you, Courtney," said Delia. But Courtney was already tucked into the arm of her benefactor. Delia picked up her bag and left the room. In the entryway, the workman had unscrewed a light switch and wires poked out. How long had he been there? Had he heard the conversation or just the music from her phone?

"These older buildings need a lot of upkeep," he said, keeping his head down and pointing a screwdriver at the socket. His hands were pale and soft. He wore a kind of aftershave or cologne; if it had a color, Delia would have to say it was burgundy, the color of spilled wine ruining a new sweater. Heavy, cloying, and if a smell could be belligerent, this one had its fists up.

Delia left The Phoenix House and hurried to the safety of her red rental car, letting the thick air drape over her. She had a name! Hayley's mother had a name and it felt like music. But now Delia had to betray John and take away the tiny thread of connection to his son. Courtney had participated in a crime, kidnapping Claire and Hayley. She had to tell Mike, which would start the dominoes falling, one after the other, for Courtney.

She pictured police entering The Phoenix House, taking her away in handcuffs, the terror on Courtney's face, the skinny girl wedged between two cops, her mind vacillating between reality and the crumbling structure that Delia had just witnessed. One phone call would put it all into motion. She pulled her phone out of her bag and tapped the protective edge of it with her finger. John would stay with Courtney longer, she was sure of it. Once he saw how upset Courtney was he would call his wife again, beg for more time due to more traffic delays, and keep a comforting arm around Courtney. Delia could give them the benefit of a few more hours. She put the phone back on the passenger seat.

All the talk about donuts stirred rumblings from her belly. She hadn't eaten since morning and now the last rays of daylight slanted off the sides of the Phoenix House. She had to find something to eat on the way to the motel that she'd booked. The address to her motel was already entered into her phone GPS. She'd find something to eat along the way and then she'd make the call to Mike.

# CHAPTER 41

*Juniper*

As Juniper watched Ben drive away, her core turned molten, refusing to firm along her spine. If Delia sat beside her instead of Baxter, Juniper would turn the whole problem over to her, like she had so often done in the past. The six years between them felt generational when she'd been a teenager. But now at twenty-six couldn't she handle a crisis by herself at least for one day while Delia was out of state? Besides, she was worried about Delia.

How could Ben have slipped into addiction with pain meds? Street oxys, for God's sake. It wasn't like Juniper hadn't been around drugs before; the restaurant world was dusted with cocaine. She'd known more than a few restaurant owners whose successful businesses floundered while they were facedown in a pile of coke. But if you had a parent with schizophrenia, you didn't have the freedom to experiment. That's what Delia had drilled into her. "What if one street drug was all it took to derail our brains like Dad's? Don't ever do it, J Bird." Juniper had kept her drug sampling to a minimum.

Ben, their father's best and last friend, had been the rock, the one she could always turn to. He had swept in after the fire, making sure the girls were safely housed, attending all the events that warranted graduation gowns, always saying, "I'm so proud of you!"

Had she been too harsh with him? She knew enough about drugs to realize that Ben had to be the one to take the reins of this galloping addiction. She couldn't force him to do anything. But she wouldn't stand by and let him lose everything.

She could just text Delia. And say what? "Our super-uber stand-in dad is addicted to oxy and he's buying street drugs in front of the J Bird Café and I'm so terrified that I can't stop shaking. Love, J Bird."

No. Delia was transporting a child from Denver. She had enough on her hands and she'd be back soon enough. Her sister might even be past her maximum safe stress levels. When Delia wasn't available, she'd always gone to Ben. Now what? Should she say something to his colleagues at the vet practice? Was he no longer competent to take care of his furry patients? She had to give him more time to wrestle with this on his own. She'd given him an ultimatum and she would hold him to it.

Juniper wasn't due at the Bayside Bakery today. It was Monday, her day off, the slow day for restaurants and bakeries, if they were open at all.

Restless energy gripped her. Baxter sat in the passenger seat, offering his commiserating look, his head tipped to one side.

"Your answer for everything is a walk on the beach," she said.

The golden heard *walk* and *beach*, part of his essential lexicon, and joy returned to his world. He stood up in the seat, congratulating Juniper on her wise choice by wagging his tail and igniting his best retriever smile.

She drove from the parking lot of the convenience store, across town, and over the short expanse of Casco Bay Bridge, out to the edge of land in South Portland. Willard Beach was bracketed on either end by lighthouses, both stationed high on rocky promontories. Juniper knew every inch of the beach, was in tune with the rhythms of the high and low tides, but today she saw none of it. She threw sticks for Baxter like an automaton, and her thoughts whirled around Ben, who was sick and struggling and, from the looks of it, losing the fight. She couldn't lose another dad.

J Bird Café was three blocks from Willard Beach. After collecting a reluctant Baxter from his personal paradise, she toweled him off and drove to the café. There was more painting to be done and she could put in a day's work. Painting would help her think. Or not think, which might be better. Greg wouldn't be coming by until noon so she'd have a few hours to herself.

She started with the last unpainted wall, the one closest to the street. Everything was a hard gloss. "Easier to clean," she'd told Delia. That's why it felt good to be here. This was Juniper's world. This was the place where she was more than the little sister, more than the looked-after one.

Juniper had worked in cafés since her first year of college. She knew the best baking ovens, how to buy them used, where to get the best winter wheat, when to buy Canadian flour, and how to negotiate bulk items. She knew that the walls with high gloss paint stood up to the heavy traffic of a café and the constant moisture of baking.

She relaxed into the brush strokes around the door trim, edging it with a steady hand. Her favorite blue scarf held her hair in a wild pile on top of her head, a style that Delia called retro gypsy. She was safe here, amid the paint, the ovens, the new café tables and chairs, the wet dog by the back door. She opened the front door to freshen the air as she painted. The front bay window was still covered in brown paper, with declarations of the opening day drawn in bright red letters.

A car drove by so slowly that she at first thought the driver was lost, not unheard of in the curving streets of South Portland. A black car, four-door Nissan Maxima standing out like a Maserati against all the Subaru and Honda four-wheel drives and GMCs that muscled through the Maine winters. Before the man had even put one foot on the sidewalk, Baxter was at her side, then as the man approached, in front of her. The man stopped and smiled, looking at the dog.

"That must be Baxter," he said. "Delia told me about him. I'm Mike. And you must be Juniper."

Baxter trotted forward and sniffed the man's outstretched palm. Mike gave every indication that he knew about dogs, that he understood his access into the pack was allowed only with a formal greeting. Baxter put the guy's scent through his master snout and immediately relaxed so much that he found a discarded tennis ball next to the sidewalk and pushed it into Mike's hands.

He tossed it lightly into the backyard, and Baxter took off at full speed, returning it before Mike had finished wiping the ball goop off in the grass. "Sorry, boy. I'm working. I just stopped by to see if Delia was here. She and I are collaborating on an abandoned child situation." He took a few steps and extended his dog-scented hand to her paint-speckled hand.

This was the detective? Delia had failed to mention that a breeze could jostle the top hank of his deep brown hair, that dogs liked him, that his eyes lit up when he mentioned Delia's name. Of course, because her sister wouldn't have noticed. J Bird knew men, felt the warm edges of his palm that swallowed her hand, noticed the hair along his arm that emerged from the rolled-up sleeves of his shirt, the breadth of his shoulders. Why didn't Delia go for a guy like this?

"She's working today, traveling out of state, something about bringing a child from Denver, but she'll be back tomorrow," she said.

Mike stopped. His forehead furrowed. "Oh. I thought she was . . . never mind. Nice to meet you. Say hi to Greg. You're in good hands with him." He turned to go.

She understood what ingredients blended perfectly, how to keep butter at room temperature for most baking but ice cold for pie crusts, how to add a few flakes of Maldon Sea Salt to chocolate to heighten the experience, and how to torch the top of crème brûlée so that the sugars caramelized into a glassy brittle. Food was her finest expression of love, not unlike sex, yet longer lasting and more abundant. If she were going to purchase ingredients to enhance her sister, she'd buy a fifty-pound sack of Mike.

Baxter sat on the front step with the tennis ball between his jaws and watched Mike walk away. He gave a canine sigh of disappointment and dropped the ball.

"Wait a minute, Mike. Nice to meet you too. You can call me J Bird," she said. She reserved J Bird for family, boyfriends, and friends. The kind of people she wanted to keep in her life. He wouldn't know all that. It was too bad that Delia lacked mating instincts.

She needed to know one more thing about Mike. "I forgot to ask you something important. What's your favorite thing to eat?"

Mike looked at her across the roof of his car. "I'm sorry to say this, J Bird, but I'm a pasta man. Bread and pasta."

She knew it. "We're going to need a taster when we open. Delia's perfecting lemon pasta. She learned to make it in Italy." J Bird felt eerily like an Old World matchmaker selling the attributes of a young woman. But she knew men. Mike would remember this about Delia.

"You mean she makes the actual pasta? It doesn't come out of a box?" He smiled and put his hands over his heart. "Be still my heart."

J Bird put her hands on her hips, jutting one to the side. He was a tall man and even with the car between them, she saw the sturdy spread of his shoulders. "That's right. You'd be surprised what she can cook up." She knew when to stop, when a homeopathic dose of romantic promise was enough.

"I'm learning not to be surprised by Delia," he said. There it was, the thread of longing and attachment, the reference to the future. "And put my name on the list of pasta tasters," he said as he gave a wave. He ducked into the driver's seat.

J Bird turned around to walk back, until she heard the whir of his car window. "J Bird? Put me on the top of the list." For a woman who had to be dragged into online dating, Delia was attracting a lot of attention today.

The flirtatious encounter buoyed her mood. Watching Mike and Delia discover each other was going to be fun.

She resumed painting for another hour, putting the last touches on the doorframe to the back deck, lost in the details of opening the café, giving her time to think about Ben. Who did she know who could help him? She stopped in midthought, paintbrush held high. Tyler! He might be verging on weird old boyfriend behavior, but he was an ER doc. They saw addictions every day.

Juniper wrapped her paintbrush in a plastic bag and washed up in the new stainless steel kitchen sink. She did not want to be surprised about anything in Tyler's West Coast background so she tapped away at her phone, Googling the daylights out of Tyler Greene, MD. Their newly installed Wi-Fi connection opened up a window of reassuring employment references about Tyler. A photo of the young doctor at a fundraiser for a homeless shelter in San Jose. No news articles about stalking. She had to be able to trust him completely if she was going to pull Tyler into Ben's world. He wasn't right for Delia anymore, but she needed to know if she could depend on him with her next most important person.

She called his cell. "Tyler? Can I see you today? Yeah, it's J Bird. I need your fancy medical brain for something important. Can we find a time? Great. I'll meet you out in front of Bayside Bakery in Portland around noon."

Greg should be on hand for the last oven delivery and could also take care of the sign painter who would arrive later today. Had Greg arranged for the plumber to arrive today so the stove could get hooked up to the gas line? Was it too early to put in an order for cleaning supplies?

A car pulled into the small parking lot of Bayside Bakery in Portland with the bright cheerfulness of California license plates. Tyler. Juniper hadn't seen Tyler in his blue scrubs before.

Dark circles cupped his eyes. Exhaustion etched lines on either side of his face. Despite that, blue was a good color for him.

They settled onto a park bench that bordered the parking lot. Small birds, accustomed to a bounty of crumbs from baguettes and croissants, hopped by their feet in anticipation. She had not yet returned Baxter to his solitary confinement at home. Called to duty, the dog rose from a spot outside the bakery door and greeted Tyler with a hand sniff and settled in between the two people.

"What's up? Is there something wrong with you or Delia? I called her phone but she hasn't answered yet. I couldn't sleep last night and I'm going to have to pull a double today. Most days we don't really get a lunch break but I talked someone into covering for me."

"She's doing a quick transport of a child from Denver. I guess Ira has her doing the extreme stuff that no one else with full caseloads can handle. She's never had to do this before. That's all I know. The gasket on Delia's confidentiality jar never leaks. I learned never to press her for details about her work."

Tyler's shoulders drooped. Was Tyler the same handsome guy Juniper had had a secret childhood crush on, the guy her big sister dated back before their world blew up? Or had he changed, pushing Delia too hard, trying to please her in a manner that reeked of desperation, and generally acting like the kind of guy who'd earn the overbearing boyfriend badge? But the man in front of her right now was deflated and exhausted.

He pressed his hands together. They were scrubbed clean. The fingernails were clipped and filed to perfection. He covered his face and ran his fingers through his hair.

"Thanks, J Bird. I'm not doing so great today. I made a huge mistake and I don't know what to do. I know you want medical advice, but I've blown it with Delia, haven't I?"

This had to be her day for male mentoring. Baxter wedged his damp body closer to J Bird.

"When I first saw Delia at The Daily Grind, I couldn't believe it. I knew I'd probably run into her, but I didn't know it would feel like a collision with the past, and all of a sudden I was a kid again. I haven't felt that kind of sweetness since . . ." He paused. "Before the fire."

Since the fire? Were they talking about the fire or Delia? "I was only a kid. But you and Delia seemed so into each other. I always wondered what happened. Your family moved across the country, but that didn't have to end the relationship."

"No, but it made a perfect excuse. I couldn't live with what I had done. I couldn't face Delia."

A chill ran through her. "What? Did you cheat on her?"

Tyler wedged his elbows into his thighs and lowered his head into his hands. "No. I never would have cheated on her; there wasn't anyone like her." He lifted his head and looked puzzled. "Didn't she ever tell you?"

What the hell were they talking about? "Tell me what?"

"About the fire, that I tried to reach your dad, I could hear your mom. Delia was on the floor. A wall of fire shot up between the living room and your dad's office. I had to choose. . . ."

Tyler squeezed his eyes shut and pressed his lips together until they were a hard, flat line. When he opened his eyes, the bloodshot lines created a red and white mandala around his irises. "After that, I kept my head down, finished college, and tried to forget that I had ever lived here. I tried to forget Delia. Medical school and the training after it had a profound way of obliterating anything else. And then a homing beacon went off in me, like one of these blinking lighthouses. When I saw the job opening for emergency medicine in Portland, I wanted to come back. I wanted to rewrite the past," he said. Tyler stood up and rubbed his hands along the back of his neck. "I saw Delia. And you. And I got this idea that I could make it all better."

Baxter stood up and pressed his body against her thigh. What could she say to Tyler that would penetrate his guilt?

"I'm going to talk straight to you. I looked up to you when I was a kid and you were Delia's boyfriend. When you showed up here again, I was glad to see you. But then you started acting like a weird semistalker, asking Delia to check out houses with you, pick out furniture. And then you showed her a table that looked just like our table in our old house and freaked her out.

You've been back for a few weeks and in anyone's world, that is too fast."

Baxter's ears twitched.

Tyler raised his hands in surrender, palms out. "I know, I know. I feel like an idiot. We have to slow down, that's what I want to tell her."

"I don't think the both of you have to slow down. *You* have to slow down. And tell her what's going on with you, tell her why you left. It will be hard but you can do it," she said. Juniper didn't have a lot of experience giving advice to people who had once seemed older and wiser. She had left all psychological advice to Delia. But she had already run into one addiction calamity with Ben and one emotional superstorm with Tyler, and it wasn't even noon. She was in new territory.

She felt a sudden surge of compassion for this man, one more wounded survivor of the disaster that left two sisters orphaned. "She'll be home tomorrow, probably late," she said. "And I probably shouldn't be the one to tell you this, but I'm pretty sure Delia isn't going to be your girlfriend, all grown up. Not that Delia knows yet, but this is my area of expertise. I'm saving you from heartache. You saved Delia from being killed along with my parents. I'm grateful beyond belief. If I didn't have my sister, I don't know if I would have lasted. You couldn't save my parents and neither could she. Give yourself a break." She reached out and took his hand. "Thank you for saving my sister."

He wiped moisture from his eyes and looked at his watch. "You really are officially grown up, aren't you?" He patted her hand. "But you shouldn't speculate about Delia and me. Now that I've said all that about the fire out loud, it's still hideous, but we can't all be at blame. Can we?"

"No. If I could change anything, I'd wish my parents here, mental disorders included. But that's not the way it went down and here we are." Her voice trembled. Baxter lifted his head and looked up at J Bird. "But I have a problem brewing where you could really help."

He rearranged his body, shoulders pulled back, face relaxed.

This was Tyler the doctor, not the guilt-ridden, love-confused man of a few seconds ago.

"I have a family friend who is addicted to pain meds. You might remember him. Ben. He's a vet, a big hero in the animal community. He's addicted to opioids and he doesn't know where to turn. He had a knee surgery six months ago. He's advanced to street oxy and he's in a world of hurt."

"Send him to the ER and tell him to ask for me. It's what we do in emergency medicine. Plus all of the accidents and poor life choices related to alcohol."

He stood up.

Tyler smiled for the first time. "Finally something that's in my ballpark. I might finally be able to do something useful for you and Delia. I have to run."

She watched him jog back across the parking lot, lighter and more put together. The teenage Tyler had less of a stranglehold on him. But how would Delia take this? It was clear to Juniper that his interest in Delia had been driven by absolving his misplaced guilt. Delia could be crushed again.

# CHAPTER 42

How could she get lost with GPS? Wasn't the sky filled with satellites, circling the planet and beaming down directions to motels and restaurants? Delia wouldn't give Ira the satisfaction of knowing that she traveled without a paper map. At this very moment, his beloved road atlas sat idle on her kitchen counter in Portland. Despite GPS, she had circled the outskirts of Nashville in a misguided attempt to find her motel halfway between Dalton and the city.

A sack of fried chicken, coleslaw, and french fries sat on the nightstand near the bed of the Quality Inn. Not the kind of image she imagined for a soon-to-be baker for J Bird Café.

It was past nine o'clock. Delia had to override the misplaced sympathy for Courtney. Yes, she was broken. Yes, Ray had manipulated the daylights out of the girl. Yes, she was swamped with guilt. But Delia still had to turn her in. She tapped in Mike's number.

"Hello." He had a good voice. Solid, sure. His form of *hello* was a statement, not a question.

"It's Delia." She knew her name had come up on his phone. It was hard to say what she needed to tell him.

"I called your office and heard you were taking a sick day. Is this a mental health day or are you really sick? I'm wondering if you're okay. Are you?"

The hints of tenderness made her wince, caught in a lie.

"I found out some information. Hayley's mother's name is Claire. Her father could be a pharmacist," she said, letting the information rush out from the burst dam of her chest. "And the naughty place is a tobacco barn somewhere between New York and Connecticut or Massachusetts. That last part is more conjecture on my part. And Claire and Hayley were kidnapped sometime in March. Six months ago. And yes, Raymond was trying to build a heroin empire."

She was greeted by silence on the other end. "Wait a minute, I have to go into another room." She heard a door closing. "My daughter just went to bed. You gathered all of this from Hayley when you took your dog to visit? That's one incredible dog. Why didn't you call me right away?"

The smell of oil from the white KFC bag went from soothing to disgusting. Delia stood up and dropped the bag into the plastic-lined wastebasket. "I didn't get this from Hayley. I'm in Tennessee."

"This must be a bad connection. It sounded like you said Tennessee." Mike's voice dropped into a new layer of concern.

"I'm flying home early tomorrow morning; my flight leaves early but I won't be in Portland until early evening. I wasn't able to find a straight shot from Nashville to Boston on short notice. No direct flights," she said, still dancing around what she needed to tell him.

"Stop avoiding my questions and tell me what you're doing there. You told your boss that you needed a sick day and you told your sister that you were accompanying a minor on a flight from Denver. What's going on?"

Delia sat back on the bed and pressed her back against the headboard. "You talked to my sister? You don't even know my sister."

"I was driving past your café. It's not that far from Erica's house, which is under heavy surveillance. So I stopped and introduced myself to Juniper. I asked how you were feeling. She said I should call her J Bird."

The sooner that she told him, the better. He had easily uncovered her pitiful attempt at covering her tracks.

Her bare toes wiggled on the bed. "I followed a hunch that there was a reason for me to come to Tennessee. A feeling. Never mind, that part isn't important to understand. I talked to Raymond's father, John Blanchard."

"Delia, this is a police investigation that you are screwing with. Why did you talk with him? The state police in Tennessee talked with him already."

"Do you want me to tell you or not? Just listen and lecture me later."

"I'm making no promises about the lecture. Talk," he said.

"Raymond found someone to help him and it wasn't Emma Gilbert. It was a young woman named Courtney. She was Hayley's nanny. Lord only knows how anyone thought she'd be a good nanny, but she probably wasn't yet addicted to heroin when Claire hired her." She took a breath.

"And how do you know all this?"

"Because I talked to Courtney. She's in a treatment center. She's in bad shape, vacillating between being lucid and on the edge of a breakdown. The treatment center sounded ready to find a psychiatric setting for her. And they should," she said. Courtney had ignited a thread of compassion in Delia that she was wasn't sure Mike would understand. "I know the police will have to talk with her, but at least let her have one more day. Or tonight. John has become her benefactor. A friend. One last night of solace won't get us closer to Claire, I promise you that."

"This is not your decision. You are letting something other than the law influence you. If this is because she has a mental illness and your father had schizophrenia . . ."

His voice was urgent, reaching out to her. How had she let him get so close to her?

Was he right? Was she acting like a kid whose parents had just died, engaging in magical thinking that if only she could get something right, she'd have them back again? "Maybe you're right; you can't live with a schizophrenic father without bearing scars that influence everything. But this is different. Here's the important part. Courtney told me that Raymond had purchased property and that there was a tobacco barn on it. That's where the naughty place is. That's where Hayley's mother is."

"So we need to find out the real estate records for New York, Connecticut, and Massachusetts for the last year, and in particular, properties that had tobacco barns on them. It's nearly ten o'clock! I can't pry these records out tonight no matter how connected we all are to the Internet."

"One of Raymond's drop-off places was that library in West Hartford. Remember? The Lillian Tiger Library. Do you have a map in front of you? I left Ira's road atlas at home. Won't that kind of narrow it down if you follow a route that Raymond might have taken?"

"Delia, you don't have to tell me how to do my job. I'm on Google Maps right now. If Raymond has a property that he thought was perfect, it likely had to do with access to the main heroin highway. He was an idiot if he thought he'd make his way into this business. He must have had no idea that major crime organizations on the East Coast are jumping all over this. Or he had a giant ego and he thought he could be the smartest guy in the business. When are you coming home?"

This last question was different, less like the detective, more like a slipstream that Delia wanted to flow into.

"I fly into Boston around three tomorrow. I leave here super early. Last-minute flights only offer terrible connections."

"Call me in the morning. You know that Courtney committed a crime, whether she was addicted to heroin or not, whether she is mentally disabled now. She has to be arrested."

"I know. First thing in the morning."

"You didn't tell me what happened that was so important

that you decided to lie to your sister and Ira and fly to Tennessee," he said.

Could she tell him about her father's voice startling her in her sleep? "I'm not harboring police information. It wasn't like that. I promise. I'll tell you when I see you," she said. And she truly wanted to see him.

# CHAPTER 43

Delia might have slept during the worst hours of night, between two and four a.m. Those were the hours when the mind perseverated, running in loops of calamity. But by four thirty she was wide awake. She prayed that the powers of a hot shower would revive her for the drive to the airport.

The steam from the shower curled her hair. She hadn't brought much in the line of toiletries, only body lotion, toothbrush, and toothpaste. The sliver of generic soap sealed in a plastic wrapper did its job. She kept the bathroom door open, not wanting to be surprised by a knife-wielding intruder, a holdover precaution from her father when they traveled as a family. Wasn't that why she had pushed the heavy lounge chair against the door and wedged it under the door handle? Would that truly stop an intruder?

The motel room was equipped with a single serve coffeemaker. Was she doomed to be followed by the plastic version of coffeemakers? She refused the packet of powdered nondairy substance. The watery brew would hold her until she got back on the highway, past town, and stopped at a convenience store for coffee. She remembered passing a store about ten miles out-side of town, the kind that opened early and closed late. The airport was an easy one hour drive.

She stepped into a clean skirt, a pair of slip-on shoes for easy driving and airport security, and a black, long-sleeved T-shirt. By seven a.m., she pulled the heavy chair away from the door, grabbed her small backpack, tossed the key next to the coffee-maker, and opened the door. Her rental car was parked right outside her door. The gray light of morning heralded hope and another link to Hayley's family. In eight hours she'd be home, munching on whatever delectable goodie J Bird experimented with that morning.

She wasn't the only early riser from the motel. The lights were on in number six. An older Volvo sat outside their door. True travelers hit the road early.

Delia settled into her car and decided to leave Mike another message. She knew that he'd want to know that she was leaving for the airport. The call went to voice mail. He had to be in the shower; it was the only time he didn't answer, or the only time Delia knew about. An image unbidden by her conscious mind saw a soaped-up Mike, with water cascading over his shoulders.

"Hi, Mike. It's Delia, and I'm just leaving my motel and head-ing for the airport. The place where Courtney is in treatment is called The Phoenix House in Nashville. They are going to need an immediate psych assessment for her. And they'll want to talk with Raymond's father, too. He was paying for Courtney's treat-ment. He said his wife didn't know anything about it. Give me a call when you get out of the shower. I mean, I just guessed that you were in the shower."

She set the cell phone on the seat next to her and pulled out of the parking lot. She had a huge backlog of phone and text messages that she would get to later. J Bird would have already walked Baxter by now and set multiple trays of muffins cooling on the racks at the Bayside Bakery. Ira and his wife would be in their kitchen, sipping coffee before their day started. What would Tyler be up to? He would have escorted his landlord's dog outdoors; there was no getting away from the morning needs of a dog. Would he be thinking about Delia at all or would he already be in doctor mode, assessing broken bodies, stethoscope draped around his neck? It would be time to have an honest talk with him when she returned, and she didn't look forward to it. Hayley would be getting dressed for kindergarten, watching Erica pack her lunch, with Louie rubbing against her legs. The detective was apparently still in the shower. Was he a thirty minute shower kind of guy? She turned on the radio and set it to search for a news station.

Delia looked up from her radio, and her rearview mirror was filled with the front end of a Volvo, a tank of a car. Was this the same car from her motel? Volvos were the cars that middle-aged women and parents of teenagers chose, saying, "I feel so safe in them." Of course they were safer in the lumbering Volvos; she guessed they were second only to a Hummer in damage inflicted on other vehicles.

Someone was tailgating her, a guy with sunglasses, not a middle-aged woman at all. If he was late for work, why didn't he pass her? The speedometer read forty miles per hour. She had been daydreaming, projecting herself into the near future of home in Portland, and missed the sign that said speed limit fifty. She was dawdling and she needed to pay attention. She accelerated to fifty, then a cavalier fifty-five.

The space between her and the car behind her opened up, but a slice of electricity rankled the back of her neck. She was several miles from town and from the convenience store, an in-between land governed by thick groves of trees and no houses. Her eyes flicked from the road in front of her to the car in her rearview mirror. She reached for her cell, looking down long enough to hit the little phone icon on her screen.

The scream of metal on metal, or metal on fiberglass, filled her ears. She was thrown forward, straining against the seat belt. The phone leapt from her hands. Just as quickly, the back of her head ricocheted against the headrest. He had rear-ended her on purpose. Either that or he was texting his sweetie. Should she keep driving until she got to the store? She looked in the mirror again and saw that he had one palm against his cheek in a look of "Oh, no." Delia pulled over and so did the idiot behind her.

The jolt of the impact rang throughout her body with a full-out release of adrenaline. Two nights of little sleep, compounded by the shock of the crash, left her dazed. Her hands shook as she opened the door and stepped out. The sun crested the hill and morning birds ruffled through the trees. Waves of warm air already flowed over the blacktop. The man in the Volvo walking toward her held his palms out in the *whoops, I'm so sorry* position. He wore a jacket, which would be too hot for a day like this. Something about the way he moved was familiar, but how could it be?

She thought, *I want to get back in my car now. I should get back in my car and lock the doors and call 911.* But she didn't. Not even when she detected a scent of cologne that pounded at her memory. Lack of sleep and the shock of the collision jumbled her thoughts.

"Hey, sorry about that, dude. I was texting. Let's take a look at the damage and we can settle up with insurance," he said. He must be on his way to work. But wasn't that the same car from the motel?

He was in his twenties, dark hair short and combed forward, culminating in a peak in the center, a blue shirt with a collar and a little green alligator on the pocket. He took off his sunglasses. His mouth pulled into a smile but his eyes darted down the road from where they had just driven and ahead. Then he bent slightly to look at the damage, so Delia approached the rear of her car also. She leaned forward, her center of gravity pulling in front of her, and she saw his shoes. Gray New Balance running shoes with a big blue N on the side. She recognized him: the carpenter from The Phoenix House.

He grabbed her around the neck. He was thin with tight, metallic muscles.

"Delia, don't you know you shouldn't stop on strange country roads?" He threw her against the back of her car and pressed hard against her. She felt the beating of his heart on her back.

Her body exploded, kicking, moving any part that wasn't

gripped by his arm. "Get off me, you asshole!" If ever there was a time for profanity, it was now. Why did he know her name? Had Courtney talked to him? She smelled a spicy deodorant scent coming from him, ripe with his own sweat. This was a man who showered and put on deodorant before ramming into a woman's car. And over all that was the cologne, dark and cloying, the color of burgundy, fists up. All of her senses came back on line.

"We want you off our backs, and I have the green light to choose how to take care of you." He bent one knee and pressed it hard into her back, pressing most of the air out of her lungs. "You never should have talked to Courtney." Delia felt him reach into his jacket pocket. With his elbow, he bent her head to one side with crushing power.

He paused and pressed his cheek against her neck. "I wasn't like this before," he whispered. Could she possibly keep him talking? Surely another car would come along this road.

His iron grip loosened minutely and Delia was sure that the universe was going to tilt in her direction again, that he would release her, jump in his car, and she'd never see him again, that the goodness in people would prevail and she would get back in her car and drive away. Her life in Portland was only inches beyond her reach. She could hear the gulls along the port on Commercial Street, taste the salt air on the back of throat.

"But that was before Ray started up such a nice business for us to take over. Little boys shouldn't try to play with the big boys, and Ray was a little boy," he said. He tapped the side of her neck hard with his finger and her jugular vein throbbed. "You might just like this. So many people do." He pulled his hand out of his jacket pocket and from one eye, she saw the syringe. She vaulted into overdrive, struggling wildly, the way a cat wiggles when it is picked up against its will, twisting in all directions with the hope that one of the moves will secure her release.

"No! Help me! Don't do this. Whoever you were before is still you," she cried.

He pressed against her harder. "That's a nice idea but you

can't stop business. Heroin rules us and now it's going to rule you. Meet the king," he said, kissing her neck, running the tip of his tongue from her ear to her collarbone. He slid the needle into her neck.

Warm syrup washed through her torso, loosening her legs, the tight muscles along her arms, and her jaw. The syrup stormed into her stomach and she felt seasick, unbalanced and ready to vomit.

His arms softened. "There you go. It won't be so bad. I promise," he said.

The honey of his voice covered her in warmth. The goodness in him had prevailed and everything was going to be okay. Was she falling? If she was, she was falling from a higher place, floating like a leaf. An immense weight lifted from her body and her mind. The relief was unlike anything she had ever experienced. She floated down and away from the weight of her father, J Bird, all the children marching through foster care, and the last child, Hayley.

He held her as her knees melted.

"You only get one first time. I envy you, Delia. That was a mighty hit," he said, letting her sink to the ground. He propped her up against the back wheel. How kind of him. She turned her head and the smell of asphalt and wet grass braided into a ribbon, flapping in the air. He walked back to his car, opened the door, and reached in. The back of her head flopped against the wheel. She thought of Baxter and how the dog could sniff anyone and tell where they'd been, their mood, and what they had for breakfast. She thought of J Bird and her retro gypsy hairdo when she baked. Would her parents have liked Mike? She was sure of it.

His car door slammed. His body blocked the morning sun as he stood over her.

"It looks like you are going to need one more hit, so enjoy your moment," he said. He bent over and pulled her away from the car, put his hands under her armpits, and dragged her to the front of her car.

Her head rolled against his shoulder. What was so familiar

about him, the way he hesitated, something about his lack of attachment to earth? Of course. "You're looking for your family too, like me," she said. Her words sounded thick, nearly incomprehensible. Her shoes fell off as he pulled her along. She understood the world of searching for families, her own, Hayley's. Oh, Hayley. Louie the cat would be walking her down the stairs now, ready for school.

He stopped. "What did you say?"

She smiled. "Your family, you want to find them. We all do," she said, her words slurring.

He folded her into the driver's seat. "They don't want me," he said.

This seemed incredible that his family wouldn't want him. Yet she had seen this again and again, and it was far sadder than losing the ones who loved you. She'd have to tell J Bird how lucky they had been, how loved.

She heard a car approaching and at the same time a beautiful ringing sound pealed from under the seat. It was her phone.

"Shit!" He pushed her head back on the seat and injected her again. He was so close to her face. He was afraid, she could smell it pulsing off him. And then she fell through space, toppling head over heels, bumping gently into clouds until she was gone.

# CHAPTER 44

Delia was hunched over the steering wheel, her forehead pressed against the black molded plastic. Had she pulled to the side of the road and fallen asleep? If so, she hadn't done a very good job of pulling over. The front end of her car was nosed into a thicket of bushes. She turned her head toward the side window; she had to be thirty feet from the road.

"Delia, we've just administered Narcan. I hope to God that this syringe we found on your car seat was really heroin."

Delia's vision pulled back together, turning fragmented pixels into a face. Two faces. Pat from Dalton. The man behind her was a cop. What was going on?

"Did I have an accident? Wait a minute." Delia sat up straighter. A dull pain traveled along her neck as she turned to the left. Why wasn't she thinking more clearly? It was as if she couldn't quite wake up. Had she hit a deer and swerved off the road? She touched her neck and flecks of dried blood stuck to her right hand. She tilted the visor down, slid the cover off the mirror, and tilted her head to look at her neck. A needle mark, and a bruise blossomed. And something extra was pulsing through her body, a wanting, a demanding visitor, hammering in her throat.

"There was a man who rear-ended my car. I got out to see the damage and when I looked he grabbed me." Delia looked down; she didn't have her seat belt on. She was a zealous seat belt wearer. She swung her legs out. Pain shot out and traveled up from her heels and feet. Where were her shoes? She reached down and felt one foot. It was streaked with blood; bits of asphalt and pebbles were stuck in the open grooves. The backs of her feet were raw. She had been in an accident? People often had amnesia about the actual impact and the time prior to the accident. Retrograde amnesia. Her heart thumped faster and her hands shook.

"Ma'am, I'd like you to stay seated for a few more minutes. There's an ambulance on the way," said the uniformed officer. "And please don't touch anything else in your car."

"Like what? Don't touch what?" Delia tried to remember. It was early morning but the air was warm and humid. Tennessee, she was still in Tennessee. A loud peel rang out, the cry of a raptor, likely a hawk. She looked up and a hawk sat on a telephone pole. The bird turned his head to one side and peered down at her with one eye.

The cop wore blue plastic gloves. He pointed to the passenger seat. "Like that," he said. On the seat was her purse, a hypodermic needle, and a small packet of white powder.

She wanted her brain back again and it was apparently MIA. A sound entered her skull, rolling through it, reverberating around the rounded bones, not unlike the warning cry of a hawk or crow. What was it? It was getting louder and louder, which meant it was coming closer. It was a siren. Police, fire, or ambulance. The good guys. But these good guys only arrived when something terrible happened.

Pat put her hand on Delia's shoulder. "Honey, I was on my way to work and I saw this little red car. Well, I wasn't sure it was your car, but I stopped when I saw a guy peeling out and your car rolling into the bushes. I called 911 and these guys were close by. Look, I don't know what happened or why, but we almost lost you. They just started carrying Narcan a few months ago. You were pulled back from the brink."

She had to stand up; she had to move.

"Hold on a minute, let me take your arm. You look all wobbly," said Pat, giving a stop hand signal to the cop. "You're going to need your shoes. There's a bit of everything along these shoulders, but mostly broken glass."

"Excuse me, Pat," said the officer, "but the shoes are evidence. Don't touch them."

Evidence? What the hell was going on?

"Stay here for a minute and I'll bring you my best flip-flops, purchased for the gym that I never go to," said Pat.

Delia slid her feet into plastic thongs that were too short, but they kept her feet from further damage. With Pat holding along one elbow, she walked to the back of the car. Yes, another car had rear-ended her. Her brain sloshed in liquid waves, forcing her to lean her entire upper body against the rear of the car. Not an unpleasant sensation at all. It felt like the car shared some its solar gain and nestled against her. She could sleep here like this, her face pressed against the warm rental car. Oh, no, the guy with the New Balance shoes, the workman from The Phoenix House. Chunks of memory danced together. She had to tell the police now, there was no turning back. What if he tried to harm Courtney? What if he already had?

Pat put her hand on Delia's arm. "Here's your phone. It was ringing like crazy when I stopped. After I called 911, I answered your phone. Seems like your friend, Mike Moretti, is ready for his head to explode. I like a man who can curse, and your guy is among the top contenders. If I understood him correctly, he's going to rearrange particular body parts of whoever did this to you."

She wished Mike were here with her right now. Why did the clarifying moments in life veer toward the disastrous? Nothing could be clearer to her; Delia wanted to stretch out her arms from this highway in Tennessee and connect with Mike. She pictured a difficult talk with Tyler, squashing his strange assumptions about them getting back together.

Her thinking was buckling back into a cohesive chronology. She pushed off the side of the car. "Officer, I need to talk to you about a case in Maine. But first, there is a woman at a treatment center in Nashville who is in danger right now. It's called The Phoenix House. The man who hit my car and attacked me works there. He's part of a heroin trafficking system."

Four things happened at once. The young cop looked questioningly at Pat, Delia's phone rang again, Pat tossed the phone to Delia, and she shouted at the cop, "Did you hear the woman? Call Nashville and get someone to The Phoenix House!"

Responding as if his high school principal had just reprimanded him, he turned away and called in the request. Graduate degrees and compassion were not the only reasons that Pat ran the department. The woman could run a Marine boot camp with that voice.

Delia looked down at the screen of her phone. It was Mike's personal line. "I'm okay," she said. "Please just talk to me a little before you start telling me about interfering with police business. Talk to me about the Dalai Lama, or Igor the Rabbit, or anything. I want to hear your voice."

The pause was long enough that she wondered if he had heard her. The breath that she had been holding caught in her throat and couldn't find its way out. "Come home, Delia. Give the local cops everything they need, then come home."

A whoosh of breath escaped. "I should have told you everything last night." Pat said Mike was furious. She waited for the barrage of recriminations. Surely she deserved it. What if Courtney was hurt by the man who had just assaulted her? Or what if he sent someone like him to the Phoenix House?

"Come home, Delia," he said, softer this time. "Is there an officer there? I want to talk to him."

# CHAPTER 45

Shirley was out for her afternoon walk in Southwick, Massachusetts, with her rambunctious young dog, Chelsea. Her daughter told her that according to the Internet, no one named girls Shirley anymore, just in case she was wondering. "It's gone out of fashion," said her daughter on one of their weekly phone calls. "You're the last of your kind." So Shirley was careful to name her dog, a rascal of a labradoodle with a champagne-colored coat, a contemporary name that would have lasting power.

But how contemporary could she hope to remain? She was seventy-five this October and had arthritis in all her joints. Exercise was the best thing for arthritis, plus yoga and a cortisone shot every few months. Chelsea was her ultimate physical therapist, enticing Shirley out for walks across fields, up the steep trails, and along the dirt roads of rural Massachusetts.

Chelsea had been on edge for days, scratching at the door to go out all hours of the day and night, delivering her lead to Shirley. The usual local walks did not satisfy Chelsea's sudden canine angst. The walk along Southwick's Congamond

Lakes had always been Chelsea's favorite, with opportunities for swimming and stick fetching. Not this week. After a long walk along the lake, Chelsea had balked at getting back in the car. What was wrong with that dog? Her regular hike along the M&M Trail that ran from Connecticut right into Massachusetts proved disappointing as well.

In order to keep peace, Shirley picked a new place to walk, the Huddleston farm that sold six months ago. She was sure that the new owners hadn't moved in yet, and being on the zoning board, she tried to keep tabs on every new person who moved to Southwick. She hoped this wasn't a new owner who wanted to break up the farm and build a flotilla of houses.

The farm bordered conservation land, and she could get double her money by walking the periphery of the old tobacco fields and the protected land. Maybe that would satisfy her energetic dog.

She parked along the side of the dirt road that bordered the old farm. No one liked seeing the old farms sold. But what could you do?

Shirley opened the back door for Chelsea, and the dog sprang past her, knocking the woman to the ground. From her position on her back, she looked up at the sky. Was anything broken? If so, it could be a long time before anyone came by. She pushed up on one arm. No, nothing broken. But maybe her daughter was right; Chelsea was too much dog for a woman her age. She should have picked out a smaller dog, a basset hound with their absurdly short legs. They didn't need so much walking.

She stood up, shaking the dirt off her backside. A flash of her cream-colored dog streaked across the field and headed for one of the old tobacco barns like a missile. She grabbed the dog's blue lead from the front seat and swore she was taking Chelsea back to dog training school.

By the time she made it to the elongated tobacco barn, Chelsea ran to greet her, determinedly staying out of reach, then ran back to the barn door, throwing her front paws at the door and whining. Then the dog backed up and barked.

Shirley had had dogs all her life and knew the difference between a bark of alarm and a bark of excited happiness. On a scale of one to ten, Chelsea's bark was a ten on the alarm scale. Still, this was someone else's property, and she had never broken into another's person house or barn before. The dog launched her body at the old barn door again, dragged her claws, digging at it.

"Okay, girl, I guess you're either going to break down the door or I'm going to open it for you." Shirley lifted the long plank set in iron *u*-shaped hooks. She pulled one door open. Chelsea tore into the long barn, barking, heralding an announcement.

There wasn't much to a tobacco barn. They were large, long rectangles, made to hang and dry tobacco. And here in Southwick, they grew a special leaf variety used to wrap cigars. Or they did in the days when cigar smoking was a sign of prestige. The cigar market had crashed. The sides of the barn were adjustable so that they could be opened to let in air when the weather was nice and dry. Shirley had seen enough of them over her time, growing up in Southwick. Her husband had picked tobacco when he was in high school. Stripes of light hit the dirt floor, and Chelsea kicked up a dust storm as she ran to the back of the barn.

Shirley squinted while her eyes grew accustomed to the interior light, and followed Chelsea. Someone had built a shed right in the barn. Must have been the new owner because it was new wood, full sheets of plywood with enough resin left in the sheets to give off the scent of pitch. Her nose twitched at a sewage smell. The new owners had a backed-up septic system from the smell of it.

There must have been something precious in the shed; the door had a padlock on it. And they'd even poured a section of concrete to set the whole shed on. Looked to be ten by eight. Not a very good job of it; the concrete extended past the perimeter of the shed and the edges were sloppy, not squared off like they should have been.

Chelsea barked as if the sky were falling in, scratching at the door.

"Chelsea, the door is locked! Whatever is in there will have to stay there. Now, come on! Heel!"

In a massive display of frustration, the dog complied, trotting to Shirley's left side. But her ears were as agitated as Shirley had ever seen them, as if she was listening to something from the shed. Then she heard it too. A guttural moan and a scraping along one wall. Oh, no, someone had locked an animal in the shed and left it behind.

Another moan, this one louder, clearly human. Shirley pressed her ear to the wood. Shirley knocked on the plywood door. "Hello. Is anyone in there?"

"Help me, please help me," said a whispered voice from the shed. Deep, rasping.

"Oh, dear God!" said Shirley, staggering back. "The door has a padlock on it," she shouted. "I'm calling for help."

She pulled her cell phone out of her pocket. Her daughter had insisted that she take the phone with her on the daily jaunts for fear that her mother would end up in a ravine, unable to call for help. She punched in 911. "There is someone trapped in a shed in one of Huddleston's tobacco barns. No, I don't know how long. From the sounds of it, we're going to need an ambulance."

She should wait for the police and ambulance. Southwick was spread out amid old farms. The police could take up to twenty minutes. Shirley looked around for a tool, anything to dislodge the padlock. Her phone had a flashlight app, and she turned it on and shined it at the far corners of the barn, looking for anything that might have been left behind. In the far corner, her flashlight caught the outline of a wood splitting maul, likely left behind by the Huddleston family, back when they spilt and stacked wood and sold it in the spring. The head of it was rusted, but sharp as an axe on one side and thick as a sledgehammer on the other. The long handle was wood, not fiberglass like the new ones. This would do.

Shirley went straight for the padlock and after a dozen blows, each one vibrating down her arms until she feared her bones would shatter, the padlock gave up its job. She dropped the maul. "I'm coming in, I've got a dog with me," as if anybody within half a mile hadn't heard the dog barking or the crashing thud of the maul.

She pulled open the door. "Oh, no." A woman lay on a wooden pallet covered by vinyl pillows that used to be part of someone's lawn furniture. Her handcuffed arm was attached to a metal pipe anchored into the wall. On one side of her was a white five-gallon bucket, a slop bucket from the smell of it, and on the other were the remains of a case of bottled water and a half dozen Luna Bar wrappers. Her eyes were huge and dark, like the pictures of prisoners of war. Her skin pulled tight across her face. Her fingers on both hands were bloodied. The woman had tried to dig her way out, scratching at the unyielding plywood.

"My daughter . . . help me," she said, croaking out the words, unable to even sit up.

# CHAPTER 46

The airplane bumped to a landing in Boston.

While Delia at first tried to persuade Pat that she didn't have to accompany her back to Boston, she was secretly relieved that Pat rebuked all of her rationale. Her initial protests about Pat traveling with her had been weak. "I'll just sit on the plane and when I get to Boston, I'll pick up my car and drive home."

Throughout the protest, Pat looked unimpressed. "I might be inclined to believe you except Detective Mike made me promise to accompany you, and he said not to tell you that it was his idea. But there is only so much deception that I swallow in one day."

Her stomach still curdled from not only the heroin, but also the Narcan. It wasn't only the infusion of chemicals, but the shock of the assault. After working with traumatized children and parents, she knew the effects of the attack could topple her without warning, even if she denied it to Pat and Mike. The airport was an easy one hour drive.

"The doctor said it would be better if you took it easy. It's hard to know what the effects of heroin can be. He said in rare instances, breathing can stop even after Narcan. So I'm coming with you," said Pat, in her final, steely argument.

Delia was split between gratitude for Pat's kindness and the need to see herself as she had been before the attack. The ease with which the man had upended her life and made her a victim of a crime was disorienting. She struggled against the feeling that the man made her less than she had been before.

Delia didn't like being the one who needed help. It was uncomfortable, like putting on clothing that didn't fit, studded with prickly thorns.

When the plane touched down, Delia's phone dinged with a text from Mike. "Look for me. We'll meet you outside security."

Mike and Ira were meeting them at the airport. Delia insisted that she could drive her own car, thank you. Then Pat said she was fully capable of driving Delia's car back to Portland. In the end, the two women gave in to Mike's insistence and somehow Ira was now included.

"I've never been this far east," said Pat, looking out the small airplane window. "You wouldn't know it by my cosmopolitan airs, but I haven't traveled all that much." She reached across the empty seat between them and patted Delia's hand. "I can't wait to meet your Mike. I have the unique ability to read boyfriend potential at first glance. Not for myself, mind you, but my girlfriends use me as a litmus test all the time."

All of Delia's clothing, including her luggage, remained with the police in Tennessee. Pat, who was a good four inches shorter than Delia, provided black pants, underwear, and a tunic top a few sizes too big. The pants came to an ungainly high water mark, so Delia rolled them up to just below her knees, which wasn't all that much of an improvement. J Bird recently told her that the tunic look was so over, a fashion critique that she did not share with Pat.

She couldn't imagine what she looked like: pants rolled up like clamdiggers, Pat's floppy tunic, plastic thongs, hair pulled back in a ponytail. Her sensitive nose was sure that her body odor, laced with fear and adrenaline, formed a pulsing, three-foot perimeter around her.

They filed out of the plane and followed the signs to the passenger exit. "If Mike hits the gong with my boyfriend radar, I'm going to use a code word," said Pat as they followed the herd of passengers through the corridors. "What's a special word for you that Mike won't know?"

"Spring lamb," said Delia.

"Like the kind you eat rare or the Disney kind?" Pat pulled a small carry-on suitcase.

"It's too complicated to explain. Let's just say it has to do with my father when he was a food columnist," said Delia. A flicker of panic gripped her stomach. What would Mike say to her?

Immediately outside the cordoned-off area for ticketed passengers, Mike and Ira stood at alert, like African meerkats on sentry duty, scanning the area for predators.

"There they are," whispered Delia, nudging Pat's elbow with her own.

"Which one is Mike?"

"Not the one with the mustache; that's my boss. I can't believe Ira drove all this way with Mike."

As they emerged into the general area where lovers and family waited to greet the arrivals, Delia pushed the panic down, where it cowered in her lower gut. She was safe here. No one was going to stab her with a hypodermic needle; no one was going to ram her car. Although she was less sure of the latter, knowing that they would be headed into Boston traffic.

Ira pushed his way through a parade of baby carriages and pulled her into a hug. "What were you thinking? This isn't part of your job. This was insane! If you weren't resigning, I'd fire you right now!"

"Hello, Ira. Nice to see you too," said Delia. They were not customarily huggers, and she wiggled out of his anxious hold.

Delia turned and looked at Mike as a river of passengers passed between them. When she saw an opening, she crossed over.

"Come here," he said softly.

Somewhere in her absence, they had skipped a step. When she left Portland, Mike was still the detective, a handsome detective with a good sense of humor who was good with kids. But he was still the detective. In the twenty-four hours of her escapade in Tennessee, they had crossed over, and they both knew it. He exhaled as he wrapped his arms around her, a tremor running through him, the stale accumulation of adrenaline. With her head tucked neatly beneath his jaw, she didn't want him to let go.

"Excuse me, gentlemen, but I'm Pat Garvey, chaperone and director of Family Services in Dalton, Tennessee."

Delia jumped back slightly. "I'm sorry. Pat, this is Detective Mike Moretti."

The foursome moved near a large concrete column, forming an island with their bodies and Pat's suitcase wedged between them. "Pat, it's good to meet you," said Mike. He reached out and shook her hand.

"And this is my boss, Ira, who, as you can see, is a little irritated with me," said Delia.

Pat surveyed the faces of her companions. "Well, as I see it, we have four people and two cars, and we are all driving to Portland." The woman took control like a true director. "I have two days emergency leave from my job, and I plan to make the most of it. Ira, if you can hold off on your discussion with Delia, I'd take it as a personal favor if I could ride with you. I've never been to the East Coast before, and you can educate me in the ways of Maine. I'm looking for a place to dine on spring lamb while I'm here." She looked at Delia and winked. "And lobster, of course. Who could visit Portland without trying your famed lobster?"

Ira's mustache jumped in agitation. Delia didn't know if he could bear delaying his lecture to her. The man might implode, and yet he took a breath and said, "I'll be glad to have you along, Pat. But I shall not be denied my moment with you, Delia. Tomorrow morning, my office." He reached down to grab Pat's suitcase. "May I?"

"Why, thank you, Ira. Who said northerners lack hospitality?"

"Ira, you can drive my car back; it's in long term parking. I'll show you where," said Delia. She had already made the assumption that she'd ride back with Mike. She looked over at him to double check, and he smiled. "We'll meet at my place. Pat is staying with me," she said.

The air around Boston airport, filled with exhaust, anxiety, and moisture from the Atlantic, smelled like heaven.

# CHAPTER 47

The inside of Mike's car felt like the cockpit of a rocket. Faint lights glowed around her feet. "Your daughter must love this car. How old did you say she was?"

Mike turned his head momentarily as they slowed through a toll booth and the green light registered his E-ZPass. "She's old enough that even this car might not make me cool that much longer. I'm on borrowed time with the teen years on the horizon. She's ten."

Delia's brain buzzed with a new chemical stowaway, and she fought to ignore it. "You deserve to feel better than this," said the voice, whispering along her neural pathways. It must have been the safety of Mike's car after all the hustle of the hospital and traveling with Pat that allowed her to hear the disquieting voice. It was the shadow of heroin, she was sure of it. Is this what her father battled, a voice that competed with family and friends?

"They haven't apprehended the guy who attacked you. And Delia, this is a very large drug cartel, far beyond the likes of

Raymond Blanchard. That's why he's dead. That's why Emma Gilbert is dead. That's why they tried to kill you when you meddled with their arrangement in Tennessee. And that third victim? He was likely an intermediary, trying to hone in on Raymond, someone who was expendable. The big boys didn't like Raymond's entrepreneurial spirit. So that is why you and Pat are not driving back alone. They could have easily found out you were on the flight to Boston," said Mike.

He tapped the steering wheel with one finger. There was more he wanted to tell her, but he was hesitating.

"What?" she said. "What else?"

"Maine Drug Enforcement Agency has decided to keep a man at Erica's house twenty-four seven. After you were attacked, they don't want to take any chances with Hayley. Erica was freaked out at first until she realized that they were all a lot safer with their new resident cop. I stopped by this afternoon, and Hayley's teaching him to draw with her marking pens."

"Oh, my God, Hayley. This thing just keeps snowballing. Are you sure she's okay?" Delia struggled to keep up with the thundering pace of the situation. She longed to go home, slip into her own bed.

"Believe me, South Portland PD, Maine State Police, and the MDEA are fully aware of the level of danger. And now thanks to you, the cops in Tennessee have ratcheted up their game," he said. He merged the car into the left lane, accelerating.

She was sure that they needed to keep talking, to avoid the wordless leap that they made while she'd been in Tennessee. Now they were something not like a couple yet, but like two people who had agreed that they both wanted more.

"I'm convinced," she said. "I don't ever want to be that vulnerable again. I was terrified." Delia wrapped her arms around herself and bent her head forward.

Mike set the car to drive in cruise control, and he relaxed his right leg. "You have to be careful for the next few days, and maybe longer. An attack like that can sneak up on you. Back when I worked in Rhode Island, a bunch of drunks blindsided me one night outside a club before my backup could arrive. They got in some wicked punches. I thought I was okay, no big deal, until two weeks later when I was walking through the aisles of CVS. My heart started racing and I broke out in a sweat. I thought I was having a heart attack. Or going crazy because there was nothing scary going on in the tissue aisle of the store."

"Panic attack," said Delia. She unfolded and turned to look at his profile in the dim light of the car. Typical panic attack, although no one liked to be told that they were typical. "Did it happen again? Once they get started, they can sort of spread like a grass fire."

"That's what they told me at the hospital. But they gave me good news and bad news. I was way too young to have a heart attack, that's the good news. The bad news for me was that those idiot drunk guys could have such an effect on me. So I'm just saying, take it easy. And no, it never happened again."

Interstate 95 was thick with large trucks and a never-ending stream of cars. The road signs offered exits for Danvers. Traffic always started to thin after Danvers, taking them due north to Maine. She could almost smell J Bird's scones. What about J Bird? Delia should have had multiple text messages from her by now in the text pileup. She'd rather explain the whole thing in person. J Bird would insist on details.

"Was Courtney arrested? Did anyone try to harm her?" asked Delia.

"She was arrested. And you were right about her mental state. The state police have been able to get very little information from her."

A sudden fear gripped her. "They have to put her on suicide watch!"

Mike placed his right hand on her thigh, lightly, making no assumptions. "They know that, Delia. They know how to do their job. And just in case they didn't, John Blanchard was still at the Phoenix House when they arrived and he was as protective as a bullmastiff. He was ready to take the blame for everything that happened after Courtney surfaced in Nashville."

"Thank you," she said.

Mike turned his head and appeared puzzled. "Thank you for what?"

"For coming to get me. For making Pat come with me on the plane, even though I kicked up a fuss. I'm not used to people taking care of me like that. Well, except for our family friend, Ben, but we were still kids when he started taking care of us. So this feels weird. But good." She squeezed his hand.

"Is this by any chance a date?" he asked. "I mean, it has some of the same details as a date. I picked you up in my car, we talked by phone beforehand. We could stop and get something to eat. That would really make it a date."

Something like a laugh worked its way up her throat. "We skipped several steps to an official date. This is more like emergency transport."

Mike's phone rang. "Mike here. What? Are you sure? Do they have a positive ID? What hospital? I'm still in Mass. Yeah, on 95 North. I can get there in under two hours."

Delia's skin prickled. "What's happening?" she said.

Mike disabled the cruise control and accelerated. "A woman was found in an old tobacco barn in Massachusetts, north of Hartford. Some lady was out walking her dog and the dog led her to the barn. She's in a hospital in Springfield." He passed a row of three trucks. "We're taking the first exit and heading back to the pike. Call Ira and tell him that we'll meet him later."

Mike rearranged his entire body in the driver's seat, rolled his shoulders around, and pushed his spine into the back of the seat, like he was getting ready to ride a horse. "She's not conscious now, but the last thing she said to her rescuers was, 'My daughter.' This could be Claire. How many other women could be locked up in a tobacco barn?"

Delia didn't dare hope that this was Hayley's mother. And yet there was nothing that she wanted more.

# CHAPTER 48

Once they hit the Mass Pike, Mike flowed in and around trucks and cars, merging the way water does, going for the open spaces, the places of least resistance. They'd been thirty miles south of the Maine border when he'd taken the call. They pulled into Baystate Medical Center in Springfield in under two hours. The digital clock on the console said ten p.m.

Delia didn't know if it was the residual effects of the attack in Tennessee that made time crack and fragment or if it was that time changed with her perception of it. Every article she'd ever read on the subject in *Scientific American* said time was not finite. When a five-year-old agonized about waiting thirty minutes, those minutes stretched out in unbearable Einsteinian taffy; when that same kid was engrossed in digging a hole in a sandbox with a soul mate, the thirty minutes flickered by, snap, like that. Delia speculated about this while Mike parked his car/ hovercraft and they made their way through the parking lot to the wide electronic doors of the hospital entrance.

Mike flipped open his police ID at the information desk.

They took the elevator to the fourth floor. Room 417, Intensive Care.

Funny thing about hospitals; nobody really wants to be there. Every able-bodied visitor is cinched tight by concern, sadness, regret, and the field marshal, fear. Two people got off on the second floor, and one elderly man stepped on the elevator on the third. Mike said, "We're going up."

The man said, "It doesn't matter."

On the fourth floor they followed the arrows to 417, leaving the bewildered-looking man alone in the elevator.

"What if it's not her?" said Delia. "What if it's not Claire and it's a homeless person who took shelter in a tobacco barn?"

The sense of timeless urgency was everywhere in the wide hallway. Patient rooms were left open, with only blanketed feet visible as they walked by. Delia still had on Pat Garvey's flip-flops, and they made a sucking sound as she walked. They walked past the nursing station, the command central. A woman seated at the station typed into a laptop and looked up at them. They kept walking.

At the end of the hall, a uniformed police officer stood outside the room. Southwick Police. Delia's heart raced. She wanted to run straight into the room and come to the end of not knowing. She wanted to see a woman sitting up in bed, an overbed table swung over her chest as she sipped orange juice in a plastic cup. Delia would shout, "Claire! We've found you. We have Hayley, we've got your girl!"

The cop moved into the doorway and filled the space. Mike showed his ID again: detective, South Portland, Maine.

"How did you get here so fast?" said the Southwick cop. He said his name was Rob. Officer Hernandez.

Mike said, "We were in the neighborhood. What's the status?"

The two men moved slightly to the right and Delia saw a space open in front of her, and like water, she flowed into it, sliding along the back of Mike, skimming him with her palm as she moved into the room.

There were two beds in the room. The one by the window was empty. In the bed nearest the door, a woman lay with eyes closed, IV lines in her arms, white cotton blankets draped over her from the chest down, snug without a wrinkle. A woman in blue scrubs looked up at an array of beeps and blinks, then placed her palm on the woman's forehead. She turned as Delia took one step closer.

"Are you a family member?"

Did she expect the woman to look like Hayley? The woman in the bed had shoulder length hair, darker than the little girl, but it was also filthy, weighing heavy on the pillow.

"No, but I'm from Foster Services in Maine. We think this might be a woman we've been searching for who was kidnapped. This might be her. Claire. She has a daughter who was kidnapped along with her. We've been taking care of the child and searching for her mother."

Delia spoke quickly. The deeper voices from Mike and the cop rumbled outside the door. Given the guidelines of confidentiality, Delia doubted that the woman in scrubs would offer more.

Mike stepped into the room. He spoke quietly to Delia. "They found a half dozen Luna Bar wrappers and the remains of a case of bottled water. We have confirmation that Ray Blanchard owns the property where she was found. If Ray stashed her in the barn, he was planning on returning in a few days. Make his drop-off in Maine, return and check on Claire on the way back through. Given that, plus what Courtney told you, and what Rob just told me, this is our Claire."

He showed his ID to the woman in scrubs. She looked at the Southwick cop and he nodded.

"I'm Julia, critical care nurse. I've been with her since she came in. We're assessing the damage to her kidneys. Can we step outside, please? I don't like to talk in front of patients."

"Why is she unconscious?" asked Delia. The four of them took a few steps away from the room and spoke quietly.

"We are introducing fluids into her system but it's going to take time to reverse the direction that her body took to cope with the lack of food and water. The human body can survive longer than you might imagine without food. A woman was lost in a wilderness area of California and survived for fifty-five days without food. Water is more critical."

The two men and Delia leaned into Julia to catch every word. "But why is she unconscious?" repeated Delia.

"We aren't sure. The metabolism had to slow down to deal with starvation. Her body was mining muscles and organs, primarily the kidneys, for energy, and she may have run out of steam. Or she may have given up. If someone critically ill gives up, that is the worst thing that can happen."

"Is there any question that this is not Claire?" said Delia.

The Southwick cop pulled out his phone. "The report from the EMT said she stayed conscious long enough to say her daughter had been taken and that her name was Claire something, he couldn't make out the last name."

The last membrane of doubt lifted off. "Let me tell her that we have Hayley. I have to tell her," said Delia. Without waiting for permission, she turned around and went back into the room and stood close to Claire. She bent over and put her head close to Claire's ear. Delia wrinkled her nose and squeezed her eyes shut against a powerfully sour odor.

Julia was by her side. "The sour smell is from ketosis. The body creates toxic byproducts while it devours muscle and organs in order to survive. She'll smell better soon."

Delia put her lips next to the sleeping woman's ear. "Claire, Hayley is safe. We are taking care of her. You are in a hospital and they are going to make you better again. Hayley is waiting for you. You have to wake up. Hayley made me promise that I would find you."

Nothing. Why couldn't Claire wake up, pop open her eyes? Julia touched Delia's arm. "Sometimes the psychic trauma is as devastating as the physical trauma. We are doing everything we can. There's no physical reason why she can't wake up." Julia placed Claire's hand in her own and squeezed gently. "Many of us are trained in therapeutic touch, or Reiki. If she was in that shed for almost three weeks, she had also been deprived of human touch." She stroked Claire's hand.

Delia wondered if it would be rude to touch someone she didn't know in such an intimate way. But the desire to reunite mother and child was so strong that her bones trembled. She tried to think of the least invasive place to touch Claire. "May I touch her feet?"

Julia smiled. "Yes, I think that would be okay. Wash your hands, please."

Delia scrubbed her hands in the bathroom sink, dried them with paper towels, and returned to the bedside. Mike leaned against the back wall, hands held together in front of his pelvis the way men do. Julia pulled back the layers of cotton blankets from Claire's feet. It looked like her feet had been given a cursory wash, but the skin was dry and cracked. Delia rubbed her hands together to warm them. She had no idea what she was doing, yet felt compelled to try this form of touch if it would help. She gave one questioning glance at Julia, who nodded encouragement.

Hands and feet are rich with nerve endings. Every massage therapist she knew said the same thing. J Bird had suggested that Delia needed to loosen up a bit and often gave her gift certificates for massages. Delia pictured a massive nerve ending collision as she closed her eyes and pressed the heels of her palms into Claire's arches and wrapped her fingers around the tops of the feet, feeling the thin bones that radiated down to the toes. She assumed that thinking about Hayley would be the best thing, but as she held on to Claire's feet, she pictured bread dough, warm and filled with a universe of yeast, breathing, moving, sighing on the exhale. Bread filled her nose with its intoxicating aroma. Food. Her father exalting in the joy of eating good food. The happiness of learning to make pasta in the Italian seaside village of Minori. Her mother's fierce love. She was filled with the opposite of what had happened to Claire.

J Bird said that making delicious food was ultimately about the transfer of energy. Her love of food was transferred to people who savored it. Delia prayed that therapeutic touch, practiced by a neophyte, might have a similar effect on Claire.

Delia's knees turned rubbery and she listed to one side.

"Hold on there," said Mike. He gripped her with his hands, nearly encircling her rib cage. "They're taking good care of her, Delia. Rob said he'd call the second that she wakes up. We've done everything we can here."

She released the feet and the lush, food-filled vision vanished. "I want to leave her a note, with my phone number on it." A colossal fatigue descended on her, thumping along on the pathways carved by heroin, the way the man had licked her neck, Narcan, the attack, the Phoenix House, Courtney, and Hayley's desperate longing for her mother.

Mike reached in his pants pocket and handed her his ever-present notepad. She wrote, "Claire, Hayley is safe and in South Portland, Maine. Call me as soon as you can."

"Time to go," said Mike. "I promise to drive a little slower, but I'm getting you home."

# CHAPTER 49

*Juniper*

Juniper did the only thing she knew how to do to help her sister. After she got the call from Ira that Delia wouldn't be home until three a.m., she chopped candied ginger, took a quart of buttermilk out of the fridge and allowed it to come to room temperature, cut butter into the flour, sugar, salt, and baking powder, and mixed the ingredients into a dough for scones. She let it rest for fifteen minutes. Only when she stopped did she notice the acidic taste in her throat, the way her hands vibrated with static electricity. She gripped the counter and let out a sob. She should have known that Ira would never ask Delia to go to Denver to pick up a child. Even she knew that was beyond the responsibility of Foster Services. More importantly now, she needed to take care of Delia.

She had never seen Delia undone before, not even after the fire, after Tyler disappeared. But from Ira's tone of voice, Delia was shaken to the core. He warned her that there had been a car accident, but he rushed to say Delia had not been badly injured, no broken parts. But something else had happened: She had been drugged, injected with a large dose of heroin. And correction, it hadn't been an accident. Her car had been intentionally rammed.

"Wait. Did you just say Delia and heroin in the same sentence?" Juniper was stuck on the first part of the unthinkable news. "Where was she? I thought she was bringing a kid back from Denver for you guys."

"Not exactly," he said. Juniper knew Ira for the entire time that Delia worked for him at Foster Services. "She went to Tennessee."

Why would Delia have lied to her?

"There's more. The guy who rear-ended her car and attacked her is part of a large drug ring. She was injected with a nearly lethal dose of heroin. She was saved only because one of the few people she knew in Tennessee saw her rental car and stopped."

"What?" Juniper's sky broke open, turned to glass, and shattered. "What is going on?" Her big sister, the steady one, was the captain of their ship.

Ira continued. "The detective from South Portland PD will bring her home. They made a side trip to Springfield because they may have found the mother of the little girl in the news. Mike just called and gave me the ETA. Oh, and the director of DCF in Tennessee escorted Delia back to Boston and she's going to spend the night at our house. I thought you might have enough on your hands."

J Bird still couldn't entirely grasp the picture. "Are you sure you're talking about our Delia?"

"She's going to be okay. She's been checked out at the hospital in Tennessee. The Portland PD is now working with the Tennessee PD. Delia discovered a lead to a kidnapping and disturbed a nest of major drug dealers."

J Bird thought she was going to throw up.

"I saw her at the Boston airport. She looks a little rough around the edges, but you know how solid she it. Please try to get some sleep. What am I saying? I know you and Baxter will be pacing around your house until your sister is home. I'll call you around noon tomorrow after everyone has had some rest."

Now it was the middle of the night, the awful time of night when the only people awake were drunken revelers or people deep in the midst of an emergency. Juniper wiped the kitchen counter with a yellow sponge for the one hundredth time and dried it with a dish towel, unable to sit down. Baxter stood up before she heard the rustle at the door, the murmuring voices. He moved to the front door, tail swishing in his usual greeting for Delia.

Delia stepped in the door, followed by Mike. A rush of brisk air followed them in. Juniper, despite not wanting to cry, wanting to surround her sister with an arsenal of protection from all that she had endured, pulled Delia into a tight embrace and sobbed. "Tell me you're okay, please, Delia. Tell me you're okay."

Delia's body felt rigid to the touch, thick with shock and something else. She tried to push away, but Juniper fought to keep a grip on her sister. "You don't have to say anything now. You're home. No, you do have to say something. What the hell were you doing? Why did you lie to me?"

Juniper released her sister and took a careful look at her. She wore clothes that didn't fit her. Baggy pants rolled up just below her knees, a long-sleeved tunic top that hung off her torso. Flip-flops, several sizes too small. Speechless, Juniper took another step back and turned both her hands up in question.

Mike, still as a post behind Delia, said, "She had to borrow clothes. Her clothing is evidence back with the state police in Tennessee." His voice was low and quiet.

Baxter pushed his golden retriever nose between the sisters and whined in a high-pitched sound of alarm. A keening sound rose from his throat.

Baxter was an obedient dog, well-mannered by any standards, and he had not jumped up on anyone since his adolescent days. Puppy training and his breed's desire to please motivated him to do the things that the sisters wanted from him. And yet now, without hesitation, he stood to his full height on his back legs and found a bit of exposed flesh along Delia's forearms and licked tenderly as if she were a baby and he were the nursemaid.

Delia sank to the floor with the dog. "Oh, Baxter," she said, her face pushed into the russet fur of his neck. "I was so afraid." He stood firmly, taking in the tremors that wracked her.

Juniper wiped her eyes and nose and looked at Mike, who stood frozen in the doorway, dark circles around his eyes. He tried to control a quiver in his bottom lip by swiping one hand across it. In that instant, with her sister collapsed on the floor, crying into Baxter's fur, J Bird saw the future. J Bird Café. And Mike. Here he was at last, the one for Delia. Her sister would have to break the news to Tyler.

Delia took a huge breath and exhaled with a shudder. "I've never in all my life smelled anything as good as our house. Ginger scones, right? It's three a.m. and you made scones. You're amazing."

Did Delia know that Mike was the perfect fit? She was exceedingly slow about matters of the heart. She'd know soon enough.

Juniper walked past the dog/woman love fest on the floor and gave Mike a hug. "Thank you for bringing her home."

# CHAPTER 50

Delia woke with a start. Where was she? She struggled out of a deep quagmire of sleep and rose up on her elbows. She was home, in her bedroom. The curtains were closed, but a vertical shaft of brilliant light found an open slit and illuminated the headboard, her pillow, and her face. What time was it? She smelled coffee and something else. Apples, cinnamon, and a particular arrangement of sugared flour. Why was J Bird baking so early in the morning? She rolled to one side and looked at the red digital numbers of her clock. Twelve thirty. Half past noon? She made a cursory search for her cell phone and couldn't find it.

As soon as her feet hit the floor, she heard Baxter's bark, the knock on the front door, and voices. She grabbed a pair of jeans from the corner chair and stepped into them. A tank top hung on the doorknob of her closet, and she wiggled into it.

The rush of air from the front door greeted her at the top of the stairway. Usually she galloped lightly down the stairs. Today her body offered resistance at every front: a stiff neck, the shadow of a headache, and complaints from all major muscle groups. She held onto the railing and walked awkwardly down the stairs. She padded barefoot into the kitchen.

Surrounding the kitchen island was a crowd of J Bird, Mike, Ira, and Pat Garvey, a configuration that had never occurred in their house before. Baxter caught sight of her, clattered across the wood floor, and whirled around her legs. All four people turned in her direction at once.

"What's wrong? What's happened now?" said Delia. She ran one hand through uncombed hair.

All four of them were smiling. Mike said, "Claire is awake. She's been awake since early this morning. She is campaigning hard to be released from the hospital. But how are you? Your sister wouldn't allow any of us to come until noon, and she is a force to be reckoned with."

No wonder they were all smiling like Cheshire Cats. Delia exhaled and put her hands over her face. "I was so afraid we'd never find her. And then last night I thought she'd been found too late. Why didn't she call me? I left my number." Her legs felt rubbery. Mike pushed a stool in her direction and she perched on it, her feet hooked around the highest rung.

J Bird removed muffins from a sturdy baking tin and set them on a blue platter. "My fault. Once you fell asleep, I took your phone away. Enforced sleeping. I also refrained from making coffee at my usual time and waited as long as I could to bake the muffins. I knew your nose would wake you. And I begged Baxter to be extra quiet, which translated into extra dog treats." She pointed to the cell phone on the counter.

Delia looked at Ira and Mike. "Does Hayley know yet?" The last time she'd seen Hayley was with Baxter just a few days ago, but time since then felt dense and dark.

Ira reached for a golden muffin. "By the time Mike called me, Hayley was already in school. I told Erica. I didn't know that woman could squeal that loud." He paused, muffin in hand. "We were all waiting for you, Delia." He looked at his watch. "Hayley will be home in two hours. Are you up to it? I thought you'd want to tell her."

"Are you kidding me? Of course I want to tell her that we found her mother!"

Pat Garvey leaned against the fridge and crossed her arms. "Then, darling, you need to go take a shower before you scare that little girl witless. We'll wait right here for you. I need to eat some muffins." She turned to Juniper. "I've heard quite a bit about your culinary skills from Ira. My name is Pat Garvey. It's a pleasure to meet you." She stepped forward and extended her hand. "I offer myself as your tester."

"Get in line," said Ira. Crumbs from the muffin accumulated on the lower tips of his mustache.

"Right after me," said Mike.

Delia could have swooned, floated away, adrift on this very moment of cinnamon and love. This could have all been ripped away on a roadside in Tennessee. But it wasn't. She pushed off the stool and wrapped an arm around Pat.

"J Bird, this is who saved me, and I won't ever know how she happened along the highway at exactly the right time. But if it weren't for Pat, you'd all be having a different kind of get-together." She kissed Pat on her forehead.

Pat put her hand up in the stop signal, palm out. "Okay, enough of that. I'm only asking for lifetime rights at your new café. J Bird Café, is that it? Portland could be my new vacation destination."

Delia showered, scrubbing away every hint of her attacker from her arms and neck. The hot water felt medicinal, melting the tight spots in her muscles. She rubbed an ointment into the surface wounds on her heels and covered them with Band-Aids, found a clean pair of jeans, and pulled a sky blue blouse out of her closet and rolled up the sleeves. She slipped on her best sandals, which left the backs of her heels untouched. All she could think about was Hayley.

Downstairs, the group had powered through almost a dozen muffins. Mike was back on his phone, as was Ira. Pat and J Bird had their heads together over the recipe page of her laptop.

Mike smiled as soon as he saw her. "You could have taken

time to dry your hair. We still have time before Hayley comes home from school."

"I can't think of anything else besides Hayley. I'm too excited to dry my hair!" She fingered wet strands behind her ears.

Ira tapped his phone off and looked at Mike. "You two can share the news at Erica's. Life goes on back at Foster Services and my presence is required. New kids are coming in." He looked at Pat. "My wife made reservations for us at the best lobster place in town. We expect to dazzle you with our crustaceans."

Pat laughed. "We have crustaceans, too. They just happen to live in creeks. Crawdads."

"Would you care to take a look at our upscale office?" Ira and Pat came with a built-in special language of insider jokes that were the same in Tennessee as Maine; they both knew their offices were far from beautiful.

Mike and Delia headed for the door. Juniper frowned and said, "Delia, can I talk to you for a minute?" She grabbed Delia's elbow and guided her into the living room. "I've got to talk to you later. I don't want to burst your happiness balloon, but we have to talk about Ben."

Delia frowned. "Ben? Is he okay? What's going on?" She felt the air whizzing out of her balloon.

"He's sick. Or more exactly, he's addicted to pain meds. Tyler has agreed to help him. I called Ben and left a message for him yesterday to go to the ER and ask for Tyler. I hope that he made it. Our guy is going to need help."

J Bird seemed to be choosing her words carefully. Unusual for her sister. "There's more to it than that. It will all hold until you get back from the good news fest with Hayley. But today, I need to talk with you today." She released Delia's elbow and shouted, "Hey, Pat. How about I show you the new café tomorrow?"

Something was wrong. She had been so consumed by ending her job at Foster Services and finding Hayley's mother that she ignored the one person who was the constant in their lives since their parents died. Ben.

# CHAPTER 51

*Juniper*

First things first. J Bird called the vet clinic to see if Ben was there.

"He just came in," said Jill, "and his wife is with him. I don't know what's up, but Michelle rarely comes by anymore now that she's teaching."

J Bird heard the concern in the receptionist's voice. "Tell him I'm on my way to the clinic," she said.

He must have told his wife. But she had to be sure.

Her eager dog sat expectantly at the door. "Baxter, my apologies, big guy, but you have to stay home. I promise a double walk later."

She pushed open the doors to the clinic. Jill looked up from the four-foot-tall counter. "They're in a meeting with the other two vets, Dr. Stanley and Dr. Maloney. They should be coming out soon. I've got patients backed up."

J Bird looked around at the two waiting rooms on either side of the counter, dogs on one side, cats on the other, with annoyed humans holding on to leashes and cat carriers.

The other two vets emerged from the back room, and both spoke quietly to Jill before they retreated to patient rooms, one with a German shepherd tugging on a leash and the other with a howling cat.

"Can I go back to his office?" asked Juniper.

Jill tipped her head and gestured with her thumb to the back room.

The door was ajar, but she gave a polite knock anyhow. Her stomach protested from too much coffee, and despite all her bravado, confrontations were frightening. Her well-thought-out speech disintegrated in her dry throat.

"Come in, J Bird," said Ben.

He sat on a stainless steel stool. Michelle looked too upset to sit. Her eyes were bloodshot and the flesh around them was swollen. She knew.

"I talked to Michelle last night and told her everything," he said. "In case you think I left anything out, I told her that I've been addicted to pain meds for several months, I've been buying oxy off the street, and I've lost control of this thing."

Michelle squeezed her eyes shut, pressed her lips together, and turned her face away. "That is everything, isn't it? Please tell me there's nothing else," she said, wiping under her eyes with the back of her hand.

The air in the small room vibrated with pain. "That's everything I know," said Juniper.

Ben exhaled with a shudder. "I've just explained the situation to my colleagues. I told them that I'll be going into treatment for six weeks."

Juniper rushed across the room and hugged the exhausted man. "Oh, thank you, thank you. I was so afraid that we were going to lose you. Did Tyler help you get set up with a treatment center?"

Nothing. Ben and Michelle didn't say a word, and the silence boomed through her chest. It was hard to tell if something new was wrong when she couldn't imagine anything worse happening than her family hero in the grips of addiction.

"I'll let you tell her," said Michelle. She put one hand on Ben's shoulder before gathering her purse and leaving the room.

"What do you need to tell me? You went to see Tyler, right?"

"I did. I met him at the ER. Honey, he not only wrote me a scrip for more pain meds, but he gave me a bottle of oxy 160 milligrams. Do you know how powerful those are? Every molecule in my body wanted to swallow those pills. He said for me to come back any time."

"Are you sure you saw Tyler? Did his name tag say Dr. Greene?"

"I'm as sure as I've ever been. Believe me, I was sick, the effects of withdrawal are overwhelming, but every alarm in my system was going off, and if Tyler had anything to do with you and Delia, I had to find out. I thanked him and left. At least he thought I left. I hung around and waited to see who asked for him. You don't normally ask for a particular doctor in the emergency department; you get who's available. But a steady stream of people came through in the next hour and asked for Dr. Greene."

"He told me that he understood addictions," she said, leaning against the wall, hands pressed flat on the wallboard to support her. Her mind spun full tilt, trying to reckon with what Ben said.

Ben tapped one foot. "He understands them perfectly, that's what I'm saying. He's perpetuating them. And there's got to be a reason. I don't want him anywhere near Delia, or you."

"What are you going to do?" She was frozen, her insides thickening like cement. Where was Delia?

"I'm calling the Maine Drug Enforcement Agency. We'll let them take care of this."

"I've got to tell Delia," she said, and then paused. She was no fool. "Ben, where's the bottle of oxy that Tyler gave you? And the scrip?"

He smiled. "I'm always proud of you, J Bird. You don't miss a beat." He pointed to a plastic bag on the far side of his desk. "It's evidence. Michelle knows it's here, believe me." Ben stood up. "I don't have much self-esteem left right now, and I'm going to have to work hard to win back trust from the people I love, but I want you to know I still have your back. I would never let your parents down."

He opened the door. Michelle waited in the hallway. "Are you ready?" she asked.

He took his wife's hand, the way J Bird's father used to hold her mother's hand, as if she tethered him to earth.

"You're leaving right now?" asked J Bird.

Ben closed his office door, as if sealing up a part of his life that he may or may not be able to return to. "My doctor found a treatment center with an opening and he said I shouldn't wait."

For the first time in her life, it was Ben who was leaving, not J Bird, not Delia. He was the one who was going to need every bit of their help.

Ben said, "Walk out with us, would you? I have a dignity deficit today, and I need you two to bolster me up for this walk through the clinic." He wrapped one arm around her shoulder. "I'm counting on a special discount at the café when I come home from treatment."

J Bird watched them drive off. The entire staff of the clinic was at the front window. Jill was crying. Ben was still J Bird's hero.

At times like this, she yearned to bake. If the gas was hooked up to the new stove at the café, she could give it the inaugural test run. She'd run home and pick up Baxter and take him to the beach later.

J Bird pictured Tyler at the hospital, handing out pain meds, feeding addictions like ducks at a pond. What was wrong with him? She wanted to go toe-to-toe with him, to have him explain what was going on. Should she say something to him? She wanted to hear this from Tyler, but she couldn't. Baking. Just do what she knew to do. She only wished that she'd never said anything to him about Delia. If Tyler was unstable or in trouble, how would he respond to a rejection from Delia?

She'd let Delia have her fantastic moment with Hayley and break the news to her later.

# CHAPTER 52

Erica left Delia and Mike in the house while she drove to school to pick Hayley up. For a foster mom, these next moments would be mixed with the bittersweet knowledge of Hayley moving on, reuniting with her mother. Delia had seen foster parents negotiate this path hundreds of times, and she still didn't fully comprehend how they bore the pain with the hope. Erica had to be a fully compassionate foster mother, yet let Hayley go.

The Maine DEA guy, Dustin, asked Mike if he was going to be there for at least a half hour, because he needed to pick up a book that his wife ordered over at the mall.

"I've got it covered," Mike said.

While they waited in the living room, seated near the coffee table where Hayley first drew the naughty place, Mike told Delia as much as he could about the case. Louie hopped on the couch and sat next to Delia as if he wanted to hear the details also.

Mike stretched out his long legs, then reconsidered and

pulled his feet in closer to the couch. "The state police have already interviewed Claire once today. Her name is Claire Higgins and her husband, Joshua, is a pharmacist in Nashville. Claire said she knew nothing about her husband's activities, only that he had worked longer and longer hours. She gave them all of her husband's information. Social Security number, password to the home computer, work address. Claire has had a hard time taking all of this in, that her husband was somehow involved. As of three hours ago, he was in custody."

She found the sweet spot along Louie's jaw and ran the edge of her hand along it. "Do you believe that she was the victim, kidnapped with Hayley, or do you think she was part of the drug business?" She had to ask. It was still her job to keep Hayley safe.

"They're interrogating her husband right now. If there is a shred of him left that isn't destroyed, and if Claire was in the dark about his connection with the heroin trade, then he can do the last best thing for his family by telling the truth. I'm expecting a call from those guys later today."

Delia's cell phone rang. It was a Connecticut number. She tapped on immediately. "This is Claire Higgins. Is this Delia?"

How strange to finally hear the voice of someone who had been the target of their search for weeks. "This is Delia. You can't imagine how good it is to hear your voice. You must be feeling a lot better than when I saw you last night."

"The best that I've been in three weeks, since Ray took Hayley from me. And then the best since March. Is Hayley there? I mean, thank you, Delia. Thank you." Her voice sounded unused, as if the words scraped her throat.

"She'll be coming back from kindergarten soon. Do you have access to Skype? Hayley is going to need to see you. We're going to tell her that you've been found as soon as she gets home, but believe me, she wants to see you."

"You're on speaker phone here. One of the nurses said she'll help me Skype later. Is Hayley okay? Was she hurt in any way? I'm only learning bits of things from the police now."

"She was never injured. I promise. And she never gave up on finding you. She motivated a small army of us to find you. Please try to rest until we can set up the Skype."

As she signed off, Mike said, "Thank you. Delaying the call with Hayley will give the cops from Tennessee a chance to verify what she's saying. I'm going to feel a lot better about all this after we hear from them."

Thirty minutes later, Louie stood up, hopped off the couch, and headed for the front door. Delia heard the sound of a car, then two doors closing, and then the sound of Erica's key in the lock.

Hayley, dressed in shorts and a T-shirt with a snowy owl on the front, dropped her small school pack and knelt next to Louie. "You missed me today, didn't you, Louie? I'm home now."

Erica bit down on her lower lip and looked away. "Let's invite our guests for a snack," she said, her voice cracking into shards. Anyone could hear the way Hayley said *home,* could see the ease with which she snuggled into Louie. And anyone could see the chasm ahead when Hayley left.

Mike's phone rang. He answered it, smiled, and gave Delia the thumbs-up sign. Claire was cleared with the police.

"Hi, Hayley. I see that Louie comes before all of us," said Delia, smiling, watching this dream unfold. "Come in the living room with me and Detective Mike. We have very good news for you." Anything she said was going to sound trite, not enough for the moment. Delia flipped open her laptop on the coffee table. "We found your mommy. Just like you said, she was in the bacca barn. She didn't have much food in the barn, which meant she had to go to a hospital so the doctors could give her lots of food and water. But today she is much better, and she's going to Skype with you. Are you ready?"

Five-year-olds have only the slimmest film covering their emotions, their hopes and agonies. Whatever ephemeral mask Hayley had constructed to get through her day peeled off. "Mommy? You found my mommy?" Louie was unceremoniously abandoned as she stood up.

Mike sniffed behind Delia and without looking, she reached one hand back to him.

"A lady who was out walking her dog found your mommy. She is going to call us back in a few minutes when a nurse brings her a laptop. Let's get you all set up over here so you can see your mommy."

Mike put the laptop on the coffee table and pushed it away from the couch so that Hayley could sit on the floor right in front of the table with her back against the lower part of the couch. Louie hopped on the back edge of the couch to see what all the fuss was about.

The familiar chimes of Skype announced the incoming call. Mike leaned over and answered the call request. Claire must have put her laptop on the table that swung over the bed. She had pulled her hair back and scrubbed her face. Her skin was pulled as tight as a drum. But she was smiling and someone had given her lipstick.

They both spoke at once. "Mommy!" "Hayley, are you okay?"

The child put both her hands on the laptop screen as if to touch either side of Claire's face. "Oh, sweetie," said Claire, and she touched her fingertips to her screen. She laughed and said, "If we put our hands all over the screen, we won't be able to see each other."

Erica had to leave the room, crying. Who would not love this determined child who had crossed over a demarcation zone with the foster mom, sliding along the chambers of her heart? Delia heard water running in the kitchen and she pictured Erica splashing water on her face.

Hayley and her mother spoke softly to each other. Delia and Mike stepped toward the large window that faced the street, close enough to hear the conversation but far enough away to give the mother and daughter the illusion of privacy.

Hayley said into the monitor, "Mommy, can you see Louie the cat? He likes to sleep on my bed."

Mike spoke softly with Delia. "She'll be able to come to Portland tomorrow. The state police are interviewing her again later today at the hospital."

From across the room, Claire's voice asked, "Is Delia there?"

Delia squeezed in next to Hayley. "I'm here, Claire. Hayley has so much to tell you that I didn't want to take up any of your time." She sat so close to Hayley that their ears rubbed together. Her heart swelled at the warm touch of the child.

"I'm going to be released tomorrow. The state police will drive me to South Portland," she said.

Erica walked in on the last few sentences, a plate of sliced apples in one hand. She slid the plate along the coffee table and squeezed in on the other side of Hayley. "Hi, Claire, I'm Erica, resident foster mom and the biggest Hayley fan. Will you please stay with us when you come to Portland? I don't know what your plans are after that, but I'd feel terrible if you two had to go to a hotel."

No one could ever doubt this woman as a foster parent. She was going to make the transition easier for Hayley.

Claire looked too exhausted to refuse. "Thank you. It's going to take time to get our life back in order, and being able to thank you in person for keeping Hayley is one way for me to start."

Details were worked out: street address, arrival times. As they got ready to say good-bye, Hayley said, "Did you hear our song?"

"What song, sweetie?"

Mike left the room as his phone rang again.

Delia and Erica looked at each other, momentarily puzzled. "Oh, that song," said Delia as she remembered the canine/human howling on the deck. "Um, we might have to do a repeat performance for your mommy when she gets here. I'll bring my dog, Baxter." Delia could picture Baxter stealing the show, the way he did when he entered a room. But his singing was a showstopper.

This was what it felt like when everything went right, when a child was reunited with a parent, a perfectly good parent. This was the end, how her days with Foster Services would end: a few more days of paperwork, the compulsory surprise going away party with Ira still giving her the stink eye about leaving, but the horizon opened before her as it never had before. The feeling was remarkable.

What awaited her was bread, glorious bread. And once the café gained its own rhythm, she'd make lemon pasta once a week. She might even try to learn the fancy stuff like chocolate éclairs from J Bird.

They stayed until Dustin returned from his mission at the bookstore. As they were leaving, Erica said, "I almost forgot. Your doctor friend stopped by first thing this morning and said he would help us any way that he could. We haven't ever had a home visit from a doctor before. Thanks for the personal touch."

"What doctor friend?" said Delia.

"Dr. Greene. The one with California surfer good looks."

The bottom began to fall out of Delia's stomach. She was falling through space, ejected from a plane without a parachute. Foster Services would never send a doctor to a home without notifying the family first. "The location of your house is confidential. What did he say? Did he have contact with Hayley?"

Erica caught the change in atmosphere. "What's wrong? He showed us his identification and everything. He even showed his hospital ID to my resident cop."

Delia put up her hand in the stop pose. She tapped into her phone. "Ira? Did you send a doctor to Erica's house? Okay, I didn't think so. We'll figure it out here. Yes, Mike is here. And the cop from MDEA."

Erica's body contracted. She put her hand on the doorframe. "What's going on? We were on our way out when he came by. I mean, he was so nice. He told me to bring Hayley to the hospital and he'd update her vaccinations. He said we wouldn't need an appointment; just walk in and ask for him in the ER."

Mike hadn't moved, except for his eyes flicking back and forth between Erica and Delia. "Did you give him this address?"

"No! Wait; he might have overheard a conversation I had with Ira, but I'm sure that I only mentioned the neighborhood, not the exact address," she said. She thought back to the day on the beach with Tyler, the excitement of seeing him again.

"Then why would he come here? And who is he? Do you know him?"

She put her hand on Mike's arm. "Let's go outside. Erica, no one has your address except Foster Services and the police. We will always let you know if we are coming over. And do not take Hayley to the hospital. Okay?"

Mike stepped inside and spoke with Dustin, who put down his wife's book and began to check all the doors.

Delia and Mike opened the doors to his car. "Please tell me this isn't the old boyfriend," he said, starting the car.

She snapped her seatbelt into place. "His name is Tyler, and yes, this is the old boyfriend."

"Why didn't I ask you before? I didn't want to seem like an overbearing cop, poking around in your private business. I need all of his information right now: cell, address, anything else that you have." Mike backed out of the driveway. "I'm taking you home and then I'm going to the hospital. Time to have a conversation with him."

Delia bent her head down and rubbed her temples. A giant headache was blooming. The doctor in Tennessee had warned her about this. "This makes no sense to me. Why would Tyler violate confidentiality like this? Does this have something to do with me?"

They drove through the old downtown of South Portland.

When Mike didn't answer her immediately, she said, "What are you thinking? Your brain is boiling away, I can feel it."

He took a big breath and exhaled. "The drug enforcement guys told me they were exploring a link with the hospital, that one of their informants said there was doctor who would give pain meds out as long as you said your pinky finger hurt. If that someone is Tyler, then we've got a very big problem."

Delia looked at the clock on his dashboard. Four thirty, just when traffic started to thicken up.

# CHAPTER 53

Mike and Delia entered the traffic across the Casco Bay Bridge, and Portland spanned in front of them.

The sirens came from Portland. Red and white fire trucks screamed in the city. Cars pulled over to the right to let them pass. She turned around and caught the glimpse of fire trucks from the South Portland side.

The skin along the back of her neck prickled in alarm. The reptilian part of her brain went on wordless alert, its tongue flicking the air for signs.

Mike's phone rang. "What?" He looked Delia. "Jesus. How bad is it? Are you sure? Have you checked inside? Yeah, I'm on the bridge. I'll turn around as soon as we cross over."

Delia gripped his arm. "What is it? Is it Hayley? Do not tell me it's Hayley."

Mike accelerated, pushed his spine into the back of the seat, and took a U-turn as soon as they hit the Portland side.

"It's J Bird Café. It's engulfed."

Delia plummeted from an amazing height, her ancient brain

squealing like a raptor, all of her senses taking on a dizzying magnification.

Mike's skin poured out a mixture of fresh soap, the remnants of J Bird's muffins, adrenaline, metallic testosterone, all awash in the lush scent of his hair. A leftover sandwich sent a tendril of mayo and roast beef from the confines of a foil package in the backseat.

Time turned into a thick custard, and even as she turned her head to the left to look at the logjam of cars leaving South Portland, she spotted him, as if there were no one else to see. As if all the other drivers were puppets, wooden-jawed, mothers with kids strapped into booster seats, men in pickup trucks with red-flagged two-by-fours slanting out of the truck beds. The carpenter from The Phoenix House.

This couldn't be possible.

Did an unsuccessful attempt at murder create a horrific bond between two people? He had pressed his body against hers, licked her neck. She had smelled the soap he used, the aftershave. He saw Delia and filtered out every other car on the bridge. His young, dark eyes looked first at her, then Mike, then he scanned ahead, seeming to calculate how to get around the traffic on the bridge, how to leap over the solid traffic jam so that he could go north, go south, disappear into the dark abyss of western Maine, or slip through to Canada. He'd been in South Portland. Hayley!

"Mike," she said. Words came out thick and hard because J Bird Café was burning, Hayley and Erica were back in a little ranch house with one cop between them and the likes of the man across the bridge, and she suddenly wanted to know where her sister was. Across the median was the man who had rammed her car, stabbed her with a syringe filled with heroin, intending to kill her. She forced the words out. "That's the man, the one from the Phoenix House, the one who attacked me. Over there."

Mike fixed the man across the road with his gaze, reached into the glove box for a gun. His phone was on the console between them. He put it on speaker and, never taking his eyes off the man, he said, "I need backup immediately. I'm on the bridge. I have visual contact with the suspect from Tennessee. He is headed into Portland, traffic is solid and not moving. I am approaching him on foot."

With a huge effort, she pulled her eyes off the man. She put her hand on the door handle.

"What are you doing?" Mike said. "Stay in the car and get down!"

There was a fire and she knew exactly where she had to go. Before Mike could react, she pushed open the door and started to run. Two miles to the café.

# CHAPTER 54

This was not her body pumping arms and running. This body was stiff and foreign. Her neck and spine screamed in protest as she ran the length of the bridge, dodging the cars in gridlock. Fire trucks from the Portland side blared in protest, urging cars to squeeze together tighter, to make room. She looked back once and saw police cars with their lights flashing on the Portland side. Mike wanted this guy and now he had help.

The sandals hindered her and would never make it all the way. She kicked them off and ran harder, up on her toes, trying to stay off the bandaged heels. The slight hill past downtown felt like a mountain. Storefront windows announced KNITTING CLASSES STARTING NOW and FIRST EDITION USED BOOKS in another. She flew past them.

*You can do anything for two weeks,* she had told kids who were desperate to get back with their parents in that appointed time. Delia could do anything for two miles, including running full out.

She crested a hill. The smoke from the fire was all that she could smell. Where was J Bird? And Baxter?

Another rise in the road that might make her lungs explode. Her heart thundered against her chest. A massive plume of smoke rose up, wide and angry. J Bird Café. Four fire trucks blocked the street, firefighters in heavy gear surrounded the café, some dragging hoses, others brandishing hatchets. Flames shot out of the bathroom window, glass exploded. And in front of the café was J Bird's car.

Delia didn't pause; she knew the drill. She was nineteen again. She shed her older body and ran straight for the side yard. She could get in the back and find J Bird.

Strong arms tackled her, lifting her off the ground. "What the hell are you doing? Get away from there. No one's going in." All she could see of the firefighter was part of his face, from his eyebrows to his chin, smoke-smudged cheeks, lips drawn tight.

The firefighter deposited her behind a barricade across the street. "That's my bakery. My sister could be in there!" she screamed.

"Your sister? There was only one person inside and she's right over there." He pointed to the open back of an ambulance, half a block down the street. J Bird leaned against the back of the vehicle as an EMT pressed an oxygen mask to her face. Baxter lay at her feet. Greg stood next to her and looked up as Delia ran to them, gasping for breath.

J Bird took off the mask. "I'm okay, Delia." Baxter sat up as soon as Delia approached. "And so is Baxter. But I don't know what would have happened if Baxter hadn't started barking. I was filling shelves in the supply closet when he started to bark. I had just mixed some dough and set it aside. I knew Greg was coming soon and I couldn't understand why he'd bark at Greg, but then I knew something was wrong. It was the way he was barking."

The woman in a deep blue uniform, EMT emblem across her shirt, big, muscled thighs pressed against tight pants, said, "Put this back on." She meant it. She held the mask up to J Bird's face and slid an elastic band over her head.

Greg said, "Do what the lady says." He turned to Delia. "When I drove up, there was smoke coming out of the bathroom window, and from the back of the café, and this is weird, from the shed." He rubbed his eyes. The smoke was black and thick. "Someone set this fire."

What had the fire chief said long ago about her parents' house? "It's like the fire was set all over, not just one place." Delia could smell nothing but smoke and with her most trusted sense overwhelmed, a rusty, dark door hinged open in her brain. What would her father say, who had never once shown an inclination toward fire, not even in the midst of the worst psychotic breaks? "Simple ingredients are the most important. Look for the simple answer first."

Sirens screamed the arrival of more fire trucks traveling on any route but the bridge. Neighbors pushed their way to the barricades.

Delia fought the rattling chains that threatened to pull her back to the fire of long ago. She was never going to save her parents. J Bird was safe. But she could find who started the fire.

She looked at her sister and said, "He's here. I know he is. He's watching because he can't stop himself."

J Bird snapped off the oxygen mask, her eyes wide. A moment passed between them as they traveled back in time and then raced to the present. Would Delia ever feel as close to anyone as J Bird?

"I know what you're thinking. Tyler. He's handing out pain meds at the hospital to anyone who asks for them. Ben told me," said J Bird.

"Ben? How would he know that?"

"Because our guy is sick and he tried to give them to Ben."

J Bird tossed the mask to the EMT.

"I know what you're going to do and you're not going without me," said J Bird.

Greg stood at the far corner of the ambulance, his gray hair, stiff with smoke, poking up erratically. "This is a police matter. You two aren't going anywhere. If you know who started this fire, tell the police. . . ."

"You tell them, Greg. His name is Tyler Greene. Dr. Tyler

Greene. We have history with him. Tell them to look for a car with California plates. There shouldn't be too many of those around."

The two sisters made their way past the neighbors, now three deep along the barricades, scanning for Tyler. Baxter hugged J Bird's left side. He could be anywhere, but Delia knew that he'd be close, just like he'd been close once before, so close that he'd seen her run into her family home trying to save her parents.

A teenage boy with a baseball cap said, "Hey, your feet are bleeding." She couldn't look down at her feet, couldn't think about anything except where he would be, what vantage point he'd take. They were a block away from the fire, moving toward the beach.

Delia grabbed J Bird's arm. "We're all creatures of habit. He might have parked at the Willard Beach lot. If he parked there, he won't be able to get out now; the streets are blocked."

Two short blocks remained between the sisters and the beach parking lot. They jogged to the entrance of the lot with Baxter leading the way. At the corner closest to the beach path was a car with California plates.

An explosion made them both jump. "The gas to the stoves! There must have been gas still in the lines," said Delia. "One of us has got to go back. J Bird, please go back and see if anyone is hurt. I'll keep Baxter with me."

There it was again, the look between them, the dead serious, taking-everything-into-account look. They would never go back again to J Bird being the little sister and Delia taking the place of a parent. They were tracking down Tyler and they both knew why.

"I'll be right back. I'll tell them Tyler's car is here. He can't go anywhere," she said.

"And he can't take everything away from us, not our home, our parents, and our livelihood," said Delia. "I'll stay here where I can see his car. Go."

Once J Bird was out of sight, Delia walked directly to Tyler's car. "Heel," she said to the dog. J Bird didn't have time to search for the dog's leash when she escaped the fire. The car was empty and locked.

Delia knew where he was, where he'd go if he thought he couldn't get away. She didn't doubt that she'd find him or that J Bird would send police. What she wanted was time.

"Come on, Baxter. We're going to the beach."

The path to the beach went from blacktop to sand, lined with dense shrubbery along both sides. Sand, well-seasoned with salt, quickly found the open skin on her feet, grinding into her wounds. The beach was not wide, not like the massive beaches along Ogunquit. She walked past the play structures, looked left, then right.

"Hello, Delia. Are you alone?"

She turned to face him, this old lover and destroyer of dreams.

"I am alone. But not alone the way you are. Am I right? You've been alone for a very long time." Delia finally understood who she was talking to.

Tyler's face cracked, his mask of good looks falling away. "You know I tried to help you once. I wanted to do something for you, to free you from your father. Remember how you used to cry and tell me how screwed up your family was, that your father was sucking the lifeblood from all of you?"

Anger shot up her spine. "My father was brilliant and he was sick. My mother could wither the political machines to dust with her analysis. She chose to take care of him; she would have done the same for any of us."

The wind started to whip up as it did in the late afternoons. He took one step closer.

"Stay there. Baxter is a very obedient dog. Do you understand me?"

Tyler stopped. "But sweetheart, I remember that you said she should divorce him, that he was bringing all of you down."

The way he said "sweetheart" made her shiver. "My mother was devoted to him. There were times when I thought life would be so much easier without Dad's illness, but I knew she'd never leave him. And we would always love him."

Baxter moved in front of her, head slightly down, staring at Tyler, steadying himself.

"Your house wasn't my first fire, but it was the only one where people died. Your mother saw me come into the house after you. I might have been able to save her, but she begged me to pull you out," he said.

A deep chill ran through her. "My mother was alive when you pulled me out of the house?"

"Oh, Delia, fires are beautiful, powerful beasts that will have their way. By the time I dragged you to the lawn, the fire had taken her," he said, tilting his head slightly and smiling.

She thought she'd want to kill him; he had taken so much from them. But the rage that flared up in her chest was quelled by her parents' love. Her father had been in the midst of a psychotic episode, and her mother died protecting her.

Now she only had to keep Tyler talking until the cops came. She could stop searching.

"Why J Bird Café? What did that have to do with anything?"

He took another step toward her. Baxter's fur along his spine rose up. Tyler exhaled loudly and let his lips flutter, as if exasperated by a trifle. "There was such a chance for money, truly big money. I saw the potential when I worked in the clinic in San Jose. Who would need me more than the guys selling heroin if I supplied people with a steady flow of opioids, and then cut them off? I was the one at the starting gate of addiction. The money was intoxicating."

Delia must have looked shocked. He continued, as if explaining to a patient. "Doctors don't make that much money, not like I deserved after college, med school, the ridiculous monastic life of a medical student. It should have resulted in much more for me."

This was not the time to diagnose, but the man standing in front of her was checking off a serious list of disorders.

Tyler looked around from one end of the beach to the other. "But these are very bad people, not like me. And since I couldn't do what they asked me to do, I suspect that they are coming for me."

"What did they ask you to do? You've torched J Bird Café, my sister's dream. My dream!"

"They told me to kill you, that you had caused a terrible amount of trouble for them, disrupting a situation in Tennessee, leading drug enforcement cops closer to them. But I couldn't do it. I could never do that to you."

How much time had passed since J Bird ran back to the fire scene? If Tyler didn't see a way out of this, the last tether to his humanity could snap. She looked behind her; there was a family at the far end of the beach, a father bouncing a toddler on his shoulders, a mother and child dragging driftwood from the water. They would only see a man, woman, and dog at this end of the beach.

"You could have hurt J Bird. She was in the café when you torched it."

Tyler shrugged so minutely that another person might have missed it, someone who hadn't lost a mother and a father to an arsonist. "But I wouldn't hurt you, Delia."

He would have killed J Bird. It wouldn't have mattered to him. She no longer cared if he was sick. If she had a stick she'd have bludgeoned him. What was that on his neck? A red dot of light suddenly appeared.

"Tyler—

She heard the shot and at the same moment, saw Tyler's neck spurt blood. He looked stunned, genuinely surprised. He put his hand on his neck and dropped to his knees. He opened his mouth to speak but nothing came out except for a trickle of blood. He crumpled sideways into the sand.

Delia dove to his side and pressed her hand against his neck. For a moment, he looked like a boy again. He held her gaze as blood gushed out of both sides of his neck until his muscles sagged.

She heard J Bird calling her. "I'm here," she yelled as loudly as she could, which was little more than a whisper. Baxter barked. "You are such a good dog," she said.

Mike, breathing heavily, followed by J Bird and Greg, found

her. Mike squatted down next to her. "You are a terrible listener," he said, looking over her body quickly. "Are you hurt?"

Delia pointed and said only, "Tyler. Did you shoot him?"

Mike urged her up. "No, but I saw the direction of the flash." He pointed to the ridge where the lighthouse pulsed out its unmanned, automatic beacon.

She looked down at her hands, covered with Tyler's blood. A tiny sound came from J Bird, high-pitched, carried off quickly by the growing wind. Mike pulled off his shirt and let Delia wipe her hands.

"We've got the guy from Tennessee. He's already ready to talk. He said he knew Tyler was targeted."

"And Hayley?"

Mike smiled. "Back at Erica's watching *Clifford the Big Red Dog* with Louie."

# CHAPTER 55

*May*

May in Maine is an unpredictable month, filled with sleet and freezing rain or spring flowers, usually both. Delia and Juniper picked Mother's Day for their grand opening and the weather cooperated. They had been up since four a.m., preparing for the eight a.m. opening. The sunrise greeted them with a vibrant peach color, moody with fog. Now the sky was blue with a soft breeze waving the daffodils in the window boxes. Next year the daffodils would be in the ground, but they couldn't do everything the first year.

The only things that remained after the fire were the foundation and some hardy root stock from the lilac bushes. They started rebuilding even before the insurance money arrived. Greg said, "I always wanted to be a silent partner. IBM was generous with me. What good is money doing in mutual funds when I could be earning muffin credits with you two? I promise not to interfere with your expertise. Let's get the café framed in by December and we'll spend the winter finishing the inside."

Today, he wore a white apron, and he cleared dishes from the tables and ran the dishwasher. He was also the dog watcher of the day. Baxter lay on the deck and Greg checked on him constantly.

The new J Bird Café was like the old one on the outside, but the windows were triple glazed and the south-facing roof had solar panels. The building extended twenty feet farther in the back and the new deck had an awning for hardy customers who liked the rain.

Ben had been waiting at the doorstep as soon as the café opened. He was back at work half time. "You know they won't let me work today unless I come back loaded with several cardboard bakery boxes from J Bird Café," he said. "My staff can forgive my former addiction, but they'll lock me out if I deny them the scone of the day."

They had not lost Ben, and every time Delia saw him she was grateful.

It was almost noon, and the glass cases that had been filled to capacity with breads, muffins, scones, and croissants were now alarmingly sparse.

"Maybe they're not coming," said Delia.

"Erica said they were going to stop at her house first. That might have taken longer than expected. And you know how traffic can be on the turnpike," said J Bird. She wore her favorite blue scarf around her head, holding back her hair and adding a burst of contrast to the fuchsia and coral walls.

The café had ten tables, and every one of them was filled with patrons. "Can you manage the counter for a few minutes?" asked Delia. She ducked into the bathroom, locked the door, and leaned against the wall. New plumbing was a blessing. Everything worked better; toilets didn't clog, sinks drained, and the café was designed exactly to their specifications.

Was this what had drawn Tyler to fire? Was it a desire to cleanse and start anew? His father had tried to hide Tyler's addiction to fire. The move to the West Coast was a last-ditch effort to save his son. Delia would never know how many other fires Tyler started, and how much his dual life as doctor and arsonist had cost him. He was dead by the time the EMT raced to the beach. He had nearly cost her everyone that she loved.

*Knock, knock.* Someone needed to use the bathroom. "Just a minute," she said. There were moments when she felt like this was a dream, prepping dough, chopping ginger for J Bird, that any moment she'd wake up and see Tyler on the beach again, his blood soaking into the sand.

Delia took a big breath and then exhaled. She opened the door. Mike filled the doorway. He smiled and pushed into the small room, pulling the door closed behind him, and kissed her. It was one of the things that she loved most about him; he was a champion kisser.

"I'm sorry I couldn't get here sooner but I was on a shopping mission."

Delia hooked her fingers around the belt loops of his jeans and pulled him closer. "I had a moment of panic," she said. "Is this really my life now? J Bird knows this terrain like the back of her hand. I'm new at the bakery world. I feel like a big fake."

Mike took both of her hands in his, folded them together, and kissed them. "Face it, she's the leader of the pack. For now. You've been breaking the trail long enough."

*Knock, knock.* "They're here!"

Delia pulled her hands back. "I thought they weren't coming!" She pulled open the door and looked past the diners, out the new, sturdy windows that Greg said would withstand a hurricane. Coming up the walkway were Ira and Pat Garvey. Ira campaigned for two months for Pat to take over Delia's job. He had even promised her one lobster roll a week for the first year until she accepted and gave her notice in Dalton. "Totally worth it for the lobster rolls," Pat said. Behind them was Erica, and then a woman and little girl. Claire and Hayley.

J Bird handed change to a customer. "Go. I can take care of business."

Delia met them on the front steps. She wouldn't have recognized Claire, whose face was soft and filled out, all the sharp edges of her jawline tempered with food and safety. A blue skirt, leggings, and short boots.

Delia knelt down and said, "Hello, Hayley. I'm so glad to see you." Her heart caught on each word and her throat tightened. Hayley looked older, the way kids can so suddenly. She had on stretch pants and a hoodie. Her hair was longer and fluttered in the breeze.

Mike bent down and said, "Hi, there. I have someone in the bag who would like to speak with you. Igor sent him." He pulled out a long-eared stuffed rabbit, silver and tan with pink satin lining the ears. He wiggled the rabbit near his ear. "What? You want to go live with Hayley? Let me ask."

Hayley looked up at her mother. "I told you about Igor, Mom."

Mike sat the rabbit on his shoulders. "He wants to know if he could come and live with you at your house."

Hayley reached over and ran one hand along the rabbit's face. "What's his name?"

Mike looked stumped. As wonderful as he was, he hadn't thought to give the rabbit a name. "Igor said you should name him."

Hayley held the rabbit in her arms. "I think his name is Louie."

Delia caught Erica's eye. "We brought Louie. He loves car rides." They had parked across the street and there was Louie, standing on the seat, paws on the window.

"I never had a chance to properly thank you," said Claire. "Ira filled me in on what you did for us." Delia stood up. "Hayley and I brought you something for the café." She reached into a Whole Foods Market bag and pulled out a six-pack of plant starts. "They're cucumbers. Hayley thinks you can grow them and use them for the café." She stepped forward and hugged Delia. She whispered, "Thank you for taking care of my daughter. All of you."

The café closed at two. By three, even Greg was gone, the floor was swept and mopped, dough was prepped for the next day, J Bird had a long list of supplies to order, the closed sign was out, and Delia sank into one of the chairs. "So this is what a bakery is like. When is my first day off?"

J Bird laughed. "Welcome to my world." Baxter lay in the doorway to the deck, half in, half out, a sleepy contentment on his face. Hayley had asked to see him, and she threw his gooey tennis ball off the back deck. The child was still more comfortable with animals than humans. Now J Bird slid down and sat next to him, rubbing his belly. Someone knocked on the front door.

"Oh, no," said J Bird. "Another customer. Tell them we're closed; there's not a crumb to be had."

An older woman with a dog on a leash pressed her face against the window. Delia stood up, intending to mouth the words through the glass door to the woman. There was something about the dog, its champagne color, the exuberance.

"I've driven for hours," shouted the woman. "I read that you were opening today. Are they gone?"

J Bird and Baxter came to either side of her, shoring her up as they had done for months. Delia unlocked the door. "Who are you talking about?" said Delia.

The woman gripped the blue leash, but when the door opened, Baxter trotted forward with such assurance, his chest out, tail high, and the woman's dog startled, as if seeing something amazing, like the Grand Canyon. Then the dog whirled around the woman, injected with a canine euphoria. In the excitement, she dropped the leash and both dogs twirled around each other.

"It's okay," said J Bird. "They seem to like each other. A lot."

"My name is Shirley, and I was hoping to see the woman I found in the barn last year. Claire? I've not wanted to interfere, but when I learned the café was opening today, I just took a chance. . . ."

Delia reached out and took Shirley's hand. "They were here, Claire and her daughter, Hayley. But I'm sorry; they're gone. Do you want to leave a message for them? I'm sure I can contact them."

Shirley's hair was short and stuck out thickly beneath a baseball cap. "I wanted to know if they were okay. I felt compelled to see how the story turned out. That's ridiculous, isn't it? You never really know how a story turns out."

Baxter rolled on his back as the other dog leapt over him.

"I see your dog isn't neutered," said Shirley.

J Bird put her hand up, apologetically, palm out. "He has an appointment next week. He will soon be among the legions of neutered dogs."

Shirley smiled. "I knew there was another reason for us coming all the way up here. Chelsea is a hero. There may not be another dog like her with all that heart, and persistence, and bravery. If she hadn't found Claire, if she hadn't defied me, we'd be having a different discussion right now. She's come into one heat and will soon do so again. Would you consider breeding your dog? Before he joins the neutered legions, I mean."

Delia and J Bird looked at each other. "We do love to deal in heart, persistence, and bravery," said Delia.

By the time Shirley and her dog, Chelsea, left, the sisters had agreed to bring Baxter to Massachusetts soon as Shirley called them. Would Claire let Hayley have a puppy? If there were puppies.

They locked the café doors again and walked to Willard Beach.

They could talk about anything now. Delia was flooded with questions now that she had allowed the pileup of roadblocks to be disassembled, all the barriers that had grown after their parents' deaths. "I used to worry all the time that you'd go crazy like Dad," she said, stopping to sit on a massive tree trunk that had washed ashore.

J Bird stretched her legs out. "I never thought I was crazy, but I had serious doubts about you." She rolled her head from side to side, stretching out tight muscles. She untied the scarf and loosened her long hair.

"What if Dad left us the part that is just crazy enough to hear bread rising, methane gas escaping from the yeast mixture? Do you remember what he said about truly great food being a conductor of energy from the cook to the patron?" asked Delia.

"None of that is crazy. It's just who we are, not normal at all. Who would want to be normal?"

"You're right," said Delia, feeling lighter than she ever had before. "I like who we are." And she was sure that their parents would be cheering for them.

# Acknowledgments

My most heartfelt thanks to:

My agent, Jenny Bent, and her team at The Bent Agency. We are in it for the long haul.

My editor, Michaela Hamilton, publicist Lulu Martinez, and the powerful network of people at Kensington Books. What a joy to have found you.

The two writing groups that support me. Members Marianne Banks, Jeanne Borfitz, Jennifer Jacobson, Celia Jeffries, Kris Holloway, Lisa Drnec Kerr, Patricia Lee Lewis, Alan and Edie Lipp, Brenda Marsian, Ellen Meeropol, Lydia Nettler, Patricia Riggs, Morgan Sheehan-Bubla, and Marion VanArsdell.

The women who gave me insight into the complex emotion and spirit of food: Julie Copoulos and Amanda Milazzo of Small Oven, Unmi Abkin of Coco's, and Anna Fessenden of AnnaBread.

The people who represent the best of social work and foster care: Mia Alves, Linda Dugas (Linnie), and Pat Riggs.

Detective Sergeant Steven Webster of the South Portland Police Department, who helped me through the layers of investigative work.

Tom Foley, for your brave and generous heart.

My medical references, Kim Connly, who understood the medical consequences of starvation, and Bryna Greenspan, who walked me through addictions.

Tom Clark, friend, neighbor, and captain in the Northampton Fire Department.

And lastly, to my friends and family who were still there when I emerged after disappearing into the world of this novel. You may never know how good it was to see you all when I surfaced again.

# THE TIGER IN THE HOUSE

## Jacqueline Sheehan

## ABOUT THIS GUIDE

Here are some questions that may help you start
a lively conversation with your book-loving friends.

# Discussion Questions

1. What would you do if you spotted a little girl, splattered with blood, walking alone down a road where you were driving?

2. Who do you think is responsible for children who have been separated from their parents? Is their protection only the job of government agencies? Or do we each have some personal responsibility for such children?

3. How would you describe the relationship between Delia and J Bird? How was their relationship changed by the deaths of their parents? How have their adult lives been affected by the relationship forced on them by the tragedy?

4. How are the sisters' differing characters shown in the choices they make in the book?

5. How do the big sister/little sister dynamics change over the course of the story?

6. Were you surprised by any of the revelations you learned about the book's characters and their past?

7. Do you think communities are taking the right steps to halt the spread of prescription drug addiction? What do you think society can do about this problem?

8. In the course of the story, the sisters must face the consequences of crimes committed by others, including some they loved. What personal qualities help them to face those consequences? What lessons do they learn through this process?

9. Do you think animals have the power to help children (and adults) get through difficult times?

10. How does Louie, the Maine coon cat, offer comfort to Hayley?

11. How would you describe Baxter's personality? What essential qualities does he offer to Delia and Juniper?

12. What treatment modalities are used to help Hayley talk about traumatic events?

*Here's a recipe for an easy-to-make treat that*
*will add a tasty dimension to your conversation.*

# J Bird's Famous Recipe
# for Apricot Ginger Scones

*Ingredients . . .*

3¼ cups unbleached all-purpose flour
⅓ cup sugar
2½ teaspoons baking powder
½ teaspoon baking soda
⅔ teaspoon salt
¾ cup butter, room temperature
¾ cup dried apricots, diced
⅓ cup candied ginger, diced
2 tablespoons grated lemon peel
1 cup buttermilk
Parchment paper (optional)

Preheat oven to 400 degrees Fahrenheit. Mix dry ingredients in a large bowl. Cut in butter. Add the apricots, ginger, and lemon peel. Add the buttermilk and stir until just mixed. You may need to add a little more buttermilk, depending on the humidity level of the day. Knead for five turns, folding and pressing with the heels of your hands. Form into two logs and place on greased baking sheets (or use parchment paper instead). Bake at 400 degrees for 25 minutes. Cut into hearty triangular wedges. Serves one entire book group. Enjoy!

—Recipe from Morgan Sheehan

# Connect with Us

Visit us online at
**KensingtonBooks.com**
to read more from your favorite authors, see books
by series, view reading group guides, and more.

**Join us on social media**

for sneak peeks, chances to win books and prize packs,
and to share your thoughts with other readers.

facebook.com/kensingtonpublishing
twitter.com/kensingtonbooks

## Tell us what you think!

To share your thoughts, submit a review,
or sign up for our eNewsletters, please visit:
**KensingtonBooks.com/TellUs.**